Born Dark

Unfortunate Blood Book one

H.G Lynch

Copyright of H.G Lynch 2012
All rights reserved

The right of H.G Lynch to be identified as the author of this work has been asserted by her in accordance with the Copyright, Designs and Patents Act 1988

Published by Vamptasy Publishing

Cover Design by

Nicola Ormerod

For my crazy best friend

I want to thank my funky family, my adoring grandparents, my insane best friend, and, of course, my awesome literary agent and editor for their hard work! Couldn't have done it without you all!

To Grandma

Happy Birthday

Lots of love,

Holly xxx

Born Dark

Born Dark

HATE AT FIRST SIGHT

Reid

It was a new term at Acorn Hills Academy and Reid Ashton was sitting with his friends at one of the rotting wooden benches in front of the looming, grey school building. Many of the girls who walked past in high heels wiggled their fingers in flirtatious waves at Reid. He ignored them. He was busy watching the new girl he'd spotted. New girl meant fresh flesh for his games. It had been a while since he'd had a new challenge and this girl looked just perfect for his intentions.

The light August wind blew stray strands of her fine hair around her face. The steely clouds above threatened rain, which would ruin the textbook she held. The tall, thin pine trees that surrounded the school campus rustled over the chatter and bustle of the milling students. The scent of wet earth, girls' perfumes and vibrant teenage vitality filled his nose with an exquisite fragrance.

The new girl wasn't Reid's usual type. His type were tall and busty, with a tendency to drink too much and a few too many bruised brain cells. But as soon as he saw this girl he knew he just had to mess with her, as he'd messed with almost every other girl on campus at one time or another. This girl was short and skinny, but she was quite pretty too with light freckles across pale cheeks and long, caramel-blonde hair tied up in a tight ponytail. He couldn't see properly from here, but he was sure she had blue eyes. Despite her small stature, there was something intriguing about her. Maybe it was because she seemed so out of place amongst the other students, like a mouse amidst a group of cats.

She walked quickly, hugging her biology textbook to her chest, and looking around like she was lost. Her oversized black hoodie and skinny jeans made it clear this girl was trying to be Goth, but that little freckled face just clashed with all the black. Sweet, innocent, little newcomer. He couldn't resist, he just had to corrupt that innocence.

He took this as his chance to get acquainted.

Ember

Ember Jennings was new at this school and she was looking for Sherry, her roommate and best friend of thirteen years. They'd both transferred here, only agreeing to it so long as they were together.

Born Dark

Sherry had said she'd meet her here in front of the school, but she couldn't see the blonde-haired, green-eyed girl anywhere. Ember absently admired - for the sixteenth time since she arrived at the school two days ago - the huge, castle-like building, with its towering, grey stonewalls and old, Gothic architecture. It was an imposing building, built from large blocks of unruly granite that sparkled like it had glitter embedded in it if it caught the light just right. All around the school were swaying, fragrant pine trees, encroaching on the campus with their wiry, needle-laden arms. As was usual in this part of the world, the sky was grey, just a few shades lighter than the granite rock, but the bright splashes of colour that were the students added liveliness to the dreary place. The school building was centred between the adjoining students' dorm building and the visitors' and teachers' dorm building, and the whole place was set in a remote, little, forest-swathed town called Acorn Hills - hence the uncreative name of the school. It was really quite beautiful in a way, even with the gravel expanse of the car park leading down to the single main road in and out of Acorn Hills.

Students loitered about in front of the school around her, girls in miniskirts chatting up guys who ought to have had 'sleazy' printed on their foreheads. A handful of kids in dark clothes, with dyed-black hair, lingered by the rustling trees on the edge of campus. A couple was seated on one of the mouldy benches, passionately kissing, in the open for all to see. It all made Ember want to crawl under a rock… or bang her head on one. And she still couldn't see Sherry.

Ember was just about to give up waiting and make her way back to the dorm room she was sharing with Sherry, when a tap on the shoulder made her jump.

"Hello there. Sorry, I didn't mean to scare you." There was a boy grinning down at her, not looking very apologetic at all. He was gorgeous with scruffy blonde hair and lovely blue eyes. He was dressed like a skater with a sleeveless hoodie zipped over a long-sleeved grey top and baggy jeans. But it was clear to her immediately that no matter how gorgeous he was, he was trouble. His smile was just full of mischief. She could see two guys at a table behind him snickering, while a third grimaced. His friends presumably. How lovely, she thought sarcastically. She tried not to scowl.

"Hi," she said shyly, forcing herself to smile politely. Even if he was trouble, she had manners; no need to go making enemies just yet.

"I'm Reid. And you are?" He shrugged one shoulder and waited expectantly, his eyes raking her over in a way that made her want to shudder.

"Ember," she answered, then quickly glanced off to the side, hoping to catch a glimpse of Sherry. No such luck. She wanted to get out of here. This guy was undoubtedly messing with her, judging by his friends' laughter, and she wasn't going to be made a fool of.

"You're new here, right? Maybe you'd like to come out tonight and I could show you around?" Reid asked, obviously trying to look innocent and helpful and failing miserably. The half-hidden smirk gave it away. This sort of thing had happened to her many times before and she'd learned never to trust a good-looking guy, or really, any guy for that matter.

"Thanks but no thanks. Now, if you'll excuse me, I have to go." She muttered briskly, though politely. She brushed past him, moving swiftly toward the familiar figure looking in her direction.

Perfect timing Sherz, she thought thankfully. She didn't turn back to see what the boy, Reid, had thought of her declining his mocking invitation. But she could hear whoops of laughter from his friends. She smirked to herself vindictively. Good. She was new here, but she wasn't a pushover.

"So, who was that boy you were talking to before? He was hot," Sherry asked teasingly as she slipped into their dorm room's en-suite bathroom to change into her pyjamas. The room was at least three times the size of Ember's room back home, and it was nicely decorated, with pale blue walls and cream carpeting. Pine furniture sat around the room including a wardrobe, bookcase, desk and dresser. There was one wide window that looked out over the front of the school where you could see the wooden benches on the green grass below, then the cold, black cement of the parking lot, and beyond that there was the slick river of tar that formed the main road. Past the road there were only more trees, as far as Ember could see. It wasn't the best view ever but it most certainly wasn't the worst she'd seen.

"His name's Reid, but he's obviously an asshole," Ember replied to Sherry with a sigh, folding herself on the end of her bed. The bedspreads on the wood-framed beds were cream and brown with splashes of blue to match the walls. Not very exciting, but at least there wasn't floral wallpaper.

"Really? But he looked so nice." Sherry's muffled voice came from behind the bathroom door. Ember rolled her eyes though Sherry couldn't see it – unless the other girl had developed x-ray vision and forgotten to mention it.

"You mean he looked sexy. If you want him, go for it. I'll be right here if he messes you about, waiting with a baseball bat," Ember laughed quietly. As small as she was, Ember had a fierce temper and she was very protective of her best friend. Nobody screwed with Sherry and got off with it lightly.

"Nah, you saw him first and you might change your mind. I'd settle for the dark-haired one that was at the table behind him. You know, the one that wasn't laughing." Sherry was grinning as she exited the bathroom in a set of brand new purple pyjamas with 'Kiss me, I'm dreaming' written across the front.

"Like the new jim-jams," Ember snickered, glancing down at her own pathetic ensemble which consisted of an oversized grey t-shirt and pink pyjama bottoms that hid her feet because they were too long. They both laughed quietly and got into their beds, wishing each other goodnight. Then Sherry turned out the light, plunging the room into darkness and signalling the end of their third day at Acorn Hills.

Chemistry the next day was awful. Ember enjoyed Chemistry on occasion, but she was hopeless at it. She hated working with chemicals in experiments unless they were doing titrations, and though she could understand most of the stuff she was taught in the classroom, she never remembered it in the exams. Also, she hated the calculations. Who really needed to know how many atoms were in two litres of hydrochloric acid? She sucked at maths.

Biology and Art went fine and she thought it would be an OK day until she was making her way back to her dorm room after the last class of the day. She was trying to remember the exact density of Mercury and what the second level in a fractional distillation tower was – she needed to know for the Chemistry homework - when she bumped into someone and dropped her textbooks.

"Oh, I'm sorry," she said automatically, bending down to get her books. A smooth, elegant hand reached out and picked up her Chemistry textbook for her, handing it to her. "Thanks," she muttered shyly, and looked up to see whom she was thanking.

"No problem." It was Reid, the boy from yesterday. She groaned internally. Annoying boys were not a top priority right now. He needed to get out of her way.

"Oh, hi," she mumbled, shifting her books in her hands. She didn't want to look at him; if she looked at him, she might forget why she'd declined his offer yesterday. Surely he was too pretty to really be an asshole?

"Hey. Have a good day?" he asked, his hands wrapped in black, fingerless gloves and shoved in his pockets. I was, until now, she thought, perhaps harshly. After all, he hadn't actually done anything outwardly mean yet. He just happened to come across as particularly arrogant.

"Yeah, it was alright," she replied quietly, flipping her ponytail impatiently. Hello, I have homework. Go away.

He didn't budge. The hallways were almost empty now, the fluorescent lights buzzing overhead. The wood panelling on the lower half of the walls was scuffed and stained, the dark wallpaper covered in graffiti. Various proclamations of love and creative insults drawn in coloured marker pen made for interesting reading on the way to and from class. Reid didn't seem to realise she wasn't paying attention to him anymore. "So, any chance you might want to re-consider my offer?" He sounded confident as she lifted her gaze to his. His eyes really were lovely, but then again, she had a weakness for blue eyes. And damn, he was persistent.

Ember began to shut him down again. "Actually, I... ," she started and stopped, an idea suddenly hitting her like lightning, "Sure, why not? But only if my roommate can come too." She smiled sweetly, looking as innocent as possible. Well, she might as well have some fun, and her plots were always more fun when Sherry was around to witness her genius.

Reid grinned like the cat that'd had the cream. "Sure. That'd be great. What dorm room are you?"

Ember repressed a giggle, "2-10".

Reid smirked and said he'd be there to pick them up at half eight, then sauntered off down the hall. This was going to be an interesting evening.

Later that evening, Ember got the chance to inform Sherry of their plans.

"Guess what? We've got a date tonight." Ember sang as she stepped out of the bathroom, drying her hair with a towel, and saw Sherry was finally back from the library. She was scribbling away on her notepad, curled on her bed by the window.

"What?" Sherry's green eyes lit up with surprise. She dropped her pen onto her bed, shoving aside the maths homework she'd been doing. Ember dumped her towel onto her dresser, nearly knocking over the bottles of perfume that rested there, and flung open the doors to the pine wardrobe.

She explained what had happened earlier while she dug around for nice clothes. "Yeah, Reid asked if I'd reconsider his offer, and I said only if you could come too. He's going to pick us up here at half eight. Better get ready." Ember smirked, pulling out a selection of clothes from the wardrobe and tossing them across her bed. Sherry grinned excitedly.

When there was a knock on their door at twenty-five to nine, they glanced up at each other from their books and choked on silent laughter. Something fluttered in Ember's stomach and she ignored it. This wasn't a real date. She had no reason to get all giddy.
"Do you think it's really him?" Sherry breathed excitedly.
"Only one way to find out," Ember whispered back and went to the door. She pulled it open and just about bent double with laughter.
Reid was indeed standing at the door, his blonde hair tamped down by a black beanie and a charming smile on his face. Ember felt suddenly a little nervous, seeing the way Reid's eyes appraised her outfit like an artist admiring a particularly fine painting. She was dressed in her favourite skinny jeans, black three-inch heels and a stylish red top that set off her eyes. Sherry was dressed in a pretty, aqua-green top and boot-cut jeans with cute black boots.
Once he was done eyeing her over, Reid gave a wicked half-smile to show his approval. "Ready to go?" he asked, gesturing with one gloved hand. She had to turn away, biting down on her lower lip to keep from laughing, and nodded toward Sherry.
They followed Reid, the hot blonde, out to his car in the parking lot - a sleek black Aston Martin DB9 - Ember's all-time favourite car. "Wow! That's your car?" she breathed reverently, looking over the expensive, sexy car.
"Yup. Who wants shotgun?" Reid smiled a smile that looked almost genuine, but at the same time just a little creepy.
Ember turned to Sherry with pleading eyes. "Do you mind?" she asked softly. Sherry shook her head. "Of course not. I know it's your dream car."
Ember gave her friend's hand a quick squeeze and rushed round to the passenger's seat while Sherry slid in the back and Reid got in the driver's seat.
The car journey to the club was amazing - she was sure she was in love with that car - but the club itself wasn't so much fun. Ember really wasn't a party girl. Big crowds made her uneasy, and drunken teenagers didn't amuse her.
"This is Santos. One of the hottest clubs in town," Reid announced proudly, getting out of the car. Ember lingered for a moment, trying to memorise the fresh smell of the leather seats, and then stepped out, feeling like a movie star stepping

out of a limo at a big Hollywood event. Sherry was right beside her as they followed Reid into the club.

The inside of the club was dim, the air filled with the cloying heat of dozens of sweating bodies. The perimeter of the room was lined with cosy booths, while the centre of the room sported a massive dance floor. Girls wearing practically nothing writhed around sensually, guys with Mohawks and leather jackets nodded their heads to the fast techno beat, gaggles of people swung their hips and laughed at nothing. Flashes of neon colours from tutus and headbands were caught in the erratic strobe lights. Ember and Sherry selected a booth near the door, declining Reid's offers to dance until he got bored and finally wandered off somewhere.

They'd been at the club for a little over half an hour, when Ember decided it was time to leave. "So, I say it's time to run. What do you think?" Ember snickered. They hadn't driven far to this club, and Ember was sure walking in these shoes back to the dorms wouldn't be a problem. Hopefully, Reid would leave her alone if he thought they'd ditched him.

"Do you think he'll even notice we're gone?" Sherry muttered over the pulsing music. Ember shrugged and looked about. No sign of tall, blonde and mischievous. She jerked her head toward the door and they headed out discreetly.

They couldn't help but laugh as they jogged down the road to the school, Ember's heels clicking on the rough pavement. The chilly breeze lifted her hair and raised goosebumps on her skin, but she was satisfied that Reid would get the message that she wasn't going to be messed around by some guy. Even if that guy was totally cute.

Reid

Reid wasn't surprised to see Brandon and the guys lounging in a booth at the back of the club. It was their usual hang out spot, good for admiring girls from. It was the darkest corner of the room, back behind the dance floor, away from the flashing lights and prying eyes of humans.

"Hey Reid, I thought you had a date tonight?" Perry Romalli asked, raising his glass. His white teeth flashed in a bright smile as Reid joined his friends. Perry was cheerful, but he was also Brandon's lapdog, which meant Reid didn't get along with him all the time. Ricky Sanders was the quiet one of the group really; he didn't say much and didn't stand up to Reid or Brandon when there were arguments. Brandon Morris was the golden boy of the gang, moral conscience and all that jazz.

They, along with himself, Reid Ashton, were the most popular boys at Acorn Hills. Their families had helped found the town and only their families had the awesome 'genetic quirk' that made the boys what they were. It was unknown to most that these four boys, were vampires. Born vampires, with centuries of history in their blood. They didn't feed on blood often - once a week usually - and only used their magic when necessary. Well, the others did. Reid occasionally used his vamp-magic just for the fun of it. Maybe to unlock the door to the girls changing rooms so he could sneak in and spy. Brandon gave him crap for it every time he used his magic, telling him he would blow their cover or something. Reid mostly ignored him.

"Yeah, actually I've got two." Reid smirked, giving Perry a high-five. Brandon looked disapproving, as always. Ricky just shook his head indulgently.

"How did you wrangle that?" Perry laughed.

"She wanted to bring her roommate along." Reid shrugged. That got Ricky's attention. He lifted his head and straightened his shoulders.

"Her roommate? The blonde one with the green eyes?" Ricky asked quietly.

Brandon grinned. "I think Kee here has a crush." He used Ricky's much-hated nickname. The boys had given him that nickname because, when they were seven, he'd lost his front teeth and couldn't say Ricky properly - he kept saying Kee-Kee. So they'd started just calling him Kee. Ricky smiled weakly and shrugged, blushing. He was the baby of their crowd, the youngest, with almost as strong a moral compass as Brandon, but sometimes Reid could persuade him to have some fun.

"Well, bring them over here to meet us!" Perry suggested. Brandon was shaking his head, frowning slightly, while Ricky was snickering and Perry was roaring with laughter.

"Wait, are you going to feed on them?" Brandon hissed, tugging on Reid's arm as he was about to leave. He kept his voice low. His dark eyes issued a warning that Reid understood all too easily. He considered making a smart-ass remark just to piss Brandon off, but he refrained.

Instead, he just said, "I've fed this week already. I just want to corrupt the little one." Reid smirked and wandered off to collect his dates.

Unfortunately, they were gone. He scanned the crowd for them, but they weren't there.

He returned to his friends unhappily. "I think some prick picked up my dates." He slid into the booth next to Brandon, and smacked the table with a fist. Perry was grinning like an idiot, making Reid wonder how much the larger boy had had to drink this evening, but Brandon, being the golden wonder, was worried.

"That's not good. We don't know who might've gotten them or maybe the girls were taken. You should go look for them and make sure they're OK. We can't afford any disappearances linked with any of us." Brandon sounded concerned, but his point was logical. Even Perry had stopped grinning now. Brandon was right of course; they couldn't afford anyone digging into their business because of missing girls. Reid hated it when Brandon was right.

"Fine, I'll ask Bernie if he saw them leave, and check their dorm room later. Happy?" Reid hissed and got up to ask Bernie the Bartender if he'd seen anyone make off with his dates.

Bernie had seen them swipe out of the club laughing, earlier. Reid cursed the girls mentally, not impressed. So they thought they'd make a fool of him, did they? Well, he had ways of getting payback on that account.

Ember

It was 3am when Ember woke up to banging on the dorm room door. She blinked her tired eyes, then threw a slipper at Sherry to wake her,

"Sherz, wake up! I think Reid noticed we were gone," she whispered, and heard Sherry giggle under her breath from across the room.

She went and opened the door, blinking sleepily and then trying to look surprised at seeing Reid behind the door. She was too tired to resist her reaction. She simply burst out laughing, her hand covering her mouth as she saw the anxious look on Reid's face. He looked genuinely worried and then almost hurt when she started laughing. She could hear Sherry's muffled laughter in the bed at the far wall behind her.

"I'm… I'm sorry. I just… I just," Ember gasped, unable to stop laughing. Reid was no longer looking worried, he looked angry.

"You just what?" His voice immediately dimmed her laughter to hiccupping giggles. It was cold and hard, frightening almost. She looked up and saw something icy glint in his eyes. She guessed he'd never been made a fool of by a girl before.

"Look, I'm sorry. We were just having some fun. Messing with you. I just thought I should make it clear that...well, I'm not stupid. I thought I should make that obvious right from the start here, so nobody gets the wrong impression of me. Sorry for running out on you like that, though." She did feel a little bad about it, thinking he might have actually been pretty worried when he discovered the two new girls had vanished in a busy club. Even an asshole would worry that they'd been kidnapped, right? It was only human.

"Well, I was just, you know, worried. As long as you're OK, I guess it's alright." Reid was suddenly quiet and bashful. He changed attitude faster than she could track. Freaky.

"Yeah. Sorry again. Night." Ember smiled at him and watched him turn to head down the hall. She closed the door and immediately burst into hysterical giggles again, Sherry joining in.

It took them a long time to get back to sleep after that and they'd regret it the next day.

"Ember, Sit up! Unless you want detention, I suggest you stay awake," Dr Callums cautioned her and she pulled her head up from her desk. It was halfway through the day, and halfway through Chemistry, and she could barely keep her eyes open. She was starting to think this was karma's work. She'd made a fool of Reid, when he'd only been trying to be helpful. She had to admit that it really did seem like he had actually been being nice. After all, he really had shown up to take them out. She'd had no reason to blow him off the way she had and now it was coming back to bite her in the butt.

She was contemplating finding a way to make it up to Reid, a real date maybe, when there was knock on the Chemistry lab door. Dr Callums, a short, mousy man who had a habit of digressing into random stories in the middle of a lesson, went to the door, opened it and spoke to whoever was outside. She couldn't see who it was, because Dr Callums was blocking her view.

"OK, Reid, you'll have to catch up on notes from someone," the teacher said in a patient voice. She could hardly believe what she was hearing. Weird coincidence. The blonde boy sauntered into the class, shooting a smile at her, and taking the empty seat next to her.

"Mind if I copy your notes?" he asked simply, a tiny smile on his face and his eyes kind. She just nodded and passed him her notebook. Dr Callums was droning on about the experiment they were about to do. Honestly, she'd done it before and it wasn't difficult.

She collected all the equipment and chemicals, lighting the Bunsen burner and setting the chemicals in the little white bowl on top of the tripod. She turned to get the iron chips to put into the bowl, and heard a whizzing pop. She turned back quickly and saw the contents of the bowl were alight, and a wad of paper was burning in it. She instantly doused it with a beaker of water, causing a plume of steam to puff out. She turned off the gas tap and coughed, beating at the thick steam.

"Ember, what's going on here?" Dr Callums came over, looking stern. He examined the half-charred, half-soaked crumpled paper in the bowl. He picked it up and carefully unfolded it. He read whatever was written on the paper, and then glared at Ember. "Detention, after school today. Half an hour," he said in a cold voice and shredded the paper before dropping it in the bin.

Ember stood in shock with her mouth open for several minutes before the bell rang. She could hear soft chuckling as she tidied up her equipment. She had been thinking about how she simply couldn't get detention, she couldn't! She'd never had detention in her life, and she'd only been in this school for a few days! But when she heard the chuckles, she began thinking about what had really just happened.

She finished tidying and grabbed the arm of the person snickering. "What did the paper say?" she hissed at Reid, not bothering to ask if it had been him who'd messed with her experiment. She knew it was. She didn't know how she knew, but she did.

"What do you mean?" he asked innocently, but he was having trouble keeping a straight face.

"You know what I mean. What did the note say?" She was still gripping his arm, quite tightly. He looked down at her hand on his arm and looked faintly surprised for a moment.

"Does it matter what the note said? You've still got detention anyway," he smirked at her.

"I was right with my first impression of you," she said coolly, letting go of his arm and swinging her bag onto her back.

"Oh, really?" Reid said vaguely.

"Yeah. I thought you were an ass and I was right." She shoved him out of the way as she strolled out the door, planning to have lunch in her dorm room today.

"Well done. You're a genius...Wait, aren't you going to tell Dr Callums I was the one who wrote the note, like a good little tattle-tale?" He was walking right alongside her, even though she was clearly trying to get away from him.

"There would be no point. You already have detention. And I can't prove you wrote it. It was in my experiment and you were supposed to be busy copying my notes," she spoke shortly and coolly, glaring at him out of the corner of her eye.

"How do you know I've already got detention? Are you stalking me or something?" He was looking at her oddly, like she'd said something astounding.

"No, but you're the kind of guy who has detention at least four days a week," she muttered, slamming open the door to the dorms, hoping to hit him with it.

"And you're the kind of girl who's never had a detention. Innocent little angel, aren't you?" Reid's voice was scathing, but his words hit her like a knife in the gut. Shredding her pride. She whirled on him with fire in her blue eyes and a growl in her throat.

"I am not an innocent little angel. Don't make the mistake of thinking that because I'm small, I can't hurt you. Believe me, I am willing to give it a go," she snarled in his face, feeling a spark of satisfaction as he flinched back from her unexpected fury. His blue eyes narrowed and they were glaring at each other from a distance of six inches. The hallway was empty now, only the distant sound of fading laughter echoing down the stone-floored corridor. Then rapid footsteps, coming in their direction. Neither of them moved, though Ember wanted to slap Reid and walk away before anyone was around to see it.

"Hey Reid, what are you...?" someone shouted, and then in a whisper to someone next to him, "Oh, I think he's about to kiss the girl!"

Ember whipped her glare round to aim it at a boy she now recognised as Perry Romalli. "No. He's not. 'Cause if he does, I'll punch him in the face!" she yelled at Perry, turning her glare back on Reid. Perry murmured something and Reid didn't move as she hissed and stormed off toward her room, planning on skipping Maths. She'd rarely skipped class before, but she was suddenly feeling tired again and had a headache. She'd have Sherry explain her absence to their Maths teacher.

"What time is it?" Ember mumbled later that afternoon, as Sherry came in, rolling over in her bed. Sherry frowned, dumping her bag on the floor. Ember pushed her hair out of her face and sat up.

"Three thirty. Why?" Sherry groaned and collapsed on her own bed, and started pulling off her trainers.

"Shite! I was meant to be in detention fifteen minutes ago!" Ember threw back the covers and tugged a brush through her hair. She was still dressed from earlier and she grabbed her bag from the floor where she'd left it.

"You? Detention?" Sherry was staring at her like she'd just admitted to being a leper.

"I'll explain later. Bye!" Ember rushed out the door, giving her friend a quick wave, and started down the hall at a run.

She burst into the detention room, gasping. Asthmatics shouldn't run, she thought as she tried to catch her breath, leaning in the doorway for a moment.

"Ah, Miss Jennings. You're twenty minutes late. You'll be here an extra twenty minutes to make up for lost time." The teacher, a brown-haired, stocky woman in her mid-thirties who always wore thin-rimmed glasses, was slouching over a copy of Hello magazine at her desk in the front of the class.

Ember resisted the urge to argue and took a seat at the back of the class. She pulled out her notepad and started scribbling. There was only one other person there, a girl a few years younger with black hair and too many piercings, and she left ten minutes after Ember arrived. The detention room looked like any other classroom, with dull grey-green walls and rough blue-grey carpeting. Behind the teacher's desk at the front of the class, there was a giant chalkboard, smeared with chalk dust. The paint on the walls was cracking and peeling, and the corners of the room were webbed with silver nets of cobwebs. Rows of plastic-topped tables, all spaced out, spanned across the room.

"Hey, I half expected you wouldn't show up. What're you still doing here? Your time should be up by now," Reid's voice mocked from the doorway as he came in.

"I was late. Had to sleep off a headache," she remarked shortly, sending the boy a glower. He sauntered into the room like he owned every inch of it, as if it were as comfortable to him as home. From what she could tell, it probably was.

"Mr Ashton, take a seat. No talking," Miss Hollander commanded from the front of the class. Of course, Reid sat a few seats down from Ember, winking at her as he dumped his school bag. She glared at him and returned to her sketching. She was drawing a rose, one of her favourite things to draw.

Born Dark

Five minutes later, she was just finishing her shading, using her fingertip to smudge the pencil appropriately, when a note landed on her page.

What are you drawing?

The note read. She glanced up at the teacher who still had her nose stuck in her magazine.

Why do you care?

She wrote back and tossed the paper at him with a glare.

She saw his mouth twitch as he read it, and then he glanced up at her. He scribbled something on the note before sliding it back to her. She took another glance at the teacher, and grabbed the note, stuffing it in her pocket as Miss Hollander looked up suspiciously. Ember pretended to be focused on her drawing, until the teacher grumbled and returned to her magazine. She un-crumpled the note and read it.

Seriously, what're you drawing?

She sighed and wrote back swiftly.

A rose. What does it matter to you?

She threw the note back and took out a sharp-edged rubber, and began defining light points on her drawing. She did it slowly and carefully, making sure her hand didn't smudge the page. The note came back to her.

Didn't figure you for the romantic roses type.

He was really starting to piss her off. She wrote back once more.

You don't know me. You have no idea what 'type' I am.

She tossed the note back a little viciously, hitting him in the head. She let out a giggle and then clamped her hand over her mouth.

"Something funny Miss Jennings?" Miss Hollander was glaring at her over her magazine.

Ember shook her head, looking merely disinterested and solemn. The teacher went back to her magazine, and Ember glared at Reid. He made a shrugging motion as if to say, 'What did I do?' She tilted her head sharply and gave him a look that said, 'You know what'.

She went back to her drawing and felt her phone vibrate in her pocket. She stole a look at Miss Hollander and pulled out her mobile. She had a text from Sherz.

Having fun in detention? Is your boyfriend there? X

She was about to reply when she felt something hit her in the head. She yelped and glanced down at the offending object: a crumpled ball of paper.

"Mr Ashton, I saw that. You'll spend an extra fifteen minutes with me for that." Miss Hollander spoke without glancing up from her magazine, and Ember bit down on a victorious grin. Reid grumbled and sighed.

The last fifteen minutes of her detention went without interruption. She finished her drawing and replied to Sherry's text with a witty, biting remark.

"You're free to go Miss Jennings," Miss Hollander said dully, dismissing her. She packed up her stuff and sent Reid a vicious smirk and a sharp wave as she left the classroom.

Once she was down the hall she could laugh at how pissed off he'd looked.

She was still smirking about it when she got to her room. "Hey, did you get my text?" Ember tossed her bag on the floor and shook her phone at Sherry, who replied with a mock-hurt expression.

"Yeah. No need to be so cruel. Detention made you cold," Sherry pouted sulkily. They both giggled. "So what did you two get up to in detention?" Sherry wiggled her brows suggestively.

"Hit each other in the head with paper." She smiled and kicked off her shoes, shoving them under her bed.

Sherry laughed and put down her book. "Seriously? Why?"

Ember rolled her eyes and sat down on the floor. "He was passing me notes and I got annoyed and kind of threw it at him. I didn't really mean to though. But I'm glad I did it. Then he threw it back at me and he got caught. So he's still stuck there." Ember shrugged amusedly. She was sure he'd get payback somehow, but she revelled in having won this round. It was kind of fun fighting with Reid, the same way it was fun fighting with her little brother. It reminded her of how, when they'd been little, her and Josh - her brother - would pick fights with each other, pull nasty pranks on each other, and if one of them went to tattle, it would turn into a competition to see who could lie better. Ember had been very good at it, but Josh had often been better, simply because their parents thought he was adorable. And they knew Ember had an evil streak in her.

"Well, you know what they say. Boys bully you when they like you." Sherry grinned, picking up her book again. Ember didn't believe that for one second, never had. Boys bullied you because they were mean or because they thought it made them look cool.

"Yeah, yeah. You and I both know that's a load of bull," Ember snorted, pulling her MP3 off the bedside table and plugging the headphones into her ears.

Born Dark

Reid

When Reid eventually got out of detention, he was angry. Really angry. He couldn't believe it; the little new girl wasn't nearly as innocent as she looked. She was a demon, he was sure. There had been flames flickering in those wide, blue eyes when she'd tossed that smirk at him going out the door.

This wasn't just about gaining another notch on his bedpost anymore, another conquest, another challenge; now, this was about beating this girl at her own game, making her miserable until she caved and admitted she wanted him. Every girl wanted him, no matter how good they were at pretending they didn't. It was just a matter of making them admit it, to themselves and to him. No girl had ever held out longer than two weeks before. And neither would Ember, he'd make sure of that.

"Reid? Reid!" Brandon's voice hissed in his ear, startling him awake. He groaned and sat back, leaning his head on the back of his seat.

"You got to stop falling' asleep in these lectures, man," Perry chuckled from his other side. They were in class, sitting through another tedious lecture. The air in the room was stifling, stale and warm, which Reid always found conducive to sleep.

"Can't help it. History's too damn boring," he muttered, stifling a yawn.

"Dude, we're in English," Ricky laughed under his breath, sitting next to Brandon. The room was filled with half-asleep students, some of whom were lazily copying notes, but most were texting slyly under their desks or doodling on their notepads. With his enhanced vampire sight, Reid could see at least three versions of 'so-and-so loves Reid' scribbled on girls' notepads. It made him smile, knowing he was so well adored by the ladies.

The teacher, Mr Waysworth, was droning on and scrawling some illegible notes onto the blackboard. The man was tall and spaghetti-skinny, with a beaky nose and rectangular glasses. He looked every bit the geek he was. And he had a real grudge against Reid ever since he tore the pages out of a Romeo and Juliet book to write notes to girls in the middle of class.

He was just starting to tune out the teacher's rambling again when he heard a mocking snort from about two rows back. Whispering, and then a familiar giggle.

He grimaced and leaned over to Perry, "Since when was Ember in this class?" he muttered.

"Huh?" Perry murmured dumbly, turning to glance up at the girl.

Reid yanked his arm, "Don't look!" he hissed.

Perry yawned. "Oh, her. She's been here the whole time. I thought you'd noticed." He shrugged, putting his head on the desk. Oh, this was too good to pass up. He had to find a way to mess with her here, ruin her day.

And then he saw his chance. Mr Waysworth was interrupted by a knock at the door. "Mr Waysworth, they need you at the office." A tall, dull girl he knew to work in the main office peaked in the door. Mr Waysworth nodded, commanded silence of the class, and left.

Reid immediately got up and shuffled past Perry. He wasn't sure exactly what he was planning on doing but he was sure that just seeing him would be enough to annoy Ember.

"Where are you going Reid?" Brandon questioned tiredly. Reid just chuckled and winked before heading up the two rows to his target.

He slid onto Ember's desk and perched there in front of her, legs crossed. She glared up at him with piercing blue eyes. Her mouth was set in a hard frown, clearly not happy to see him.

"So, did you enjoy your extra-long detention?" she muttered icily, arching one brow in a defiant expression. He flashed a dazzling smile, determined not to let her see that it irritated him. Her expression darkened further.

"Not really. Would've been more fun if you'd stuck around. I didn't get the chance to…," He was cut off by the green-eyed girl sitting next to Ember.

"Ember, why is your boyfriend sitting on the desk?" The girl laughed, nudging Ember with her elbow. Ember turned and hissed at her friend, turning a cute shade of pink.

"Shut up or I'll burn your precious new book," Ember threatened the girl, lowering her lashes to glare sidelong at Reid. It was somewhere between a shy and a vicious look.

"Ooh, boyfriend? What have you been saying about me behind my back little one?" Reid chuckled, watching her blush and squirm. Inside, he wondered if she'd really called him her boyfriend. The thought made a funny little shiver run down his spine. He couldn't identify what that meant exactly. Bizarre.

Ember shot a glare at her friend, who shrunk away, clutching a book to her side. "For the record, what I actually called you was an annoying asshole. It's just that some people like to romanticise everything." Ember was still glaring at her friend viciously.

"Sorry. Don't burn my book please!" Sherry pleaded in a mock-frightened voice. Reid watched them with growing amusement, and also curiosity. There was something so… intriguing about Ember, even in the way she interacted with her friend. It was like she had every defence imaginable up around herself, but what she was protecting herself from, Reid couldn't guess.

Ember was still glowering at her friend, some meaningful expression on her face. Sherry abruptly sighed and turned to Reid, tipping her head back to look up at him with green, green eyes. "OK, she really did call you an asshole," Sherry admitted ruefully, then pouted sulkily, like saying that had ruined all her fun. But, Ember looked satisfied. She smirked a little up at Reid, and for some reason, he really didn't like that smirk.

"Oh, really?" He tilted his head, pulling on a sceptical expression, teasing her.

"Yes, really. Now go away before we get in trouble. I do not want another detention," Ember said coldly, glaring at him. He didn't move a muscle. "Move!" she commanded harshly. He just grinned, staying put.

Abruptly, she looked about the room swiftly and he wondered what she was looking for. She leaned around him and glanced down. He figured she was probably glaring at Brandon and the guys, who must've been laughing by now.

After a moment, she pulled back and looked at him tiredly. "I think your friends want your attention." He turned to smirk down at the guys, but saw they weren't even looking up. He was about to make a snarky comment to the blonde demon but found himself yelping as he was shoved off the desk.

He fell onto the desk a row down, banging his elbow and knees in the process and making the unsuspecting girls behind the desk shriek. He heard Ember and Sherry laugh, Ember vindictively and Sherry indulgently, as if she'd expected Ember to do something like that. And then there was the laughter of everyone else in the room, including his own friends, who were laughing almost as hard as the girls.

"Excuse me, special delivery. Did you order a pig-headed idiot?" The blonde demon girl was leaning forward and speaking to the girls in front of him now. They burst into piercing giggles and Reid watched one of them high-five the demon. Ember looked pleased with herself, flashed Reid a smirk and winked at him - actually winked at him, mockingly.

"Dude, she's totally evil!" Perry was roaring from the next row down. Brandon looked like he was trying very hard not to laugh, and Ricky had his hand clamped over his mouth, his face turning red from stifling his own laughter. Reid, indignant and embarrassed, struggled to sit up, sneering as the giggling girls in front of him flinched away.

"REID ASHTON! GET OFF THAT DESK AND SIT DOWN!" The bellowing voice of Mr Waysworth roared through the room, and Reid resisted the urge to groan at his bad luck. Everyone in the room quieted their laughter with the teacher back in the room, but he could see the way everyone was looking at him, with bright, amused eyes. He repressed a blush with all his will, growling under his breath. He would not show he was embarrassed. He would not let the demon girl win this one. Thing was, though, she already had. And he knew it.

Unhappily, Reid took his seat next to Perry and buried his head in his arms while his friends continued to chuckle around him. Snickers were still running through the room, whispers passing from person to person. "Oh my God, can you believe that new girl? The nerve!"

"Honestly, if that'd been me, I would've been all too glad to have Reid Ashton sitting on my desk. What's wrong with her?"

That's what the girls were whispering. The guys were much more enthusiastic.

"Dude, did you see that? I always knew that guy would get what was coming to him, but I never thought it'd be a chick that gave it to him!"

"Well, the greatest prick in the school gets beat on by the new girl. Never thought I'd see the day." Yeah, of course the guys in the class were enjoying this. They'd probably have the whole football team informed by lunchtime that Reid Ashton not only got turned down by a girl, but that girl threw him over a desk and humiliated him. Great.

"Mr Ashton, you have a two-hour detention after school today. Would you like to explain why you were offering yourself on that desk?" Mr Waysworth spoke up again. He was nothing if not cruel. But Reid, an idea occurring to him, took the chance to incriminate Ember.

"Actually, I was just getting notes for Chemistry from Ember and she pushed me over the desk." He explained, trying to keep the smugness from his voice. If he was going to be stuck in detention, so was she.

Born Dark

Mr Waysworth looked up at the blonde demon over the rim of his glasses, and Reid followed his gaze with a sneer. She was bent over her work silently writing, and looked up with a surprised and angel-innocent expression, as if to say, 'Me? Why would I do something so mean?'

Mr Waysworth nodded to himself, as if confirming an inner suspicion, and looked back to Reid, his jaw set.

"That's an extra hour for trying to blame Ember. I hardly believe someone of her stature would be able to shove you of all people over a desk, Mr Ashton. Apologise to her now and meet me after class." The teacher gave him a reproachful glare and began to turn away.

Stunned, Reid gaped, and heard at least half the room let a few chuckles slip. He could imagine the victorious flames in the demon girl's eyes, the smug expression on her face. He didn't even need to turn around to see it. Just the thought of it irritated him.

"Yeah, Reid, apologise to the poor girl." A high voice squeaked from behind him. One of the girls he'd nearly fallen onto. He continued gaping, unsure exactly what to do. He'd never been beaten at his own game like this before. It took him a moment to regain any semblance of composure, and then he got really angry.

"No! I'm not going to apologise to her!" he almost shouted it in his outrage. That's it, He thought, this means war. No holds barred all-out war.

"Mr Ashton, outside! Now!" Mr Waysworth yelled, pointing sharply towards the door. The teacher had turned an unattractive red.

"What!?" He knew he sounded like an idiot, continuing to argue but he couldn't honestly believe what he was hearing. How could he be the one in trouble here? She was the one who'd pushed him! Eventually, hoping to retain some semblance of his dignity, he sighed and gave up. He grabbed his bag and stormed out of the class, ignoring the chuckles and giggles. It didn't matter. He was already planning his revenge.

Ember

"Did you see his face?" Sherry was still laughing as they made their way back to their room. Ember couldn't stop grinning. She couldn't believe how well everything had panned out. Reid's plan to incriminate her had backfired most spectacularly. It was brilliant how her innocent, tiny appearance made her almost immune to blame. She had used it to her advantage many times in her previous school.

She was contemplating her own brilliance as they rounded the corner on the hallway where they resided and her self-satisfied basking was cut short right there. Ember suddenly wished she had something to throw at the scowling blonde leaning in front of their door. She groaned and mumbled. "Does he ever give up?"

She put on a smug expression to piss him off as she walked up to Reid. "Don't you have a three hour detention to get to?" she smirked. He glared. He had his arms crossed over his chest, his blonde hair falling into his eyes in a way that made him look dangerous.

"I've... I forgot my... notebook..." Sherry murmured slowly, awkwardly, and then rushed off back down the hall. Ember pulled out her key and tried to shove Reid to the side so she could unlock the door. He didn't budge. She sighed and looked up at him, exasperated already.

"What do you want?" she snapped, moving back and leaning against the wall opposite him. He was the one to smirk this time. He peered around as if making sure they were alone. They pretty much were by now, with only a few people milling about at the far end of the hallway.

"Revenge," he replied slowly with a mischievous smile.

"Right," she muttered, rolling her eyes. "And just how do you plan on getting revenge on me..." she began tiredly, and then squeaked. He cut her off by pinning her against the wall. He'd moved so fast she hadn't even seen it coming, and now she was trapped between him and the wall. He held one of her forearms against the wall, his fingers like iron bands around her wrist.

"You have no idea who you're messing with!" he almost snarled the words and she was very nearly scared just for a second. His soft mouth was just inches from hers, something predatory in the shape of it. His blue eyes glinted. He was just so pretty, so unpredictably impulsive - Ember could feel her heart beating hard in her chest, but she couldn't tell if it was because of fear or because of something else.

"I don't care who you are! Let go of me, you stupid, arrogant tosser!" She tried to thrash, tried to free her wrist from his grasp, but his grip was unbreakable. Her voice came out just a little breathless, and she hoped he'd assume it was due to anger and surprise.

He smirked, just a little quirk of his lips. "Why? Am I making you uncomfortable? Getting a little hot under the collar, are we?" he taunted, his fingers playing lightly with the collar of her shirt. Her breath caught her throat and she made a small choking noise, trying to twist away from him. It was no use. The painted brick wall at her back was solid, and he was too strong - incredibly strong.

"In your dreams! Did you hit your head when I shoved you over that desk or are you just incredibly stupid?" she hissed as his elegant fingers tapped on the top button of her shirt. One fingertip brushed her skin, just above the collar, and it felt like someone had pressed a heated metal coin to that spot on her skin. It tingled with warm needles. "Let go of me before I cause a scene," she spat, even as she felt heat flooding her face. She kicked out at him, and he neatly dodged her foot. He trapped her legs against the wall with one of his and laughed quietly, blue eyes bright. Ember glanced down the hall and saw a boy she knew to be Joseph Rian, walking down the adjoining hallway. Reid hadn't noticed him.

Ember saw an escape, and took a deep breath. Then she screamed. It was loud and ear piercing, and it caught Joseph's attention immediately. It also caught Reid by surprise and he actually jumped backwards, throwing his hands over his ears, releasing her.

"Get away from me! Let me go! Get away!" Ember shrieked, slapping at Reid, though he was standing there with a stunned look on his face. He really hadn't been expecting that.

Joseph came rushing down the hall. "Hey, what's going on here?" he yelled. Ember stumbled into Joseph's protective arms, faking a sob. "Reid, what did you do to her?" Joseph sounded furious. Ember pretended to sob into Joseph's chest, and peaked out at Reid's shocked, angry expression with a smirk. She saw Reid's jaw was set and there was fire in his eyes. He was raging. And she was enjoying this much more than she ought to have been. After all, Joseph was cute and well muscled. Not a bad saviour really.

She looked up at Joseph's face and saw he had nice green eyes, currently glowing with fury. Ember let Reid see her admiration for her protector, hoping it would irritate him. She assumed it was likely he had never been turned down by a girl before and here she was ogling another guy, right after rejecting him.

"What did he do, Ember?" Joseph asked her gently, looking down at her, his green eyes soft.

"He... he wouldn't let me go. I thought he was going to hurt me!" her voice cracked, and tears streamed down her face. She buried her face back in his chest. She knew her act was completely convincing.

"Reid, get the hell out of here! Now! And if you come near her again, I'm sure the headmaster would be glad to hear what you get up to when nobody's around!" Joseph's voice was cold and threatening, but his arms were gentle around her. Ember glanced at Reid and smirked again. She resisted the urge to stick out her tongue.

Reid hissed something at her and stormed off down the hall. She could practically see the waves of fury rolling off him as he went, and felt sorry for whomever he ran into in the hallway next.

That's when Sherry reappeared, at last. She turned the corner, her head bowed over her open bag. "Hey, Emz, Where did..." Sherry started, not looking up from riffling in her schoolbag as she walked towards them. She stopped when she caught sight of Joseph and Ember in his arms. "Oh. I...Uh." Sherry looked confused and embarrassed, "I hope I'm not interrupting anything?"

"I was just leaving. Are you going to be OK? I'll make sure he doesn't come back," Joseph muttered hastily, letting go of Ember and shifting uncomfortably. Ember just nodded and sniffled.

"Thank you," she murmured sweetly. Joseph nodded, blushing faintly, and walked off.

"Would you like explain what happened while I was gone?" Sherry grinned as she unlocked their door and stepped in.

"Would you like to explain why you left? I was nearly freaking attacked!" Ember almost shrieked.

"I thought you two would either scream at each other or end up tearing each other's clothes off. Either way, I didn't want to be there," Sherry chuckled. Ember glared at her.

"So you left me alone to deal with him? Seriously? And just for the record, you couldn't pay me enough to tear his clothes off!" she lied, not really expecting Sherry to buy it. True to form, Sherry raised a brow at her in a sceptical expression.

"I'm sure," was all she said, but the tone of her voice was laden with so much sarcasm, it could've sunk a battleship. Sometimes, Ember wished Sherry didn't know her so well.

"Shut up. Do you want to know what happened or not?" Ember sighed, collapsing on her bed.

"Fine. What happened?" Sherry was looking at her with that expression that said she wanted every detail. She wasn't getting every detail.

"After you left, Reid pinned me against the wall…" Ember started, and saw Sherry's eyebrows go up, a grin flashing across her lips. Ember ignored her, knowing what she was undoubtedly thinking. "He said I didn't know who I was messing with. I told him I don't care who he is, told him to let go. He just smirked at me, the asshole, and I implied that… well, he was being arrogant. Then I saw Joseph, so I screamed. Then I did my angelic act and Reid got really pissed off. Joseph told him to go, threatened him, and told him not to come near me again. Reid looked like he was going to pick a fight right there but he just turned and left. And then you showed up in time to see me in the arms of my saviour," Ember grinned. Sherry laughed, shaking her head.

"God! You two are going to end up in a coliseum with shields and swords, stuck in a fight to the death," she joked. Ember couldn't argue with that, because at this point she was ready to kill Reid.

"Well, yeah. But I'd use matches, not a sword." Ember smirked. Then she remembered something. "Oh, by the way, I overheard some girls chatting in the bathroom earlier, and one of them said that Ricky Sanders might like you."

Sherry's face lit up with excitement. She'd been admiring Ricky from afar all week. "Ricky? The hot one with the dark hair? Ooh!" Sherz giggled. Ember rolled her eyes and relaxed back on her pillows. She wondered vaguely how Reid was enjoying his detention right now.

H.G. Lynch

The Game of Desire

H.G. Lynch

Born Dark

Ember

The next few days passed without incident. The girls spent the weekend exploring the town, even buying some new books and clothes. Monday was boring, Tuesday was dull, but Wednesday... well, that was the day that Reid reappeared.

It was Wednesday evening, and the girls were out in the courtyard, sitting at one of the crumbling wooden picnic tables. The weather was nice, calm, warm and dry, so they'd decided to get away from their stuffy dorm room to do their homework. The trees muttered, shaking their leaves in the light breeze, and the air tasted of impending autumn. The girls chatted about the Maths homework a little, but mainly Ember listened to Sherry gushing over how hot Ricky was. Again. Ever since she'd told her that Ricky supposedly had a thing for her, Sherry had been keeping her eye on the brunette boy, listening out for any scraps of gossip that might give her some more information about him.

"What did you get for question... seven? I couldn't find the..." Ember said, looking up and abruptly ending her sentence with a growl. She glared over Sherry's shoulder and Sherz turned to follow her gaze. Reid and Ricky were walking toward them across the grass, Reid with his usual smirk and Ricky with an endearingly nervous expression.

"What the hell does he want I wonder?" Ember hissed, slamming her pen down on the picnic table.

"Who cares? Ricky's with him!" Sherry whispered, turning back to the table with a faint blush. Ember chuckled at her friend and hesitantly returned to her work, hoping that maybe the annoying guy walking in their direction would take a nice, long detour and end up in the sea.

A shadow fell across the table and Reid's voice interrupted her concentration. "Hello, little one," he said casually.

"What do you want Reid?" she spat back, not looking up from her calculations. Her fingers tightened on her pen, and she willed it not to snap. The last thing she needed was to ruin her Maths homework with spilled ink.

"Actually, it's not what I want, but what Ricky here wants." She caught Reid waving his hand toward his friend. She looked up suspiciously and saw Ricky blushing a little. Sherry, with her back to the boys, had her hair over one side of her face but Ember could see her biting her lip on a smile.

"And just what does Ricky want?" Ember asked kindly, directing the question at Ricky himself. The brunette boy shifted uncomfortably and smiled, bowing his head. For the first time, Ember noticed he was good-looking. His eyes were a very bright blue-green colour, surrounded by thick lashes. She supposed she hadn't noticed that before because she was always busy looking at Reid. It was hard not to - Reid was quite an overwhelming person sometimes, with his arrogance and commanding beauty. Right now, he was watching the scene before him casually, as if it was all mildly amusing but had nothing to do with him. He had a graceful way of standing that made it seem like he was almost lounging against the air, his body language just screaming insolence to anyone who looked at him.

Ricky, on the other hand, had his hands shoved into his jeans pockets and was fidgeting nervously. "Well... I just... wanted to ask Sherry if maybe... she might... want to go on a date with me tonight?" Ricky stuttered, his eyes sliding to rest on Sherry's back. The green-eyed girl's face lit up, a bright smile coming to her lips. She appeared to be speechless.

Ember laughed under her breath and replied on Sherry's behalf. "She'd love to." Ricky smiled a surprisingly boyish smile that made his blue-green eyes shine. Reid just shrugged, nudged Ricky's arm and turned to leave. He stalked off without waiting for his friend and Ember tried not to watch his retreating back.

Ricky lingered for a moment. "Uh, I'll see you at eight... Sherry." It was a pity Sherry couldn't see Ricky's face. The boy was flushed like he'd just won a date with a supermodel. In Ember's opinion, her best friend was a hundred times more beautiful than any model. Ricky was right to be happy.

Once the boys were safely out of earshot, Sherry let out a few high-pitched, excited squeals, bouncing on the spot. Her cheeks were pink, and she paused in her squealing to put a hand over her mouth. Her eyes widened. "Oh my God! I've got a date with Ricky Sanders tonight!" she squeaked, clapping her hands together, her green eyes glittering.

"Yes. I know. I was right here the whole time," Ember chuckled, shutting her Maths textbook, knowing they weren't going to get any more work done today. A brisk wind had picked up anyway, making it too cold to stay outside. She started to gather up her stuff and Sherry did the same.

After a ten minute squealing session on the way back inside, Sherry finally calmed down enough to talk in full sentences again. She turned to Ember with a pleading smile. "Do you think you could help me get ready? Please? What should I do with my hair?"

Ember grinned as Sherry clutched her hair in her hands with a worried expression. "Of course I'll help you." Ember patted her friend's shoulder lightly. "Come on then, we'd better get started. You're going to look so good tonight, Ricky will be stunned!"

As excited as she was for Sherry, Ember wondered what she was going to do all evening, stuck in her room by herself. She could draw, or read a book, but she suddenly felt like doing something fun herself. Maybe she could take a trip to the library, and maybe she'd bump into Reid. She stopped the thought right there. No. Why would she want to bump into Reid? She wouldn't. She would spend the evening in her room, with one of her books, she promised herself. No thinking about Reid.

"OK, you can look now," Ember instructed her friend, who was sitting in a chair in front of the desk. Ember had set up a couple of free-standing cosmetic mirrors so Sherry could see what she looked like once Ember was done with the primping and preening. It was quarter to eight, and Ember had just finished with Sherry's hair. She had to admit, the girl looked amazing. Sherry opened her eyes and immediately beamed at her reflection in the mirrors.

"Oh my God, thank you! I never would've been able to get it to sit like this on my own!" Sherry reached up to touch her loose curls, tucking one behind her ear to show the delicate silver earrings she was wearing tonight.

Ember shrugged; all she'd done was brandish a pair of curling tongs, some hair mousse and a few Kirby grips. Now Sherry's blonde hair sat in cute ringlets on her shoulders, a few tiny curls falling across her forehead, and a little apricot bow clipped onto one side. It matched the pearly apricot silk shirt she was wearing, making her look sexy yet sophisticated at once. She'd donned a stylish black skirt and black leggings, along with some creamy three-inch heels and a pale jacket. All in all, she looked like a model from an ad for the new autumn collection.

"You look great. I'm sure Ricky will be drooling over you by the end of the night. And be sure to text me if anything important happens." Ember gave her friend a quick hug and smoothed out a stray curl before they heard a knock on the door.

Ember went to open it, and gave Ricky a smile. The boy was dressed in jeans and smart powder-blue shirt that looked really good with his faintly bronze skin and dark hair.

"Hi Ricky," Ember greeted him, before standing back to let Sherry past. Ricky's eyes went wide as he took in his chic date. It was a moment before he found his voice.

"Um, wow. You look… really great, Sherry," he said softly, tugging at the sleeve of his shirt. Ember patted Sherry on the arm as she stepped into the hallway.

"You two have fun. And Ricky, look after my friend," Ember added in a quiet voice. It sounded good-humoured enough, but she put a real warning behind it. It was her standard for any guy that took Sherry out; she wanted to protect her best friend.

Ricky just nodded solemnly, obviously catching the warning. "Of course. Goodnight Ember."

Ember watched as they walked, hand in hand, down the corridor. Sighing happily, she closed the door. It was going to be a dull evening all on her own, but she'd deal with it.

Two hours later, Ember found herself stretched out on her bed, staring at the ceiling with nothing to do. The ceiling was painted a dull grey-white, with thin brown cracks running through it like veins of quartz through rock. She'd finished her newest book over half an hour ago, and she wasn't in the mood for music. She wondered about how her best friend's date was going, but decided it was probably going great and she shouldn't worry. What is there to do at ten on a Wednesday night? She thought sullenly.

She sighed, rolling off her bed and glaring at her stack of books on the bedside table. She'd read them all at least twice. So, there wasn't much else for her to do. A shower. That's something to do. She shook her head at herself, knowing how sad it was to have nothing better to do than brush up on personal hygiene when you'd already had a shower the same day. Despairingly, she grabbed some clean underwear and her favourite pyjamas from the dresser, and dumped them in the bathroom before scrambling around for a fresh towel.

It was just as she was precariously tugging on a clean towel from the top shelf of the wardrobe with one hand, while holding back the surrounding pile of towels that wanted to fall on her, and balancing on her tiptoes, that there was a knock on the door. Without thinking, Ember immediately answered the knock. "Come in." She gave the towel in her hand another careful tug. Almost got it, she thought, biting her tongue.

"I think you need to grow," a warm, arrogant voice taunted from behind her. She whipped her head round in surprise, losing her balance and squeaking as a pile of towels fell on her head. She tumbled onto the floor, landing in a mass of fluffy white fabric and glaring up at Reid. He was almost bent double in fits of laughter, clutching his sides like he couldn't stop them splitting. Ember furiously swallowed a giggle, realising that if it had been anyone else in the room, she would've been laughing too. It was pretty funny, but she refused to let the offending blonde guy see that.

Instead, with a grim expression, she got to her feet and began folding the towels to put them back in the cupboard. Reid was still laughing at her when she folded her third towel, and she got fed up. She lobbed the towel at him, hitting him square in the face. She would have laughed at that as well, if she hadn't been so angry.

"What the hell? Why'd you do that?" he asked, sounding honestly confused. Ember scoffed; almost let her jaw drop in disbelief. She was astounded that he seemed to have no idea why she'd hit him with the towel. Like he'd done nothing wrong at all. Idiot.

"You were laughing at me! Why do you think I threw it at you, you moron?" She lifted her arms and her eyebrows to show her incredulity. He looked faintly surprised for a moment and then recovered his pig-headed arrogance.

He leaned back against the doorway, putting one hand in his pocket. "Well, it was funny. You said 'Come in' so I came in and then you jumped like you'd just heard a monster behind you. And then you landed on your butt on the floor with towels on your head. What about that situation isn't funny?" he said with a charming smile and a chuckle. If she hadn't been so irritated with him, she might've taken the time to admire how sweet he looked when he smiled like that, but she glared at him instead.

"The fact that I did hear a monster behind me," she muttered sharply as he tossed the towel back at her, and she caught it. Reid rolled his eyes and simply watched her folding the mountain of towels. "Why the hell are you here anyway? I would've thought you'd be off chaperoning Ricky on his date, maybe giving him tips on how to be an arrogant, chauvinistic pig." Ember folded the last towel and piled them all into the cupboard carefully, keeping one on her bed to use.

"Ricky Boy knows how to get along on a date just fine," he said, ignoring the insult, "And I thought you might be lonely all on your own with nothing to do. Decided to give you some company. You missed one," he added, nodding toward the towel on her bed.

"Actually I'm just fine on my own and I was about to go have a shower when you showed up. I thought Joseph made it clear you weren't to come near me again?" Ember picked up her towel and tossed it into the bathroom before turning back to Reid. She vaguely noticed how the towel she'd hit him with had mussed his hair, making him look like a half-woken puppy. But the next words out of his mouth ruined the cute simile.

He smirked slowly, sensually. "A shower, huh? Well, I did come here to give you company, didn't I?"

Ember made a sound of disgust at the tauntingly sleazy remark. "Not in this lifetime, moron." She really hoped she wasn't blushing as much as it felt like she was.

She grabbed his arm, spun him round and tried to shove him out the door. But she could only budge him a few inches before he realised what she was doing and dug his heels in.

"Whoa, whoa, whoa. Chill. I was kidding!" He turned and held up his hands in mock surrender. Some unreadable expression crossed his face briefly, but Ember thought she must've imagined it.

"I know you were. Now get out." She resumed shoving him, pushing against his chest now.

He barely moved, taking only one slight step back and saying, "Would you like me to be serious about it?" A smirk played across his mouth. That final comment gave Ember the strength to give one last good shove, sending the boy stumbling into the hallway. She slammed the door on his face and sighed.

"Jesus. Someone lock that boy in a cellar," she muttered to herself, stomping to the bathroom. She was beginning to wonder why he wouldn't just leave her alone. But apparently, she'd gotten herself into some battle of wills and wits that she couldn't escape.

Stripping off and stepping into the shower, she blessed the warm water and hoped Sherry would be back soon. She needed a distraction before she started thinking about Reid in an admiring way, rather than a hateful way. Loneliness was messing with her head.

Friday. Biology. Boredom. Three words to describe Ember's afternoon so far. She was doodling aimlessly on her essay paper since she'd finished the essay nearly ten minutes ago and everyone else was still writing. She tried to think of things to do tomorrow night, seeing as Sherry was going out with Ricky again and she'd have nothing to do again. Not that she wasn't happy for her friend, truly she was. Sherry had come home buzzing with excitement at half eleven on Wednesday night.

She'd come in and reeled off her whole evening to Ember, who'd been half-asleep, and Ember had tried to seem interested. She was interested, really, just not fully awake to seem it. Sherry had described how Ricky had been polite and shy, but flattering and sweet, dancing with her a couple of times and even giving her a kiss on the cheek before he said goodnight at their dorm room door. Ember had congratulated the green-eyed girl and gossiped with her for all of fifteen minutes before falling asleep again.

They'd picked up the gossip several times over the next couple of days, in between chatting about how they might have to kill Reid and how they couldn't wait for the second season of their favourite TV show, out next month. It was a thrilling prospect to them. Sad? Maybe.

"Ember? Are you finished with your essay?" Her Biology teacher's voice interrupted her typically teenage thoughts.

"Uh, yeah. I'm done." Ember shook herself mentally and handed her paper over to the teacher. The teacher went back to her desk with the paper and began grading it, but thankfully the bell rang before she could finish. Save that horror for next time, Ember thought, grabbing her bag and heading out the door.

Reid

Reid was walking leisurely down the hallway, whistling to himself. Having just talked his way out of another detention for falling asleep in Modern Studies, he was feeling pretty chuffed with himself. It was all too easy to wind the newer teachers, mainly the females, around his little finger. All he had to do was pout and look repentant, and spout a couple of lies, and they let him go without so much as a warning. He didn't even have to compel them. Suckers, He thought gleefully.

But, his afternoon was about to get even better. Who should appear in his line of sight but Ember, the very devil spawn he'd been hoping to run into. With a mischievous grin, he watched her slipping into the library down the hall. Even from here, he could smell the natural perfume of her skin and blood. For a human, she had a particularly delightful aroma. One usually encountered such sweet scents when dealing with various kinds of Fae, or occasionally the tasty witch. Drawn to her by both her scent and the urge to tease her some more, Reid followed her into the library.

The school library was a fairly large place, with sections boxed in by the layout of the shelves. Each section had a set of low, leather-upholstered seats and a small coffee table for students to stack books on. Reid always liked the library, despite his lack of inclination to read any of the books. If he wanted to read, there were dozens of centuries-old books about mythology and history in the meeting den; which was where the vampires met up and had meetings to discuss important things like intrusions onto their territory by hostile brownies, or the odd visit from an unwelcome banshee. So, nope, it wasn't for the books that Reid enjoyed spending time in the library. It was the quiet that he liked, the solitude. The musty smell of dust and wood polish and paper. And, right now, the view.

Straight ahead of him as he pushed open the heavy wooden door to the library, Ember was standing on her tiptoes, trying to reach a book from a high shelf. With the way she was stretching, her t-shirt rode up to show a strip of smooth, pale flesh between the hem and the waistband of her jeans. She had her tongue caught in the corner of her mouth as she tickled the spine of some book, not quite tall enough to pull it down.

Unable to resist the temptation, Reid skulked up behind her. She didn't even notice. Her hair shone like brass under the dim lights of the library, the watery light coming in the window barely brushing its fingers on her. This close, her strange scent was yet more intoxicating, and he could feel the body heat coming off her. *Wonderful*, He thought with a wicked smile, *what better snack than a pretty girl? Too bad I can't snack on her. Yet, anyway.* He'd never encountered a girl like Ember before; a girl who could spurn his advances. Oh, it was only a matter of time, he knew, but meanwhile, her rejection just made him want her more.

Born Dark

So, still with the urge to tease her, and now with the urge to touch her, Reid looped one arm around her waist while simultaneously plucking down the book she was reaching for. Instantly, Ember yelped and tried to leap free of his grasp, but he had her pinned against him. His hand was resting on her bare flesh, so warm and soft, and he could hear her heart thrumming in her chest. Yes, he'd surprised her, but he'd surprised himself, too. Normally, it took more than just touching a girl's skin to turn him on, yet, with Ember held against him and his fingers brushing the waistband of her jeans, he was undeniably hot for her.

"Reid! Let go of me!" Ember snarled in a low whisper, obviously not wanting to attract attention. She wriggled in his grasp and it did nothing for his self-control. Chuckling in her ear, Reid released his grip around her waist, and she leapt away from him, straightening her t-shirt and holding it down as if he might try to take it off her. He'd like to, but he wouldn't. He preferred girls to come to him willingly. "You daft, sneaky, arrogant tosser! What do you think you're doing?" Ember hissed, her blue eyes aglow with fury. Her heart was still hammering, and he could see her fluttering pulse beating away at the base of her throat.

"I thought," he said slowly, deliberately eyeing her up and down, much to her obvious irritation. She folded her arms across her chest and blushed slightly. The faint pink was startlingly lovely against her pale skin and freckles. "That I was helping you out by getting down this book for you." Casually, Reid held out the book he'd taken down from the shelf, balancing it on his palm. Ember snatched it from him, and then hastily tried to back away. She fetched up against the bookcase behind her, though, and her eyes widened as she realised she was trapped. He was blocking the only way to the door.

"Get out of the way," she commanded but Reid shook his head. He wasn't letting her go anywhere, not when he had her right where he wanted her. Instead, he stalked forward until he was right in front of her, only inches away, and placed his hands on the bookshelf on either side of her head. Now she really was trapped, between the books and his body. And she clearly didn't want to be there. Her pulse jumped up a few notches, and at the same time, so did his. In the dimness, her face was cast in light shadows as she glowered up at him, but he could still see every eyelash and every freckle, and the curve of her mouth. "Reid, grow up and get away from me before I scream," she warned in a low voice. Reid couldn't help it. All his naughtiest nerves lit to a blaze. It was her accent that undid him.

Normally, that husky Scottish lilt to her words was attractive, but when she was angry, it turned every 'R' into a sexy growl.

Reid dug his fingers into the wood of the bookshelf he was holding and bit back his fangs, which were throbbing insistently. Ember continued to glare at him, oblivious to the effect she was having. *What, in God's name, is this!* Reid thought, half-desperately. This was a wildfire attraction he'd never experienced in his life, and it was driving him nuts. She was only a girl, like any other. Not even particularly stunning; she was short, blonde and lacked curves, but still, somehow, he wanted her like he'd never wanted another girl. *Kill it*, a voice whispered in his head, the voice that always got him into trouble, *Kill the desire for her. You mustn't pant after one girl like this. It isn't in your nature.* Obedient to the voice, Reid tried to douse the desire, but with her still so close, it was impossible.

He shoved away from her, still grinning just to annoy her, and purred. "As you wish. But there are other ways I could make you scream if you so choose." At that, Ember turned a very bright shade of pink and she looked inclined to lob her book at him. With a visible effort, she clamped her jaw shut, digging her nails into the cover of the book she was holding hard enough to leave marks. Then she turned and walked away, flipping her hair indignantly.

Reid waited until she was out of the library and her scent was no longer teasing his senses, and then he collapsed back against the bookcase and heaved a sigh. Slowly, his skin began to cool, and his fangs stopped throbbing. He stared mournfully at the high, beamed ceiling of the library, watching dust motes spiralling in the light. *Why couldn't she just be like every other girl?* He thought pleadingly. *Why does she affect me like she does?*

Ember

"Hey, Emz. You okay?" Sherry asked her, strolling into the room after the final bell. Ember was spread on her bed, still thinking of things to do when Sherz went out on her date.

"Yeah, just tired. I had to dodge Reid twice today. I think he followed me into the library earlier, because I doubt he was there to find a copy of Pride and Prejudice for English." Ember chuckled, leaving out the part where she'd actually talked to the blonde boy. It wasn't a conversation she wanted to relay to her friend, who already thought she was secretly in love with the guy.

"Maybe you should put that scheming mind to work instead of avoiding him. Make a trap for him or something, or come up with a plot to embarrass him. After all, it's a war you're in. He might take avoidance as forfeit," Sherry said smartly, dumping her textbooks on the desk and slipping off her shoes. But her words sparked an idea in Ember, an idea of what to do tomorrow night.

"You're a genius, Sherz!" Ember cried, launching herself off the bed to hug her friend, and then pulling out her sketchpad to make plans.

Sherry laughed. "I know," she said but didn't ask why. Sherry knew by now that she'd find out in time whatever Ember had planned. And this was going to be one hell of a plan.

After Ember bid Sherry good luck on her date, giving Ricky a smile, she began to put her plan into action. It was going to take a lot of sneaking, and some real caution. But she thought she could pull it off. Just as long as Reid was where he was meant to be. She'd heard from Ricky that Reid was supposed to be at the pool, practicing for the swimming meet next week. Since it was late, she hoped there wouldn't be too many people milling about.

She got lucky. She reached the pool, and found that it was empty aside from Reid and an uninterested lifeguard who barely glanced up from his magazine. The smell of chlorine in the air was choking, and the white walls were irritatingly sterile. Ember kept her eyes off the pool itself, not wanting to see Reid and not wanting him to see her. She swiftly ducked past the lifeguard, and round the corner, stopping at the Boys' Locker room door. She took a deep breath and knocked, hoping to hell nobody answered.

After a few minutes with no response from inside the locker room, she slipped in. It was exactly like the Girls' Locker room, the only difference being the pile of clothes sitting on the bench. It was more than she'd dared hope for. She'd assumed she'd have to scramble with a locker to get at his clothes. But, being Reid, he didn't bother with one.

Ember giggled as she bundled the clothes into her arms knowing full well that this was the oldest trick in the book, and if she got caught…Well, she didn't waste time thinking about that, unlikely as it was and rushed out of the Locker room.

She snuck past the lifeguard easily, and stashed the clothes in a safe place under the bleachers. He'd never find them. Then, hiding in the stands with her camera, she waited. She crouched and watched the blonde-haired phenomenon that was Reid Ashton swimming. He was a brilliant swimmer, Ember had to admit.

She didn't have to wait long in her hiding place, because Reid did only a few more laps before climbing out of the tepid, green-blue water of the pool.

Ember ignored the way his smooth muscles rippled as he padded round the pool, didn't notice the way the water glistened on his chiselled, lovely chest, and she completely missed the fact that he looked amazingly gorgeous with his blonde hair dark and wet and dripping over his sculpted face. Ember didn't care about any of that. Or at least that's what she told herself. She was here for her great plot. And it was show time. She watched the dripping Reid saunter off to the Boys' Locker room.

She followed after him carefully, waiting at the door to hear the rushing of the shower. Perfect. She slipped in silently, and nicked the wet swimming shorts sitting on the bench. He mustn't have noticed his clothes were missing. Idiot. She crept out of the room, and took the shorts back to her hiding place behind the stands. She knew it wouldn't be long before she got her snapshot, so she lifted her camera to her eye and bit back a giggle.

Sure enough, three and a half minutes later, Reid came rushing out of the Locker room, clutching a towel round his waist. Ember starting clicking the camera, catching Reid's bewildered, angry expression perfectly. She watched him stride over to the lifeguard, who still hadn't looked up from his magazine, and she could hear him saying something to the poor guy in the high chair. She couldn't catch words, but she could tell his tone was furious. Reid was gesturing wildly, and the lifeguard just looked nonplussed.

Then, the money-shot! Reid looked down and paused, bent onto one knee to pick something up and held it up to the light while the lifeguard looked down, baffled. All in all, it looked very much like a half-naked Reid proposing to the poor lifeguard.

She snapped the camera once more, capturing the scene, and took off.

She waited until she was back in her room before she burst out in hysterical laughter. She could feel tears rolling down her cheeks she was laughing so hard as she flicked through her digital camera to her favourite photo.

She'd left his shorts sitting behind the stands, and God if she could see his face if he found them there. But she'd gotten what she needed, and she instantly plugged the camera into her laptop and transferred the photos across.

It was only after she'd gone through the photos and laughed herself out that Ember realised something: her necklace was missing. Uh oh. While she'd been taking the photos, she hadn't stopped to think about what Reid had been picking up. It had just been a better pose than she could've hoped for in her life. It must've been my necklace! She thought with sudden panic; it must've gotten snagged on the bundle of clothes when she'd stolen them and then fallen off.

Ember bit her lip, pondering over what to do for a moment, before deciding it didn't matter. Reid was going to know it was her anyway; necklace or no necklace, he'd have figured it out. It just meant she had to work faster. She printed out copies of her money-shot on A4 paper, lots of copies. And, grabbing a little box of thumbtacks, along with the stack of papers, got to work on the final part of her plan.

Sherry

Hey, how's your date going? Be back soon? U might want to brace yourself when u return. X.

Sherry glanced at the bizarre text from Ember. She knew already that whatever prank Ember had pulled, was going to have severely pissed off Reid. She replied swiftly.

It's going great. Kee's so sweet. Whatever u did, give me details when I get back. X.

Sherry shook her head, smiling to herself.

"What's funny?" Ricky asked quietly, a sensitive smile on his mouth. He really had been so sweet all evening. He'd taken her to a cute little restaurant that his parents owned, and he'd complimented her a hundred times over and now they were just chatting about little things, getting to know each other a bit better. Sherry was enjoying every minute of it. The dim, cosy atmosphere of the restaurant added a romantic air that sent silly little shivers down her spine.

"Oh, just Ember, being Ember." Sherry replied to him vaguely, not daring to mention her friend's undoubted cruelty to his roommate.

"Yeah, she seems quite… loyal. She really cares about you doesn't she?" Ricky asked, his eyes the soft aquamarine colour of the Mediterranean ocean in sunlight.

"Mh-hm. We've been best friends since nursery. Ember can be a little overprotective sometimes. She worries that it's her responsibility to take care of me, but she's a great friend. I can always trust her," Sherry replied calmly despite the butterflies in her stomach. She always got a little nervous just looking at Ricky. He was really overwhelmingly gorgeous, with his soft dark hair and deep blue-green eyes.

"That's sort of like me and the guys. We're really close since we sort of grew up together. We're like brothers really. Although you wouldn't know it with the way Brandon and Reid fight sometimes. Like lions in a cage." Ricky hesitated, and then said, "I know you and Ember don't think much of Reid, but he's really not all that bad. He acts like the ultimate man-whore, and the world's champion asshole, but he's secretly a nice guy. You won't believe that, I know. But I think his war with Ember is his way of saying he likes her." Ricky flashed a dazzling smile, and wrapped his fingers round her hand on the table. She blushed and repressed a giggle. The giggle wasn't borne of shyness, but from the very idea that Reid liked Ember. If Sherry were to tell her that, Ember would have a fit. Sherry, personally, didn't doubt what Ricky said, but she knew her friend would think she'd gone crazy. Ember didn't respond well to seemingly ludicrous ideas like that.

"It's late. We should probably get going," Ricky said, glancing at his watch and grimacing. Sherry was reluctant to leave, but he was right; it was late. And she supposed she should find out what it was that her roommate had done while she was away. She shuddered at the possibilities.

They were just pulling up to the dorms when Sherry thought to check her phone again for a reply from Ember. Sure enough, there was a text.

Trust me, I won't need to explain. You'll see. X

The text read. Sherry rolled her eyes, mentally questioning the idea of placing Ember in some sort protective home. As in to protect the rest of the world from Ember.

Ricky walked her to the big wooden doors of the students' dorm and led her in, giving a quick smile and a dip of his head, looking as charming as could be. It wasn't until they reached the staircase at the end of the hall, that Sherry spotted something out of place. There was piece of A4 paper pinned to the wall at the base of the stairs. She leaned over to take a look, and almost bent double with laughter. Ricky looked back at her questioningly, and walked back to see what she was laughing at.

"Uh oh. Reid won't be happy." Ricky's voice was strained; he was fighting to contain his own laughter. And failing. His mouth was bent into a funny line, but his eyes were bright with humour. "Ember's work?" he asked, nearly gasping the words through silent laughter. Sherry could only nod, her sides aching from laughing so much. Well, Ember had really outdone herself this time.

Sherry and Ricky climbed the stairs, Sherry wiping tears off her face and Ricky biting his lip to silence his chuckles. When they reached the second floor, they found many more posters pinned along the walls. And several people gathered round each of them, laughing. They made their way past the chortling students to Ember and Sherry's room. Ricky placed a quick kiss on her cheek, but lingered with her for a moment, looking like he had something to say. Sherry waited patiently for him to speak.

"You know, I really like you. And I know Reid isn't going to like Ember's newest battle position… So, I thought I should say right off, that I'm going to try to make him give up. I can't have him at war with my gi… with your best friend… if we're going to keep dating. It would be awkward. Not to mention possibly dangerous." Ricky pulled an expression of mock fright, and then smiled weakly, blushing just faintly. Sherry felt her heart slam into her ribs. He wanted to keep dating her. And he was going to try to talk Reid out of trying to kill Ember… for her sake. Awww! How sweet.

Sherry smiled helplessly at him and he kissed her again. This time on the mouth, chastely. She almost reeled from the intoxicating sweetness.

"Goodnight," Ricky whispered into her hair, and then strode away past the still-chuckling students in the hall.

"Oh, wow," Sherry breathed, feeling dizzy. Somehow, she managed to push open the door and get over to her bed before she collapsed with a happy sigh. She buried her face in her soft pillow.

"Good night?" Ember's voice was gentle, but edged with excitement.

"Mh-hm," Sherry nodded, her voice dreamy.

"Like my prank?" Ember let out a small giggle.

"It's hilarious. Reid's going to go… nuts." She was interrupted by a yawn. She let her eyes slide shut, not caring that she was still fully dressed. She suddenly felt dead tired and seeking peaceful dreams. She felt a hand on her shoulder, patting her lightly.

"Good. On both counts. You deserve some sleep," Ember's voice was little more than a whisper. Sherry rolled over, kicking off her shoes and lazily slipping under the covers. She was sure her dreams would be full of Ricky tonight, and she looked forward to it. She just had to get to sleep first.

Reid

"Uh, hi Reid," Ricky greeted him, coming in from his date. Reid himself was half asleep, resting off the aches from a trying swimming practice. He mumbled a vague response to Ricky and groaned when he turned his head to see his friend. "I take it you haven't left the room recently?" Ricky asked him, his voice oddly mocking, causing a kind of stupefied suspicion to rise in Reid.

"No. I did some laps in the pool and came back here to sleep. Why would I bother leaving?" Reid propped himself on his elbows, wincing as his shoulders protested to the movement. He supposed that extra two hours of practice had been a couple hours more than were strictly necessary.

"Well, um… did anything… you know, weird, happen at the pool?" Ricky hedged cautiously, strolling into the bathroom to change out of his date-clothes.

Reid pretended to think for a moment, and then nodded slowly. "Actually, yeah. Some prick stole my clothes." Reid rolled his eyes, making it clear by his tone that he knew exactly who had stolen his clothes. There was only one person who would have the nerve to pull that kind of prank on him.

"Really? Well, uh… anything else?" Ricky's voice was suddenly quick and light, like he was trying not to laugh. "You know, like maybe… you proposed to Steve the lifeguard?" Ricky burst out into laughter, coming back into the room with his eyes bright.

Reid bolted up with a snarl. "What? What the hell are you talking about?" he yelled, flinging himself off his bed. Oh, no, she hadn't, had she? There was no way that Ember was that good.

Ricky stumbled back a step in his fit of chuckles and tumbled onto his bed. "Just… I just think you shouldn't leave the room for a while. Like a few days… or weeks," Ricky gasped, pulling a clean t-shirt on with some difficulty. Reid just gave him an angry glance and stormed to the door. "No Reid, seriously!" Ricky shouted after him as he flung the door open and stepped into the hallway, aiming to make for Ember's room.

But as soon as he got out the door, he was assaulted by laughter from both sides. He whipped his head around, seeing dozens of students crowded in groups around posters on the walls. With a vicious growl that sent the nearest group of girls fleeing, he stalked up to the closest poster. Then he stared in horror. That little bitch! He glared at the poster; a photo of him, kneeling on one knee by the lifeguard chair - Steve the lifeguard looking down at him with a confounded expression - and holding something glinting up to the light. It looked exactly like Ricky had said. No way. Nobody, not even Ember could be this good. Even he wasn't this good, and that was really saying something.

"This is going to mean serious payback," he muttered to himself, tearing the poster off the wall and proceeding back into his room.

"Hey, I warned you!" Ricky exclaimed, trying futilely to hide a grin. Reid tossed the crumpled poster at the window and rummaged in his desk drawers for the necklace he'd put there earlier. He scrambled it out from beneath a stash of firecrackers and shoved it in his pocket, slamming the drawer shut hard enough to make the desk rattle. A bottle of wooden runes toppled over. He didn't bother setting it right again.

"Hey, where are you going?" Ricky yelled after him as he left the room again, slamming the door behind him. Some of the remaining groups of students jumped and scattered. Reid knew he was giving off waves of fury and menace and he hoped it would keep them from laughing. Despite that, he felt an infuriating blush creep up his face. He couldn't remember the last time he'd blushed with embarrassment like that. It only made him angrier.

By the time he reached Ember's door - only down the damned hall - he'd yelled at three kids, almost punched a guy and turned as red as beetroot, both from humiliation and fury. He practically punched the door, slamming it with the side of his fist so hard it shook.

When it finally came open, it revealed a dark room, seemingly empty. But he didn't fall for it, he wasn't stupid. "Ember, get your butt out here now!" he shouted, not caring that he could probably be heard on the next floor up. He clenched his fists until his knuckles hurt.

When she didn't come to the door after five seconds, he took a quick look in the room, ensuring there weren't video cameras or something set up, and stormed inside. The door whammed shut behind him and he turned, opening his mouth to give the offending demon an earful. But there was nobody there, just an empty space and silence. He was livid, too angry to care about keeping up appearances right now, so he reached out with his mind. He vaguely heard books rattle on the shelves - using magic while he was this angry was generally a bad idea because it could be hard to control. He wasn't supposed to do it, and Brandon would kill him if found out about this. But, he could feel and pinpoint the bright minds of two girls in the room. One was in the bathroom; the other was under the nearest bed. He could tell by the fire and sparkles in the mind under the bed that it was Ember, and she was finding this all very funny indeed.

He reeled his magic back in and, with superhuman speed, whipped the mattress off the bed to reveal Ember, curled up and shaking with silent laughter. Until she realised she'd been found. Then her laughter became audible and she crawled out from under the bed, tears rolling down her cheeks. He was almost too angry to care that he could feel his fangs extending impulsively, but the key word 'almost' meant he kept enough sense of mind to retract them. With some effort. What would it hurt her if he drained just a little blood? Maybe planted some bizarre notion or urge in her brain while he was at it? Make her dive into the outdoor pool naked or confess her love for him in front of the whole school? It would feel good to make her embarrass herself like that, and it'd be exactly what he wanted most right now: Revenge.

"I guess you saw the posters?" Ember gasped between fits of giggles, bringing him out of his devilish plotting.

Now that he was really looking at the giggling girl, he knew he couldn't mess with her head that way; he couldn't control her like that. If he hadn't been who he was, he might've thought he felt guilt at the idea. But, really, his mind supplied a much more likely answer; Brandon would find out if he compelled Ember, and then they'd get into another big argument and… God, who could be bothered. Surely she wasn't worth that stress, even for revenge.

"Next time you play a prank on me, you might want to make sure you don't lose anything!" Reid snarled, holding up her necklace, crushing the chain in his fingers. Ember was slowly sobering, and she reached out to snatch the necklace from him. He raised it above his head and watched her expression become sour in an instant. Her jaw was set and her eyes were cold.

"Give me my necklace, asshole," she hissed, clearly unhappy with his keep-away technique.

"I'll give you it if you can reach it," he smirked, feeling his calm arrogance returning as she got angrier with him. Well, well. Good to know what really got to her. The most childish of actions - such as playing keep-away with her belongings - could really rattle her temper. And here he'd been trying to think of complicated plots and traps to get his retribution.

Ember sighed, but it was more like a sharp hiss. Her blue eyes glinted with growing fury, and her little hands were curled into fists. Reid thought it might've been the first time he'd ever expected a girl to honestly punch him. For some reason, the idea intrigued him. "Is this your revenge? Acting like a twelve-year-old?" she asked, her voice deadly.

"Oh no, not even close. This is just giving me an idea is all," Reid replied with a shrug, still holding her necklace over his head. She glanced up at the dangling chain and then at him. The briefest of smirks flashed across her lips, a dark flicker in the depths of those blue eyes.

She darted forward, her leg swinging out to kick him where it would really hurt. But he was faster, grabbing her leg behind the knee and flipping her against the wall. She huffed sharply and lashed out with her hand, aiming for his face. He dodged neatly, pinning her to the wall with one hand while his other hand clasped her knee. As for the necklace… he wasn't sure where it had gone, but it didn't matter. He hitched her knee up on his hip, leaning close so she couldn't fight. Oddly, his own pulse quickened at the contact.

"Déjà vu? And this time Joseph isn't around to save you," Reid whispered, listening to her heartbeat racing. He wasn't sure whether that was fear or something else driving her insane pulse but either way, it worked in his favour. And as for Ember's expression, well, she looked utterly murderous.

"Let go of me. Now," she spat, but he noticed she didn't make a move to escape.

"Now why would I do that? I'm rather enjoying this. I know you just hate to be overpowered… and right now, you radiate discomfort. Or maybe it's not discomfort as such… Maybe it's something else entirely?" He leaned in further, testing, teasing. And he watched her pupils dilate, pooling out to leave just a ring of sapphire in her eyes. Interesting.

"Like what? Why don't you just let go of me? Get out! Get off me!" she shrieked, getting louder as she continued. But it wasn't going to work this time. Last time, he'd been caught off-guard, but now he was ready for her to scream and shriek as loud as she liked and he wasn't going to let go.

That was, until something hit him in the head from behind, causing him to jerk in surprise and lose his grip on Ember's knee. Damn it! He'd forgotten the roommate was hiding in the bathroom. Why was this girl never alone when he needed her to be? Reid turned, dodging a fierce kick and ducking to avoid a hard slap, and then looked down at what had hit him; a hardback book and a good thick one at that. Ouch. And Sherry, green eyes glowing indignantly, glared at him with another book in hand. Ember ducked round him and picked up the one on the floor, handling it carefully like it was some precious object, gently smoothing out a bend in the cover.

"Get out," Sherry said only those two words, but her voice was hot with fierce protectiveness for her friend. Reid knew he couldn't win this one. After all, he didn't want a war with both girls - just with the little demon.

"Fine," he shrugged, sending a wink to the little blonde girl, who was shaking with fury. Then he slouched out of the room, ignoring the sniggers and glances he got on the way back to his room. It didn't matter. He'd noticed the way Ember treated her books, almost with reverence, and it had given him the perfect idea for revenge. That girl would learn what it meant to mess with Reid Ashton.

Reid groaned when he got into his room, closing the door behind him.

"Reid! Why were you using magic? You know not to use it when you're pissed off! You could've exposed us all!" He was met by Brandon's furious expression.

"Yeah, well I didn't," he retorted fiercely, brushing past Brandon and Perry to collapse on his bed.

"Reid, I'm serious…" Brandon started again, persistently angry over nothing.

"You're always serious. It's part of your problem," Reid grumbled, not bothering with his taunting grin for once. Brandon sighed and Perry shifted to sit on the floor by Ricky's bed. Ricky himself was looking sheepish, obviously having been the one to tell Brandon what was going on. Reid shot him a dark glance and Ricky shrugged defensively.

"Okay man, what's going on with you lately?" Perry yawned, glancing at the digital clock that told them all it was after two am. Reid looked at him questioningly, not sure what he meant. "Oh come on Reid! You've been tense and hung up for two weeks now. I can't remember the last time you ditched a class, and not to mention you've been doing swimming practice instead of doing girls!" Perry chuckled half-heartedly, but there was worry in his dark eyes, which Reid didn't understand. So what if he was behaving for once? Shouldn't Brandon and his lapdog be happy about it?

"He hasn't conquered the blonde demon yet. Hence the posters," Ricky chipped in, looking smug and unfolding the crumpled poster from the windowsill. Brandon and Perry glanced at the piece of paper briefly. Both boys then burst into laughter. Reid wanted to punch all three of his friends at that point.

"Now I know why you nicknamed her the demon." Perry was clutching his ribs.

"This is brilliant. The first girl you haven't been able to charm. It could be good for you." Brandon sounded truly impressed, his laughter dying down. Reid hissed, and pulled a pillow over his face. "She's certainly different isn't she? You wanted her just for the thrill of messing with yet another girl. But now... you want her because she's unique. Right?" It appeared that Brandon was thinking out loud. Reid had half a mind to throw the pillow at his face and hold it there. Not that that would do any good, seeing as none of the vampire boys needed to breathe. But still. It might shut Brandon up if he was coughing up pillow feathers for a while.

"Why, Reid, are you starting to actually like this girl?" Brandon sounded pleased by the idea, and Reid pulled the pillow off his face just enough to see Brandon's grin spread to the other boys. Reid shot up angrily, the pillow flying across the room and hitting Brandon in the gut - Which got him a dirty look, but no retaliation.

"No, I don't like her! She's just a girl! I'm still messing with her, and I've got a plan already for ultimate revenge. She's just another girl!" The words felt wrong and clumsy coming out of his mouth, and left a hollow tingling in his throat. Brandon and Perry looked at him with suspicion and disgrace, while Ricky hid his expression by flopping down onto his pillows. Brandon slumped, pinching the bridge of his nose, sighing.

"Look, Reid. I'm not going to keep lecturing you for using magic. You know it's stupid, and it'll be your own fault if you get caught. Just try at least to keep it from the girl. Whether or not you like her, it's safer for everyone if the secret stays secret. Whatever it is you have planned for Ember... just don't emotionally cripple the girl." Brandon's voice was tired, and he was obviously giving up the fight for tonight.

Perry got off the floor and stretched. "Cripple her? Reid wouldn't do that," he muttered sarcastically, giving Reid a quick three-fingered wave before following Brandon out the door.

Ricky groaned into his pillow and glanced up at Reid.

"They would've seen the posters anyway. The only reason they didn't before I showed them was 'cause they came in the window," Ricky muttered defensively, seeing how pissed off Reid was.

"Whatever Kee. I don't care. Can we just drop it?" Reid groaned, using Ricky's hated nickname and retrieving his pillow from the floor and tossing it onto his bed again. It had been a long night, and he just wanted to get some sleep. Tomorrow was going to be hell, thanks to Ember, and he'd need time to refine his revenge plans.

Ember

"Did you hear? Apparently it was that new girl, Ember, who stuck up the posters." Some random girl was whispering in the row behind her in English.

"Yeah, I know. Someone told me that she slept with him, and he told her she was just another one-night stand, and she got pissed off so that's why she took the pictures." Another girl was whispering back. Ember groaned inwardly, cursing whoever invented rumours. Being as short-tempered as she was, Ember whirled round in her seat.

"I did not sleep with that asshole. I'd rather gouge my eyes out with a burning fork. And yes, I took the pictures but it was because I hate the guy and wanted to humiliate him. Got it?" She knew her voice was dangerous, and the girls who'd been chatting looked honestly shocked. Ember turned back to her desk, Sherry giving her a knowing look and a nod.

It was the third time today Ember had had to quash the start of a rumour. Everyone knew it was her who'd put up the posters, but they were speculating wrongly as to why she'd done it. Maybe she'd have to make an outright statement to the whole school before they got the message.

And, by all hell's demons, who should walk into the room right at that moment, but the blonde hottie of the hour himself. He looked rough today, his face drawn and dark circles under his eyes. His soft mouth was pinched and his brows pitched down in an angry, tired expression.

She almost felt sorry for him as the whole class burst into quiet giggles. His eyes immediately flicked to her, fixing on her without hesitation. It was really kind of creepy the way he did that - and the blue depths were icy and dark. She watched him hand a late slip to the teacher and start up the stairs toward her. Please don't sit near us, please don't sit near us! She prayed silently.

Unfortunately karma was not on her side today, and her prayers went unanswered. Reid sat down in the empty seat right in front of her. Crap! She hissed mentally. There were murmurs and chuckles and called-out comments to Reid. "Hey Reid, Where's your fiancé today?" and "A womaniser is a gay in denial!" were among the more civil slurs. Reid was apparently ignoring them all. The only thing he seemed to hear was Ember's whisper to Sherry. "If he wasn't such an ass, I'd feel a little bad for him right now."

At which point, Reid turned round and met her startled gaze. "You should feel bad. Because you have no idea what kind of mess you've gotten yourself in to. You're going to regret this," he almost snarled the words, his lovely face contorting viciously. For just a second he looked... almost inhuman. Ember flinched back and watched a satisfied smirk spread across his mouth.

Before she could reply, he turned round, grabbed his stuff and stormed out of the room thirty seconds before the bell rang. What was the point in him even coming to class so late? Idiot.

"Oookay. I think he's nuts," Sherry muttered, shoving her notebook into her bag.

"Yeah, I'm with you there," Ember agreed, slinging her own bag on her back. But there was something bothering her about the way his eyes had glinted and his teeth had seemed... too sharp... just for that single split second. Stop being stupid, she told herself. Maybe I ought to stop reading so many vampire books.

It wasn't until after school, stepping into their room, that the girls realised just how nuts Reid might be. Ember knew something was off the second she stepped into the room. Hadn't she left one of her books on the nightstand? And why was the top drawer of her dresser half open? That was her underwear drawer and she always made sure she shut it properly, just in case.

"Hey, do you know where I put my book? I could've sworn I left it by the lamp," Ember asked Sherry almost absently, shrugging off her schoolbag. It wasn't a huge deal really, she was always forgetting where she put things, but she had an odd feeling that the room had been disturbed. But the plain bed sheets were unruffled, the papers on the desk untouched, the laptop - still turned on from the night before - was where she'd left it. The only thing out of the ordinary was the half-open drawer.

"Not a clue but I…" Sherry started and then cut off with a gasp, as she turned to face Ember. The green-eyed girl was staring wide-eyed past Ember to the bookshelf behind her. "Ember, you might want to sit down," Sherry suggested, moving to hold Ember by the shoulders. Ember was immediately worried by Sherry's reaction and she wondered what the hell was wrong.

She whirled around and just about fell to her knees with horror. Her bookshelf was completely empty. That morning there had been over twenty books on that bookshelf, and now there were none. Ember suddenly had a horrid dropping feeling in her stomach, like she was suddenly falling backwards. She gritted her teeth and rushed to her dresser, flinging open the top drawer all the way, almost sending the wooden drawer flying onto the floor. She felt sick, staring into the empty white-painted drawer. This was the most horrifying thing that could've happened and she began to truly regret having pinned up those posters of Reid. Because she knew it was him who'd done this. Who else would have reason? And after all, he'd told her not two hours ago that she'd regret her actions.

Ember turned, utterly panic-stricken, and faced Sherry. Neither of them knew what to say. Ember knew she ought to be furious, but she was too appalled to be angry for the moment. She carefully shut the empty drawer and slumped to the floor, putting her head in her hands.

"What do you think he's done with my stuff?" Ember managed to choke weakly. She had no doubt that he'd probably tossed her underwear around the school and most likely torn the pages out of her books, but she needed to hear Sherry's theories, just in case she might be able to cast a little hope on the situation.

"I have no idea. You know him better than I do, and my theories might be affected by what Ricky's told me," Sherry sounded uncertain, and worried and very much like she didn't want to answer directly. Ember just looked up at her despairingly. Sherry sighed. "I think he'll blackmail you, but I don't think he'll do anything too awful. Ricky said last night that he thought Reid's war with you was his way of saying he likes you. I don't think Reid would…" Sherry stopped talking, looking very sheepish and backing away. So she'd noticed Ember's expression: murderous and venomously sceptical.

"So you're saying that Reid is torturing me, stealing my books and underwear, because he likes me?" Her voice was deadly calm, and she knew her eyes were glinting dangerously.

"I didn't say that. I said that's what Ricky thinks. I just think he'll blackmail you rather than hang your underwear out in public," Sherry replied quickly, sounding like she wished she'd swallowed her words. Ember gave her a long, dark look and got to her feet. The green-eyed girl stayed out of the way as Ember stormed out of the room.

The hallway was nearly empty, only a few students lingered, keeping their eyes averted as Ember made her way to Reid's room.

Reid

"Uh-oh. I think she discovered her missing items," Reid muttered to Ricky, holding up a pair of lacy pink panties on his little finger. Ricky shook his head and perched on the windowsill by the open window. The brunette boy didn't want to be here to see this, and he didn't completely agree with Reid's method of revenge. Stealing Ember's underwear was going a little too far in his opinion - and Reid knew this because Ricky hadn't hesitated in telling him. Three times. Thing was, though, that Reid didn't care what Ricky thought. He wasn't the one who'd been humiliated by the demon girl.

And right now, Reid could literally feel the fiery aura of fury heading towards their room.

Ricky sighed and flung himself out the window, and Reid heard him land neatly three storeys down. Lucky for them all, nobody hung around outside when it was raining like it was today.

He sat up and braced himself for the violent knocking at his door. He couldn't help the grin of anticipation that spread across his mouth.

Ember

Ember reached her intended destination, but she wasn't as stupid as Reid and she was far too angry to bother knocking. She simply threw the door open with brutal force, causing it to groan on its hinges before crashing against the wall. The room beyond the door was set out differently from her and Sherry's, and it was much dimmer, probably due to the half-closed curtains draped in front of the window. It was surprisingly neat without even a poster on the pale-blue wall.

Clear glass bottles sat in a row along the desk, and the beds were made with dark blue sheets.

"Give me my stuff, Reid!" Ember demanded, striding into the room, feeling like she could almost spit fire at the blonde boy, who was leaning casually against the desk in front of the window. He looked just faintly surprised. He'd probably expected her to at least knock first, the idiot, but otherwise he looked completely bored.

"What stuff?" He replied calmly, watching his own hand playing along the edge of the desk absently.

"You know damn well what stuff! Just give me it back!" she screamed, prowling toward him. He didn't so much as flinch when she got right up in his face and growled through her teeth. "Give me my stuff back. And I swear to God if you've so much as ripped a single page in a single book… I'll come back with a pair of scissors and a box of matches," She didn't add that she'd be removing the most precious part of his anatomy and then burning his hands off.

Reid simply looked at her patiently. "Try it."

Ember stepped back just a little and, before she knew what she was doing, her hand collided with the side of Reid's face. It was good, hard slap and she saw blood rise to a hand-shaped print on his fair skin. She wasn't surprised at herself for having done that, but she was surprised at Reid's reaction; he gave none. He seemed to simply accept it. It infuriated her even more. But of course, she'd forgotten Reid probably got slapped several times a month, plus the odd scrap with unhappy boyfriends of the girls who slapped him. This was nothing to him. Ember made an incomprehensible noise of frustration, and threw her hands up.

"Reid, just give me my stuff!" She hated that her voice was almost a whine. Her anger was dying down now, threatening to dissolve into tears. She even had to bite her tongue on a humiliated sob as Reid tugged a pair of her more delicate panties out of his pocket and dangled them on his finger. She instantly lunged for the fabric and ended up trapped in Reid's grasp. He wrapped one arm round her tightly as soon as she got close enough and he held the pink lacy underwear up out of her reach. She was so close to tears, she decided to stop fighting and focus on breathing steadily instead. She needed to compose herself before she could find a way out of this. She was desperately uncomfortable, being pressed against Reid's chest this way, having him smirking down at her from a distance of just a few inches. She refused to look at him.

"Now then. Let's talk." Reid grinned, tossing the panties in his upraised hand onto Ricky's bed.

Ember nearly screamed as he whipped her into his arms, carrying her, bridal-style, to his bed. He sat down on the edge of the bed and placed her on his lap. She felt like a very unhappy small child, being soothed by a big brother. Except this situation was the opposite of soothing, and being treated like a child was one thing that Ember just couldn't stand. But if she tried to escape now, she'd never get her stuff back.

"OK. So you want your stuff back, undamaged, and you'd rather I didn't expose your underwear to the whole school, right? What are you willing to give me in order for that to happen?" Reid's voice was taunting, his fingers even more so. He trailed his fingertips up and down her spine, making her shiver involuntarily. Sherry's guess had been right; He was blackmailing her. Damn it. She just glared at the door… and something about it seemed off. Her mind tucked that little suspicion to the back of her head, focusing on the current problem at hand.

"What do you want?" she asked emotionlessly, keeping her voice dead so she didn't start screaming or crying.

There was a tiny pause as Reid considered his options, and then murmured, "Hmm…A kiss." Ember flinched but didn't respond. She had expected something along the lines of admitting 'her undying love for him' in front of the whole school, something to cause her almost physically painful humiliation. But not this. This was so much worse. She'd been too angry and upset before to register how tantalising it was to be pressed against his chest, but now, with her anger going numb, simply from emotional overload, she could feel the tingling shocks his fingertips were shooting down her spine. Damn her stupid teenage hormones! And damn him for being so freaking gorgeous!

"Come on, it's just one little kiss. You get your books back, unharmed. You get your underwear back, without it being revealed to the world." Reid's voice had taken on a new quality, one she hadn't heard before - persuasiveness. He sounded almost too lovely when his voice was warm like that. Ember glanced around the room, looking for hidden cameras. She couldn't see any and, knowing she didn't have much of a choice, she sighed, giving in. She was going to have to wash her mouth out with soap and maybe bleach after this, and she'd hate herself for it too.

"Fine. You win. This is the last battle, because I can't keep doing this. My schoolwork is suffering and I'm not risking another detention. After this, I'll leave you alone and you've got to leave me alone. OK?" Ember struggled to say the words, feeling her pride race up to stop her. But she really couldn't keep fighting him pointlessly. It was a stupid battle to have started and now she was holding up a white flag. Reid seemed to have been taken off-guard by her surrender.

"You… you're actually giving up? No more games or pranks or fights?" he asked, sounding suddenly uncertain. His expression gave nothing away, though.

"Yup, I surrender. I'll kiss you, you give me my stuff back, and then we stay away from each other for good." Her voice shook as she said it, because she hated to let him win and she wondered how she'd get her kicks from now on. And maybe, just a little, because she enjoyed having an excuse to see him. No! Don't be stupid Ember! She mentally whacked herself. She was not going to fall for this guy. Ever. Ember Jennings simply did not fall for guys, and she wouldn't dare even think of going soft on this one.

"I… OK," Reid muttered, sounding, oddly, a little disappointed. Ember sighed and felt his arms go round her, strong and lean, holding her firmly to him. Then his lips found hers, and the world vanished. It was just her and Reid, and she could feel her heart fluttering in her throat.

The second their lips met, Ember was washed with heady sparks. It was an extraordinary feeling, like being in a dream where everything was too real. Her thoughts melted away to pure sensation, and she barely knew what she was doing when her hands snaked their way in his silky blonde hair. His mouth was so soft and warm, as the light kiss turned deep. He smelled so good, like spiced apple. She didn't want to move, didn't want to stop, she could just sit here and kiss Reid and never worry about anything else ever again…

Rap tap tap. A rapping at the window knocked her out of her entranced state. She gasped and threw herself out of Reid's lap, irrationally thinking they'd been caught. Of course, as she turned to the window, all she saw was a plump nightingale. She silently thanked the bird fervently and closed her eyes briefly, breathing hard. Jesus, she was an idiot. 'One little kiss' was all that was needed, and she had just about lost herself in kissing Reid. Reid of all people!

"OK, give me my stuff so I can go wash my mouth out with boiling water." She tried to make her voice sharp and scathing but it came out shaky. Reid looked like some forgotten sex angel, sitting with rumpled blonde hair, a faint pink flush across his cheeks and his soft mouth slightly swollen. Now she understood why even when he broke their hearts, girls came crawling after him again. He was almost inhumanly beautiful… and one hell of a kisser. But that devilish smirk spread across his mouth and the angel in him melted away.

"Fine," he said with a shrug, before scrambling around in the pine wardrobe - an exact match to the one in her own room - for a moment. He came back over, holding out a plastic bag filled with books and underwear.

She blushed and muttered a quick, "Thanks." Before snatching the bag from his outstretched hand and heading for the door. Her fingers closed on the cool metal handle just as Reid spoke.

"No. Thank you," he chuckled as she closed the door behind her.

Sherry was waiting when she got back to her room. She looked worried as Ember came in.

"I got my stuff back. But you were right. He blackmailed me." Ember could feel a blush creep up her face, not wanting to explain to Sherry what exactly happened. But it seemed she didn't need to.

"He made you kiss him?" Sherry's voice was tinted with surprise, but otherwise perfectly relaxed. She perched on the edge of her bed and crossed her legs, clasping her hands over her knee. Ember dumped the bag on the floor and turned to her friend in shock. "You might want to take a look in the mirror. It's kind of obvious. I'm just surprised you actually did it." Sherry was smiling now, and Ember wondered just how surprised Sherry actually was. But she did as instructed. The mirror revealed a girl with slightly ruffled hair, bright eyes, pink-tinted cheeks and a darkened, swollen mouth. For a second, Ember almost didn't recognise herself. Yeah, it really is obvious. Damn. She hoped nobody had seen her leaving Reid's room in that case. That would be bad.

"Well, it was the only way to get my stuff back and… I surrendered. I gave up. No more battles or pranks or anything. We're going to stay away from each other from now on." Ember sighed, and began piling her underwear back into the top drawer of her dresser.

"Seriously? You gave up? That's not like you." Sherry frowned, then added, "And Reid's OK with that?" she sounded sceptical for some reason Ember couldn't fathom.

"Well, I'd assume so. He won, didn't he? He won the battle and he got me to kiss him. He ought to be OK with it. He can move on to his next target." Ember shrugged, but something in the back of her mind told her she was wrong. It seemed that the back of her mind was getting a little crowded as she ignored the little voice. Sherry said nothing more as Ember started lining her books back on her bookshelf.

Reid

"So, how'd it go?" Ricky grinned, wandering up to Reid, who was lingering by the pool. The sharp smell of chlorine and sweat mingled in the air unpleasantly, but Reid was used to it by now. The high, small windows set in the walls cast fragile beams of pale light across the rippling, blue-green surface of the pool, making it shimmer.

"She surrendered." Reid shrugged, pretending to watch Brandon swim. He tried to sound nonchalant at least, knowing he should really sound smug and victorious. He just couldn't sound that way, because he really didn't feel that way. He felt... obscurely disappointed.

"You don't sound too happy about that? You won. What did you make her do to get her stuff back?" Kee gave him a suspicious look, searching his expression.

"Kiss me," Reid replied shortly, rolling his eyes heavenward and forcing a smirk. He folded his arms over his bare chest, and absently toed at a puddle on the floor.

"And she did it? That explains why she surrendered. I guess it was too high a price to keep playing," Ricky muttered, leaning back against the tiled wall. Reid didn't answer.

He was glad that he'd won, he was ecstatic he'd gotten her to kiss him - but he was truly disappointed that from now she'd be avoiding him. And he didn't understand why he felt like that. He'd won. He hadn't exactly gotten what he'd wanted from her, hadn't bedded her like he'd planned, but he'd made her give in; which he was sure was one hell of a victory, considering the girl's pride and ferociousness. Plus, that kiss… It was the strangest thing. He'd never experienced something like that before. It had been like there were sparks flying down his nerves, leaving hot tingles in their wake. If he didn't know any better, he'd think maybe Ricky and the guys were right about him liking the girl. But that wasn't his style. It couldn't be.

"Reid? Reid! Dude, back to Earth." Perry was waving a dripping hand in front of his face. The taller boy's dark hair straggled wetly around his face, and his eyes were bright with laughter.

"Yeah, what? I was just…." Reid frowned.

"Thinking about Ember?" Ricky asked wryly. Yes. Reid looked past his friend. Motes of dust swirled in the shafts of light, and Reid could see every particle. Sometimes, vampire sight was quite amazing. For instance, when Ember had been right up in his face, blazing with fury, he'd been able to see the shades of blue and chips of silver that made up her pretty eyes. He'd been able to see her pale freckles, even in the dimness. He'd been able to see the soft curve of her mouth, and the silkiness of her hair…

"More like daydreaming about what she'd look like in a miniskirt and heels," Reid retorted devilishly, hoping his thoughts hadn't shown on his face.

But Ricky called his bluff. "Liar. You wish she'd kept fighting and hadn't given in. You have no reason to see her anymore. And that upsets you." Reid had forgotten how good Ricky was at reading him sometimes. Reid just glared at him and walked to the pool's edge. The pool tiles were cool and slick under his feet, and he focused on feeling the physical surroundings rather than thinking. If he started thinking again, he knew what he'd think about.

As he stood on the edge of the pool, he heard Ricky and Perry's chuckles. Then he dived, the cool water enveloping him. He fell into the easy, natural rhythm of strokes as he swam, pushing the demon girl out of his mind.

H.G. Lynch

Unexpected Saviour

H.G. Lynch

Born Dark

Ember

It was Friday night, and Ember was bored to death. It had been four days since she'd surrendered to Reid, and she'd barely caught glimpses of him all week. It seemed he was keeping his side of the deal. He was avoiding her, and she was avoiding him. It wasn't that she missed him, or his arrogant attitude - not at all - it was just that she had nothing to do without plotting against him.

All too much lately, she'd been thinking about that kiss. She found herself replaying it in her head whenever she was alone - and she'd been alone an increasing amount of time since Sherry had been out with Ricky twice more this week - and it was driving her nuts. She hated that she could still feel his soft lips on hers, and the tingles running down her spine. It was maddening to be able to still smell his spiced-apple scent, and feel his fingertips sliding down her back. She could still see the way his eyes had darkened before he'd kissed her, see the delicate cheekbones and the shadowy crescents of his long lashes…

SHUT UP! She commanded her mind, shaking her head violently as if she could shake away the memories. There was something else nagging at her in her subconscious. But every time she got close to tracking it down, it escaped her.

Ember sighed, and flopped back on her bed, puzzled and frustrated. It was late, and Sherry was already asleep - she'd gone to bed early with a headache. Staring at the ceiling, watching shadows move with the shifting of the moonlight sinking through the curtains, it wasn't long before Ember herself fell asleep, drifting away, still lying on top of her duvet.

***

She was in Reid's room, and it was dark. The curtains were closed. She was facing the door, but there was someone else in the room, she could feel it. Her shoulder blades prickled with a feeling of being watched. She turned to see Reid, leaning on the desk just like he had been on Monday when she'd burst in furiously. Only now, his shoulders were tense, his fingers curled tightly round the edge of the desk.

"Why am I here?" Ember asked, her voice echoing like it always did in dreams. Reid looked up at her, but his eyes weren't their usual blue. They were brighter, almost glowing, piercing. It was eerily beautiful. And he looked… haunted. There was something dark behind his expression, something scary in his fine features.

"You shouldn't be here. I could hurt you." Reid's voice was cold and floating; the words almost coalesced into mist and wrapped round her.

"Reid, I'm not scared of you." Ember let acid seep into her voice. But something inside her told her she really ought to be scared of him.

"You should be," he replied icily, waving one hand in an abstract motion in the air. She just raised one brow questioningly. Suddenly, the door - which had been open - slammed shut. Something about it was familiar.

The dream cut to a flash from Monday, when she'd noticed the door was closed… She'd left it open when she'd stormed in, and Reid hadn't had time to close it before she tried to attack him. That was what had bothered her that day, the detail she'd tucked away in the back of her mind.

And then she was back in the dream room, Reid looking at her with a dangerous glint in his eyes.

"Reid, what's going on here?" Ember asked, confused and irrationally worried about being stuck in this room with him. It's the darkness, she told herself, the dark is freaking you out. You know his eyes don't really glow like that, you know he doesn't really look so… predatory. The shadows played across his face, collecting in the hollows at his temples and under his cheekbones, catching in his fair hair in a way that made her itch to draw him with charcoal pencil.

"I told you. I could hurt you," he said, his face twisting in an expression that was almost scary. A gleam shone in his eyes and his teeth took on an edge that looked too sharp.

Flashback again. English on Monday, when he'd turned to her and sworn she'd regret humiliating him. He'd had that same scary, almost inhuman expression. She wondered about it then, and she wondered about it now. It frightened her a little. Surely she was imagining things?

But she was back in the dream room with Reid, and he was muttering something over and over. "What?" She couldn't hear what he was saying. He didn't look at her; he was looking past her, with blank eyes now. He kept muttering. It was creepy.

"Reid-" She was abruptly flung back to reality

***

Born Dark

Ember was sitting up in her bed, staring into dizzying darkness. What the hell? That was one of the weirdest dreams she'd ever had. It had also felt amazingly real. Her nerves were jangling, and she eyed the corners of the room where the shadows lurked at their darkest. But there was nothing there. Of course there was nothing there.

"Great," she sighed almost silently. "I'm dreaming about the guy now." She groaned and drew up her duvet, crawling under it and praying Reid would stay out of the rest of her dreams. What was the point in avoiding him, if he still popped into her mind all the time?

Reid

What Ember didn't know was that, down the hall, Reid had just had the same dream. Only he knew what he'd been muttering at the end…'Vampire'.

Sitting up in bed, he pushed his hair off his face, taking a deep breath. His eyes flickered to the doorway, where he half-expected Ember to be standing, glowering at him accusingly. The door was closed, though; nobody was there. The rest of the dark room looked exactly like it had in the dream, exactly how it looked every night. He had no reason to think anything would be different, but he almost wished it were, wished it didn't look so exactly like the dream. He didn't like the shivery feeling slithering down his spine. Reid didn't usually dream, and when he did, it was rarely a good thing. It was a sign of his distress when he dreamed, an indication of his restlessness.

He was starting to think there was problem developing here, but until Ember came to him screaming that he was a blood-drinking monster, he didn't have to let anyone know. No matter how much he wanted to see her again, he'd avoid her for a while. To keep her safe from his secret. To keep his friends safe from her.

Ember

"Ember? Uh, Ember?" A male voice drifted into her blank reverie. She snapped out of it and looked up to see Joseph Rian standing there, looking sheepish. His dark hair was tousled, and his cheekbones were flushed faintly pink with a blush, but his green eyes sparkled at her.

"Oh, hi Joseph." Ember smiled politely. She hadn't realised before that he was in her Biology class.

"Uh, we have to pair up for the microscope slides and I was just wondering if I could partner with you?" Joseph gave a shy, sweet smile and a shrug. Ember looked around and saw that everyone else was paired up already, flipping through their textbooks and chatting quietly at their benches.

"Yeah, of course." Ember shifted her work over so Joseph could sit down. The teacher handed out microscopes and slides.

"Right. I want you to identify which type of plant is under your slide. Onion cells, pond weed, or fern cells," Ms. Bowie instructed, slipping back to her desk at the front of the lab.

Ember watched Joseph clip the slide under the microscope and examine it for a moment. "I think it's the… fern?" he said uncertainly, glancing at her sideways. He moved aside to let her look. She glanced down the scope and adjusted the lens size.

"Mh… I think it's the onion. See the way the cells are long and thin instead of short and blocky?" Ember smiled lightly, letting him know she wasn't criticising him.

He took another look and smiled up at her. "Yeah. I see. Have you done this one before or am I just a little slow?" He grinned bashfully. Ember took pity on the boy.

"It's an easy mistake to make, but I actually have done this before. I did it at my last school." She dropped her gaze to the desk and fiddled with her pen. She could feel Joseph's green eyes watching her, and it seemed he was about to say something when the teacher interrupted.

"Ember, Joseph. Have you identified your plant cells?" Ms. Bowie asked, pushing a lock of dark hair behind her ear. Ember looked up and nodded mutely. She didn't talk to teachers, unless they pissed her off enough to elicit a snarky comment from her. "And?" The teacher turned to Joseph, knowing too well that Ember wasn't likely to answer.

"The onion cells?" Joseph shot an uncertain glance at Ember.

The teacher took a fleeting glance down the scope and nodded, "Well done."

The teacher walked away, leaving Joseph looking sheepish, "I guess you were right," he muttered quietly. Ember smiled and shrugged, and then the bell rang.

Born Dark

"So, uh, I... I was just wondering- I mean, if you're not doing anything tomorrow night...Would you maybe consider, you know, going out, like on a-a date with me?" Joseph had walked her to her room and now he blushed scarlet, dropping his green eyes to the floor and twisting his hands nervously. He really was very cute, and maybe a night out would do her some good. She'd have to explain to Sherry though; they'd been planning to have a movie night tomorrow.

Sherz would understand, but Ember still felt just a little bad as she said, "Yeah. I'd love to." Smiling as sweetly as possible. Joseph suddenly lit up like a light bulb, his green eyes almost glowing and his whole demeanour seemed more confident.

"Great. Thanks. I'll, uh, pick you up here at eight. That OK?" He grinned, running a hand through his dark hair. Ember nodded and blushed as he turned and wandered back down the hall, giving her a glance over his shoulder. A few people lingering around followed his gaze and started whispering. Fabulous. The whole school was going to know she had a date with Joseph Rian by tomorrow afternoon. Then again, that idea had a certain appeal. Maybe if Reid found out, he'd... No. Don't even go there, she told herself, cutting the thought short. She didn't know where it was going, but she was sure she didn't want to finish it.

With a sigh, she turned the door handle and slipped into her room. She dropped her bag on the floor, dumped her textbooks on her bed, and beamed at Sherry. Sherry looked up from her book and raised her eyebrows, apparently surprised by Ember's expression. "I've got a date tomorrow night!"

Friday night at TipTap was interesting, to say the least. A bar packed full of tipsy teenagers and writhing couples on the dance floor, music buzzing from a jukebox and friendly betting at the pool table. Ember was dressed casually in dark jeans and a graffiti-print grey t-shirt, with her best black hoodie and favourite Vans trainers. She had her hair down for once, handy to hide behind when she got nervous or paranoid. And in a crowded bar, with a cute guy, that happened a lot.

They were sitting at the bar, on high stools, overlooked by warm lights and the pretty bartender girl who was polishing glasses behind the counter. Ember was halfway through her glass of coke while Joseph was halfway through his third can of beer. She hadn't suspected he was a drinker, but as long as he didn't get plastered, she didn't really mind. 'Joey', as she'd learned his friends called him, was currently blabbering about some Biology homework she must've forgotten about and Ember was less than interested in what he was saying. He was a nice guy, but not particularly fascinating. Now, if he was as impulsive or curious as Reid, he might… Stop thinking about Reid! You're here with Joseph!

"Hey, uh, Ember… Do you want to dance?" Joseph's voice was almost lazy with the alcohol he'd consumed but his eyes were alight with bashful curiosity. She hadn't realised she'd been staring blankly at the dance floor for at least ten minutes now. Scantily clad girls were swaying now with various boys scattered across the dance floor, the coloured spotlights beaming down on them from above. The music had turned soft and slow, and Ember tried not to grimace. She couldn't imagine slow dancing with anyone, let alone with Joseph.

"Oh, no. No, I don't dance." She turned to him with a polite smile. Joseph looked relieved and then grinned at her before gulping down the rest of his beer. She let him put an arm around her, not too bothered about it because it was an innocent enough gesture between two people on a date. He said something indistinctly about how nice she smelled. Lightweight, she thought absently, noting the slur of his voice. She let him plant a gentle kiss on her forehead as he traced her arm with his fingertips, feeling just a little uncomfortable. He was warm and smelled good under the faint scent of booze, and he was such a nice guy after all.

He seemed surprised when she suddenly flinched away, gasping. Not because of anything he'd done, but because her eyes had been lingering distractedly on the doorway and someone of interest had just walked in. Reid.

He looked great tonight, his blonde hair tucked under a black beanie, and his slim hands folded in those fingerless gloves of his. It had been five days since she'd really seen him, and she'd forgotten how gorgeous he was, with his high cheekbones and sculpted mouth. Ember was glad at that moment that she couldn't see his eyes from here, knowing full well how his lovely eyes could mesmerise her - though she rarely admitted it, even to herself.

Joseph was looking over his shoulder at Reid, with something like disgust in his expression. A dark, reflected light glimmered in his green eyes. "Ignore him. He comes here all the time to play pool with his buddies." Joseph didn't sound happy about that. Ember just shrugged, tearing her eyes away from the blond bad boy to smile at the gentle dark-haired boy next to her.

Joseph resumed nuzzling at her neck, making her want to squirm away but she tried to enjoy it instead. He kissed his way up her jaw and planted just a tiny kiss on her lips. It felt good, warm and sweet, and she let him do it again. And again, until he decided he wanted a real kiss. His fingers touched her spine and she almost jerked away, remembering how it had felt when Reid had done the same thing when he'd kissed her. She pushed the thought away and let Joseph kiss her, feeling paranoid that people might be watching, but otherwise not minding. It was a tame kiss, slow, calm and gentle - not like the intense, electric kiss she'd had with Reid. It didn't make her tingle, and she didn't feel like she was going to abandon herself to the feeling of his lips on hers.

Abruptly, Joseph broke away and looked around with excited emerald eyes. Ember had a sudden wrenching feeling in her stomach, a feeling of impending trouble... and of being watched.

Instinctively her eyes fell on Reid at the pool table, and sure enough, he was watching her. He didn't look away when she caught him, his blue eyes sending a shiver through her despite the distance. His expression was unreadable, but it was somehow intense enough to make her wish he were the one sitting next to her, instead of Joseph. Banishing that thought quickly, Ember turned back to her date with a brighter-than-needed smile.

"Hey, can I show you something? Come on, I'll show you something cool around back. But you've got to keep it a secret." Joseph grabbed her hand before she could answer, and started tugging her toward the side door. Behind that door was an alleyway that led round the back of the bar, and something in her gut lurched in protest.

"Wait, I'd rather just stay here." Ember tried to pull her hand away but Joseph was stronger than he looked.

"Come on, I promise it's OK. I just want to show you something I found the other day back there. I've been hiding it but I think you'll like it." Joseph looked like he'd sobered up, calmness returning to his eyes and his grip on her hand loosening a little. She frowned but nodded, looking around nervously. *Stop being stupid,* She told herself as Joseph led her out into the empty alleyway, *You're being paranoid again, but this is Joseph remember? Sweet, nice guy. Hardly the type to hurt you.* She thought the words with a kind of panic, almost willing them to be true. But of course, wanting things to be one way doesn't make them so.

As she'd suspected, Joseph dragged her around to the back of TipTap, in the pouring rain, insisting there was an abandoned kitten that he'd been looking after. It was dark and dank and stank due to the massive dumpsters shoved against the corrugated metal-plated wall. A chain-link fence blocked off the alleyway to the left of her, and a building formed a solid wall behind the bar.

Unsurprisingly, Joseph pinned Ember to the wall. She'd almost expected that. *For God's sake, this is the third time I've been pinned to a wall in the last three* weeks. Strange that that was her first thought. Maybe she was getting used to it. What she wasn't used to was having someone pressing up against her and trying to shove a tongue down her throat. She pushed at Joseph's chest, and when he didn't move, she yanked his head back by his hair.

"Joseph, stop it!" She didn't quite yell the words, too out of breath to yell. Joseph looked furious, a hazy light in his eyes. He slammed her back against the metal wall of the bar and gripped her sides hard enough to bruise. Her head smacked off the wall, sending a lancing pain through her skull. Water dripped down her back, soaking her clothes. Her wet hair fell into her eyes like dripping ropes. "Joseph! Stop! Stop it! Don't!" she gasped, writhing to get free. His hands were creeping under her t-shirt, his rough fingers scrabbling across her skin, and she felt her mind screech to a halt in the middle of panic mode.

This was so different from having Reid pinning her tauntingly, having other people in earshot just in case. Having Joseph Rian, the sober nice guy, wandering helpfully down the hall. That was a different Joseph Rian than the one currently trying to tug her t-shirt up. Ember got ready to scream, swung her leg up to kick him where it would really hurt. He yelped and fell back, groaning. He recovered quickly, and then snarled. There was a dangerous light in his eyes. He almost looked feral.

Ember bolted right, making for the front of the bar, her scream sticking in her throat. She thanked whatever greater force was out there that she'd chosen to wear Vans tonight and not heels, but she still wasn't fast enough. Joseph seemed to move at the speed of a racing animal, grabbing her wrist as she ran. He tossed her to the filthy ground easily, and she shrieked. Pain shot up her arm; the rough ground scraped the skin from her hands and elbows. Oddly enough, under her fear and panic, she was just purely furious at herself. Furious that she was so small and so weak. And so stupid to have come here like this with him. She'd known better and ignored her instincts. Idiot!

"Goddamn it! Would people stop treating me like a damned rag doll!" she screamed, losing control of her temper. Anger was always her default emotion, especially when she was terrified. Joseph didn't seem to even hear her, his eyes glinting silver in the dim moonlight. Along with his mussed dark hair, it made him look truly animalistic. She half expected a feral snarl to tear from his lips. That would certainly petrify her.

Ember got ready to roll away as soon as Joseph pounced, hoping her surging adrenalin would give her enough strength to break his leg. She knew it'd be risky, though. Joseph was fast and strong, and she didn't stand a chance if he got his arms around her.

Just as Joseph got ready to pounce, a dark smirk spreading across his face and his eyes turning to mercury, something astounding happened. A blur of shadows and light streaked across the alley behind Joseph, and suddenly the dark-haired boy yelled out in pain and anger. His arms were trapped behind his back, twisted at a painful angle. Ember couldn't see well in the darkness and that frustrated her as Joseph fell to his knees, his arms still twisted behind his back. She heard a thud, like someone kicking flesh, and Joseph arched his back, yowling in agony. An indistinct voice murmured something in a vicious tone, but she couldn't hear the words.

Joseph was flung abruptly to the side, hitting the metal wall with a surprising amount of force, and he slid down onto the dirty ground, clearly unconscious.

Ember, breathing quickly and raggedly, fixed her attention on the figure shrouded in shadows. The one who'd saved her. With adrenalin and fear rushing through her veins, she scrambled backwards when the figure stepped toward her. She vaguely noticed for the first time that tears were pouring down her face, and her arm hurt. A lot. She must've whacked it when Joseph had tossed her to the ground.

"Hey, look, it's me. I'm not going to hurt you. It's OK. See, it's just me."

Ember nearly fainted at the sound of that voice, her whole body going numb with relief when Reid walked into the stream of light so she could see him.

At that moment, she would've sworn he was an angel. He didn't have a scratch on him, his clothes and hair were barely ruffled and it was clear it was no sweat for him to have tossed Joseph around like that. Seeing him standing there like some powerful, gorgeous saviour, Ember just cried more. Completely breaking down as she saw the concern lingering in Reid's deep blue eyes, not a hint of arrogance in his expression. There was anger, but it wasn't aimed at her. It was aimed at the unconscious son of bitch lying on the ground six feet away. The rain had stopped now, but she was still soaked and covered in filth. Her scrapes stung, and her sides ached with impending bruises.

"Shh, Shh. Calm down. It's OK." Reid came toward her with his hands held up in a non-threatening gesture, palms toward her. He crouched next to her and she let him help her to her feet.

She was still crying, but more quietly, as she limped alongside Reid to his car. She didn't protest when he folded her into the passenger seat and strapped her in.

He got in the driver seat and turned the key in the ignition, and the car hummed to life. The sound was soothing, so were the familiar scent of leather seats and the warmth of the car. Neither of them spoke as Reid drove back to the dorms.

By the time they pulled into the parking lot outside the dorms, Ember had recovered enough to have smoothed out her hair, wiped her face on her sleeve, and stopped whimpering like an injured puppy.

Reid turned off the ignition and just leaned his head back on the headrest, sighing. Ember looked at him, thinking of how to word what she had to say. She stared at his sharp profile, the line of his jaw, the outline of his straight nose, the curve of his mouth. He seemed to sense her eyes on him because he opened his eyes and turned to look at her searchingly. Ember swallowed and settled for saying the simplest thing she could think of.

"Thank you," she said the two words with as much gratitude as she could put into her shaking voice. Reid continued to look at her, and nodded once in acknowledgement. She took a steadying breath and looked at her scraped hands in her lap. The edges of the wound were black with dirt, and the scrapes were full of ground-in filth. She knew she ought to clean that out as soon as possible. But she didn't want to move.

"Are you OK? He didn't break anything did he? Will you be OK?" Reid asked suddenly, his quiet voice full of concern; honest and open concern. Ember looked up at him.

"I'm fine. Just a bit shaken is all. I've had worse bruises falling off horses." She tried to smile, wiping a stray tear off her face quickly.

Reid looked unconvinced. "But are you really OK?" There was something lingering in his voice that made her think that maybe Reid wasn't quite as bad as he made out to be. She nodded, rubbing her hands on her jeans.

"Sorry I ruined your night out. I should've known better than to follow him into the alley. That was so stupid," her voice wavered and she swallowed back more tears.

Reid's face showed astonishment and fury as he gazed at her. "Sorry? You're… you can't be serious! It's not like you asked to get attacked, is it? Everyone makes stupid mistakes, and it's not as if you could've fought him off. He would've dragged you out there no matter what you said or did. It's the third time Joseph's done that kind of thing. I'm surprised nobody warned you!" Reid clamped his mouth shut with an audible snap, grinding his teeth. He looked away, his eyes blazing. Ember watched with shock; She hadn't realised he cared enough to get angry over her this way. She felt a quivering smile tug at her lips, her sodden hair hiding it from Reid. He was busy glaring out the window, his knuckles white as he curled his hands into fists.

Ember, realising it was time to go, took a shuddering breath and pushed the car door open. Reid sighed and got out too, coming round to help her stumble into the dorms.

He helped her to her room and lingered cautiously at the door while she tried to make herself look less... wrecked. She didn't want to worry Sherry. But she realised it was a lost cause; Sherry was going to know something had happened, because there was no way of hiding the scrapes on her hands or the dirt that blackened her jeans.

"You sure you'll be OK?" Reid asked quietly. He was looking at her so intently, as if he were trying to read her mind. It was unnerving, but at the same time, it made her mouth go dry so her tongue stuck to her teeth.

She nodded. "Thanks again. You really saved me." She chuckled under her breath at the slight irony of that. He'd saved her from Joseph, but before, Joseph had saved her from him.

Reid shrugged. "No problem. That guy needed a beat down anyway." He grinned, his usual devil-may-care smile, and she smiled too. It was strangely good to see that smile again. Comforting in a way she didn't really understand.

"Well, goodnight," she muttered, turning to open the door. She carefully twisted the door handle, trying not to injure her hand further.

"Goodnight, Ember." Reid's voice was gentle, the words hanging in the air after he strolled away down the hall.

Ember crept into her room, slouched over to her bed, and collapsed. The soft duvet hugged her, and she didn't care if she got it wet or dirty. Sherry looked up from her desk, glasses perched on her nose - must've gotten tired of her contacts, Ember thought vaguely - and gasped.

"What happened to you? Are you OK? Oh my God." Sherry rushed over to her and covered her mouth with her hands in a gesture of shock.

Painfully, Ember reeled out the events of the evening while Sherry listened in mute horror. By the end, Ember was crying again, and Sherry wrapped her arms around her friend soothingly. Ember cried for a little while longer, and then got up, feeling the ache of her bruised arm.

"I'm going to have a shower," she said weakly, looking down at the mangled mess of her clothes. Sherry got her a towel from the wardrobe and left her alone to clean up.

The hot water was calming and cleansing, and cleared her head. Her scraped skin stung for a while, but all the dirt got washed out at least. She was too tired and shocked to think properly, her thoughts moving sluggishly and confusingly as she watched the steam condensing on the glass wall of the shower.

Eventually, she sighed and stepped out of the shower, having scrubbed her skin raw and washed her hair twice. She dressed slowly, carefully so as not to brush the fabric of her pyjamas against her scraped skin. Retrieving the first aid kit from the cabinet over the sink, she sprayed her wounds with antiseptic and bandaged up her hands. She was going to have plenty of bruises tomorrow, but she would be OK.

At last, she curled up in her bed, with Sherry watching her closely. She tugged the cosy duvet up to her chin and curled her fingers into it. She yawned.

"Do you want me to read you a bedtime story?" Sherry smiled delicately, and Ember rolled her eyes at her friend. She was starting to warm up under the duvet, and drowsiness began to suck her in.

"I'm OK, thanks," Ember replied sarcastically, yawning again. Sherry nodded and let her drift off to sleep. Ember knew, even in unconsciousness, that her friend was keeping watch over her. And just maybe somebody else was too.

Reid

Reid had had to resist the temptation of going back to TipTap, in the hopes that Joseph was still there, and draining him dry of every last drop of blood. He'd heard Ember's terrified shrieks from inside the bar, but Perry had warned him not to get involved, saying that Ember was feisty enough to handle it herself. But when he'd tapped into her Joseph's mind, seeing Ember - crumpled on the ground, and ready to fight - and seeing what Joseph planned to do to her... Well, every one of his friends couldn't have stopped him from going out there to save her. It wasn't that he would've let any guy rape any girl on his watch anyway, but reading the images of Ember in Joseph's mind had made him feel physically sick to the point of dizzying nausea, and something in his chest had exploded in fury.

It had taken all his control not to sink his fangs into the son of a bitch and listen to him scream in agony.

After he'd left her at her door, he'd crept out his bedroom window and hung about in the tree outside her window and watched her cry while her friend comforted her. He didn't know why he'd done it, maybe because he'd wanted to make sure she was really OK, or maybe just because it was the first time he'd really seen her since Monday and, even covered in dirt with tears staining her face, he'd been unable to stop himself from staring at her like she was some precious work of art. There was something wrong with him, and he knew it. He'd let this girl get to him, and he was having trouble fighting his way back to the arrogant man-whore that everyone was used to.

"Reid, dude, what's up? You look down?" Perry nudged him, knocking him out of his depressing reverie. Ricky was watching him closely, his blue-green eyes seeing into him.

"Huh? Oh, I'm just…" Reid sighed, hanging his head. He had no reasonable answer to give. History today was incredibly boring, not holding his attention in the least. It left his mind free to drift and that was dangerous.

"You're what?" Perry enquired suspiciously. Reid ignored him, groaning and putting his head on his arms, which were folded on the desk.

Mondays always sucked but… after the weekend he'd had, this one was worse than usual. He had a headache, he was bored and tired, and he couldn't get rid of his urge to tear Joseph Rian's head off. Plus, he couldn't shake the yearning to make sure Ember was OK. He'd spent the weekend swimming and drinking and he'd been in three different girls' beds. Gotten six slaps, a kick in the shins and scratches down his left arm. And the whole time, he'd been thinking of Ember. It was like her image was burned into his mind.

"Hey Reid." A girl wandered past his desk, waving flirtatiously over her shoulder at him. She was short with dark hair and lots of curves, but he couldn't call up a name. One of the girls he'd bedded this weekend, he guessed. He rolled his eyes at Perry, who was chuckling, and picked up his bag.

"Where're you going? There's still a half hour of class left!" Brandon called after him as he headed for the door. The teacher was too absorbed in helping some dumb jock at the back of the classroom to notice as he strolled out, slinging his bag on his back. Reid wasn't sure what he was doing, but he refused to sit in some dull classroom, doing nothing, for any longer.

Ember

"What the...?" Ember sighed, crawling off her bed. She'd decided to stay off school today, not sure she could stand going to Biology and seeing Joseph again. She'd end up wielding a scalpel and some hydrochloric acid at him. Sherry ought to be in Drama and nobody else knew where she was today. And yet, someone was knocking at her door.

She opened the door cautiously and blinked in surprise. "Reid? What're you doing here? Don't you have History right now?" Ember opened the door further and stood back to let him in. She could hardly be impolite to him, what with how he'd saved her on Friday. He stepped into the room hesitantly and glanced around, but Ember had the feeling he just didn't want to meet her gaze.

"Yeah, History got boring so I decided to come check on you," he replied with an easy smile, shoving his hands into the pockets of his jeans.

"How'd you know I was here?" she asked curiously, moving to sit on her bed, putting the bookmark back in her newest book. As Reid examined her My Chemical Romance poster on the wall above her bookcase, she surreptitiously glanced around the room, ensuring she hadn't left anything lying around that she perhaps shouldn't have.

"You've got Biology this period, and I know Joseph's in your Biology class... I did the math." He shrugged.

"OK. Well, as you can see, I'm fine. Bruises are healing, hands are fine. Still perfectly sane." She held out her hands for him to see the healing pink scars, and then tapped her temple to indicate her mental status. Reid smirked a little, finally looking at her.

"That's debatable," he said. Then his smirk dropped and he gazed at her with serious concern. Ember sighed, feeling the need to reassure him.

"Seriously, I'm sane. It's not like he actually did anything to me really. A few bruises and a panic attack. Why do you care so much anyway?" She crossed her legs and waved a hand, inviting him to sit on Sherry's bed.

He sat cautiously, and ignored her question. "So, I was thinking... If you're not too busy..." Reid started, his blue eyes fixed on hers and a smile clinging about his lips.

"You've got to be kidding me, right?" she cut him off sharply, giving him a critical look.

He rolled his eyes. "I was just going to suggest we go for a drive," he said, looking as innocent as a bad boy can.

"Mh-hmm? And why?" Ember countered, suspicion rising. Reid shrugged, fidgeting with the edge of Sherry's pillowcase.

"What, you got something better to do? I promise not to attack you." He grinned his arrogant grin, and she sighed. Honestly, she figured a little time out of this room might be good for her. And really, she wanted to go with him, wanted to spend time with him… No, you don't. You just want out of this room, she scolded herself.

"Fine," she groaned and got up to look for her shoes. Reid seemed to examine her for a moment and then nodded to himself, apparently making some sort of internal decision. "What?" Ember asked nervously, feeling self-conscious.

He just shrugged. "You might want to go with the boots," he said lightly and nodded toward the pair of black boots with the slight rubber heel, sitting in the bottom of her wardrobe. She glanced down at herself; she was wearing skinny jeans and a scrappy long-sleeved top. The boots would look good, she supposed, but why Reid would care about her wardrobe choices was beyond her.

She pulled on the boots and a jumper, and followed Reid out the door.

Ember didn't ask where they were going as Reid drove the Aston Martin down some long, empty road lined with fields. She enjoyed the view, the fresh breeze coming through the open window blowing back her hair. It was a lovely, warm day and the skies were blue for once, instead of a cloudy grey.

She was surprised when Reid stopped the car at a random lay-by next to field of sunshine-yellow rapeseed oil plants. The pungent scent of them floated into the car and tickled her nose. She turned to look at Reid questioningly and saw him holding up a black bandana in one hand.

"Uh… Oookay," she muttered hesitantly as he held it out toward her. Suspicion rose inside her, and she eyed him carefully. If he was thinking what she thought he was, he had to be joking.

"Put it on. Blindfold. I've got a surprise for you." He grinned, mischief leaping in his blue eyes. Yeah, that was what she'd feared. There was just no way she was doing that.

"Nuh-uh. Not happening," she answered bluntly, shaking her head.

"Oh, come on. I'm being nice. Trust me, you'll like the surprise," Reid insisted, blue eyes pleading. It was hard to believe that just a week ago, she'd been at war with this guy. She still didn't like him, she didn't, but it was hard to hate him after he'd saved her from being raped. And it was extremely difficult to say no when he looked at her like that! He wasn't playing fair, using his looks against her like that.

Still suspicious, Ember took the bandana, sighing, and blindfolded herself with it, tying it in a knot at the back of her head. It made her uncomfortable to be unable to see what was around her, and she tensed up, anxiety building in her chest.

"Can you see how many fingers I'm holding up?" Reid asked, a chuckle in his voice. The sound eased some of her anxiety. Just a little bit.

"I can probably guess which two fingers it is," she smirked.

"Wrong. Four fingers," he laughed, making her smile. It was a warm, genuine laugh, and it did funny things to her insides.

The car started up again, buzzing, and they drove for only a few minutes before it stopped again. She heard the car door open on Reid's side and then slam shut. Her door opened, a faint breeze coasting across her thighs, and Reid helped her out. As soon as she was standing, he let go of her hand, but she could feel he was still close. An array of smells hit her at once. Some smells were familiar, evoking flashes of memory from back home. Hay. Leather. Sawdust. Apples. And an animal smell she could pick out in petting zoo. The smells that weren't so familiar, at least not mixed with the other smells, were soap bubbles and rose blossoms.

"You can take off the blindfold now. Unless you want to guess where we are?" Reid actually sounded a little nervous for some bizarre reason. She'd never heard him nervous before. It was almost endearing.

"I don't need to guess. Stables. I'd know the smell of horses anywhere." She tugged off the blindfold with an incredulous smile. Reid looked almost impressed by her assumption, because she was exactly right.

They were standing in a large clearing in a thicket of pine trees. There were three rows of stable blocks, all built with red bricks and polished mahogany doors. The ground was paved in flat, grey stones, and there were finely-clad stable hands tending to gorgeous horses of all sizes, colours and breeds. It was like a little slice of heaven in the middle of a random hidden clearing.

"What is this place?" she asked stupidly, feeling the amazed expression on her own face. The place was so beautiful, so clean and bright and cosy-looking. Reid grinned at her, his face alight with... something. Something she couldn't quite identify.

"It's just something my parents had built for me when I was younger. I used to love horses, and they always encouraged me. I got tired of it once I turned eleven," Reid replied with a shrug, "But I remembered something you'd said about falling off horses the other night and thought you might like to see it."

Ember turned and saw that they'd driven up a long, narrow pathway, through the trees. There was small tack room just to the side of the pathway, painted white with a dark, polished wooden door. It was so quaint and pretty. "It's... amazing," she breathed, turning back to look at Reid. He looked ecstatic, his blue eyes bright and a smile spreading across his mouth. The fragrant breeze lifted fair strands of his hair that shone in the light filtering through the trees.

"Glad you like it," he said, bowing gracefully. She laughed. He held out a hand elegantly, pulling off his beanie with the other hand. "Want to go for a ride?"

Had Reid Ashton just offered to go horseback riding with her? Seriously? What happened to Acorn Hills Academy's resident bad boy? Ember decided she would have fun here and pulled on an outraged expression. "What do you think I am? I'm not one of your usual whores!" She shrieked, whirling away with her arms crossed. She bit her lip on a grin.

It was all of two and a half seconds before Reid burst out, "Hey! I didn't mean it like that! I meant the horses! You know I wouldn't... Look, not that I wouldn't... What I mean is-" Reid let out his breath and she turned to see him clutching his hair, a blush creeping up his face. Ember burst into laughter, doubling over.

"Why, Reid Ashton, did you really just blush?" she gasped, seeing his astounded, puzzled expression. "I know what you meant. I was just messing with you. Chill out." She finally stopped giggling, and added, "But seriously, how many girls do you take here? Half a dozen a month?" She teased, snatching his beanie from his hand and skipping away. Something about his momentary embarrassment had made her more confident. It was a slight crack in the impenetrable force field of Reid's coolness.

"Uh, actually, the only other people who know about this place are the guys. I've never taken a girl here before. Normally, there's only one recreational activity on the schedule when I'm with a girl."

Now she knew why Reid had sounded nervous to start with. Right now he was avoiding her gaze, rubbing the back of his head absently. Ember looked around again, admiring a small bay pony being led along by a stable hand, swinging Reid's beanie in her hand. "Well... That doesn't surprise me," she said softly, not knowing just what to say exactly.

"Why is that?" he asked, wandering over and snatching the hat back. She grinned then pretended to sulk, making him grin in return.

"Because you're Reid Ashton. Resident bad boy, man-whore and asshole. Girls want you for obvious recreations because you're the kind of guy that only wants girls for the same reason." She paused, "As for why on Earth you brought me here... I'm guessing it's different when you save the girl from being raped in an alleyway and want to ensure she doesn't turn around and have a mental breakdown, right?" Ember laughed, following close behind him as he walked to the first stable block. Reid didn't reply and he didn't turn to look at her. It was disconcerting not having a Reid-like reply to her comment for once.

She followed him past three gorgeous horses in the first stable block: A grey Dartmoor pony, a chunky Shire and a perky Shetland. They stopped at the stable at the end, and Reid gestured for her to take a look inside. There was a beautiful, liver-chestnut Arab in the stable.

"Let me guess. Thirteen hands and three inches?" She guessed the pony's height expertly.

Reid nodded, clearly impressed. "I figured she'd be just your size. Her name's Sasha. She's seven years old and she's a speedy little pony." Reid grinned, and Ember had never felt closer to a guy in her life. No guy she'd ever known had had any interest in horses. Yet here was her sworn enemy.

"This is why you told me to go with these boots!" The revelation hit her and she felt dumb for not having worked that out sooner. Reid laughed and slung an arm round her shoulders. She shrugged it off good-naturedly and followed him back to the little tack room.

The tack room was a lovely, spacious room with a wooden desk at one end, and two walls lined with saddles on racks. Reid lifted a well-kept brown leather saddle off a rack and handed it to her, dumping the bridle on top.

"I'm guessing you know how to tack a horse?" he asked, but he seemed just a little sceptical.

"I could do it with my eyes closed!" She grinned, adjusting her grip on the saddle to carry it properly, and waiting for Reid to grab his own saddle. He took her back to Sasha's stable and dumped his own saddle over the door of the stable next to it. He then opened the sliding bolt to let her into Sasha's stable, and watched her tack up the beautiful pony. To her, it was the most natural thing in the world. Positioning the saddle correctly, straightening the numnah, doing up the girth, unrolling the stirrups. The bridle was next. Sasha tried to bite her on the first attempt but with a firm, steady hand, she got the bit into the pony's mouth easily, and slipped the straps over the ears. She did up the throat lash and noseband and untwisted the reins.

She finished and turned back to Reid in under ten minutes, then saw his astonished expression. His mouth was actually hanging open. "Uh… I don't think I've ever seen someone saddle a horse so fast and so easily," he commented, looking a little doubtful. He let her out and glanced at his own saddle on the neighbouring stable door. "To be honest… I've never actually tacked up a horse before. When I was younger, I always had one of the stable hands do it," he admitted sheepishly. Well, well. This was a very different Reid to the one she loved to hate.

"Seriously? Do you want to learn? I could show you if you want," she offered, feeling only too glad to show the ever-arrogant Reid Ashton how to tack a horse.

"Uh, sure. I guess so." He smiled weakly, his blonde hair falling in his eyes.

The horse Reid had chosen was a lovely, fifteen hands high, skewbald cob; chunky but friendly, and quietly docile. This one was named Harry, and he was eight years old.

Ember dragged Reid into the stable and had him carry the saddle to the horse. She showed him where to position it and helped him smooth out the saddlecloth. She showed him how to do up the girth and check whether it was tight enough. She double-checked that part herself just in case. She didn't really want his saddle to slip if they started cantering. Giving him a little leeway, she did the bridle herself, knowing he'd likely get his fingers bitten. Inexperienced stable hands did that a lot. She let him do up the throat lash, telling him which hole to buckle it on. And then they were set. But after all that, Reid was still Reid.

"Saddling a horse is a woman's job anyway." He shrugged, giving her a sideways glance.

She slapped his arm hard and scowled at him. "Just because I can do something you can't, doesn't mean you have to revert to being an asshole. You were actually decent for all of ten minutes." She shook her head, sighing. Reid chuckled and led his horse out of its stable, sliding home the bolt on the door. Ember collected Sasha and they led the horses out to the yard.

"Do you need a stepping stool?" Reid taunted as she lowered the left stirrup on Sasha's saddle.

"Actually I think what you mean is a mounting block, and no, I don't need one, thanks." She stuck her foot in the stirrup and swung up onto the horse easily. She sat tall and straight, feeling funny to be on a horse without her riding-gloves and body-protector. Reid tossed a velvet-covered riding hat up to her and she clipped it on neatly. He pulled on his own hat and tried to steady Harry, who was skittering about nervously.

Ember tried not to laugh as Reid hung his head in defeat. She swung off her own horse and held Sasha's reins in one hand while holding Harry's in the other. She steadied the nervous cob, holding the noseband underneath just for safe measure.

"OK. He should be good now." She rubbed the cob's muzzle lovingly as Reid swung on. "Well done. I half expected you to get on the wrong way," she laughed, releasing the calmed Cob and getting back on Sasha.

"Hey, it's been a few years since I've been on a horse. The last horse I rode was like twelve hands high. Sorry if I'm a little rusty," Reid said in a mockingly sarcastic tone. Ember rolled her eyes at the blonde boy.

They rode along a hidden pathway through the trees, a real hack through the forest. The smell of dirt and wildflowers and pine trees was wonderful, and the slow, smooth movement of the horse's strides under her felt as natural as breathing. Sitting with her back straight and chin up, hands just right on the reins and heels tilted down, she was in heaven. Reid didn't look quite so natural on his horse alongside her. He looked nervous, rigid and uncomfortable.

"Relax. You'll freak out poor Harry. He'll think there's something to be scared of and then he'll get jumpy. That's when you'll fall off," Ember instructed soothingly, giving a squeeze with her legs as Sasha slowed down.

Reid glanced at her quickly. "What are you, my riding instructor?" he quipped.

"For today, yes. Because you've obviously forgotten how to ride a horse. Point your heels down and sit straight. And relax. You need to absorb the movement in your hips. Otherwise, if Harry decides to duck down to eat grass, you'll go flying over his head. Trust me, I've seen it happen a dozen times." Ember shook her head, sighing. She'd seen too many nervous kids fall off that way, and then the kids were always too scared to get back on the horse. It was a pity. But Reid seemed to take her advice; he loosened up a bit and tilted his heels down.

"There. See? Now loosen the reins a little, you're pulling on Harry's mouth. He won't like that." Ember watched as he struggled to correct the reins. She sighed and pulled Sasha closer, careful to ensure neither horse would kick out at the other. She looped her own reins over one arm and reached across to help Reid. She took his hands, keeping them positioned correctly on the reins, and slid them easily back. Her fingertips were warm where they brushed his skin. "Simple. Doesn't that feel smoother?" Ember smiled, glad her voice didn't waver despite the butterflies in her stomach. She knew how bizarre this situation was: Her riding on horseback through the forest, teaching AHA's bad boy - her enemy until just a few days ago - how to ride properly. And more amazingly, she was enjoying it. Reid nodded stiffly, his blue eyes focused ahead.

Ember took up her own reins again and directed Sasha a safe distance from Harry. She looked around her at the bright wildflowers and swaying long grass, the reaching pine trees and dirt path. It was so much like the forest she'd ridden in back home.

Memories of her old riding school bombarded her; the wide spreading green fields, dotted with horses she could name and describe every detail about with her eyes closed; wandering through the main field, the fresh grass wet with dew drops, swinging a head collar in her hand; the first time she'd led three horses at once, struggling not to get tangled in all the ropes as she sloshed through the muddy track to the stables; grooming her favourite horses, chatting away to the animals while she watched the soft coat turn glossy under the body brush; the first time she'd cantered, her first real jump; laughing and partying with the gang in the tack room after darkness fell and the horses were tucked away in their fields; and, of course, her favourite pony of all time - a little grey welshie with tiny ears and huge eyes - trotting around her field and rolling in the grass.

"Ember? You OK?" Reid's gentle voice broke into her reverie and she realised her eyes were wet. She quickly wiped the tears away and put on a smile. "I'm fine. I was just remembering my riding school back home. I hadn't realised how much I missed it until now." She heard the longing and sadness in her own voice. Reid just looked at her curiously and she pointed sharply forward, reminding him to keep his eyes on where he was going. He turned his attention slowly back to the dirt path. Ember peered closely at the path up ahead, where the light seemed tilted differently. As they neared the area, she saw the path widen and the trees thinned out. Perfect.

"Can you trot?" she asked Reid, and saw him nod once. His eyes were unfocused, and brooding. A look that sat oddly on the face of the arrogant blonde. "OK then. Shorten your reins and let's go!" Ember grinned and nudged Sasha into a smooth trot.

She instantly fell into the easy rhythm of rising-trot, matching the pony's strides perfectly. Sasha had a lovely stride, too; quick and light, unsurprising for such a dainty horse. She chanced a glance at Reid over her shoulder, and saw he was much more at ease, just slightly off on his timing of movement.

After a good lengthy trot, Ember pulled back on her reins and sat back in the saddle. Reid pulled up next to her and flashed her a grin.

"Well, that was fun," he said, and Ember gave him a look, unsure if he was being serious or sarcastic. He shrugged. "I'm just glad I didn't fall off. You're a natural at this; I could never quite get the rhythm right, but you've got it perfectly. My old instructor, Miss Henna, would be impressed with you." Reid was being genuinely complimentary and she blushed. She then felt stupid for that. After all, he was still Reid. Which he proved ten minutes later when they trotted again.

He was watching her carefully as she moved with the horse, getting the rising-trot just right. When she slowed to a walk again she asked Reid what he was looking at and he replied with a typically Reid-like remark. "The way your hips move. It's giving me ideas." He grinned and gave her meaningful look, one brow arched.

She wanted to throw something at him but instead she said, "Just keep your thoughts to yourself."

With a quick glance forward at the wide, flat path ahead, she squeezed Sasha into a fast canter. She wasn't sure he would follow, but she didn't care. She loved the speed, the thudding of horses' hooves on the dead pine needle dirt. She kept her heels pressed firmly into the stirrups and tugged on the left rein to drive Sasha toward a fallen log. Ember gripped her reins and stretched her arms, almost hugging the horse's neck as they cleared the log easily. Sasha was a great jumper, and Ember felt the thrill of whooshing air past her face.

She was breathing heavily and grinning like a maniac when she pulled Sasha to a stop to wait for Reid. She hadn't realised how far they'd gone, she couldn't even see Reid anymore. She giggled breathlessly and patted Sasha's neck. "Good girl. That was brilliant. Good girl," she muttered to the excited pony, prancing about and kicking up dirt. Ember circled the hyper pony a few times and let her eat some grass, the reins just resting loosely in her fingers. She was lost in her own thoughts when Reid finally trotted up next to her.

"Finally. Too scared to canter? You missed my amazing jump over the log." Ember beamed at the flustered blonde boy. Reid looked at her with wild blue eyes.

"I was sure you were going to fall off." He shook his head, as if realising how stupid he'd been to think that.

"Pfft! Me? Fall off? Unlikely. Cantering is as easy as breathing to me." She smiled sweetly.

Reid rolled his eyes. "We should get back. Your friend will be wondering where you went. She might think I kidnapped you." Reid turned Harry round and jerked his head.

It was still light when they returned to the stables, but it was dimming slowly to a warm glow. The stable hands appeared to have gone home, and the stables were quiet but for the occasional whinny of one or two horses, and the whisper of the wind through the trees.

"You know, I think you're less of an asshole than you make out to be," Ember said to Reid, hefting the saddle off Sasha and dumping it on the door of her stable. Reid was watching her, leaning his chin on his hands over the saddle. He looked thoughtful, an odd gentleness in his features that she hadn't seen before. But the minute she spoke, the gentleness vanished, replaced by a sort of cold sharpness.

"You want a bet." He glared at her, his expression hardening. She sighed, despairing at the way he always did that; became the careless bad boy again after being fun and mischievous.

"No, I don't want a bet. We're through with games, remember? I'd ask why you really brought me here but I know I wouldn't get a straight, truthful answer." Ember slipped off Sasha's bridle and flung it over the saddle, making Reid jump back to avoid being whacked in the face. She smirked and slid out of the stable.

"Well, you got that right at least," he muttered as she hefted the saddle into her arms and headed for the tack room out front.

They tidied away the tack and groomed the horses. Ember gave Sasha a good rub down with a rubber curry comb and fed her some mints she'd swiped from the tack room desk. The horses deserved the treats more than any person did in her opinion. Sasha's stable was small and warm, the stone ground dusted with straw and a layer of sawdust. Sasha stood patiently, munching on hay in the hay-net strung by the door, while Ember groomed her. Ember felt herself drifting into that sense of peace she always felt around horses. She tried to linger in Sasha's stable for as long as she reasonably could, but eventually she had to leave. She slipped a couple of mints to Harry when Reid wasn't looking.

"Well, I guess I ought to say thank you. That's probably the most fun I've had since… well, in a long time," Ember sighed, finding it difficult to meet Reid's eyes as they lingered outside the tack room.

"I've got an idea of how you could thank me," Reid said suggestively and she whacked his arm.

"I take it back. I was wrong when I said you're not as much of an asshole as you pretend to be. There's nothing pretend about it. You're an asshole, end of story." Ember shoved him unnecessarily. But he grabbed her wrist and pulled her to him, before smashing his mouth down on hers. He kissed her roughly for a short moment and then whirled her away, flashing a killer grin at her. Ember was unsteady and breathless as she stumbled back a few steps, wide-eyed and shocked.

"What the heh-?" She gasped, her curse coming out marred due to her breathlessness. There were little sparks running all over her skin and her lips tingled, her head was spinning.

Reid just chuckled. "Just proving your point." He shrugged and started whistling casually as he sauntered back to the car. Ember was too shocked to move for a moment, and then wandered dizzily after him, mindlessly slipping into the passenger seat.

Her thoughts moved sluggishly as Reid drove back to the dorms; her mind seemed to have stalled. It did that a lot around Reid. Something about him was just so… overwhelming. He seemed to exude a kind of power, something beyond just his confidence.

It wasn't until they were parked back at the academy that Ember finally got angry. He kissed me, She thought slowly, anger rising, I can't believe he freaking kissed me! Reid turned to her, evidently to say something, but she slapped him across the face and hopped out of the car without waiting for his reaction. She didn't have to, though. He got out of the car hastily, slamming the door.

"Hey, what was that for?" he yelped, chasing after her as she made her way to the big wooden doors of the dorm building. A brisk wind had picked up and it bit at her cheeks.

"For kissing me, you idiot!" she hissed back, slamming open the wooden doors and starting up the stairs.

"Wow, slow reaction time. That was fifteen minutes ago at least! And you didn't seem to mind when I did it, you didn't exactly try to push me away," he taunted, still following her but at a safe distance.

"I was in shock. I didn't have time to react when you did it! And if you ever try it again, I'll do more than just slap you across the face!" she threatened viciously. It vaguely registered in her mind that they were back to square one, the friendly banter of the afternoon having been forgotten already. Well, almost. Rather than snapping out a harsh retort, Reid paused and tilted his head quizzically, viewing her with a look in his eyes that she couldn't - or didn't want to - identify.

"Uh-huh. Or just maybe next time you'll admit you like it," Reid teased. At least, she hoped he was teasing. She whirled on him, her mouth open to yell but she was incredulous and speechless. The look on his face wasn't one of someone who thought they were joking. "That's what I thought," Reid smirked half-heartedly, and ducked as she aimed another slap at his face. It was an action of frustration more than anger. She didn't really want to hit him, but he was confusing her, messing with her head with the way he was being so... different than usual.

"Yeah, 'cause I just love it when a guy kisses me against my will. You're no better than Joseph. In fact, you're worse. At least Joseph was drunk when he attacked me." She expected her words to bounce off him like water off a duck but she was wrong. His expression became dark, his blue eyes shadowed.

"I'm a lot of things, Ember, but I am not a wannabe-rapist like Joseph," Reid growled, getting up in her face dangerously. His mouth hardened into a sharp line, and she had the strange feeling of being in a dream again.

"Well...you're still a major asshole," she muttered, backing off. She'd seen something glint in Reid's blue eyes, something violent, sharp and scary. It was the same glint she'd caught when he'd pulled that almost inhuman face in English a week ago. He relaxed a little and turned away, sighing.

Ember let out a breath she'd hadn't realised she'd been holding. "Damn it. And here I was thinking it'd be easy to avoid you, avoid arguments and games and fights... I'm an idiot," she muttered, mostly to herself, but Reid heard her clearly.

"Yeah, well... that's not going to happen, is it? It's too much fun torturing you," he mumbled, trying to sound smug, but there was vulnerability in his expression that surprised her.

She groaned. "Why?" The word was almost a cry in her frustration and confusion. "I gave up! You won! Why don't you find someone else to torture? I'm sure there are plenty of girls just dying for your attention." Ember rolled her eyes, showing how unimpressed she was by that fact.

"I don't play games with those girls like I do with you. Like I said before, they're only up for one activity. Plus, they're all too dumb or weak to fight back." Reid flashed a smirk, "It's not a war if only one side fires shots," he added, an oddly soft light in his eyes.

"Well I'm not playing anymore. Banter is fun, war is tiring. If you want to play games with someone, go paint-balling." She made it clear the discussion was over, and started down the hall toward her room again.

Reid caught up to her just as she put her hand on the door handle. He wrapped his long, delicate fingers around her arm, making sure she didn't go anywhere. "Hey, wait a sec. Look, what do you say... maybe we could..." He abruptly took his hand off her arm as she glared up at him sharply. "I know how this is going to sound and don't take it the wrong way, but you're the first girl I've ever kind of... you know, really talked to. I've never really hung out with a girl beyond..." He shrugged, but she knew what he meant. "I guess what I'm saying is... I kind of think of you like a friend, in a really dysfunctional way." He smiled, a genuine, sweet smile. His blue eyes shone from under his blonde mop of hair.

"So... you torture me because... you want an excuse to hang out with me?" Ember hadn't missed the angle of this conversation, but Reid was obviously surprised she'd been able to read between the lines.

"Well, yeah. I guess so," he muttered, glancing away as if he was suddenly shy. Ember felt a pang of... affection? She pushed it away.

She was mildly startled by his admission but not astonished, after the day they'd spent together. Though she knew that this meant he wouldn't leave her alone: It wasn't a war or game anymore, it was a type of secret friendship, in a very dysfunctional way, as he'd said. The only way she was going to escape the torture was to find another way to hang out with him in secret. She felt stupid and unhappy about it, but she wasn't going to accept Reid's pranks and games anymore. She didn't want to hang out with him - there were hundreds of reasons against it. Or at least, that's what she was telling herself - but it was better than finding her underwear plastered about the school, which is where this would end up otherwise.

Ember bit her lip for a moment, looking around to avoid meeting his gaze. The hallway was empty; the ugly navy wallpaper that stretched down the corridor was the same colour as the mouldy carpeting. A wooden dido rail ran along the wall, and above it, spaced at odd intervals, were tarnished metal candelabras hanging like eerie decorations from a previous century. Ember had to admire the fine crafting of the metal but wondered if the school ever used the candelabras anymore. She'd always liked that kind of thing, had wanted candelabras in her room at home but her parents had been terrified she'd burn the house down. Not an unwarranted worry to be honest.

Slowly, Ember's gaze trailed back to the boy in front of her, who was waiting patiently for her to say something. She frowned. "Skateboarding." She said after some thought, and Reid looked at her, puzzled. "Instead of games and wars, we could go skateboarding. Nobody ever goes to the skate park down the road, so nobody would know and we'd be able to hang out without you giving up your bad boy reputation. I'm sure nobody would question where you were going if we did it late in the evening." Ember shrugged, noticing she'd been keeping her voice low instinctively. Reid considered it for a moment.

"What would you tell Sherry?" he asked.

"I'd make something up," Ember lied. She'd tell Sherry the truth and make her swear not to tell anyone.

"OK, skateboarding. Wait, you can skateboard?" he added distractedly, looking surprised.

"Yeah, a little. It's been a while but I still have my board. I think I can still go a few ramps." She smiled. She'd taken up skateboarding as hobby when she was younger, and since then it had been and off and on thing she'd done when she was really bored.

"And I can teach you. You teach me to ride horses, I teach you to skateboard." Reid grinned, looking proud of himself for coming up with the idea.

"Whatever. Thursday at eight?" Ember rolled her eyes, eager to get into her room now. She was afraid that if she spent any more time with him tonight, she might not want to walk away from him. Already, she was wondering if he might kiss her goodnight, just because of the way he was looking at her. Shut up and stop being so stupid, she commanded herself, you don't want him to kiss you, remember? Plus, he just said he thinks of you like a friend. He only kissed you before because he was being an ass. Somehow, that thought didn't comfort her; it sort of upset her actually.

"Sure. I'll meet you at the skate park then. See you later, Demon Girl." Reid smirked, waving as he sauntered back to his own room. She almost snapped at him, ready to ask what the hell he meant by 'Demon Girl', but she thought better of it and crept into her room.

"Where have you been?" Sherry asked playfully, grinning. Clearly, she knew Ember had been with Reid. Ember wasn't sure how Sherry knew, but didn't care enough to ask.

"Horse riding. With Reid," Ember answered truthfully. She wouldn't lie to her best friend. Tiredly, Ember pulled off her dusty boots, and shucked her hoodie, tossing them both in the wardrobe carelessly.

"Wow. Reid rides horses? I bet you raced circles round him," the green-eyed girl laughed.

"It's been a while since he's ridden. I had to teach him how to tack up a horse." Ember collapsed on her bed, feeling her thighs already beginning to ache from the horse riding.

"And…?" Sherry asked expectantly, looking at her oddly, and it took Ember a moment to click.

"You were listening at the door?" she accused, repressing a grin. Sherry just grinned back. "So we're going skateboarding. It's nothing. If you heard the whole conversation, you'd understand that I'm just doing it to avoid him stealing my underwear again." Ember grimaced.

"Unless you're using 'skateboarding' as a code word…" Sherry arched a brow insinuatingly, and Ember threw her pillow at her. Her mind flashed back to that wild, impulsive kiss back at the stables, and she hoped Sherry didn't notice her blushing.

"No! Are you nuts? I-he's-I wouldn't…We're going to the skate park. With skateboards. I'll take pictures to prove it if you want!" Ember realised she'd gotten a little defensive, but after Sherry implied the idea, she'd begun to wonder.

"OK, I believe you. But you can't deny you want to?" Sherry teased, smirking at her.

"I can actually because I don't want to. Do I look like a stupid slut? No. I will not be one of his one-night stands, just because he's…" Ember shut up, quickly catching on to Sherry's plot. She was deliberately winding her up in the hopes she'd say something complimentary about Reid. Something along the lines of 'I won't screw him just because he's the sexiest guy I've ever laid eyes on'. She so wasn't going to admit that.

"Uh-huh? Would you like to finish that sentence?" Sherry gave her an expectant look. Ember lifted her chin.

"No. I wouldn't. And now, I'm going for a shower 'cause I smell like horse and dirt." She collected clean clothes and a towel and stormed into the bathroom for a nice, long, relaxing shower.

Reid

OK, so his plan to avoid her hadn't worked out. He'd let his walls crumble around him and somehow ended up with plans for Thursday evening.

He hadn't known what he was doing when he'd stormed out of History, hadn't known what he was doing when he'd ended up standing at her door, had no idea what the hell he was saying when he suggested they go horse riding. He'd been unable to control the words pouring out of his mouth while they'd been out having fun. He'd been almost nice to her, honest for once. Worse, he hadn't been able to help himself when he'd kissed her, some inexplicable impulse driving him to put his mouth to hers, like he needed to taste her lips in order to survive. Luckily he'd quickly recovered himself and shot her some witty one-liner.

When she'd accused him of being like Joseph, he'd gotten so angry and... hurt, that he'd let his control slip. His fangs had just about slid out, and he knew his eyes had been glinting. He could only hope Ember hadn't been paying that much attention. He'd bitten back his fangs and turned away. And when she'd walked away from him with that stubborn, dark expression on her pretty little face... well, he couldn't help but feel the need to explain himself.

Reid groaned and held a pillow over his face, feeling confused and stupid. Why had he done that? Why couldn't he control himself around her? It was like something in her just drew out words and thoughts and actions from deep inside him, and he was helpless to stop it.

"Crap!" he muttered harshly into his pillow, wishing he could smother himself. Of course, being the walking undead, he didn't need to breathe anyway. Maybe he should get a wooden stake?

"What? I take it you didn't leave History to get screwed? Otherwise you'd be in a good mood."

Reid hadn't realised Ricky had come in. He pulled the pillow off his face and, without thinking, said, "I took her horse riding." After the words were out, Reid cursed himself. Obviously that part of the demon girl that dragged words out of him hadn't worn off of him yet. Maybe if he could just stop thinking about her.

Ricky did a double take and opened his mouth to speak. He closed it again without saying a word and sat down on his bed facing Reid. He made a motion with his hand indicating for Reid to expand on that.

He was fed up of keeping it all in, all the confusion and longing and desire, so, with a sigh, Reid explained. "Ever since she surrendered, I've been bored and confused and distracted. I keep thinking about her, and I tried to see her a hundred times, discreetly walking past her just so I could look at her. On Friday… well, I'm guessing Perry told you what happened?" Ricky nodded mutely. "Yeah, well, after that, I couldn't get her out of my head all weekend. And today… I don't know, I just… it just kind of happened. I took her to the stables and we talked and I was…nice to her. Sort of. And I kissed her - I don't why but it was like I couldn't help it. Then, when we came back here… Long story short, we're going skateboarding on Thursday evening." He paused to take an unnecessary breath, then said quietly. "I told her I thought of her like a friend, but I think I was lying," Reid concluded weakly, pulling the pillow over his face again.

"Oh, yeah. You were lying," Ricky chuckled, "Well, well. Reid Ashton likes a girl. For real." Ricky sounded happy about it, if only a little surprised.

"Yeah, and I hate it. I don't just want her to be another one-night stand, I want to actually hang out with her and talk to her. It's not right. And anyway, she's human. I can't tell her what I am and I can't even feed on her. I can't do that to her," Reid groaned.

"Not to mention feeding on her would involve 'one-night stand'-ing her and she wouldn't even let you unzip her jumper without slapping you across the face," Ricky chuckled again. But they both knew this was serious.

Reid was changing, and he was getting close to a human. He didn't know how to control his vampire nature, hence why he never got too close to humans - except when he fed - but whenever he fed, he'd always erase the girl's memory and hide the bite marks with a hickey so nobody looked too close. He couldn't hide the silver glint in his eyes when he got angry, the fangs that sprung out when he felt lusty, the superhuman speed and strength he struggled to contain at the best of times. Ricky, Brandon and Perry were good at containing it all, they were used to being close to humans. They could do that safely without exposing what they were or hurting the human. Reid had no practice at that. He'd never had reason to, because he'd never felt the need for prolonged social contact besides that of his friends.

"OK, Reid. I think we need to talk to the guys. There's a meeting later tonight because Brandon heard about a group of witches headed this way. Hopefully they're just passing through but we need a plan anyway. We'll bring it up then. Maybe Brandon will know how to deal with this." Ricky was serious now, and Reid sighed. He wasn't looking forward to telling Brandon and Perry that he'd discovered he had emotions after all.

"Fine. Just don't expect me to be-" Reid started sharply, but Ricky cut him off.

"Sober? Well, you'd better be. Brandon's on edge as it is, without you showing up to a meeting totally plastered," Ricky warned. There went Reid's contingency plan. Could this day get any worse?

H.G. Lynch

Born Dark

THE TREE

H.G. Lynch

Born Dark

Reid

"So, I don't think the witches are going to be much trouble, but just in case, we need to stay low. These girls aren't like the vamp-loving witches from up North. They will burn us on the spot if they find out what we are." Brandon was leaning with his elbows on his knees, looking as serious as ever in the flickering firelight. The dim, dusty room always had that faintly eerie feeling. Shadows danced on the stone walls, and the place practically screamed stereotype vamp-den. Reid loved it because of that.

"And, great leader, just how did you obtain this information?" Reid snickered, and Brandon glanced at Perry.

"Perry came across them on his bike the other night, on the edge of the forest. They were casting protective spells, sharpening stakes. It leads me to believe they might be vampire hunters, probably got a tip from one of the other witches that have passed through." Brandon sent Perry a nod, and Ricky looked worried. Reid snorted, but his friends knew he was taking this seriously. Despite his mocking demeanour, Reid always took supernatural business as seriously as Brandon did. He just didn't show it.

"OK, so do we have a game plan in case we get caught? Or are we just going to wait around like sitting ducks?" Reid raised a brow. He was itching for a fight; it'd been too long since he'd had a real fight, and he had a lot to get out of his system.

"We'll cross that bridge when we come to it, Reid. But if we lay low while the witches are in town, we won't get caught, so it won't matter." Brandon's voice had that 'I'm-warning-you-Reid-don't-mess-up' tone again, and Reid sighed. He heard that tone on a weekly basis, and he wondered if Brandon would ever loosen up.

"Meeting adjourned?" Ricky asked with a grin. Uh-oh. If official business was over, it was time for the Laugh-at-Reid session. Was it too late to back out now? He wondered.

"Yeah. I think that's it. What's up with you, Kee? You're grinning like a mad man." Brandon lightened up quickly once the real business was out of the way. It wasn't often Ricky said anything when they were down here. Secretly, Reid thought Kee was a bit creeped out by the mysterious, cobweb-dusted meeting den.

"Well, maybe Reid would like to tell you himself?" Ricky turned his excited aqua gaze on Reid, brows raised expectantly. Reid glared at him, sighed, and hung his head.

"Reid?" Perry sounded confused and, as Reid looked up at him through his blonde hair, his voice matched his expression. That wasn't anything new though; Perry often looked confused. He wasn't precisely the brightest of the bunch.

"Come on Reid, You can't keep going the way you have been. Not anymore," Ricky encouraged smugly. Reid was going to have to remember to put jelly in Ricky's pillow later. Or maybe a dead rat.

"Kee, what're you talking about? He obviously isn't going to tell us, whatever it is," Brandon sighed. Ricky chuckled, clearly enjoying this much more than he should've been in Reid's opinion, and Reid lifted his head to give the brunette boy a warning glare. Ricky ignored it.

"Reid Ashton is having…" Ricky paused for dramatic effect, so that the only noise in the hallowed stone room was the crackling of the fire and Reid's own heartbeat. "Girl troubles." Ricky finished dramatically, grinning. Reid kept his head down, hearing Brandon and Perry gasp mockingly, and then laugh.

"Seriously? What kind of troubles? Have all the girls finally banded together against you, or did you just lose your mojo?" Perry chortled. Ricky laughed harder, and Brandon was quite likely to have a brain aneurysm. Great, Reid thought bitterly, Now Brandon lightens up. At the same time, he was mentally kicking himself. Why the hell had he told Ricky? Why hadn't he kept his damn mouth shut like he should've? Maybe he was losing his mind. The idea did have a certain appeal.

"Oh no. It's not like that. I'm talking about how Reid-" Ricky started, chuckles dimming but not dying away just yet. Reid decided he'd had enough. He didn't want the others to know; he'd deal with it on his own. He got to his feet abruptly.

"-Is leaving now! And, Kee, you might want to remember we share a room." It wasn't even a concealed threat, and Reid smacked the boy in the side of the head as he stormed past, heading for the narrow staircase. Brandon, who was closest to the stairs, cut him off. He stuck out an arm to block his way and Reid vaguely considered ripping his arm off.

Born Dark

"Wait, Reid. Is this about Ember?" The dark-haired boy had sobered quickly, his mouth now set in a concerned yet attentive frown. Tell him? Break his arm? The latter sounded like a much better idea. Reid sighed.

"Yeah. It's about Ember..." Reid whirled so he could address everyone in the room at once, knowing he'd never live this down after he said it. "I like her. I actually like the girl. She's different. There. You happy now? I said it!" Reid flung out his arms in a frustrated, exasperated gesture. Nobody laughed this time, and Reid shook his head tiredly. "Can I go now? I need to go punch a tree or something," he groaned.

"Just a sec... there has to be more to it than that, otherwise Ricky wouldn't have brought it up and you wouldn't have admitted it," Brandon said analytically, searching Reid's face. When Reid didn't answer, Kee spoke up.

"He doesn't know how to deal with it. Unrequited infatuation isn't something Reid is used to." Brandon and Perry nodded in agreement with what Ricky said, and all eyes turned back to Reid. This is going to be a long night, Reid thought to himself, retiring to his perching spot back in the corner. The others took their seats too.

"OK, so... you want to know what you should do? Well, you could try acting like a human being for once?" Perry grinned.

"Yeah, well, I'm not human am I? That's part of the problem. I don't know how to be close to a human and keep the secret. She's going to find out somehow. She's a lot more perceptive than any other girl I've ever met," Reid muttered, feeling ashamed that he was having this conversation. It was an injury to his pride just to feel this way, let alone tell his friends about it.

"That's 'cause every other girl you've met has either been drunk, or just too desperate to take your clothes off to notice anything else," Perry chuckled, but Brandon made a thoughtful noise.

"I can see your problem. But first you need to establish some sort of non-hostile relationship. She needs to not hate you to start with. And, like I said earlier, we all need to lie low. Stick with that, and you won't need to deal with the vampire-human struggle for a while," Brandon said sensibly, shrugging. The firelight cast strange patterns on his face, darkening his eyes to make him look older and wiser than he was. It irritated Reid.

"Non-hostile? That won't be so easy. Ember is... vicious. And she seems to know just which buttons to push to piss me off," he explained dully.

"Just try. And who knows? Maybe you'll discover your humanity." Brandon grinned suddenly.

"And maybe he'll corrupt her, feed on her and then get over it." Perry was less optimistic, striking at what he knew was more Reid's nature. Reid almost chuckled himself, seeing the likelihood in Perry's perspective.

After all, he was still Reid Ashton, infamous man-whore and wild card. Plus, it wasn't like Ember was one of those prissy, controlling, make-their-man-a-slave girls. She had a wild side of her own; it was just more refined than his. Maybe this could work. Or maybe it would blow up in his face. He figured it was a fifty-fifty shot.

Ember

Two days passed in the blink of an eye with nothing of consequence happening. It had given Ember time to think, and now that she had, she realised she'd been an absolute idiot. She'd fallen for Reid's charm.

She was sitting in the skate park, at quarter past eight in the evening, and staring blankly at her skateboard on the ground. She wasn't sure why she'd come; she'd established with herself yesterday that Reid was messing with her. He hadn't given up his games at all, he'd just found a new way to play them. He was going for the honest-lies approach: act like a nice guy, tell her what she wants to hear, and then laugh at her behind her back because she believes your act.

"Bullshit," she hissed to herself out-loud, throwing her skateboard as far as she could. Her voice echoed and her skateboard skittered across the concrete ground. The darkening sky overhead was littered with stars, and a cool wind blew loose strands of hair around her face. She pushed them back impatiently, staring out at the humped shapes of shadowy concrete ramps and the surrounding expanse of grass, grey as cement in the dim light. Lamp posts along the street behind her were starting to flicker on.

Damn it, Reid is such an asshole! She'd actually believed him when he'd said he thought of her as a friend. She'd let the horse-riding expedition get to her, make her trusting and soft. "Stupid, hot asshole!" she muttered to the ground before sighing and heading slowly toward her bashed board.

"Who's a stupid, hot asshole?" The voice came from right behind her. She gasped and jumped in surprise, her hands flying to her chest.

"Jesus, Reid! Don't sneak up on me like that! You'll give me a heart attack!" Ember battled the blush trying to colour her face. He really didn't need to know she thought he was hot; it would only make him more arrogant.

"You didn't answer my question," he grinned, winking at her so that she felt a flutter in her ribs.

"No. I didn't," Ember replied simply, sounding cool and calm. She wasn't. She was frankly amazed he was here, but then again, he probably had to come and laugh at her for showing up. Convoluted plan. Maybe Reid wasn't that smart… or that dumb, rather?

Having just confused herself, and feeling the puzzled look on her face, Ember grabbed up her skateboard and made to leave. So what if he'd shown up? She'd known this was a bad idea to start with, and now, she just wanted to leave before she made a fool of herself.

"Hey, not leaving yet are you? I just got here." Reid held up a skateboard of his own. It had a pretty cool deck, with a flaming skull printed onto the underside.

Ember muttered appreciatively, "Ace deck."

Reid looked faintly surprised for a second and then proceeded to snatch her board from her hand. "Hey! Give me my board back, idiot!" She dived for it but he whirled it away faster than she could blink. He held up the skateboard, examining it, and snorted derisively.

"'Vampires do it better'? Seriously?" He mocked, reading the bleeding red words on the underside of her board. But there was something curious in his voice that Ember couldn't identify, an edge to his tone.

"Yeah, so I like vampires. Considering you stole my books before, I thought you just might have figured that one out." OK, so she hadn't actually expected him to take a glance at the titles of her books while he'd been snatching them.

"Hmm," said Reid, dropping her board and heading for the top of the biggest straight ramp.

Ember retrieved her abused skateboard and sighed, unsure whether or not she should leave. Part of her told her she didn't want to be here with him, but another part was curious. For some reason, she thought of the kiss at the stables on Monday. With that memory, a confusing array of emotions arose: Anger, lust, hatred, longing. In the end, the jumble just gave her the urge to slap the blonde boy flying down the ramp. And a headache. She also was developing a headache.

"Wait, come on, don't leave!" the blonde in question yelled to her, whizzing down and around the quarter-pipe. He skidded to a stop three feet in front of her, blocking her way out. "I haven't even done anything…" He held out his arms in a helpless gesture, tilting his head so his hair fell in his eyes. She just arched a brow, quirking her lips.

"Yet," he amended, sounding sheepish. She got the impression he had more to say, but he was making an effort to keep his mouth shut. Those blue eyes were wide and pleading, drawing her in. He knew just how to pull on a girl's heartstrings.

Eventually, Ember sighed, her mind too boggled with contrasting emotions and ideas and unnecessary thoughts that she wished would go away, to deal with an argument. Of course, Reid grinned, having won again. *Maybe I'd have better luck dealing with him if I was blind,* Ember thought wryly.

Half an hour later, they were both sitting atop the half-pipe, having what was almost a real conversation. It was darker now, the street lights casting pools of yellow illumination on the street. Nobody was around, except the odd passer-by too keen on getting home to notice the two teenagers in the skate park. Occasionally a car would go by, headlights sweeping across the skate park and uncovering the darkened ramps for a flash.

"So, you've really never been drunk?" Reid asked with raised brows. Ember had no idea how they'd gotten on to this topic; she'd let the discussion run away with her.

"Nope," she replied simply, leaning her head back to look at the misting clouds coasting across the dark sky. A chilly August breeze tickled her neck.

"Why not?" he persisted. For some reason, her personal life seemed to be of great interest to him. He'd already asked her what she wanted to do when she left school, what other hobbies she had, and whether or not she was seeing anyone. That last question had caught her off guard and she'd been startled into answering truthfully. Of course, she told herself he didn't mean anything by it. He was probably just trying to make her uncomfortable.

Reid was sitting on his skateboard, legs dangling over the edge of the curved ramp, gloved hands planted on the metal under them as he leaned back. Ember gave him a sidelong glance. His profile was pale and serene in the dimness, shadows hovering over his fair skin like bruises.

"Because I like my brain cells," she answered smartly, smirking at the sky. Reid chuckled at that, and they descended into silence, aside from the chirp of crickets in the grass nearby. It wasn't an awkward silence really, just… unusual. Ember tried not to look at him.

"OK, so what about the other aspects of your social life?" Reid asked suddenly, sounding truly curious. There was something specific he wanted to ask about, she could tell.

"Such as?" Ember enquired cautiously. Reid hesitated, considering whether or not to say it, probably. But, being Reid, he took the chance.

"Sex life. I mean, have you-"

Ember cut him off sharply, "That is none of your business!" She emphasised her indignant offence at his question by slapping his arm. She hated that she could feel heat in her face, burning like flames. She turned away with a hiss, glowering across the grass beyond them. The field of grey-green disappeared into blackness beyond the reaching fingers of the streetlights.

"Huh. I'll take that as a 'No' then," Reid muttered, not at all smug like she'd expected, but sort of gentle. As if he found it interesting, if not entirely unsurprising. Yet, there was a set to his jaw that made her think he was internally ridiculing her. Ember turned and made to shove him down the ramp, but he caught her wrists surprisingly easily. Twisted half-way to face him, she scowled, trying to yank her wrists back. It was a futile effort on her part. "Whoa, chill. I wasn't mocking you. But I would like to know why you haven't…?" He left the sentence hanging. She gritted her teeth and tried again to pull her wrists free.

"Let go of me," she hissed, hearing her heart beating in her ears. She didn't like being so close to him; close enough to see the lighter and darker strands in his hair even in the dim lighting, close enough to smell that odd, delicious spiced-apple scent that always surrounded him.

"Come on, it's an innocent enough question. Answer me and I'll let you go." Reid insisted, attempting to use his looks to influence her again, batting his lashes innocently and making his mouth into an irresistible pout. Luckily, she was too mortified for it to take effect. As she continued to struggle against him, he pulled her toward him until her could wrap both arms around her to keep her still. Ember was sure she'd start hyperventilating any minute now; she was too wrought up and they were far too close. Her heart was going a mile a minute.

"Let go of me!" she commanded again, in a clear voice this time, ceasing her wriggling.

"I will if you answer me." Reid was just impossibly stubborn. Ember looked for an escape, testing how tight his hold on her was, estimating how long it would take him to react if she made a dive for the ramp's edge. But somehow, she knew she wasn't getting out of his grip without some serious weaponry.

She sighed. "I hate you, you know that? I don't even know why the hell I showed up here tonight. I figured you were just messing with me again. I didn't even expect you to show up," she grumbled, uncomfortable with being close enough to him to hear his even breathing, to feel his breath in her hair.

"Well, I guess subconsciously you must've expected me to show up, or else you wouldn't be here." It was a surprisingly insightful thing for Reid to say, and she was speechless for just a moment, but then he ruined it. "So, spill. Why?" he added. For all his persistence, Ember had to wonder why he was so keen to know.

She wanted so badly to slap him across the face right then. Couldn't he just leave it alone? What did it matter to him why she wasn't a slut like every other girl he'd known? "Just because. A lot of reasons. Not the right guy, not the right situation. Not to mention, I hate romance..." Ember mumbled quickly, hoping her voice was careless and nonchalant. Unfortunately her voice shook a little and she took a shuddering breath to calm herself. "Let go now." She aimed her elbow for his ribs but he changed his grip on her, turning her to face him fully, grasping her upper arms.

His face was just inches from hers and she could feel his cool breath on her lips. His blue eyes were dark and intent on hers, reflecting light from the street lamps until she could swear his eyes shone. "I think you're just nervous. Maybe you just need the right...experience...to encourage you..." He almost whispered the words, his soft breath washing across her face, intoxicating her. She felt herself leaning toward him, helpless to break the spell he was casting. Her eyes slid shut and her lips parted, she could taste his cool breath on her tongue. Tingles were running down her spine, and shivers raised the hairs on her arms. There wasn't anything she wanted more in the world, in that moment, than to kiss Reid... until her phone buzzed against her leg, jolting her like an electric shock.

Ember was jerked out of the spell, and scrambled in her pocket for her phone. She had a text from Sherry. She would have to thank her friend fervently for that.

"I have to go." Ember threw herself off the ramp, grabbing her board as she went, and tugged out her hair bobble. She flipped her hair over her face to hide the scarlet blush and the glazed look in her eyes as she bolted for the gate to the street.

Ember got back to her room, panting and wheezing from running the whole way. Her ankle hurt from the hundred and one times she'd accidentally whacked herself with her skateboard as she ran. A few people gave her odd looks as she stumbled down the hallway to her door. Hastily, she fumbled with the handle, and toppled inside as the door swung open.

She limped to her bed, collapsed onto it and tried to catch her breath. Dropping her skateboard on the floor with a clatter, she slung her hand over her face and felt her cheeks burning, whether from running or from embarrassment, she couldn't be sure.

"Hey, how'd it go?" Sherry asked, her voice even. She didn't look at all surprised by Ember's clumsy entrance, and there was an amused spark in her eyes that made it clear she already had an idea of just 'how it went'. Great, Ember thought, still gasping, I am so screwed.

"OK, until around the time you sent me a text. Thank you so much for that. Really. I don't know what came over me. I was about to kiss him for God's sake!" Ember gasped between wheezing breaths, shaking her head at her own idiocy. Why, why, why couldn't she keep it together around him? Why did he always get to her like that? It was frustrating and annoying and it made her feel helpless. That's how it makes you feel. Don't think anything else. It just makes you feel helpless against his stupid charm, she told herself sternly before her mind conjured another word for the strange bubbly feeling she got around Reid.

Sherry seemed amused, which Ember thought was a little cruel really. "Again? When will you admit you want the boy?" The green-eyed girl grinned. She slid her laptop off her lap and twisted the cuffs of her oversized grey jumper around her fingers, clearly enthusiastic.

"I don't want... OK, he's hot. I'll admit that much. But it was different this time! He didn't just grab me or blackmail me. It was... different. It was like I was in some sort of trance and I came this close to kissing him. Until my phone buzzed. Again, thank you!" Ember sighed, feeling the beginnings of a headache. It really had been different, so slow and teasing; she'd been excitedly anticipating the touch of his mouth on hers.

She smacked herself on the forehead, groaning. No, there was no way she was going down that road. She did not want him, she did not like him. She couldn't. She refused to fall for the guy just because he was astoundingly pretty and funny and... Shut up!

Sherry chuckled from across the room, as if she could read Ember's mind. "Ember, you so want him! I'm not saying you don't dislike him, or that he isn't an asshole, but you're only human and Reid is undeniably hot. Not as hot as Ricky, but you know what I mean." Ember rolled her eyes, but she was happy that her friend had found a nice guy. She was just glad that Sherry's new relationship was clearly a lot less complicated than whatever was going on between herself and Reid.

"Yeah, yeah. Damn my teenage hormones!" Ember grinned and laughed, and Sherry joined in. OK, so what if she wanted to drag Reid into a closet and tear his clothes off? It didn't mean she would actually do it, and it didn't mean she liked him. She would deal with this issue by ignoring it. Whenever she had to be around Reid, she'd ignore her emotions and essentially all her senses. She would not fall under his spell again. She'd be a walking, talking robot from that standpoint. Surely it couldn't be that hard?

Three days later, Ember was bored to death. Sundays were usually peaceful; she'd sleep until noon and then read all day, maybe go for a walk if she felt like it. Possibly do some drawing.

Not this week though. This week, she longed for something exciting and interesting. She wanted to go out and have some fun, do something impulsive and reckless. Hell, she wanted to do anything that might get her mind off Reid. But Sherry was out with Ricky today, picnicking. So, Ember was left alone with her thoughts - which, recently, had become a dangerous thing, being alone with her thoughts. It meant she thought about things she ought not to think about. Things she didn't want to think about. Ever.

Reid

Three days later, Reid was sitting in his room, banging his head on his desk in frustration.

He'd woken up this morning in some strange girl's bed - that was normal. But he'd been having lurid dreams about Ember - that wasn't so normal. Some of the dreams had been… pleasant, to say the least. Others had really been nightmares involving the blonde girl running from him in horror after seeing him drinking from the neck of some useless bimbo. One had even been about him waking to find Ember naked and lifeless next to him, pale and marred in blood with two sharp puncture marks on her neck. That was the most bizarre and horrifying nightmare of all. He'd never had a nightmare like that, never doubted his ability to control his own blood-lust, never worried about harming or killing someone... unintentionally.

This was a bad sign, and he knew it. He didn't want to hurt Ember; he didn't want to see her pretty face twisted in horror of what he was.

She thought she loved vampires, but would she be so adoring if she knew she'd been hanging around with a real, live, blood-sucking creature?

Coming back to himself, Reid realised his head was starting to hurt from bashing it on the desk. He groaned and sat back, rubbing his forehead with the heel of his hand. Lucky for him vampires didn't bruise. Of course, if he did bruise, he could pass it off as a battle wound from a fight with a disgruntled member of the football team. The footballers didn't like him much. They said he was too pretty; really, they were just jealous because he got all the girls. Or maybe they wanted a piece of him themselves. Didn't matter either way. He wasn't scared of some brutish guys with a combined IQ of seventy-six.

The thought of taking on the whole football team amused Reid, and he grinned to himself. It was a pity Ricky would sulk with him if he did though - Reid hated it when Ricky sulked with him. It was like having a puppy dog mad at you in some ways. Too bad Ricky was out with his new girlfriend, because he could use a distraction. A boys' night out maybe: a trip to the local bar or a club. That wasn't going to happen though, not tonight anyway. So, all Reid could do was wait and hope Kee could keep his mouth shut about his crush on Ember.

Sherry

"Stop it!" Sherry giggled as Ricky tickled her mercilessly. She fell backwards, sprawling on the soft wool blanket. The weather today was warm and sunny, and they were picnicking on some remote stretch of lush green grass in the middle of nowhere. Birds chirped as they flew overhead, and the white, fluffy clouds created misty patterns across the pale-blue sky.

Ricky withdrew his hands, sitting back with a grin and tossing a grape at her. It hit her on the nose and Ricky laughed, his smile gleaming in the sunlight. Sherry picked up the grape and threw it back at him; he caught it in his mouth like the typically boyish guy he was. Cute, Sherry thought with a smile.

Then her phone buzzed and she glanced at the screen. It was another text from Ember, the third one today. Sherry sighed and slid her phone away across the picnic blanket, feeling only a little guilty about ignoring her friend's desperate attempts to relieve her own boredom.

"Ember again?" Ricky guessed, running a hand through his already-scruffy dark hair. He tipped his head back, and the sunlight caught the profile of his face, dancing along his cheekbones.

Sherry nodded. "She gets bored easily, sometimes gets lonely when she's left on her own." Sherry stifled a giggle, realising she sounded like she was speaking about a pet dog rather than her best friend.

Ricky looked thoughtful for a moment and then said, "Can you keep a secret? Like, really not say a word about it? Even to Ember?" He asked quietly, as if someone would overhear them despite the fact there wasn't a single person to be seen all around them. Sherry doubted the sparrows would tell anyone anything.

Sherry thought for a moment and then replied. "Yeah. I can. As long as it's nothing that could hurt her," she clarified. Ricky made a motion with his hand, telling her to come closer. Sherry obeyed eagerly, shifting right up to him, so close that she could smell his fresh, minty scent.

"This is top secret information. Classified. I shouldn't even be telling you this but…" Ricky shrugged, smiling faintly, sounding like an FBI agent or something, "But you have to swear to me you won't breathe a word of this to anyone, especially Ember. It's nothing that could hurt her, but it could hurt the other person involved." Ricky gazed down at her with amused aqua eyes. Sherry felt a ripple in her ribs, staring into those endlessly deep eyes. She just nodded, smiling sweetly up at him while he wrapped an arm around her waist, pulling her against his chest. She rested her head on his shoulder, sighing and letting her eyes drift closed.

"OK, well, here goes… Reid likes Ember. I mean, he really likes her. Reid has never actually liked a girl like this before, and it's driving him nuts now. He wants Ember to like him, but at the same time he likes that she's the only girl he's ever met who's able to resist him." Ricky paused then added, "He's conflicted in so many ways." Ricky laughed, a heavenly sound to Sherry's ears, especially with his breath shuddering across her forehead. This distracted her from his words for a moment and then they caught up to her, and she turned to give him a sceptical look.

"Wait…what? Reid - like Reid Ashton? The man-whore, bad boy, pain in the butt Reid?" She felt her eyes widen, but she really wasn't that surprised. She'd suspected it for days now, and she would've said something to Ember, but Ember seemed intent on ignoring what was right in front of her. Sherry let her stay ignorant, mostly because she knew how Ember hated to think of anyone as having romantic motives for things related to her.

"Yup. He apparently can't stop thinking about her and, as much as he wanted to…uh, 'bed her', he doesn't want her to be just another one-night stand anymore. Which is… well, it's a big deal for Reid. He doesn't usually look past boosting his reputation when it comes to girls. I have to say, I thought I'd never see the day he would fall for a girl." Ricky's eyes were bright and his smile was genuinely brilliant. It was clear he was happy that his friend had found a girl he could stick with. The only problem was…

"But Ember… doesn't like him that way. She thinks he's hot but she wouldn't go on a date with him or anything. She still thinks he's an asshole. If he wants to get her to like him, he's going to need to work really hard at it. Otherwise Ember will just slap him every time he tries to kiss her." Sherry grinned, remembering how Ember had come in surprised and irritated, every time Reid kissed her.

"I told him to stop doing that." Ricky shook his head with a sigh.

"I think she likes it really, she just won't admit it," Sherry replied, smiling. Something changed in his eyes and Ricky dipped his head to kiss her softly. It started out slow and tender, but Sherry was soon breathless as he deepened the kiss, pushing her flat onto her back.

"Is this OK with you?" Ricky pulled away and asked her, a little breathless himself. Sherry simply nodded, not sure she could speak. Ricky put his mouth back to hers, his hands wandering along her body, making her tingle hotly. She could feel his long fingers playing along the bottom edge of her light t-shirt, and his soft lips on hers were making her dizzy with pleasure. She gasped faintly against his mouth as his fingers slipped under her top, brushing her skin so her stomach muscles jumped. His lips curled into a smile on hers and he let his fingertips trail circles around her navel. He moved his mouth to her neck, leaving hot kisses there.

And then, just as things were starting to get really interesting… it started raining. Out of nowhere, heavy clouds had magically appeared overhead and were dropping sheets of fresh, autumn rain on them. Sherry and Ricky both groaned and Ricky shifted off her, looking regretful and unhappy. Sherry herself was more than a little irritated by the fickle weather.

"Come on, we'd better get back anyway. I've got piles of homework and I bet Ember will be glad to have some company again. Assuming Reid didn't get too bored and go looking for her." Kee chuckled, but there was an edge to his voice. Sherry ignored it; she wasn't as paranoid as Ember was.

She cursed the damned weather for ruining their picnic, and hopped in the car with Ricky, watching the patters of rain on the windshield as she fastened her seatbelt.

Ricky

As he drove, Ricky was silently growling, sending out telepathic death threats to Reid that he knew the blonde boy would be laughing at. Only Reid knew where he'd been planning on taking Sherry, and it was a typically Reid-like thing to do - make it start raining when he was just enjoying himself with Sherry. No wonder the boy couldn't get Ember to like him, if he did things like that all the time. Ember was probably better off without him, and maybe the heartache would do Reid some good.

Still, Ricky would give his tosser of a friend a good talking to when he got back and maybe let Brandon know about it, if he felt like being really cruel - which he now did.

Ember

Ember was so bored with Sherry being gone that she took an afternoon nap, curled up on her bed fully dressed. She quickly fell into a bizarre dream, one that gave her a vague sense of annoying déjà vu.

***

She was in Reid's room, and he was standing by his desk with a solemn expression. It looked odd on him, so different from his usual smugness. The room was dark again, like last time, with shadows huddling in the corners like frightened creatures. The glass bottles on the desk glinted dully as she took a step forward, glancing around uneasily.

"Why am I here again?" Ember asked in that echoing, floating dream voice. Reid's blue eyes fixed on hers coolly, as if he were just now spotting her in the middle of his room.

"You shouldn't be. I told you before, I could hurt you," he warned quietly. Ember thoughtlessly stepped toward him, something inexplicable driving her closer to him. Curiosity, maybe.

"But how? You keep saying that but I don't know what you mean," she said, confused but trying to remain calm. She was apprehensive, not knowing how to deal with this solemn dream-Reid, but she wouldn't show it, refused to let him see he was freaking her out. Even in sleep, she was stubborn.

"Think about it," he replied in a distant voice, and suddenly she was shot into quick-changing memories. Just scraps of flickers of minor things. Like the night he'd saved her from Joseph; one minute Joseph had been growling at her, moonlight turning his eyes to mercury, and the next Reid was there, her personal saviour, cracking the drunk boy's spine like it was nothing.

The next flicker was of that sharp glint in his eyes when she'd accused him of being like Joseph, the glint she'd seen only twice before. His eyes turned cold and icy, shining almost metallically.

Memory number three; the way he'd appeared out of thin air silently at the skate park, making her jump. She'd never known anyone to move so quietly; his movements were all so contained.

Final memory; Flashes of the several times he'd pinned her or gripped her, seeming incredibly strong, stronger than he should be for someone with such delicate musculature. His fingers had felt like iron bands around her arms, immovable.

And then she was facing him again in the dream room, his face bleak and her mind buzzing. Sure, the flashes of memory were each odd in their own ways and together they seemed to paint a very fuzzy picture, but she still didn't understand.

"Maybe it's better you don't. But you should still stay away from me," Reid said suddenly, gazing at her evenly across the room. That was more bizarre than the flashes of memory; she'd never had someone read her mind like that, even in dreams. It was unsettling, especially after the odd flickers.

"Wait, Reid, I still-" she started, reaching out to him. But his eyes flashed darkly, and she was thrown back into the waking world.

***

"Ember? You OK?" Sherry asked worriedly as Ember sat up in her bed, her duvet tangled around her and her hair falling across her face in knots.

"Yeah. Just had a nightmare," Ember explained weakly, gazing in the general direction of Sherry's bed, unable to see in the pitch blackness of the room. Her heart was beating a rapid pace against her ribs.

"Nightmare? You were saying Reid's name so I assumed…" Sherry sounded amused and suggestive. Ember shook her head, blushing, knowing Sherry couldn't see it.

"It was a nightmare. Forget it. I'm fine," Ember muttered, lying back and tugging her covers up around her.

"If you say so. Goodnight," Sherry replied quietly.

"'Night," Ember sighed. She spent a long while after that staring at the ceiling, but eventually, she fell into a deep, dreamless sleep.

By Monday, Ember had begun to think about how to tell Reid she was just plain fed up with him; all the games and emotional strains, and the bizarre dreams. They were taking their toll on her academic performance and giving her headaches, always with the headaches.

For example, it wasn't until she got to English that she realised she hadn't done her homework. All weekend she'd been trying to figure out what her weird dreams meant, because dreams like that just had to mean something.

"Ember, have you got your homework with you?" the teacher asked in his dull voice, looking at her with steely grey eyes behind his glasses.

"Uh, Sorry. I forgot about it." She frowned to herself. The only homework she usually let slip was Maths homework, and that was often deliberate. She really had been meaning to do her English… and her Art, and her Biology. All of which she'd forgotten to do this weekend.

The English teacher frowned too and moved on, giving her a disapproving look, which made Ember bristle. She bit her tongue on her excuses.

"I thought you were all raring to get that homework done. You love the writing projects," Sherry whispered next to her, tapping her pen on the desk.

"I was, but I was too distracted," Ember replied shortly, knowing Sherz would understand. She saw, out of the corner of her eye, the green-eyed girl nodding. But nothing more was said about it.

Born Dark

Ember and Sherry hadn't spoken much lately, partly because Ember was so caught up in her problems with Reid and partly because Sherry was so caught up in her new relationship with Ricky. Ember was sure that once things cooled down, her and Sherry would be just like before. Or, at least she hoped so. Maybe Sherry would finally get bored of her and go off with her new boyfriend, leaving Ember to her own devices.

She was pondering this miserably when something hit her in the back of the head and landed on her desk. She turned to give Reid a quick glare, knowing only he would throw notes at her - just like in detention. Then she un-crumpled the ball of paper on her desk and read it:

Hey, what happened with you the other night? You took off so fast I wondered where the fire was.

Ember sighed, not wanting to be reminded of the near disaster on Thursday night. She wrote back quickly.

I had to go before I did something stupid that I'd regret.

She put it bluntly, positive he'd know what she meant. Then she threw it back up at him, first ensuring that the teacher wasn't looking. Sherry nudged her and raised a brow questioningly, mouthing 'What was that about?'

"He asked why I left so fast the other night," Ember whispered back. Sherry smiled a little. "What did you say?"

Ember quickly bent her head back to her work as Mr Waysworth passed by. Once he'd scanned the class from the back row, he returned to his chalkboard and began scribbling on it again with his back turned to the class. "I told him I had to leave before I did something I'd regr-Ow." The paper hit her again, a sharp corner stabbing her scalp before falling onto her notepad. She opened it up and groaned inwardly at the new words on the page.

Something like kissing me?

Sherz peered over to read the note and then giggled. Ember shot her a dark look and Sherry shrugged defensively. Watching out for the teacher, she wrote back. Just one word.

Yes

She threw the note back with more force than needed, hitting him in the chest so he scrambled with it before it could fall to the floor. Ember rolled her eyes and turned back to her work. What the hell had she been writing before? Stupid distracting boy had made her lose her train of thought. See? Her mind whispered. This is exactly why you need to get rid of him. You're going to start failing classes next.

"You know, you could give him a chance?" Sherry suggested, her voice so soft it was almost inaudible, not quite meeting Ember's eyes. Ember gaped at her friend in astonishment for a moment before she found her words again.

"What? Why would I do that? He's an annoying, arrogant asshole! I don't want to give him a chance. A chance to do what anyway? There's only one thing that guy knows what to do with a girl and I'm not idiot enough to let him try it on me. He says he thinks of me as a friend, but I still think of him as an enemy... just one that I can't openly battle with without losing my dignity," Ember hissed back, blue eyes flashing. Sherry looked almost guilty before ducking her head back to her work, her hair making a screen to hide her face.

Ember got that awful, pit-of-the-stomach churning feeling she always got when she was having a paranoid kind of day. "Unless... there's something you're not telling me?" Ember whispered gently, expecting the usual instant rebuttal of 'Stop being paranoid. You know I wouldn't keep anything from you'.

That wasn't Sherry's reply this time. Without looking up, the green-eyed girl simply said, "You're being paranoid again." Her voice was heavy, not light and playful.

"Yeah... maybe I am," Ember muttered, feeling worse than before. Her paranoia came and went, depending on how stressed she was, and how much caffeine she'd drunk. Today, she'd missed her daily dose of caffeine. Still, she never usually got too paranoid over things Sherry said or did, but right now... she wasn't having a good day today.

The note landed on her desk again and she read the fresh sentence, feeling herself blush at the words on the scrap of paper.

Come on, you know you love it really.

"Ember, passing notes in class, are we? And with Mr Ashton, too. Perhaps you'd like to share this little conversation with the class?" Crap! They'd been caught. It was always a nightmare when a teacher caught you passing notes in class. They always read the note out, and this was a bad note to have read to the whole class. She had half a mind to snatch the note from the teacher's hand and rip it to shreds. Well, she was going to get detention anyway no doubt.

"'Hey, what happened with you the other night? You took off so fast I wondered where the fire was'. Well, at least it was clearly Mr Ashton who started the note passing." My Waysworth read and commented in a dry, precise tone. Ember pressed her lips together to keep from screaming for him to give the note back. "'I had to go before I did something stupid that I'd regret' Well, well. Been spending time with the notorious bad boy, Miss Jennings?" The teacher clucked his tongue and opened his mouth to read the next line with raised brows.

Ember prayed fervently for just point two of a second, and then grabbed the paper from the teacher's hand. She could not afford this blotch on her academic record, but she couldn't stand the glances and giggles she was already getting from the whole class. It felt like someone was squeezing her lungs and her head was whirring. On her less confident days like today, Ember was easily upset and this was too much. God only knew what people would start saying about her.

"Ember! You have detention with Mr Ashton for two hours after school. And I suggest you try to keep yourselves apart," Mr Waysworth yelled, red-faced. Laughter and chuckles echoed round the room and Ember shot out of her seat, grabbing her notebook and school bag. If she already had detention, it didn't matter if she left class now. At least it would give her time to calm down before detention, so she wouldn't rip Reid's face off.

She gave Reid a truly burning glare as she dashed out the door, and from what she'd seen of his expression, he looked almost as unhappy as she was. Good. He deserved to be unhappy.

Ember, without thinking, ran straight out into the cold autumn air. It was crisp and fresh-smelling, and the leaves were just beginning to turn on the handful of deciduous trees planted amongst the pines. Ember loved autumn, it was her favourite time of year, but right now she was too upset to notice the beauty of it. She headed immediately for the cover of the nearby forest, ducking under branches and stamping through dirt and cobwebs.

Once she was a good distance into the trees, she stopped and shoved her notepad back into her bag. She leaned back against a tree with her heart hammering and tears threatening to spill. She took a few slow, deep breaths and sighed. She didn't want to go back there, because she knew what kind of gossip would be circulating already. And she wasn't sure she'd even have Sherry to help her through it anymore. Was she losing her best friend to a guy? Ember had always thought their friendship would come first forever, that guys would come and go but they'd stick together no matter what. Maybe she was wrong?

Ember shivered abruptly, her thin black hoodie not giving much protection from the cold. She didn't really care; the cold didn't bother her much. She leaned her head back against the tree and peered up through the branches of the oak tree she'd come to rest against. The branches were low and thick, and the bark was gouged with notches.

Suddenly, Ember had an idea, and decided to do something she hadn't done in months. She stuck her foot in a gouge in the bark, shrugging her bag onto her back properly, and clasped her hand around the lowest branch. Using both hands, she pulled herself up onto the branch and searched for the easiest way up further. Reaching up carefully, she grabbed a branch three feet up, to her left. She scrambled onto it and went for the sturdy branch overhead.

She continued up the tree as nimbly as a marmoset, twisting and leaping and scrambling until the branches became narrow and close together. She shrugged off her bag and lodged it in a 'V' in the branches. She climbed still higher, balancing precariously on swaying, thin branches loaded with green needles. She brushed off all manner of insects, heard the flutter of birds' wings as they took off.

Soon, she reached the highest point of the tree she could possibly get to, and settled onto the thick base of one long branch. She could see all the way back to the ground, quite a way down, and sighed. It was strange how she felt safer up here than she had down there. She smiled to herself as a large black crow landed a few branches up and cawed. Swinging her legs a little, she began to think clearly.

What did it matter what other people thought she was up to with Reid? Whatever rumours they spread, she knew they weren't true and she'd say so to anyone who questioned her on them. It sucked that she had detention, but it'd give her the chance to let Reid know she didn't appreciate his note passing, and she didn't want it to happen again. And maybe Sherry wasn't hiding anything from her; maybe she was just more observant than Ember was. She wasn't losing her friend; Sherry just had other things on her mind. She'd never abandon Ember for a guy, no matter how much she liked Ricky.

Born Dark

Ember sighed in relief, having cleared her head and feeling as if a weight had been lifted off her chest. She'd simply overreacted, that was all. She'd shoot down rumours left and right if needed, let Sherry know she was happy for her and Ricky, tell Reid to go to hell once and for all, and then she'd come back here to relax. This would be her tree from now on, and she'd be safe here.

Suddenly the crow above her cawed again, and Ember flinched in surprise. She stuck her tongue out childishly at the bird and started to climb down the tree, grabbing her bag on the way down and slinging it onto her back.

When she reached the ground, her hair was a mess and full of bits of bark, her hands were scratched and her trainers were battered, but she felt more relaxed. Glancing at her phone, she realised she'd been in the tree for quite some time, and she only had fifteen minutes before detention started. She scrambled in her bag for her hairbrush and tugged out her hair bobble, brushing the bark out and tying her hair back up neatly. She shoved the hairbrush in the bag and set off for detention, memorising the path she took so she could return to her tree later.

It was getting dim outside when she reached detention, slipping in quickly and taking a seat in the far corner. Ember reached into her bag for her notepad, planning on doing her English homework now, and came up with a crumpled piece of paper, torn in a few places. The note from earlier. She shredded it in her fingers and went to ditch the confetti in the bin up front.

"Ember, this is second time I've had you in detention. What did you do this time?" Her maths teacher, Miss Hollander, seemed in a good mood today, looking up from her magazine. Only it wasn't her usual fashion rag, it was a bridal magazine.

"I was caught passing notes in class. Reid started it." She pouted falsely and, to her surprise, Miss Hollander actually smiled.

"Reid Ashton. I'm sorry you've been burdened with his attentions." The teacher shook her head with a sympathetic expression. Ember caught a glimpse of something shiny on the teacher's hand as she turned the page of her magazine.

"Uh, if it's alright for me to ask, are you getting married Miss?" Ember was curious, wondering who on Earth would marry this woman, and why the whole school wasn't talking about it. At her last school, news like this would spread like wild fire.

"I am indeed. My boyfriend proposed at the weekend." Miss Hollander held out her hand so Ember could examine the beautiful ring on her finger.

"Wow. That's great. Congratulations." Ember smiled politely and the teacher practically giggled.

"Thank you." She nodded and turned to the doorway as someone else came in.

Ember took her seat and sighed. Why was everyone so caught up in relationships? Ember couldn't fathom it. She began to work on her English homework, thinking hard about the plot of the short story she had to write. She knew Reid had arrived - she could feel him leering at her across the room - but she vowed to keep her attention on her work as he took a seat at the other side of the room.

He tried to get her attention a few times in the first half hour, but she ignored him easily. She was on a roll with her story and she was determined to finish it quickly.

When a note flew across the room and landed on her desk, she sighed and shook her head. Didn't he ever learn? She picked up the note without looking at him, got out of her seat, and went to put it in the bin without reading it. She returned to her desk and continued writing, hoping he'd get the message. He seemed to take the hint, though she felt him glare at her.

Another half hour passed, and Ember had nearly finished her short story. She chanced a glance at Reid, who appeared to be sleeping with his head down on the desk. She rolled her eyes and kept writing.

Twenty minutes later, she was unsure of what to do now, having completed her English and then her Biology in record time. Maybe she could do her Art? But she couldn't remember any of the details about Rene Magritte, the artist she was writing her essay on. No use. Bored, she read over her story, just in case she'd missed spelling errors or grammatical mistakes. None. Checked her Biology homework. All correct as far as she knew, but she didn't have her Biology textbook with her to know for sure.

Just ten minutes to go, she thought desperately. For the last half an hour, she'd been glancing at Reid uneasily every few minutes, expecting him to do something dramatic, but he just sat with his head down on his desk, blonde hair scruffy. Maybe she wouldn't need to tell him to go to hell after all? Maybe he already planned on leaving her alone from now on. She could only hope.

"OK, detention's up. And Ember, I hope I don't see you in here again." Miss Hollander actually winked at Ember as she fled the room. Ember smiled back tightly and made a beeline in the direction of the stairs, wanting to get back to her room and change.

Unfortunately, she was caught by the wrist halfway down the hall, and whirled to face Reid, who looked slightly distraught. She snatched her wrist away and folded her arms, gazing up at him emotionlessly.

"Hey, you know I didn't mean for the teacher to get hold of the note, right?" She saw a flicker of the Reid she'd been with the day they'd gone horse riding; a less confident, gentler Reid. She could appreciate that and not be drawn in by it, because she was done with him. She'd made the decision and no matter how much she wanted to kiss those soft lips, she wasn't going to waste her time with him anymore. There were always other hot guys, ones who wouldn't screw her about – that was if she ever wanted an actual relationship.

"I know. It doesn't matter. People talk, but rumours are only rumours. They'll get over it. You can keep your man-whore reputation; tell them what you like. I don't care," Ember replied calmly, keeping her voice quiet and carefully neutral.

"Really? 'Cause it looked like you cared a lot when you stormed out of English? Like, you looked ready to cry. What happened to that?" Reid's eyes showed his surprise at her words, and his mouth held the droop of disappointment. She wasn't acting like the feisty Ember he knew and loved to torture. Good. Maybe he'd get bored quickly and leave her alone.

"Yeah, I was upset. But I got over it. Now, if you don't mind, I'd like to go and apologise to Sherry for ditching her earlier." Ember watched his expression melt into… well, something like vulnerability. She felt a quick pang of both guilt and lust at that, seeing how deep his eyes could be and how tender his mouth could look.

She turned and resolutely walked away without giving any indication of her thoughts, her expression blank. It was weird how it almost felt like walking away from someone important.

She received glances all the way back to her room - rumours spread fast around here - and giggles and whispers echoed through the halls behind her. It wasn't until she reached her room that someone actually spoke to her.

"Hey, Barbie doll, what's it like being the shortest slut in school?" Ember turned to see an ugly girl with frizzy red hair and a smirk like a donkey on crack. She tried to call up a name for the girl but couldn't find one.

"Kara, that's so mean!" Someone down the hall called, obviously having heard the girl's comment. Kara. Ember had heard stories about this one, stories to make your hair curl. She eyed the unattractive girl with disgust and contempt.

"Actually, my name's Ember and I imagine it's better than being the ugliest slut in school. But you'd have to give me details on how much that title sucks to make a real comparison," Ember replied with a smile, not backing down as the frizzy-haired girl stomped up to her, high heels clacking, and threatened to slap her, throwing in some expletives.

"I'm sorry, I don't speak donkey." Ember smiled once more and slipped into her room, leaving Kara with her big mouth hanging open. Ember had to repress the urge to make a comment on how often she must've pulled that face, what with all the guys she'd blown, but she managed to keep that remark to herself. Ember had more self-restraint than she normally liked to employ.

"Hey. I'm back. Sorry for ditching you earlier, but I needed some space." Ember wandered over to her bewildered, upset friend, standing at her desk with a frown. Sherry looked at her like she'd just said she was going cliff-diving in Acapulco.

"What? Why are you apologising to me? By all rights, you should be curled in a ball on the floor! How can you be so… so… calm?" Sherz was wide-eyed, and just a little awed.

Ember shrugged. "I sat in a tree for a while," she explained, dumping her bag on the floor and kicking off her scrappy trainers.

Sherry just stared at her for a moment before saying, "And? I mean, I know how the outdoors calms you but this is huge. You can't imagine some of the things people have been saying about you-"

Ember cut her off there briskly, "Actually I can. And I don't care. It doesn't matter what they think because I know it isn't true. And as long as you know it's not true." She gave Sherry a gentle smile, and Sherry returned it with a fierce hug.

"Of course I know it's not true! You would never do anything like that!" Sherry sounded close to tears and Ember couldn't understand why. She gave her friend a careful glance, but Sherry just smiled at her weakly.

"I think Reid might leave me alone from now on. Hopefully. I made it clear I was tired of him, and I think he's decided I'm boring. I told him he could say what he liked to everyone else about me, because I don't care. He looked disappointed," Ember said calmly, prying her friend off herself. Sherry's green eyes were bright but her mouth was pinched. She obviously wasn't so sure about

Born Dark

Reid getting bored. Ember ignored it. "So, have you got another date with Ricky any time soon?" Ember arched a brow suggestively and Sherry blushed. "Uh-huh. I thought so."

Sherry shook her head, grinning. "He's just so sweet and nice. He always compliments me, and he's such a gentleman. He even holds doors open for me." Sherry was floating her own world; Ember could see it in the haze descending over her green eyes.

"Yeah, yeah. Well, I'm glad. And right now I'm going back to my tree." Ember grabbed a pair of gloves to protect her hands this time, and pulled on her most ragged trainers, as well as a thick jumper. Sherry looked a little concerned, obviously not keen on Ember being out in the forest alone when it was getting dark, but she nodded and let her go.

It was pretty dark by now, seeing as it was a little after six o'clock, but Ember could see just fine anyway. She made her way through the forest, easily remembering which direction to go, recognising trees and bushes here and there that kept her on track - having a good artistic memory came in handy sometimes. She found her tree after a good ten minutes of hiking and she propelled herself up it much more easily than she had this afternoon, not having a schoolbag or her school uniform to worry about.

She perched on the same branch as earlier too, and closed her eyes, absorbing the smell of the freshness and chill. She could hear birds chirping in neighbouring trees and the rustle of leaves all around. She slowly lost herself to her senses, feeling the rough bark under her hands, the deep space of emptiness below her; the nip of the autumn air on her face.

But something jerked her from her peaceful trance, a noise below that wasn't animal or element. Voices. She couldn't make out exactly what they were saying, but they were female voices. She glanced down and searched the forest floor, catching a glimpse of movement headed her way. The voices got louder, but they were still too quiet for Ember to hear, thirty feet up a tree.

Then four girls appeared, walking in a group right past her tree. They seemed to be arguing, and they stopped at the tree next to Ember's, one girl whirling on another sharply.

From up here, Ember couldn't see them clearly but one had long red hair, one had cropped black hair, one had a curtain of chocolate brown hair and the other had long black hair streaked with red and blue and purple. Ginger hair was shouting at Rainbow hair, saying something about oak bark being stronger than maple bark. The Rainbow-haired girl yelled back that maple was more potent and hibiscus partnered it well. The girl with the brown hair cut in at this point saying that rose and willow bark would make a great combination. The cropped-haired girl muttered something that Ember couldn't make out.

She had no idea what these girls were talking about, sounded like they were arguing about gardening plans or something. Even that didn't make much sense though. Ember, curious as a cat, slunk down a few branches lower, careful not to make a noise. She could hear the girls better here.

"But if we don't use a strong enough one, they might figure out what's going on." Rainbow was saying earnestly to Ginger.

Ginger said back, "And if it's too strong they'll be useless. Oak bark and blossoms would be best."

Chocolate didn't like that much, judging by her twisted facial expression. "Willow and rose works just as well, and it's more predictable." There was a collective sigh and they all turned to Croppy, who looked thoughtful.

Ember had assumed up until this point that Ginger was the leader of this little group, but it was clear that Croppy made all the decisions.

"White ash and violets. Strong, predictable and most effective if we lace it with orchid petals," Croppy said, making it sound totally final. The group nodded, murmured something that sounded like a chant in another language, and wandered off. Ember wasn't sure what to make of the strange encounter, but she suddenly had a chilling feeling down her spine and wanted to get back to her room. Whatever those girls were talking about, it was creepy in some inexplicable way.

She began climbing down slowly, finding it difficult to see her handholds clearly in the ever-dimming light. She reached halfway down the tree before she made a mistake, putting her foot in a hole in the bark so she could slip onto the next branch down. The bark though, crumbled under her foot and she lost her grip on the branch she was holding.

She let out a sharp scream as she plummeted to the earth, bashing her elbow hard on the branch she'd been aiming to climb down onto. Twenty feet wasn't all that far to fall, but if she landed awkwardly, she'd snap her ankle, she was sure.

But when she landed heavily, the only pain was a dull thump behind her knees and shoulder blades. She lost her breath and felt dizzyingly disoriented for a few minutes before she realised what had happened. Really, it was the blue eyes gazing at her worriedly that gave it away.

"Nice catch," she commented lightly to Reid, who quickly set her on her feet, seeing she was clearly OK enough to make witty remarks.

"What were you doing up there? Trying to fly?" Reid retorted, the worry in his eyes fading and becoming cold. That was a look she hadn't seen from him in a while.

"I was thinking," Ember answered simply and then said, "What are you doing out here? Stalking me now?" She brushed the twigs and dirt from her jeans, wincing when she tried to move her right arm. She'd really given it a good whack on that branch. Reid just glared in response to her comment, his blond hair sitting in his eyes. He looked a little scary actually. "Well, thanks anyway. I should go before…" Ember started to turn to walk away.

But she never got to finish her sentence because Reid's mouth was abruptly on hers, rough and warm and demanding. His fingers closed around her upper arms, holding her in place. Ember wanted to ring his damned neck, mostly because she just couldn't help herself when she began kissing him back with just as much ferocity. His hands moved down and gripped her hips, tugging her against him and preventing her escape. The world seemed to spin, and heat flashed through her body like lightning. Why did this keep happening? She only ever got that out-of-control, burning feeling when Reid kissed her, and he kept kissing her without encouragement.

Eventually, Ember remembered how to make her body react to her brain, not her hormones, but she couldn't escape with him holding her so tightly and her sore arm aching. Instead she used her cunning and, ignoring the pain in her arm as much as possible, linked her fingers through his to slyly take his hands off her.

She broke the kiss to whisper in his ear breathlessly, "Stop doing this. I'm tired of you." And with that she pulled her hands back to herself and shoved him, making him stumble back against a tree behind him.

She took off in the direction of the dorms, trying to push away the sensations rippling through her like melted silver. She'd made her decision and she was sticking to it, no matter what. She told herself that over and over on her way back to the dorms, but she was starting to think that she was running out of options here. She'd tried playing his games, tried to be friends with him, and now she was trying to ignore him - and failing already. There was only really one option left if this didn't work, and she didn't like it.

Reid

Reid slumped to the ground, sitting in the dirt like some abandoned puppy. He couldn't believe it. Ember had really just walked away from him. He'd saved her, kissed her until she ought to have been dizzy - until he himself was dizzy - and she was just… tired of him. It seemed that she honestly didn't want him, but he couldn't stop wanting her.

He'd thought earlier that maybe she wasn't the girl he'd thought she was, when she'd told him he could say whatever he liked about her, spread whatever rumours he wanted because she didn't care. He'd thought at first that she'd turned boring, lost her fight. But the more he'd thought about it, the more he realised she was still fighting. Fighting to get away from him, to break all ties to him. Then he'd begun to wonder about her apparent lack of emotion toward him; could it simply be a great show of control? Hiding what she really felt by acting like she'd gotten fed up of him? That was why he'd followed her scent out here, to confront her and make her crack. It was simply a coincidence that she'd fallen from the tree and he'd caught her. He wouldn't even have guessed to look up in a tree for her otherwise.

He'd kissed her like that to induce some sort of emotional reaction. He'd gotten a physical reaction, but that wasn't what he wanted. She didn't even slap him, didn't scream at him or beg him to stay with her. She'd given him a verbal slap though, one he was replaying over and over incredulously. 'I'm tired of you'. No girl he'd met had ever gotten tired of him. Could she really be completely unaffected by him, emotionally? Even after he'd saved her from Joseph, taken her horse riding, played the mental games with her?

Reid felt like a puppy kicked to the curb and, as much as he needed to feed, he didn't care enough to try. He'd have to go hunt up some other girl, seduce her, feed on her, erase her memory. It all sounded so tedious. But what else was he supposed to do now? Try to move on? He didn't want to move on; He wanted Ember.

CRUMBLING WALLS

H.G. Lynch

Brandon

"What do you think is up with him? He hasn't fed this week and it shows," Perry whispered, his voice too low for the surrounding humans to hear.

Ricky, nearby, just watched Reid swimming with a deep frown. Even Brandon himself was worried about their friend. Something was wrong with Reid, even he could tell that much.

Reid had been acting strange the past few days, and it wasn't like him not to feed. He was getting weaker by the day, and it showed in his slowed swimming times. He'd been holing himself up in his room, and Ricky had mentioned that he'd noticed he hadn't been sleeping well either.

Brandon sighed and looked at Ricky; if anyone knew what was going on with Reid, it'd be Ricky. He was the only person Reid ever talked to about things.

"Come on, Ricky, there must be something you can think of?" Brandon asked quietly. Ricky met his gaze with thoughtful aqua eyes, and shook his head slowly.

"I don't know. I mean, he's been all over the place over Ember but this is more like. Well, I'm not sure but I think Ember ditched him. I haven't seen her around much and Reid hasn't said anything about her since Monday. That was the same day they had detention. I just wonder what she said to him," Ricky muttered, glancing back at the blond boy in the pool doing laps.

Brandon thought for a moment and, reluctantly, decided they would leave Reid alone for the time being, hope he would sort out whatever his problem was on his own. He didn't like it, didn't want to leave Reid to deal with it on his own, but they couldn't be worrying about their friend when they might have to fight witches any day now. Because Brandon knew the witches were around, he'd found evidence of magic being used several times over the last few days but it was a different kind of power than vampires used. They'd all been keeping a low profile, but Brandon just hoped it would be enough.

Ember

It was Thursday again and Ember was not a happy bunny. She was lying on the floor with her feet propped up on her bed and a pillow behind her head. She had a killer headache; she was nauseous and was in about the worst mood she could be in. She was suffering caffeine withdrawal.

All this pain just because Sherry had taken her bottle of coke and hidden it from her. Something to do with how she disapproved of the way Ember had been acting toward everyone. Ember had defended herself, explaining that she was doing what was necessary. Sherry disagreed, saying that Ember didn't need to be cruel to shut people up.

For the past three days, she'd been rattling off harsh remarks to anyone who said the wrong thing about her. She'd even made a girl cry yesterday - that was just before Sherry had stolen her precious caffeine supply and hidden it somewhere. Ember had a feeling she given it to Ricky to hide in his room, but she wasn't even going to go near that room. And that was another thing Sherry wasn't happy about, though Ember couldn't understand why. Apparently, Ember was being 'unnecessarily mean to Reid' by acting like an emotionless drone whenever he so much as looked at her.

Ember sighed to herself, and groaned. This was an especially cruel punishment for something she deemed as insignificant. Just as she thought that, Sherry came back into the room, flipped on the lights, and handed her a bottle of water.

"Drink this and stop moaning," she instructed coolly, and Ember glared up at her.

"I'll stop moaning if you give me my coke back," she grumbled. Sherry ignored her. "Can you at least tell me why I should stop being mean to poor little Reid?" Ember knew her voice was scathing but she was always a total bitch without caffeine in her system. Her mother had accused her of being an addict, and then gotten angry when Ember had simply admitted it. Really, Ember couldn't understand what the big deal was.

"Because he didn't do anything wrong. You were both messing with each other, and he did save you from Joseph. And it's not his fault you got caught passing notes. And don't even start on the kissing thing because you know you liked it, whether or not you want to admit it." Sherry didn't even have to glance at her to know that that was going to be Ember's next argument.

"So, what? You want me to go and jump in his arms? Turn the rumours into truth? I just got tired of playing about with him; it was too draining. Talk about stress ulcers. And you only want everyone on the planet to be as happy as you and Ricky are." Ember regretted the words once they were out. But, Ember's slurs bounced off Sherry with as much impact as a dust particle.

Born Dark

"I just want you to stop acting like you don't have feelings. Don't you realise you've turned into Reid? Arrogant, bitchy and too big for your boots. Sure, people shouldn't be saying the things they're saying about you but you could ignore them instead of retaliating all the time. And as for Reid... Ember haven't you noticed him lately?" Sherry's voice went soft and Ember knew what was coming, a pleading session, instead of a lecture. Sherry would try to peel out her emotions to use against her. No doubt it would work, but Ember would still put up a fight.

"Nope. I've been ignoring him remember?" Ember scowled, her head thumping as she tried to sit up. She gave up quickly as her head throbbed, and laid back down again, throwing an arm over her eyes.

"Ember, he's been miserable. I don't think I've seen him flirt with a single girl all week, and Ricky's worried about him. Says he hasn't been eating right. He just wanders around with no purpose. Ember, you practically broke his heart." Sherry made the final words lilt with amusement but something lurked behind the lightness.

"He doesn't have a heart. He's got guts and nuts and that's it! I don't understand why he doesn't just go screw some dumb, D-cup ditz in a bar," Ember growled. Why did Sherry care so much whether or not Reid was upset? Seriously?

Sherry was quiet for a while and then left the room. Ember didn't question where she was going, because she already knew. She was going to see Ricky, either to escape Ember or to get her coke back from him. The latter was less likely.

Her hope peaked, though, when Sherry returned ten minutes later. Ember opened her eyes and sat up slowly, then groaned when she saw Sherry wasn't alone - and also didn't have her coke. Ricky was here for some Godforsaken reason.

"What now? If you two are planning on a hot and heavy party, use his room because I am not moving," Ember muttered, expecting Sherry to throw something at her. Instead she just sighed and sat down next to her on the floor, along with Ricky. "OK, what's this all about?" Ember sighed, propping herself against her bed to look at the happy couple properly. They exchanged a look and Ricky gave a slight nod. Ember felt an irrational bout of jealousy at that, like they were using an unspoken code, the way Sherry and herself usually did. Then Sherry met Ember's eyes with cautious green ones.

"Look, I've wanted to tell you this for a while but Ricky thought it would hurt Reid, so I promised not to tell you." Oh, great! She'd been right when she thought

Sherry had been hiding something from her. "But Reid's hurting now anyway so it doesn't matter. Telling you can only make things better as far as we figure." Also the 'we' part of that irritated Ember. She knew Sherry could feel the waves of hurt and anger rolling off her. "Just listen without killing me and you can have your coke back," Sherry sighed, looking just a little guilty - which meant she was feeling really guilty right about now, but she was trying to be stern.

"Fine," Ember grumbled and she saw them both pause for a moment.

Then Ricky started talking. "Reid likes you," he said bluntly. "And I mean, really likes you. Ever since you started playing games with him, he's barely shut up about you. He hated it to start with because it wasn't like him to fall for a girl. He told me he kept kissing you because he couldn't help it. You fascinate him and annoy him at the same time, but mainly he likes how feisty and cunning you are. And ever since you started acting like he was nothing to you, he's been... almost depressed I'd say. You said something to him on Monday, didn't you? I know he followed you out to the forest - he'd been thinking for ages with a confounded expression on his face, before he just leaped up and left the room, so I figured he'd gone to see you. Where else would he go? Anyway, what did you say to him that upset him so much?"

Ricky finally shut up and, after a few seconds, Ember burst into hysterical laughter. Ricky frowned and Sherry hit her with a pillow but it didn't make a difference. She couldn't stop laughing, even though her sides soon ached and she had to gasp for air.

"I think she's loopy from caffeine withdrawal. That's my fault," Sherry said quietly to Ricky, grimacing.

"Yeah, that is your fault. But that's not it. Is this some kind of idiotic plan to make me go running to Reid and finally admit that he's the love of my life and I can't stand not having him around?" Ember said with as much biting sarcasm as she could put in her shaky still-gasping voice, along with overdramatic hand gestures that showed she wasn't impressed.

"No. That's why I got Ricky to tell you. He knows all this because Reid told him. Most of it anyway. And I knew you wouldn't believe it if it just came from me," Sherry explained tiredly.

Ember slowly sobered enough to regard them with relative calmness. Well, it was more like barely concealed animosity but it wasn't hysterical giggles at least. She examined them both for telltale signs they were lying or joking, but found none. Ricky's eyes were sober and calm, but that meant nothing to Ember. What mattered was what Sherry's face held. Sherry's green eyes were as honest and kind as ever, willing her to believe them. Ember broke.

"You're really serious," she stated needlessly. Ember thought for a moment, confused and shocked. She really didn't know what they expected her to do and she told them so. Sherry regarded Ricky questioningly, and Ricky was the one to answer.

"Tell him how you really feel."

Ember gaped, open-mouthed, like an idiot. "And you think that'll help him?" She let out an incredulous chuckle. But seeing the seriousness in both their faces, she stopped grinning.

"Ember, you know you don't honestly hate him," Sherry said softly. There was so much gentle certainty in her green eyes that Ember found herself wondering if she was right. Was there more than just physical attraction to Reid? Did she really feel something for him? She'd spent so much time ignoring what she might or might not feel for Reid, that it was hard, now, to really tell.

Ember, although happy for her friend, felt physically sick at the lovey-dovey air between Sherry and Ricky sometimes. Of course, Sherry did know that. That was just how much Ember hated romance. She couldn't stand the idea of her and Reid like that. It was enough to make her feel queasy - queasier than she already did from the caffeine withdrawal.

But there had been some spark of emotion there the day he'd taken her horse riding, but every time it built, Reid had smashed it down with one of his typical comments. Maybe there was reason why she tingled whenever he touched her or kissed her? Only he could elicit those sensations from her.

"So will you give him a chance?" Ricky looked inquiring. Ember sighed.

"I don't know. I just... I mean he's physically attractive, there's no denying that but emotionally, I don't know what there is to work with." She directed her words at Sherry, knowing she'd understand in a way Ricky obviously couldn't.

Ricky must've sensed the girl-to-girl bond going on, so he gave himself an excuse to leave, and promptly left, giving Sherry a kiss on the forehead as he went. Ember sneered, but hid it from Sherry.

"I know you don't like getting all romantic and stuff, but Reid really likes you and I wasn't entirely kidding when I said you practically broke his heart," Sherry said quietly, seeing the turmoil inside her friend. Ember groaned and wished she could dissolve into atoms right then and there. This was the kind of stuff she avoided at all costs because it was just too emotional. Sickly sweet and real.

"Just give me some time and maybe… maybe I'll figure it out. Just don't bet on it being a good answer." Ember hung her head and almost asked where Sherry was going when she left the room abruptly.

Her unspoken question was answered when Sherry returned, holding - mercy of all mercies - her coke. She grabbed it, gulped some of it down, and felt instantly so much better. Her mind was still buzzing in confusion but at least her headache was clearing.

She stopped feeling nauseous soon after, and decided it was late enough to go to bed. Her dreams had been talking to her lately and she just hoped they might be less vague tonight.

***

She was dreaming, but she wasn't in Reid's room this time. She was in the forest, standing by her tree, and Reid was facing her. He looked awful, or as awful as a boy who usually looks like a vengeful blond angel can look; tired, pale and rigid, as well as completely miserable.

"Reid," Ember whispered, not knowing what she was supposed to say. Did he know she knew how he felt about her? Was this her chance to ask questions or her chance to practice what to say to him?

His blue eyes were dark and shadowed, his soft mouth turned down. He didn't look like the infamous, arrogant Reid Ashton anymore; he looked like a little lost Labrador puppy. He didn't seem inclined to say anything though, and Ember simply sighed.

She looked around, at the dark night sky clouded with grey mist and at the swaying trees around them. It was peaceful and beautiful, if only a little eerie. Ember had always appreciated eeriness.

"Ember." Reid's voice came to her in a broken whisper, but it was still his voice. She felt something in her heart twitch painfully as she heard his defeated, dejected tone. It was almost painful to hear. She looked at him and noticed for the first time that tears were rolling down her face. She wiped them away hastily, unsure why she was crying.

"Sorry. I think my emotions are in overdrive." She smiled weakly at the dream-Reid. He gazed back solemnly, blue eyes fixed on her face, unblinking.

"Follow me," he said simply, but with conviction. It was a cool command that expected to be obeyed. Normally, Ember would've bristled at it - she hated being told what to do - but now, with Reid gazing at her as if she were causing him pain just by being here, she felt no anger.

"What?" Ember asked, confused more than anything else.

"Follow me," he repeated, yet he didn't move. She just looked at him blankly, waiting. And then he did move. He vanished into thin air.

"What the-" she gasped. That hadn't happened in her dreams before.

Four seconds later, she saw him walking toward her, coming through the trees, out of the blackness of the creeping shadows. "Wh-what was that?" she asked hesitantly.

"I told you to follow me." Reid almost smiled, but it seemed to take him a lot of effort. She opened her mouth to ask again what that had been about, but she decided not to bother, confused as she was. It was something in his eyes that made her think he wouldn't tell her anyway. And why should he? It was clear to her now, impossible not to see, that she'd hurt him. She'd done this to him without even knowing it.

Guiltily, she swallowed and tried to speak, her voice coming out hoarse with choked-back tears. "Reid, look, I didn't mean to- I mean, I didn't realise that... I don't even know how to..." She was aware her tears had started up again but she couldn't stop them. Reid seemed to defrost just a little, something bright flashing in his blue eyes. "I'm so sorry," she choked, bowing her head and letting her tears fall into the dirt.

This was why she pushed these emotions back, ignored them, hid them away in the back of her mind and pretended they didn't exist; once she'd let them loose, they took over and she had to fight for control again. They hurt. It hurt to care for someone the way that she was starting to realise, she cared for Reid.

Reid still didn't say anything and he didn't move. He was a pale, haunted statue in the milky moonlight.

Ember slowly got a hold of herself, and breathed deeply. She leaned her back against her tree and gazed up at the night sky. She wiped the tears off her face, not entirely sure why she'd broken down like that. She was going to chalk it up to emotional overload, stress and lack of caffeine.

"I don't know why I'm even here," she muttered, mainly to herself. She choked on a noise halfway between a scoff and a chuckle, put a hand to her head tiredly.

"Follow me. Find me," Reid said softly, his voice carried on the breeze. Ember frowned, tipped her head down a bit to look at him. His pale skin seemed to shimmer in the silvery moonlight, but his expression was taut with strain and worry.

Ember shook her head. "What does that even mean?" she wailed in frustration, her head beginning to pound, "You keep giving me cryptic remarks that I can't make any damn sense of." She almost broke down again, his comments just making her more bewildered than ever.

"I can't tell you. I can't have you. It's dangerous. But you have to find me, follow me and find me," he repeated dully, like a chant. She caught a glimpse of that inhuman glint in his eyes, and something almost… predatory about his soft mouth. She was used to strange morphing flashes in her dreams, even if they didn't mean anything to her.

She clutched her head in her hands, resisting the urge to rip her hair out by the roots. "Stop telling me that! Say something that… that makes sense, for a start! Maybe something that lets me know whether or not you really care about me, huh? Because I don't know what to believe! If you really care, then maybe I have feelings for you. I don't know. If not, if you don't really feel like that about me, then… then whether or not I've got feelings for you will be irrelevant and I can keep on ignoring them!" Ember sprang to her feet placing herself right in front of him, close enough to kiss him if she just leaned in. She didn't.

Reid hesitated. He met her furious gaze evenly, his face abruptly wiped clean of emotion. But slowly, his eyes softened, and then he spoke in a soft, lovely voice. "I do care. I do care about you. But I shouldn't. It could put you in danger, because of what I am," he murmured. OK, so half of it was great to hear and the other half was frustrating and, admittedly, a little creepy.

"And what are you?" she asked, following the logical path instead of melting into the sound of his voice.

He frowned and backed away. "Follow me. Find me," he repeated and Ember sighed. She was getting more irritated by the second, but her heart was leaping over the previous words he'd said; 'I do care about you'. Her head was hurting, and she felt dizzy with bafflement and too many conflicting emotions. "You need to find me. Then you'll know what I am. Then everything will be OK. I promise."

She almost wanted to believe that for a moment, suddenly struck with a longing she'd never felt before; a longing to be held and kissed, a longing for... a relationship. To have a boyfriend, like every other teenage girl wanted. But at the same time, the idea made her queasy again. Knots formed in her stomach and a dizzy haze suddenly blurred her mind, merging all her emotions into one, big, headache-inducing pain. She wanted to scream, she was so stressed out, so confused, so angry, so… claustrophobic. Like all her churning emotions were trapped behind her ribs, thrashing to get free.

Then Reid reached out to her, his hand brushing her arm - or it should've. But his fingers vanished where he touched her, melting into her like a ghostly hand. A strange, strong gut-deep feeling washed over her, nearly knocking her back on her heels with its strength.

"You're not real," she said quietly. She didn't know where the words came from, but some inexplicable instinct inside her knew it with certainty. Reid smiled a little and bent to kiss her, but all she felt was cool fresh air on her cheeks and lips.

When she opened her eyes, he was gone. She was alone in the forest, except for the words 'Find me' written in the air, fluorescent and glowing, like they were written there with sparklers.

Irrational hurt and anger and horror and shock swept over her all at once, mingling with her bewilderment and tiredness and frustration and there was another feeling muddled beneath the crashing waves of her tidal emotions, a gentler, warmer one that made her chest ache a little. She locked that one away just before another wave of anxious, loud emotions drowned her. She screamed as a sudden, sharp pain lanced through her skull.

***

Ember was in her bed, sweating and shaking and gasping. She could feel her heart racing, and vertigo swept over her as she sat up quickly. Letting out her breath slowly, she lifted her hand to brush the lank, damp strands of hair off her face, and realised her hand was trembling violently. The claustrophobia from the dream had followed her into reality, and the inky darkness of the small room felt oppressive, smothering her.

She leaped out of bed, hardly knowing what she was doing, and pulled on jeans and a jumper. Hastily, quietly, she tugged on her boots, and riffled in the drawer of the bedside table. Her fingers closed on a cool cylinder of plastic. She pulled out the little torch, and shut the drawer. Carefully, she slipped out the door - without realising Sherry wasn't even there.

Thoughtlessly, she headed straight for the forest, torch in hand. A cold wind tore at her clothes and hair, unusually harsh for a summer night. The sky overhead was chalky with clouds, the stars fighting to peek through the fog. It was silent except for the scratching rattle of the trees.

Ember didn't care that it was the middle of the night, she didn't care that there could well be dangerous animals out there. She just needed to get to her tree - she didn't even care that she had no idea why she needed to get there. She just kept going, stumbling over raised tree roots, sometimes falling so her hands slid on the muddy carpet of dead pine needles. She wiped her hands on her jeans and continued, ducking and dodging branches and bushes. She ignored the rustles around her, forgot the idiocy of what she was doing. She let the night surround her, and let it absorb her. But she didn't lose focus. She had one destination in mind, and she felt that if she could just get to her tree, all the confusion, all these whirling emotions inside her, could be eradicated. Tonight she was on a mission of sorts.

By the time she reached her tree, she was feeling ridiculous for having come out here like this. She didn't usually let dreams get to her, but this one had driven her to the forest in the middle of the night, and now she felt like an idiot for it. What did she expect to find? Reid propped against the tree with a doting expression, dying to spill his heart to her? Or maybe Reid, smug as ever, taunting her and telling her how he'd messed with her dreams somehow? Reid wasn't here, though. Well, she thought bitterly, Of course not. Why would he be? You are quite clearly losing your mind.

Ember sighed and yawned, looking around her at the dark trees and smoky night sky. The trees, as they stretched deeper into the forest beyond her, melted into endless darkness and she couldn't see anything past maybe twenty feet away. It was creepy but Ember wasn't really scared. The darkness didn't scare her, not even the things lurking in the darkness scared her - Unless they were people. People could do a lot of harm. A fox, for example, couldn't follow her up the tree like a person could.

With that thought, Ember swung up onto the lowest branch of her tree and sat there. It meant that her feet hung only a short distance above the ground, but it was enough to comfort her. Exhausted, she leaned her back against the trunk and clasped her hands around one knee while her other leg dangled.

Born Dark

Her claustrophobia, the buzzing feeling of her emotions trying to escape from under her skin, began to fade. So maybe it wasn't completely pointless, her coming out here. She could think more clearly with the cold air blowing on her face and the rustling of the leaves around her.

Sighing, Ember closed her eyes, and thought. She thought about Reid. She thought about everything he'd said and done to her since she'd met him. It wasn't fun, replaying the memories of every prank and smirk and arrogant comment he'd made to her; each memory evoked the same emotions they had when they'd first occurred; anger, embarrassment…and a slight thrill. Reid was somehow dangerous, unpredictable and wild. The wildness in him seemed to call to the wildness inside herself. She'd never been exactly docile. She'd always been a little rebellious, always enjoyed doing things she shouldn't, like sneaking into the forbidden part of her last school when the teachers weren't looking. Like climbing out her bedroom window when she was grounded, so that she could go skateboarding with her friends. Like picking a fight with someone purely so she could get a kick out of arguing with them.

When she replayed other memories, of how Reid had saved her from Joseph and how he'd been nice to her, almost vulnerable, when they'd gone horse riding, how he'd been funny and light-hearted at the skate park. Those memories dug up less harsh emotions in her, like amusement and contentment and a little bit of fondness. But she felt all that toward Sherry too, because she was her best friend. Perhaps Reid had been right when he'd said they were friends. Maybe that was all they could be? Maybe she didn't feel anything deeper for him? But, somehow, she knew that was a lie.

Suddenly drained, too tired to keep thinking, Ember yawned once again and got ready to swing down from her branch. She was eager to go back to bed. But then she heard voices, in the distance, but heading her way. She thought of how helpless she was out here all alone at night, too far from the dorms for others to hear her scream.

She scrambled up the tree, not waiting to see if the people coming posed a threat or not. Nervous, she perched twenty-five feet up, clinging to the trunk like a koala and looking down. In the flickering light, the dimming and lightening moonlight filtering through the clouds, she had a strong sense of wrongness. Below her, she could quite clearly see four girls, carrying what appeared to be branches and grass. She couldn't tell for sure which one was which, but she knew

Croppy was at the front. Only her shorter hairstyle made it easy to tell. The others, Ember would have to guess at in the darkness.

From this height, she could hear them speaking softly but she couldn't make out words this time. The girls stopped just to the left of her tree and dropped their bundles to the ground, making a distinct clattering noise, as of wood.

Ember watched in baffled fascination as the group of girls set out the branches in some sort of shape. It looked vaguely like a circle with a star inside, but she couldn't be sure. Clouds had moved over the face of the moon, darkening the small clearing at the base of the tree.

After that, the strange girls lined the shape with pebbles - God knows where from because there wasn't a beach for miles around here. They were still talking in low voices as they spread some of the grass... No, it looked more like flowers: poppies, maybe? Or violets?

Then the girls sprinkled some grey - could've been white - petals over the bizarre construction they'd laid out on the ground. And, to Ember's surprise, they set fire to it all. She didn't see how they did it, it was like the whole thing just spontaneously combusted. The flames licked along the wood and outlined what was indeed a star inside a circle - a pentagram.

Ember suddenly felt more than just uneasy, but really scared. This was the kind of thing you heard about people doing, cults that did ceremonies and chants, but it was frightening to watch. The girls below joined hands around the circle and began chanting in some foreign tongue. They chanted over and over, getting louder and louder until Ember could clearly hear the words:

"Nai e Pai da noite,
imos traer o poder,
lanzan sobre os demos,
a maxia de vincular a vontade."

The girls chanted it with growing force, almost shouting the words until something incredible happened. Something Ember was sure she'd never forget as long as she lived.

The fire burning in the shape of the pentagram suddenly flared into a raging inferno, and four tongues of flame shot out, each hitting a girl in the chest, the orange and yellow ribbons dancing and rippling into them. Yet the girls continued chanting, staying at that near-shouting volume, putting the force of their whole beings into the words. The flames writhed on, lifting the girls off the ground.

Born Dark

Ember was too astonished to gasp, to breathe or scream or twitch, as the girls began floating inches off the ground. She had to be seeing things but between the firelight and the moon, now uncovered from the clouds, there was plenty of light for her to see by. She couldn't be imagining this, but she had to be.

And then, abruptly, everything was silent. Or not quite… the girls had stopped chanting, but there was a strange humming in the air, almost inaudible but most definitely there. Ember could feel it vibrating against her like pressure waves blasted from a concert speaker. A gust of wind that felt like it had come straight off a glacier came sweeping down, blowing out the fire in a puff. Tendrils of dark smoke rose from the ashes of the destroyed pentagram. The girls on the ground stood in silence for a long moment and then began muttering to each other, looking from one to another of their group in apparent confusion.

Again, Ember couldn't make out words but it sounded like another chant, uttered quickly in anxious tones. From her perching spot, Ember suddenly saw each girl whirl round, putting themselves back to back like they were expecting an ambush. They made strange hand gestures, light pooling in each of their palms like glowing orbs. Ember was beyond the point of shock anymore and simply stared, incapable of coherent thought.

Out of the shadows, she could see four more people approaching. No wonder the girls looked like they were being ambushed; they were being ambushed.

The intruders were distinctly male in their shapes and sharp movements, but Ember couldn't see their faces. Seeing as the lack of fire dimmed the lighting considerably, she could barely even make out their hair colours. Three of them had dark hair, one had lighter hair, but whether it was blond or just light brown she couldn't be sure of. That one though seemed to be on edge, crouched and ready to spring at the girls.

One of the guys was speaking in a low voice and Ember could only tell he sounded threatening from the tone. A girl spoke back. Ember guessed it was Croppy, judging by the way she stepped forward and made some crude gestures at the boy. Another boy replied from the far corner, but Croppy didn't turn to look at him.

Some distant part of Ember's mind was going through notions of helping the girls, wondering what these guys wanted from them. But mostly, she was just too stunned and frightened to move or think clearly. She was caught in a daze, sure she was dreaming.

The group below her was continuing to argue, the girls holding glowing balls of light in their hands, and the guys all dropping into battle stances, coiled to spring at the girls. Suddenly, Croppy threw her light at the first boy to have spoken - Ember assumed he was the leader of the boys' group - and the boy dodged with incredible speed, almost too fast to track.

And then there was chaos. The girls threw light and zaps of energy around and the boys dodged and landed blows to the girls with deadly speed and accuracy. Ember had established some time back that she was still dreaming, had never really woken up after her dream about Reid, so it had all stopped surprising her now: the superhuman speed of the boys, the impossibility of the girls and the devastating destruction of the area around them. None of it was real. It was like watching a Harry Potter movie.

Suddenly, there was a ripple of energy that felt like a shock blast, hitting her in the chest and jarring her bones. It had a much more extreme effect on the girls, who suddenly dropped to the ground like birds shot from the sky, and began writhing in agony. Their shrieks were easy to hear, and hard to listen to as the boys closed in. They secured the screaming, thrashing girls with what looked like minimum effort, holding their wrists behind their backs and forcing them to kneel. One boy produced four lengths of, what seemed to be to Ember, thick rope.

The boys hog-tied the girls and propped them up against the tree opposite Ember's. There was more shouting and shrieking and thrashing, but nothing that surprised Ember anymore. Until one dark-haired boy nodded to another and then pounced on one of the girls - Rainbow, Ember thought vaguely. Not that it mattered. The boy was nuzzling at her neck, but the girl was screaming like she was in agony. Brutally, the boy grabbed her by the hair and yanked her head to the side, her hair falling out of the way.

Then Ember gasped.

There was dark liquid running down the girl's neck, spilling onto her pale top. Ember refused to believe what she was seeing - it was just a dream after all - but everything seemed to hit her at once. Her other dreams rushed back to her; Reid warning her about himself, telling her he was dangerous because of what he was, and the way his eyes glinted when he got angry, the way he appeared out of nowhere sometimes. Her dreams linked together and, although it didn't mean a damn thing in the real world, she at least understood her dreams once again. She finally saw the picture they'd been painting to her.

Unfortunately, that gasp that had escaped her lips drew the attention of the boys or the three dark-haired ones at least. The fair-haired one
was gone. Ember looked around desperately, hoping to spot him in the shadows somewhere, but all she saw was the darkness retreating into the trees. He'd been there, with his friends, only a moment ago, Ember was sure, but now, he'd vanished.

This chilled Ember to the core, sending a creeping feeling down her spine. And the way those boys looked up at her suddenly, focusing on her so easily and certainly, with shock and hunger written across their features, was terrifying. Yet, that wasn't the most horrifying part of this endless dream because she recognised the boys now.

Brandon. Perry. Ricky.

Ember felt dizzy and sick, her mind sluggishly working through a haze of fear. Because she knew who the fair-haired, missing boy was and she had a feeling she knew where he was right now.

She stayed frozen, trying to hold back the tears that threatened to fall to the earth below. Her heart hammered in her chest and she had the quick, sure impression that she wasn't dreaming. Impossible as it seemed, she suddenly knew this wasn't a dream. It was a living nightmare.

And she knew she was right about where the fair-haired boy had gone when she heard the whisper of breathing behind her. There was a thick, sturdy branch right behind her and she knew it; she'd used it to climb higher in the tree that same day. Or rather, the previous day, since it is after midnight, her mind corrected stupidly. Ember could feel every cell in her body pulsing and bleeding fear. It felt like ice water was being poured into her veins and there was an invisible hand crushing her heart and lungs.

The girls were looking up at her now, their expressions in the moonlight were almost sympathetic, but Ember could see them shifting and whispering to each other. Trying to find a way to escape while the boys were distracted, she guessed. Whether this was a dream, a nightmare or reality, Ember had to keep the boys distracted and give those girls a chance to get free. She didn't know what the girls had done to piss off the four most popular boys at Acorn Hills, but she was sure it wasn't worth them getting their heads ripped off.

"Reid. I know it's you behind me so stop trying to be sly." Ember put as much belligerence in her voice as possible, summoning up every ounce of bravery she had. That wasn't much though, and her voice shook.

"What are you doing here Ember? You shouldn't be here!" That voice, Reid's voice, was sharp and cold, almost a hiss.

"I came to find you," she replied instantly, the words spilling out before she thought them through. There was a silence for six heartbeats. Seven. Eight. She waited, every muscle tense, listening to the whistle of the wind through the whipping treetops and the uneven breathing of the boy behind her.

"What do you mean you came to find me?" Reid asked harshly, suddenly appearing on the branch in front of her. The branch he perched on was lower than hers, forcing him to look up at her. In the light, she could see him clearly. His expression was dark and icy, but his eyes glinted dangerously like fire reflecting off a sword, and he had, honest-to-goodness, fangs. Real, long, delicate fangs, biting into his soft lower lip.

If she hadn't been so terrified, if she hadn't been so sure this was all real, and if Reid hadn't been looking at her like she was the thing he most loathed in the world, she would've said the fangs were sexy. After all, she had a sort of obsession with vampires. But right now, the fangs just terrified her more.

"What do you mean you came to find me?" Reid spat viciously, speaking as though she was mentally impaired. That condescending tone sparked irritation in her, and she glowered down at him.

"Don't talk to me like I'm stupid. You're the one who was giving me cryptic little clues! You told me to come here!" She was aware of how insane it sounded, Reid's expression showing clearly that he thought she was utterly nuts. Ember wanted to hit him, and she would've if she hadn't been so scared of him.

"I haven't spoken to you since you told me you were tired of me on Monday! What the hell are you talking about?" he roared back, bitterness underscoring his words. Ember was feeling less frightened and more irritated by the second. How dare he sound so hurt? How dare he look so angry with her when he was the one who'd forgotten to mention that he was a freaking blood-sucking, mythical creature of the night?

"In my damned dreams, you were telling me you were dangerous and you could hurt me! And there were flashes of you like this." She waved a hand in front of his face. "Except without the fangs. And then, in my dream tonight you were saying I had to find you. As if I would want to! As if I didn't get enough of you during the day, you just had to pop up in my goddamned dreams!" Ember slammed her fists into her knees, hard enough to bruise, growling. She didn't care that she sounded insane, she didn't care that none of this made sense and that, if this was indeed reality and she honestly wasn't still dreaming, it changed everything she'd ever believed was real. She just wanted to figure out what the hell was going on between her and the blond boy currently staring at her with a mix of hatred and shock.

"Damn it! This is why I hate dealing with guys!" she spat at nobody in particular, thumping the tree trunk with the side of her fist so hard it hurt. Reid just continued to stare at her with a half-cold, half-shocked expression.

Ember glanced down to find that everyone else had vanished, and there were drag marks in the dirt. The boys must've dragged the girls off before they could escape. So much for me helping to save the girls, Ember thought bitterly, tiredly. Her head was aching.

"You hate dealing with guys because you expect them to, what, turn out to be supernatural monsters?" Reid asked scathingly. Ember just glared at him, curling her fingers into her palms until her nails dug into her skin.

"Shut up. Just shut up, Reid," Ember replied, biting off the words.

"No. I don't think I will. I think I have a right to know what you think you're doing out here," Reid replied savagely, gritting his teeth. The wind blew his fair hair around his pale face, and for the first time, Ember noticed the dark circles under his eyes, and the faint lines of his veins at his temples.

"No, you don't. And anyway, I already told you! My dream told me to come out here, so I did." She paused, hissed through her teeth, and squeezed her eyes closed. "If, if you'd just freaking left me alone in the first place, neither of us would in this position and you wouldn't be hurting and I wouldn't be going insane and..." Ember had no idea what she was saying, but it seemed that whether or not they were in the real world, she was speaking uncontrollably like she did in dreams. She huffed, her breath making a white cloud in the freezing air.

Reid looked taken aback, and she could swear he even blushed. Between the blush and the fangs, he looked a hundred and ten per cent sexier than ever. Furiously, Ember pretended she didn't notice, told herself she didn't care how sexy he was.

"Uh... who told you... who said I was hurting?" Reid said it as if it were not only an impossible, but also a ridiculous, idea. Only, his voice came out a little choked.

Ember sighed. "Ricky and Sherry. I got a whole lecture for being a bitch to you, and then Ricky came and started telling me how much you apparently like me. Oh, and he said I should tell you how I really feel, as if that would help anything," Ember scoffed. She shook her head, tipped her head back to look up at the sky. She couldn't believe she was having this discussion, couldn't believe she was telling him this. But, she supposed, it was a lot less senseless than the idea of Reid being, you know, a vampire. Because, really, that's what he looked like right now. That's what her instincts were screaming at her, along with the word RUN!

She guessed that it didn't matter what she said anymore, because this whole thing was just too insane and she was going to get locked up in an asylum the minute she climbed out of this tree. She'd always known she would snap one day, but she hadn't expected it to be like this. So, this is my new reality, Ember thought to herself, Welcome to Crazyville.

"… and?" Reid gazed at her with deep, almost pleading blue eyes that seemed to glow in the darkness.

"And what?" she snapped, folding her arms and sighing.

"And… are you going to? Tell me how you really feel, I mean?" He looked uncomfortable and dropped his gaze, still perching on his branch like an owl. For a second, Ember thought she'd misheard him. There was no way he was asking that… but he was. Astounded, Ember stared at him.

"I wasn't going to. At first, I didn't think it would help you any because I was fairly sure I hated you. Or at least, disliked you intensely. Then I got to thinking, and…" She paused, shook her head. "But considering all of this," She made a wide gesture to indicate the whole chaotic situation she'd just witnessed. "I have no freaking idea if I'm even sane anymore. In fact, I'm not sure I'm even really awake."

Reid's eyes narrowed. "You're awake. Trust me," he said quietly.

Ember rolled her eyes. "Why the hell would I trust you? If I'm not insane, and I'm not dreaming, then you're really a vampire, right? I don't trust anyone who might want to, you know, eat me." She arched a brow, folded her arms stubbornly across her chest. Reid's lips curled in a faint smile, a spark of amusement lighting his face. But it faded quickly, and he looked entirely too serious again.

"I'm not going to eat you. I won't hurt you, Ember," he said softly, his expression willing her to believe him. The thing was, she didn't need him to tell her that; somehow, she already knew it.

"I know," Ember replied gently. "Plus, if you tried, I'd just stake you," she smirked.

Reid didn't answer right away, so she decided she was tired of sitting in this tree. She slipped down to hang onto the branch by her hands, swinging slightly. As she was dropping onto the next branch down, though, Reid caught her wrist and pulled her back up with one hand.

"Hey! I'm trying to get down from here!" she protested. He frowned at her, a crease forming between his brows.

"How can you be so casual about…?" He didn't have to say it so Ember did, watching him flinch at her choice of words.

"The fact you're a bloodsucking monster?" She grinned gleefully. Distantly, she wondered if lack of sleep hadn't made her at least a little crazy. But, she did believe she wasn't dreaming now at least.

"Yeah, that," he said darkly, dumping her back on her branch. Ember grunted unhappily and stared longingly at the ground. The ashes of the burned pentagram had scattered in the wind, and aside from a few scorch marks on nearby trees, there were no signs of what had gone on tonight. It was disorienting in a way.

"Like I've said before, I've got a thing for vampires. Whether or not you drink blood and have fangs…well, it probably won't have much effect on how I feel about you. You don't scare me, Reid." Ember could feel a blush creep up her face as her anger fizzled away. What did scare her was the fact that, at any moment, he might ask her how she did feel about him, and this really wasn't the time, or the place, for that discussion.

"Seriously? You're not scared of me? Maybe you really are nuts," he muttered, and she snapped off a twig on her branch and threw it at him. It got caught in his blonde hair and he brushed it out, mussing his hair at the same time. Damn, he looked so cute with his hair in his eyes like that. Not, she told herself, that I care.

"Hey, would you rather I jumped out of the tree and ran screaming? I'd say I'm handling this situation fairly well. Especially considering it's the middle of the night and I'm exhausted. And it's technically your fault I'm even out here," Ember shot back, swinging out her leg to kick him in the chest. He caught her leg and tugged her, causing her to fall off her branch and land in his lap. "Whoa! Was that really necessary? If you want to play Santa, you could at least get the costume right," Ember gasped, a little breathless in surprise. A blush crept up her face, and she hoped he couldn't see it in the darkness. Suspected he could anyway.

"Ha, ha." He rolled his eyes, now their normal bright blue instead of that odd, glinting colour, "Why would I pretend to be something that doesn't exist?" He grinned, flashing his fangs. In response, Ember felt something hot stir inside her, and felt the desperate need to get off his lap before she ended up doing something she shouldn't.

Reid tilted his head, gazing at her thoughtfully. He lifted his hand and ran one fingertip over her cheekbone. Surprised, Ember could help the little shudder she gave at his delicate touch. A smile tugged at the corner of Reid's mouth.

"Funny. It appears you're not so tired of me anymore. Could that have something to do with me being an immortal, superhuman bloodsucker?" He gently brushed her hair off her face. The touch tingled against her skin and sent little shocks through her hair to her scalp. His other arm was wrapped around her waist to prevent her falling off his lap and plummeting to the ground.

"How do you do that? Is that some sort of vamp trick?" she asked tightly, trying to ignore the knot in her stomach.

"Do what?" he asked, seeming honestly confused.

"Oh, come on. You must know 'what'?" She had the feeling that maybe it was just the weird, sharp sexual tension between them that made her respond to him that way. But she had to be sure.

"Actually, for once, I honestly have no idea what you're talking about." His blue eyes were truthful.

Feeling her cheeks burn, Ember sighed. "Never mind." But she'd peaked Reid's curiosity, and he narrowed his eyes to scan her face, looking for answers. Then a thoughtful gleam came to his eyes and Ember could practically see the light that went on in his head.

"You mean…this?" he asked quietly. He drew his fingertips down her spine, making her shiver. He brought that hand back up to brush the curve of her jaw. She refused to meet his probing gaze. But obviously, he could hear her heartbeat skip, and she imagined her expression wasn't hard to read. "Ah… I see. That explains why you were always so reluctant to kiss me. It wasn't because you hate me after all; it's because you don't like the way I can make you feel. That's right isn't it?" His voice held all his old, arrogant manner and she wanted so badly to hit him and tell him he was wrong. But she didn't see the point. Not anymore. And anyway, he was at least partly right.

"Yeah, you're right," she forced out the words, staring very hard at a groove in the bark of the branch they were sitting on. Reid chuckled seductively in her ear and her heart jumped, her breathing hitching. She was fully, painfully aware that she was sitting on his lap, and they were alone - alone half way up a tree, in the middle of the forest, in the middle of the night. Really alone.

She swallowed nervously. If he wanted, he could do anything he wanted to her. Like bite her. The thought made her heart contract, whether in fear or excitement she wasn't really sure.

"I suppose this has been clouding your... judgement of me?" he whispered, his mouth so close to her ear.

"Um... well, it doesn't help. Please stop it. I'm... I'm a little dizzy," Ember heard her voice as if it didn't belong to her, didn't recognise it. She sounded different... breathless and somehow teasing.

In a show of what was surely great restraint for Reid, he pulled back and lifted her off his lap, dumping her onto the branch so she could sit next to him rather than on him. Then he grinned at her charmingly, and she looked away shyly. She couldn't help it. All of a sudden, it felt like things had changed between them. Like a coin had finally dropped. As if all the arguments and pranks and stresses they'd put each other through had been leading up to this... whatever this really was. Ember wasn't sure if she meant this, as in, finding out what Reid was... or this, as in, finally giving in to how she felt about Reid. It was all a little much to deal with, especially in the middle of the night.

"Can we get down from here now? I've got a lot of questions but if I don't get on solid ground soon, I'll faint. Not a good thing to do twenty feet up in a tree." Ember shifted, getting ready to climb down.

"Oh, so my presence has that much impact on you, does it? I'm sexy enough to make you faint?"

Ember had to admit that she was kind of glad to hear the smug, taunting quality back in his voice as a flicker of that broken Reid from her dream passed through her mind. She scoffed at him. "Not exactly. I'm not a nocturnal creature, though, and I'm tired." She grinned, making it clear she was giving a dig at his vampirism, despite the fact he was obviously not afraid of daylight. She'd seen him out during the day a dozen times, and he'd never seemed affected by it in the least.

"You're so funny," he said sarcastically, raising one brow. "I don't sleep in a coffin just to let you know. Garlic doesn't bug me. Holy water is great for super-soaker fights inside a church, and if you even think about suggesting I turn into a bat, I'll toss you to the dirt from up here." He gave her a sidelong glance and a smirk and she laughed quietly, beginning her descent down the tree.

Of course, Reid opted for the less conventional way down. In an arrogant show of his superhuman resiliency, he simply flung himself into the open air and fell the twenty feet, landing neatly in a crouch before she had even climbed down three branches. "Show off," Ember muttered, carefully watching where she put her hands and feet for the next drop down.

"I heard that," Reid called up. Ember growled under her breath, and heard him laugh below her. Anxiously, she wondered just how much he'd heard her say when she didn't think he could hear her.

Pleasant Defeat

H.G. Lynch

Born Dark

Reid

Once they were back on the ground, they continued their conversation, with Ember asking a lot of questions. She was about as curious as a two-week-old kitten and Reid couldn't help but admire her for that.

He'd been worried about her finding out his secret all along, but it had kind of taken a back seat to the more immediate issue of her reluctance to return his feelings. Now, he saw he'd been stupid to worry about it. Ember was clearly unlike any normal - or sane - teenage girl he'd ever known. When she should've run screaming from him, she'd made jokes. Where anyone else would've thrashed and yelled to get away from him, she'd sat on his lap and blushed at his touch. Amazing. Bizarre, but amazing.

As they wandered slowly, winding their way through the trees, Reid asked her about what she had prattled on about earlier, the dreams she'd talked about, and she described them to him - briefly. He had a feeling she was editing out a few things but that was okay. He could fill in the blanks. Carefully, he explained to her that Brandon, Perry, Ricky and himself were all born vampires, knowing that every word he uttered to her was another word against the boys' covenant of silence that they'd held for seventeen years. Yet, he found a sort of peace in his betrayal of his friends, in letting Ember know who he really was. Plus, his rebellious nature thrived on breaking the rules. *Brandon is going to be so pissed off*, he thought gleefully.

Answering each of her questions, Reid let her know about the impossible speed and reflexes, the ultra-hyped-up senses, the ability to levitate small objects with their minds - he didn't go into detail on how exactly that worked. It was a little confusing, and he doubted she'd understand it really. It was hard to describe to someone who didn't have the telekinetic power. He also explained that, as born vampires, they weren't really dead. They were undead. They had died in the womb, but when they'd been born, they'd come to life again through the magic in their blood. Their hearts beat, but that was an evolutionary thing; they wouldn't die if their hearts didn't beat – unless the reason their hearts didn't beat was that they'd been staked or burned - but having a pulse averted suspicion. If Reid ran around without a heartbeat, the girls he bedded would probably notice sooner or later. And that would be bad.

Lastly, he explained that they did drink human blood, but only needed to feed once a week or so.

"Is that part of why all the girls?" she asked, a taunting smile across her lips.

He nodded and replied, "But only part." He arched a brow meaningfully at her in his normal manner. It didn't bother her.

He didn't feel it was prudent to mention the compulsion he could use; he knew it would likely upset her. She might suspect him for using it on her, blah, blah, blah. Of course, he hadn't ever really used it on her, except that tiny bit of influence he'd used at the skate park to make her want to kiss him. Ember would never believe that he hadn't used it on her, though… and then he'd never get to find out how she really felt about him. That question had been left unanswered for the moment, despite his itching curiosity. It was obviously quite unimportant in light of his vampirism.

Currently, Ember was saying something he wasn't listening to. He was busy watching her mouth moving but not hearing the words coming out. Her lips were just so pink. Slowly, though, her voice came to him, like a radio tuning into the right frequency.

"Hello? Reid? Back to Earth." She waved a hand in front of his face, distracting him. She scowled at him, her mouth tilting down at the corners unhappily.

"Hmm?" he muttered absently, wondering if she'd notice if he let his gaze linger elsewhere. He tried it, letting his eyes slide down to the collar of her flimsy camisole, and got a slap across the face for the attempt. It was a good slap, it stung a little, and if he'd been human, it might've left a lasting mark.

After she'd slapped him, though, Ember briefly stared at her hand in what looked like surprise, as if the hand didn't belong to her. Then she relaxed visibly, realising she'd hit him before and he'd been vampire then too, and he hadn't eaten her.

He just grinned at her, deliberately letting his fangs show. It was a great relief to be able to show someone besides his friends a part of him that barely anyone knew existed. And Ember always had an interesting reaction to his fangs. Her heart would beat faster, and her eyes would go wide - whether in fear, anxiety or surprise he wasn't sure, but it was fun to watch her react. For days now, she'd acted like he didn't exist, ignored his attempts to talk to her or see her, and it was good to see her react to him again.

"Stop staring at me and answer the question. What was the battle with the… the witches about?" She looked awkward saying 'witches', yet she had no issues with 'vampires' who were clearly the more dangerous and mythical of the two. It amused him, and he found her fascinating that way. She was full of surprises.

"Oh, that." He shrugged. It wasn't really a big deal, but he could see from her anxious expression that it was a huge deal to her.

The guys had been planning all week without him since he'd been… distracted, but last night they'd gotten information - Brandon wouldn't reveal his sources to the rest of them, so they had no idea where from - that the witches were planning on trapping them all in a spell of sorts to lure them out and expose themselves as vampires. The boys had relayed the plan to Reid at the last minute, and he was happy to have the chance to possibly rip someone's head off. It had been too long since he'd done something destructive, and he'd hoped it would cheer him up. Sure, it hadn't turned out that way, but he felt a lot better anyway.

"Witches, as a general rule, don't like vampires. The ones you saw, they'd heard there was a group of vampires around here and they were planning to cast a spell to draw us out so they could kill us. They didn't count on us knowing about it, though. But we did." Reid smirked victoriously. He always took pleasure in it when they outwitted the enemy.

Ember thought for a moment, her blue eyes deep and swirling. "What are you going to do with them?" she asked hesitantly. Her nervous tone made it clear that she was worried how civil the vampire methods were. He couldn't help but think that she really knew him too well.

"We'll just blank their memories and let them go on their way." He realised a beat too late that he'd let something slip that he maybe shouldn't have. The problem was that he always got too comfortable around her, like she drew out a side of him nobody else could. His cool façade and abrasive comments just vanished whenever she was around.

"You can blank peoples' memories? Have you ever done that to me?" she squeaked, but he could see the sparks in her eyes, ready to burst into a flaming rage if he said the wrong thing.

"No. I've had no reason to. Though if I'd known about the dreams, I maybe would've. It really is dangerous for you to know. For us and for you." He made sure his voice was serious, knowing she'd take him seriously if he acted that way. Ember just nodded solemnly, apparently believing him for once.

After that, she went into silent, thoughtful mode again and he wondered if she was thinking about him, her feelings toward him.

He tried to take a peek, knowing it was wrong but he couldn't help himself; he needed to know. But as soon as he slipped into her mind, just brushing the edges of her thoughts, she abruptly turned on him with a fierce expression. He just looked at her evenly, showing no sign of his attempted intrusion.

"You can read minds too, can't you?" she said bluntly. Reid practically felt his jaw hit the ground in surprise. She'd shocked him again. How had she possibly figured that out, known what he was doing? Humans weren't supposed to feel that kind of magical intrusion. It was impossible.

He cautiously didn't reply and Ember spoke in a calculating tone, answering his unspoken question like she could read his mind. "I can feel it like a prickling at my temples. I'm not dumb and I have enough ideas about vampires to guess at what it means," she said brusquely, looking unhappy.

"But… you shouldn't be able to feel it. That's… it's not right." He shook his head and tried it again, preparing for her inevitable outburst. Only, it didn't work this time. Instead of easing a magical link between his mind and hers, he came up against a blank wall. Ember just arched a brow at him. He gaped. "What the… how are you doing that?" he asked incredulously, recognising the smugness on her face. She was blocking him somehow. He'd never met a human who could do that. This girl had to have a stronger will than he'd imagined, making her possibly more stubborn than he was. No wonder he hadn't been able to break her and take her like he'd originally planned.

Ember smiled wider at his reaction and replied simply, "Will you stop doing that now?"

He nodded, keeping his expression one of disappointment so that she wouldn't suspect the next time he did it. Because he did have to try again. This wasn't right. It was impossible, not only for her to be able to feel his telepathic link, but to be able to block it. It was unheard of in a human.

Five minutes later, when Ember was deep in thought, not paying any attention to anything around her - all he'd said was that witches and vampires may not be the only mythical creatures going about, and he'd been joking (sort of), and she'd completely spaced out like she was trying to unravel the mysteries of the world (which, for all he knew, she could be) - he tried again and again hit a wall, but not before catching a glimpse of something he knew he shouldn't have. It stunned him.

Born Dark

Instantly, he felt his cheeks grow warm, which was unusual for him. He didn't often blush, and he was more than used to the torrid fantasies the girls around the school had about him. He took amusement from sneaking a look into their minds just to see what they were thinking about him.

But Ember was different. He didn't expect her to think of him like that. Didn't expect to find in her head what he'd just found. He had to give her credit, though; she was very good at keeping an innocently sincere, deep-in-thought-over-complex-issues kind of expression on her face when she was thinking much less complex things. He'd never suspected she had those kinds of thoughts at all, let alone about him, but then again, she was a master at hiding behind semi-composed facades and simple anger.

Feeling the prickle at her temples, Ember slammed up her mental walls. She blushed but she tried to look smug, obviously hoping to hell that he hadn't caught any of what she'd been picturing. "Will you stop doing that! It's annoying. If you want to know what I'm thinking, just ask like a normal person," she raged, but she was still blushing.

He grinned. "But you'd lie. There's no way in hell you'd have told me what you were

really just thinking about," he said in a low, intimate voice, unable to help himself. But, obviously realising he'd seen her thoughts, Ember's eyes went wide, and then she went the colour of beetroot, flushing to the roots of her caramel-blonde hair. She almost looked like she might cry. Uh-oh, Reid thought suddenly, dropping his smirk. Ember swallowed visibly and flipped her hair over her face so he couldn't see her. Damn it! He hadn't meant to upset her. What was he meant to say? She'd already figured out what he'd seen, and it would only piss her off more if he denied it. "Look, I'm sorry, I just... I can never tell what you're thinking, and you honestly looked like you were contemplating the rationality of the existence of God or something. I wouldn't have intruded if I thought... Well, I guess that's the problem. I don't think before I act..." he sighed, that last mainly being a mutter to himself. But she caught it and answered.

"Yeah, so I'd noticed," she chirped sharply, her voice like shards of glass falling.

"It wasn't like I expected... I mean I wasn't trying to find... Not that I mind, but I just..." He continued grasping at straws but he could tell it was no use. She was going to keep her guard up around him constantly now, and he'd probably never get a chance with her. *Maybe it'd be easier on her if I just-*

"It's OK," she said suddenly, her voice quiet.

Reid blinked, thought he'd misheard. "What?"

She still wouldn't look at him and he suspected she was still red under that curtain of hair but she sounded calmer at least. "It's okay. I just should've known better," she murmured. Reid wanted to ask her what she meant, why she should've known better, but he decided to let it slip. He had the feeling he'd only upset her more if he kept questioning her about it.

For some reason, it reminded him of that day at the skate park when he'd asked if she was a virgin or not, and she'd gotten all angry and flustered. Maybe there was still part of her that was too innocent, that tiny part that wasn't demonic and ferocious. The idea that there was a hidden vulnerability in her gave him a strange thrill, a desire to find that softness in her.

After that they walked in silence for a bit. Reid watched her as she watched the waving tree branches and the navy-blue expanse of sky, dusted with puffs of grey clouds. The way the moonlight caught her face made her look ethereally pale, made her hair shine like molten gold.

Suddenly, she lowered her gaze to his. Her eyes were dark as sapphires in this light. "Hey, by the way, how did you know I was in the tree? I mean, you must've known I was there before I gasped because you were already gone." She looked puzzled, an expression she had so often that he wondered if she ever stopped thinking about things. It seemed that there was always something going on in her head.

"I could smell your scent. The scent of your blood and pheromones," he explained, contemplating the idea that this information might freak her out or disgust her.

Instead, Ember considered what he'd said for a moment, and shrugged. It was astounding the way she accepted these things with nothing but interest and calmness. Surely she was in shock or something? There was no way she was really taking all this in and still didn't run screaming. Yet, he thought she was. There was something in her eyes, the thoughtfulness to the tilt of her mouth. Yes, she was absorbing it all like a sponge soaking up beads of water, and she wasn't scared. She was singularly unique, and Reid knew he'd already fallen for her, fallen so deeply that he was sure to drown if he found out she didn't return his feelings.

Finally, they reached the big wooden doors to the dorms and Reid hesitated, stopping her by gently tugging her back by the hood of her jumper. She looked disgruntled and confused but didn't lash out for once.

"I don't think we should go in together. If someone sees us, the rumours will only get worse," he explained sympathetically, feeling the frown on his own face.

He was amused by how she'd been handling the rumours so far, with witty retorts and bitchy remarks, brushing off everyone and putting some people to shame. He'd been watching her intently since Monday, despite what she'd said to him then. She was at her most demonic, and it was a little scary to watch her sometimes.

Reid focused back on the present, searching Ember's face for some sign of defensive anger, some sign that she'd lash out at him or anyone they passed in the halls but the look she gave him was far from angry. She was smiling lightly, devilishly and her blue eyes were warm and deep. "I don't care. They are only rumours after all, right?" And dear God, was that a seductive tone?

Judging by her expression, he decided that it most definitely was a seductive tone, and he was taken aback once more. His heart did a funny little jump, and if he hadn't known better, he would've pulled her to him right then and kissed her.

Ember giggled at his expression, and slipped into the dorms, not waiting for him to follow. Rolling his eyes heavenward with a silent prayer, Reid stood for a few seconds, before following her in and catching up to her. She was toying with him. The little blonde demon was playing with him like a cat with a mouse! He was sure of it. She had to know how irresistible her teasing was. The thing was... he had a feeling she didn't.

Ember

Ember ignored the whispers and stares they got as they climbed the stairs and walked to her room. She even paused at the door to talk to Reid. Distantly, she was surprised there was anyone up at this time, but of course there were plenty of students rushing to and from each other's rooms for late night recreations. A couple of people even stopped to watch what would happen as she stood to talk to Reid.

"You know the rumours are going to go out of control tomorrow, right?" Reid asked in a whisper, his blue eyes concerned. God, if he got any cuter, she'd end up wrapping her arms around him and never letting go.

"So? Rumours are only rumours. Only gossip whores believe that crap anyway," she said loudly, boldly meeting the gazes of the few who'd stopped. They immediately turned away and Ember smirked. Reid smiled faintly at her.

"You really are a tough-" he started but she cut him off,

"If you say 'kid', I'll slap you," she said, anticipating his next words.

"I was going to say 'girl' actually." Reid grinned. He shoved his hands into his pockets and glanced down, agitating the dark carpet with toe of one boot. "So," he said awkwardly, and she wondered if he would kiss her. For once, the idea didn't make her feel like running away.

"So… I'll see you tomorrow," Ember sighed, rubbing her forehead. She had one hell of a headache. Reid nodded and smiled. Then, looking around and seeing there was nobody pacing the halls since she'd scared them off, he kissed her on the mouth. A chaste, sweet kiss, just a mere brushing of lips. But it was enough to make Ember dizzy and her stomach clenched hotly. Grinning, Reid chuckled, before sauntering off down the hall with the smuggest grin she'd ever seen on him - which was saying something.

Ember got into her room and flicked on the ceiling light, regardless of Sherry. Right now, Ember was too tired to care whether or not she woke her friend.

She pulled off her boots and jumper, pulling on her pyjamas again. Standing in front of the mirror over the dresser, she brushed her hair, making sure there were no lingering bits of bark or pine needles. Her cheeks were rosy from the cold, and her freckles looked awfully dark against her pale skin.

It wasn't until she'd been to the bathroom and brushed her teeth that she noticed that Sherry wasn't in her bed. The dark covers were wrinkled, and something white rested against the pillow.

"Where the…?" Ember frowned at the empty bed, messily made up with a scribbled note on the pillow. Ember picked it up, suddenly feeling exhausted, and read:

Hey Emz. Don't worry, haven't been kidnapped. Went to see Ricky. Go back to sleep. X

Ember sighed and put the note down. She didn't want to think about whatever Sherry was doing with Ricky at this time of night. The issue of his showing up in the fight with the witches, and the fact that Reid would be back in his - and Ricky's - room by now didn't really register with Ember's sluggish, insanity-laden mind until much later.

Ten minutes later, after Ember had turned out the light and was trying to drift off, the door opened. Ember groaned, thinking that this night was never going to end, but it was only Sherry who came in, carrying her shoes in one hand and shutting the door quietly with the other. With her eyes adjusted to the darkness, Ember could see Sherry moving slowly across the room, shoulders hunched.

"I'm awake. No need to tiptoe about," Ember muttered, not moving. She was too comfortable and too tired to bother moving. Sherry jumped at the sound of Ember's voice and pulled her hair over her neck conspicuously. Ember was dead-beat tired but not stupid as not to realise why Sherry was doing that: Love bites. Or, Ember thought with her newly discovered secret in mind, Vampire bites?

"I thought you'd be dead as a log till morning," Sherry whispered apologetically. Ember reached out one arm lazily and flicked on the bedside lamp. Sherry cringed from it.

"I wish," Ember replied, her voice slow with exhaustion, "I went for a moonlight walk after having a nightmare and ended up bumping into the last person I wanted to see." She rolled her eyes, not really lying but not telling the whole truth. Even Sherry would think she was nuts if Ember told her the whole story.

"Reid, I'm guessing. Did you, uh, sort things out?" Sherry murmured, dumping her shoes by her bed and wandering over to her dresser to pull out pyjamas. Ember watched her paw through her clothes until she tugged out a camisole and began digging for the matching shorts.

"Pfft," Ember made a sound half-way between a hiss and a snort. "If anything, things just got more confusing. I didn't think it was possible." Ember almost laughed aloud at just how much more confusing things had gotten. Only, it wasn't really emotional confusion anymore, so much as psychological confusion. As in, she wasn't entirely sure if she was still sane.

"Hmm," was Sherry's simple distracted reply. She was still searching for her pyjama shorts, half tossing things out of the drawer. Ember noticed something just then and had to stifle a giggle in her duvet.

"Uh, you know your t-shirt's on the wrong way?" she stated with an irrepressible grin. Sherry whirled, blushing, and stared down at her t-shirt.

"Oh, I, uh, just…" Sherz stumbled for words and Ember just laughed tiredly.

"Hey, you do what you want. Just wait until tomorrow if you're going to get all gossipy; I don't think I can take any more news tonight." Ember waved at her dismissively and Sherz smiled sheepishly in return.

After they were both in bed and the light was out, Ember fell asleep quickly, despite the revelations and questions whirring in her brain. Thankfully, she didn't have any more goddamned dreams.

Sherry

"Ember, time to get up." Sherry prodded her friend, who was still out like light at eight o'clock in the morning. Ember groaned and rolled over, pulling a pillow over her face. Sherry sighed as she stood, hands on hips, glaring at the lump in the bed before her. "Ember, we have school. You need to get up." Ember made a muffled sound like a snort under the pillow and grumbled.

"As if I give a…" The end of her sentence was indistinct as she shifted under the covers. Sherry rolled her eyes, wondering when she'd become her best friend's mother, and grabbed the end of Ember's duvet. She flung it off the drowsy girl and to the floor, eliciting an irritated, sleepy growl from Ember.

"I'm not going to school today!" Ember sat up, rubbing her head. Sherry had to admit her friend did look awfully exhausted, with purple splodges under her hazy blue eyes, and her skin was paler than usual.

"Fine. I'll tell them you're ill, but this is the last time I'm covering for you," Sherry warned as Ember hastily bundled up her duvet from the floor and snuggled back into it. Watching her friend exasperatedly - and a little worriedly - Sherry couldn't help but wonder about what Ember had been up to with Reid, while she'd been with Ricky, which had tired her out so much?

Knowing she wouldn't get an answer from Ember, who appeared to already be asleep again, Sherry sighed and closed the curtains before grabbing her schoolbag and leaving the room, shutting the door quietly behind her.

Born Dark

Ember

It was after one in the afternoon before Ember was even awake enough to look at the clock without the numbers blurring in front of her eyes. She was glad she'd chosen to stay in bed today because she would've zonked out in class sixty times by now if she'd gone to school. But she took little comfort in the extra sleep, because she could clearly remember every detail of why she needed that extra sleep.

Groggily, she rolled out of bed and scrambled under it for her bottle of coke. She desperately needed her fix of caffeine, otherwise she'd be a mindless zombie in a bad mood for the rest of the day. She needed her head clear to think, seeing as she had a hell of a lot to think about. She chugged the coke straight from the big, two-litre bottle and got to her feet as she twisted the lid back on it. Carelessly, she dropped the bottle onto her bed and went to the bathroom to shower, hoping the hot water would wake her up.

Once she was semi-presentable, with her hair sitting neatly in golden waves and her teeth brushed, she carefully made her bed, smoothing out every wrinkle until you could've bounced a coin on it. Suddenly, it seemed the whole room was a mess. The books were out of order on their shelves, the clothes in her dresser were piled in sloppily and the make-up on the nightstand really should've been put away.

Ember vaguely noted, in the back of her mind, that none of these things really mattered. That she was finding distractions - displacement activities, as her Chemistry teacher back home had called it - because she didn't want to think about last night. But, of course, it was unavoidable, and eventually, after having put every out of place particle in the room back in order, Ember dropped onto her bed and folded her legs. It was time to think, no matter how much of a headache it would give her.

Not three minutes later, while she was staring hard at a blank spot on the wall, having skipped the actual thinking and gone straight to just mindless daydreaming, a knock came at the door. Ember knew without hesitation who it would be.

She sighed and somewhat unenthusiastically muttered, "Come in." Sure enough, it was Reid who entered, closing the door softly behind him as if frightened he might scare her off. Apparently, her casual acceptance of his vampirism last night was lost on him.

"Hey. How… how d'you feel?" he murmured, lingering by the door with his hands in his pockets. He wasn't wearing his beanie today, or his cut-off gloves, looking almost vulnerable without them.

"Apart from exhausted? I'm great. You don't have to act like I'm some terribly frightened little mouse. If I was worried about you being a vampire, I wouldn't have slapped you last night, would I?" she grumbled, flopping back tiredly onto her pillows. Reid hesitated, then, with a grin, came and bounced down onto the bed by her feet. She rolled her eyes at him. "So why are you here? A real reason or just wanted to ensure I wasn't going to run screaming 'Vampire' around the school?" Ember smirked and felt his hand close on her ankle. He tugged her down the bed, and laughed when she hissed at him. Ember struggled to fix her t-shirt, which had ridden up when he'd tugged her, feeling uncomfortable with his gaze lingering on her exposed skin.

"Stop staring at me or I might think you really will try to eat me." She jerked her ankle free and slid back up the bed, tucking her knees up to her chin and watching him carefully. Reid just smirked and shrugged.

"I don't have to be a vampire to want to do that," he stated simply, as if it were a well-known fact. Ember wanted to get angry or embarrassed but instead she just gave him a mild glare and tossed a pillow at him playfully.

"You didn't answer my question," she stated simply as he laid himself out on the bed next to her. He looked at her with lazy blue eyes and a smile.

"No. I didn't." He smirked as he said the words. Ember vaguely recalled having avoided a question of his with those words before. She reached out a hand to rap him on the forehead but he caught it easily. "Nuh-uh-uh. You don't get to do that anymore." He grinned, an astonishingly bright smile with fangs showing. Her heart jerked and her breathing caught for just an instant upon seeing those fangs. Did he really have to do that?

"I can still do this," She retorted, springing on him like a snake out of a striking coil. She landed astride his stomach, and he gazed up at her with wide, startled crystal-blue eyes. She could feel her own heart hammering on her ribs but she was determined to make him see that she wasn't scared of him, that his being a vampire didn't bother her. Far from it, in fact.

"Well, this is a nice change," she said smugly, letting her hair fall on either side of her face.

"What might that be?" Reid replied, quirking an eyebrow curiously.

"I'm the one pinning you for a change." She laughed, and felt his breathing stop for just a heartbeat.

"Only because I'm letting you. I'm enjoying this much more than you think," he chuckled, his eyes darkening with a kind of heat. That heat seemed to melt into Ember, too, and she began finding it difficult to think of a reason to ever move.

"Mh-hm. Are you going to get off, or are you going to kiss me? I'd prefer the latter but…" Reid grinned, obviously picking up on her change in mood. She quickly shifted off him and hid her blush. "C'est la vie," Reid sighed and propped himself on an elbow to look at her. He really did look like some sexy angel, lying there with warm blue eyes and a seductive smile on his soft mouth.

"If you're not here for any good reason, can you leave before I-" Ember started, leaning her head in her hand.

"Before you what exactly?" He arched a brow expectantly and she sighed, resisting the urge to smile.

Before I can't resist the urge to kiss you dizzy. "Before I fall asleep again. I'm still tired and bantering with you takes a lot of energy."

Reid looked disappointed but nodded and slipped off the bed. Ember watched him walk across the room, noting the lilt to his shoulders as he moved, and the way his t-shirt clung to his slender torso. He had a grace about him, and certain smoothness to his movements that most likely came from his confidence. Reid, Ember thought, could make a yellow jumpsuit look sexy.

"Do you mind if I come back later?" Reid asked as he put a hand on the door handle. Ember thought for a moment and shrugged. She didn't see any reason he couldn't, and honestly, she kind of wanted to talk to him. Properly. Sort out, well, everything. Particularly whatever was going on between them.

"I suppose you could," she muttered. Reid grinned at her, waved, and left. Ember groaned and crawled back into bed, the effects of the caffeine wearing off already. What harm would a couple more hours of sleep do?

"So, do I have to ask what you were up to with Ricky last night?" Ember asked Sherry, grinning knowingly. Sherry blushed but smiled, a smile that Ember knew meant there was gossip to be told here.

"Nothing happened," Sherry said quietly, turning away so Ember couldn't see her face. Which could only mean something interesting happened.

"Uh-huh? What kind of nothing happened?" Ember pressed, curious. She couldn't help but grin. Sitting on her bed, she folded her legs and leaned her elbows on her knees, resting her chin in one hand. Sherry was pretending to be occupied with folding and re-folding her sheet of Drama homework very precisely. Ember wasn't fooled. She knew Sherry had been awfully busy last night, and she thought it was her duty as Sherry's best friend to get the details.

"We just kissed for a while…" Sherry shrugged but she still wouldn't look at Ember.

"And I suppose you're going to tell me you were both fully dressed for this make-out session too?" Ember grinned and rolled her eyes, reading her friend's hesitation and fierce blush. Sherry didn't answer, which Ember interpreted as 'Clothes hit the floor'. She grinned and laughed, essentially congratulating her friend on her intensifying relationship.

"It was just his t-shirt…And mine…But that's it. He had to go for some reason…" Sherry's expression said she was disappointed and confused by that. She finally stopped folding her homework and just slipped it into her schoolbag, before tucking the bag under her bed and shrugging at Ember.

"Well, I'm sure it must've been a life-or-death thing if he just left you there, shirtless." Ember laughed again - this time though it was a nervous laugh more than anything, because she knew exactly where Ricky had gone. He'd been with Brandon, Perry and Reid, fighting the witches. Something struck Ember just then: Did Sherry know about Ricky? Should she tell her? How would she react?

"Hey, I'm sure Reid would love to throw your clothes to the floor too if you gave him the chance," Sherry said, sounding mischievous and sympathetic, misreading Ember's suddenly unhappy expression.

Ember just smiled weakly and said, "Like I'd want that." Sarcasm was heavy in her voice.

"You know you would," Sherry bantered back, flashing a smirk.

A knock on the door sounded and Reid let himself in with a lopsided grin. He'd changed his t-shirt since earlier, and now wore a grey one with 'Born Dark' written across the front in bold, red letters. Ember stifled a giggle, tried not to roll her eyes at him.

"Speak of the devil," Sherry muttered.

"You were talking about me?" Reid grinned, raising his brows and wandering over to sit himself on the end of Ember's bed. Ember ignored the way her heart did a funny little flip when he smiled at her.

"Yeah, we were just saying it's a pity you're so arrogant or you might almost be able to pass for the angel in the school's Easter play next year." Ember nudged him with her foot, and caught Sherry's meaningful glance. Ember just shook her head minutely, giving Sherz a glare.

"Oh, so you think I look like an angel now? Well, well." Reid reached out to toy with the hem of her jeans, and she smacked his hand away. He was like a kid, the way he always had to be playing with something.

"No, I think you look like a typical pretty boy. All smiles and charm around the girls, almost like you're trying to overcompensate for something?" Ember smirked, knowing he'd catch on. Sherry snickered but they ignored it, too caught up in their own easy bantering.

"Mh-hmm? Well, you could find out..." Reid leaned toward her, blue eyes hooded and warm. It was just very nearly a tempting idea. Ember bit her lip, shaking her head and pushing him away with the palm of her hand. His chest was warm under her palm, even through his t-shirt, and she felt the hardness of his muscles as he moved back.

"I think not," she said simply, watching Sherry struggle to hide her laughter. Ember rolled her eyes, "Shut up. It's not funny," she muttered, waving a dismissive hand at her friend.

"Whatever. I'll believe you." Sherry rolled her eyes, "And I'll just leave you two to figure things out alone. Have fun." The green-eyed girl smirked and skipped out of the room, giving Ember a meaningful glance as she slipped out the door. Ember glared after her, watching the door swing closed, leaving her alone in the room with Reid. For some reason, the thought filled her with a kind of nervousness she'd never felt before.

"So, do you really not want me to take your clothes off?" Reid asked, grinning, once Sherry was gone. Ember groaned and whacked his arm.

"I had a suspicion you'd been listening before you came in. You're such an eavesdropper." She rolled her eyes and lay back on her pillows. She'd only woken up - for the second time that day - an hour ago, when Sherry had come in after school. She wasn't tired anymore exactly, but she hadn't given much thought to everything. She wasn't sure what to say to him, how she should be acting.

"You didn't answer me," Reid said, arching a brow and stretching out next to her. She was aware of how they would look if anyone came in and saw them; lying together, facing each other with mischievous smirks. It would look much more intimate than it felt and it felt pretty intimate as it was.

"No, I do not want you to take my clothes off." She replied smartly, flipping off the bed backwards. Being so close to him made her feel things she didn't necessarily want to feel. So moving away seemed like a good idea.

"Liar," Reid sighed, flopping onto his back and putting his hands behind his head.

She shot him a glare. "I'm not lying! You just overestimate your own sex appeal. I get that being a vampire makes you…" Ember stopped and stood in the middle of the room, facing him with a pained expression on her face. Talking about vampires had reminded her of something she really should've thought of before.

"Makes me what?" Reid asked, smirking.

Ember shook her head, ignoring him. "It's just… does Sherry know about Ricky… you know, that he's a…?" Ember asked hesitantly almost positive of the answer to her question. Reid sat up, a genuinely serious grimace on his face.

"No, he hasn't told her. You shouldn't even know. I wouldn't have told you if you hadn't been hiding in that tree last night; Wrong place, wrong time - that's the only reason you found out. But Sherry can't know. It's too dangerous. Ricky's good at acting human, so she never has to find out… well, 'Never' being a hyperbole." His tone made it clear he knew what she was thinking. "You can't tell her. Promise me you won't tell her?" he added, verbalising his warning.

Ember frowned, feeling torn. She didn't want to expose such a big secret that wasn't hers to share, and she certainly didn't want Sherry in danger, but she never kept things from Sherry, and as far as important information went… well, this was huge. What was she supposed to do? What would be better for Sherry? That's what it came down to really. What would be better for Sherry?

"Ember? Please?" It was astonishing to hear Reid say please. Seeing his pleading expression, she knew she couldn't argue with him. Not now. She was tired of arguing with him.

Guilt washed over Ember as she replied, unhappily. "Fine. I won't tell her."

Reid sighed in relief and relaxed into an easy grin again. "Good. It really is what's best for everyone," he said, sensing her reluctance.

"Yeah, I guess so. Why are you here by the way? I mean, I know I said you could come back but I'm just wondering why you wanted to." Ember changed topic quickly, still feeling guilt lapping at her mind. Reid didn't answer right away, running a hand through his blond hair distractedly. He looked over at the window, but something told Ember he wasn't seeing what was beyond the glass. His mind was obviously focused on other things.

"I just wanted to make sure you were still handling everything OK. I mean, discovering fairy tales and monsters really exist, it's kind of a big thing and the way you just accepted it last night made me wonder if you were in shock or something." He smiled a little but she could tell he was honestly concerned about her. It was sweet, as much as she hated to admit it.

"That's it?" she asked. It wasn't what exactly what she'd expected though why else he'd be here, she had no idea. She supposed she'd thought that maybe, after last night, they might drop the pretence of being just friends. After all, it was hardly worth the energy it took to pretend anymore. "Well, you can stop worrying about me going nuts. I wasn't sane to start with. And vampires existing is not exactly my worst nightmare. Witches either. Now, you put me near clowns, that would really terrify me," she said, faking a shudder, wandering around the room aimlessly. She was full of restless energy all of a sudden. Her chest was tight, and she had the inexplicable urge to giggle for no good reason.

"Clowns? Seriously? Bloodsucking monsters, you're OK with. But guys dressed up in face paint and big shoes, meant for kids' birthday parties, they scare you?" Reid snorted. She just shrugged, and turned to look at him and he grinned at her.

For a moment, they stayed like that, just looking at each other, and Ember felt something uncurling in her stomach. It felt fuzzy and warm and she had to look away from his probing blue eyes. There was a kind of expectancy in his expression, like he was waiting for something. Waiting for her to say something. What did he expect her to say? Did he want her to tell him how she felt about him? Because she really didn't know how she felt about him. It was all so complicated.

The thing was, though, that she realised something now. Maybe she should've realised it a long time ago, because she was always making little mental notes about how he looked or how he moved or how he acted. She realised now that she noticed him like she didn't notice other people. Usually, she was so lost in the fantasy worlds in her head that she didn't really pay attention to what was really around her. She didn't want to pay attention. But something about Reid forced her to wake up and see him, really see him in front of her. It could've been simply that he was gorgeous; it could've been that he kept her on edge, but whatever it was about him, it held her attention like a butterfly trapped in a glass jar.

"You know," Reid said softly, and Ember turned to look at him. He was picking idly at the edge of duvet, watching his fingers twisting around the fabric. "I don't think I've ever noticed a girl the way I notice you either."

For a long moment, Ember wasn't sure what to say. Part of her wanted to go to him and take his hand, curl up against him and never move. And part of her was angry. How had he known... Oh. Of course. He's a bloody vampire. "Do not read my thoughts!" Ember hissed, feeling violated and irritated, and just a little flattered. He noticed her, like she noticed him. It was nice to know, at least.

"Sorry. Your expression was worrying me." He didn't seem sorry at all, which didn't surprise her. He was back to his normal, arrogant self and she could feel the acidic retorts on her tongue. But there was still that warm feeling unfurling in her stomach and chest. Damn it. Why did this have to happen to her? She had never planned, when she'd chosen to move to this school, on meeting a guy here. She'd never wanted to meet a guy, to fall for him. But she had. She'd met Reid, and she'd fallen for him, and no matter what she told herself in the middle of the night when thoughts of him floated into her mind, she liked that she'd fallen for him. Thinking about it now, Ember could hardly believe that just yesterday she'd have sworn she didn't care about the arrogant blond boy stretched out on her bed. It seemed that one little secret could change everything. She almost hated to admit to him, after all this time, that she really did care about him.

"Ember? You OK? You look confused." Reid tilted his head, examining her face curiously. In return, Ember examined him, too. She couldn't help herself. She let her eyes follow the curve of his cheekbones, the line of his jaw, and the tender shape of his mouth. There was something so captivating about him, and it went deeper than his pretty face. There was something behind those bright, inquisitive eyes that just drew her to him.

"Yeah, I'm OK. I'm just trying to figure out how to say something," Ember sighed, joining him on the bed again and meeting his wary blue gaze. He didn't say anything, and his expression was unreadable. He sat up, folding his legs in a position similar to hers, and facing her evenly. Ember braced herself, taking a deep breath and letting it out slowly.

"Is this something to do with me being a vampire?" Reid's voice was as blank as his expression, but his eyes showed how anxious he was. She wondered if he was expecting her to tell him she didn't want to see him anymore, didn't want to associate with a blood-sucking monster.

After a short hesitation Ember replied, unable to meet his gaze anymore. "No. It's about, well, I think you can guess. I mean it's not like there's any point in pretending anymore or lying to myself. So, I might as well just say it..." But she couldn't. Her tongue stuck to the roof of her mouth, and she stared down at her hands in her lap. Her long, thin fingers curled around each other, her skin startlingly pale against the dark denim of her jeans. She felt like she couldn't stand to move a muscle and the air got so thick she could hardly breathe. Reid waited patiently, and she felt his gaze on her like a weight. He'd gone tense all over, she could sense it, see it in the way his hands were laced tightly together on the duvet.

It was at least a minute and a half later before Ember got the words out – barely. "As much as it stings me to admit this I guess I owe you the truth." She stopped, wishing she could swallow her words, feeling her cheeks burning with a blush, but she proceeded with some effort. "I, I like you. OK? I said it. I like you, more than as just a friend. I thought I could keep lying to myself, to you, to everyone. I thought I could keep denying it, but I can't." Ember glanced up at his face, meeting his blue eyes. "I don't want to be enemies anymore, Reid. And I don't want to be friends. I want more than that," she almost whispered the words, her heart beating in her chest so hard she thought it might explode. She was gambling every shred of her dignity on how Reid felt about her, and if she were wrong... well, she'd probably lock herself in a cupboard until she could get over the humiliation.

But Reid didn't look inclined to laugh at her or mock her. His expression was almost enough to make her laugh though: his eyebrows shot up into his hair and his eyes went wide, glittering with surprise. Whatever he'd been expecting, it hadn't been that. Slowly, a sort of glow descended over his face and he began to smile - not his usual smirk, or mischievous grin, but a genuine, sparkling, heart-stopping smile. "You're serious, aren't you? Not even you would be cruel enough to mess with me like that. You really mean it," he sounded incredulous. Either he couldn't believe she'd fallen for him or he just couldn't believe she'd admitted it.

"Yeah, I mean it." She shrugged one shoulder, shyly avoiding his gaze, picking at the seam of her jeans. There was a long pause, and Ember wondered if he was considering getting up and just leaving. But he didn't. He just sat there, watching her. For the first time since she'd met him, Reid appeared to be speechless. Eventually, though, he found something to say.

"I meant it, what I said before. I've never noticed a girl like I notice you. Everything you do intrigues me. I watch you sometimes, when you don't think I am, when you're in class or in the library, and I just want to keep watching, because you're like some beautiful rare flower. You say things nobody else would ever say to me, and you don't treat me like I'm better than everyone else. You treat me like a person, not the infamous legend everyone thinks of me as. And every time I've kissed you, there's never been anything I've wanted more in my life than that kiss."

Astonished, Ember looked up at him, saw the light in his eyes and the vulnerable curve to his mouth as he looked right back at her. And she knew he meant it. Every word. Unsure what to say, feeling her heart fluttering behind her ribs like a bird in a cage, Ember did the one thing she'd wanted to do since he walked into the room.

She leaned forward, lifting her hand to brush her fingertips along his cheekbone, down to the corner of his mouth. Hesitantly, very lightly, she traced the shape of his lips with her fingertip. She held his gaze, watching his eyes darken to cobalt, seeing the delicate crescents of the dark lashes that framed his eyes. He sat perfectly still, barely breathing, while she bent her head and touched her lips to his. At first, she merely brushed her mouth across his, and he let her. He didn't move, didn't try to catch her lips in a kiss. Then, slowly, she pressed her mouth to his, very lightly, and felt him respond. He slid one hand into her hair, wrapping his other arm around her waist. His soft lips moved against hers, and she twined her hands around his neck, his silky hair tickling her fingers. She felt like she was trembling inside, a delicate electric current running over her skin.

Then she heard a barely-audible click, and Reid drew away from her, reaching back to unlace her fingers from behind his neck. He turned his face away from her, his eyes still closed. Confused, Ember frowned. "Reid, what is it? Did…did I do something?" She heard her voice waver, feeling the hot sting of rejection. But Reid shook his head, opened his eyes and drew in a breath. He slowly turned to look at her again, a strange expression on his face that almost looked like guilt. But not quite.

"No, it's not you. I swear. It's…" He laughed bleakly. "It's this." Cautiously, he opened his mouth and slid back his lip from his upper teeth, exposing long, sharp canines. His fangs. Now Ember understood the expression on his face. It wasn't guilt. He was ashamed. Because he wanted to bite her? "It… they come out when I'm hungry," Reid explained quietly, but he'd dropped his gaze, "And I don't mean, just for blood."

It took Ember a long moment to realise what he meant, and when she finally figured it out, she felt heat sweep up her face. She tipped her head down, hoping her hair would create a screen so he wouldn't see her blushing. "Oh," she said simply, trying not to smile.

"Don't worry; I'm not going to bite you or anything. I just…" He shrugged, and when she glanced at him, Reid was blushing too. It was so strange to see Reid blush, especially over something like this. She'd thought he was immune to this kind of thing, considering his reputation. He'd always seemed so sure of himself, so unabashed about it.

Ember couldn't help it; she giggled. And once she started, she couldn't stop. She covered her mouth with her hand, keeping her head down, but she knew Reid could see her shoulders shaking with laughter. She just couldn't believe it, couldn't believe that Reid Ashton was blushing over something like this, couldn't believe he honestly looked ashamed, thought she'd freak out over his fangs or the idea he might bite her. Clearly, the boy had no idea who he was talking to.

"Do I even want to ask what's so funny?" Reid asked, with a kind of resigned amusement in his voice.

Ember managed to gasp through her giggles. "You. I can't believe you thought that I'd… that it would…" She couldn't form a sentence, clutched at her aching sides until the giggles receded and she could breathe again. Then she looked up, wiping tears off her face, grinning helplessly. "Reid, the fangs don't bother me. Honestly. You remember that night in the skate park when I told you I like vampires? I meant I *like* vampires. As in, if you wanted to bite me, I probably wouldn't try to stop you," she explained, despite a fresh blush rising to colour her face. Here she was explaining her bizarre fetishes to a guy who, just yesterday, she was sure she hated. A guy who, incidentally, happened to be the one supernatural creature she'd ever wished to be real.

Reid stared at her wordlessly for a long moment, the colour high on his cheekbones fading. Ember couldn't read the expression on his face, but his eyes were roving her face, looking for something. Whatever he found, he was apparently satisfied with it, and a slow, sensual smile crept across his lips. Just for a second, Ember's heart stopped; He was just so pretty. For all his sins and sharp comments, he had all the beauty of an angel.

"You, Ember, are perhaps the most amazing girl I've ever met," he said softly, reaching out to tuck a lock of her hair back behind her ear. Jitters ran around in Ember's stomach.

"Unfortunately, I have to admit, you're rather amazing yourself. I'm not sure I've ever met someone as insane, frustrating, or nerve-wracking before in my life. And I'm certain I've never found a boy worth noticing before," she admitted. Then she narrowed her eyes menacingly - Reid looked faintly startled - and added in a low voice, "You are the first guy I have ever given a chance to, and if you blow it, I will personally stake you, cut off your head and then watch you burn."

"So, you finally admitted it to him? How did he react?" It was the first time all day Ember had had a chance to talk to Sherry about what had happened between her and Reid yesterday.

Sherz had been off with Ricky until late yesterday - Ember didn't ask what they were doing or even where they were - and she'd been too out of it to keep up a real conversation when she'd arrived back at just after midnight.

"He was happy, I guess. I expected him to smirk or laugh or made some arrogant comment, but he just…" Ember shrugged.

They were walking back to their room after the final bell and, for the first time lately, Ricky was nowhere to be seen. He'd been sticking by Sherry so often these last few days that Ember was starting to consider pulling out a restraining order on him. Ember was missing her best friend because of him and she just wanted one girls' night, with movies and popcorn.

"And? Come on, he had to say something or do something? Some kind of show of appreciation?" Sherry muttered, a meaningful gleam in her green eyes. Ember just sighed and rolled her eyes. It only spurred Sherry on more. "He did, didn't he? Did he kiss you? Stroke your hair? More? Come on, we're best friends! We need to share this stuff!" When Sherry said that, Ember felt a wash of guilt yet again at how she was hiding the true identity of Ricky and the guys from her best friend. It was something she should know, something huge and amazing and wonderful. But it was safer not to tell her; safer for everyone, especially her.

But Ember could tell her this much; after all, it was only girly gossip. "Yeah, he kissed me. Or I kissed him. Whatever. And, no, he didn't exactly stroke my hair but things got a little warm. No clothes hit the floor though, so don't even ask." Ember held up a silencing hand quickly as Sherry opened her mouth, undoubtedly to ask just that. She was grinning madly, clearly pleased. Ember almost wanted to tell her exactly what Reid had said to her yesterday, about how he noticed her and how he'd said that whenever he'd kissed her, it had been what he wanted more than anything. But, for now, she wanted his words to be her little secret. A memory she could keep locked away until it got worn with time, like a photograph taken out to be looked at too many times.

"At least now we both have boyfriends. Maybe we could go on a double date?" Sherry's green eyes sparked excitedly at the idea. Ember groaned inwardly, thinking that her friend's head-over-heels romance had turned her mind a little slushy.

"Seriously? A double date? That's about the most sickly, mind-numbingly clichéd thing you could've suggested," Ember groaned out-loud this time, feeling queasy at even the idea of a double date. It was typically romance movie-type stuff that made her want to gag.

Sherry knew that, of course, but she simply smiled. "Please? It would be fun."

Ember wasn't to be persuaded, not this time. "No way. Not in this lifetime chum. And anyway, I'm not quite sure if you'd say Reid was my boyfriend exactly. We're still working out the details of that issue." Ember felt the puzzled frown on her face and saw the disappointed look on Sherry's. She also had an air of exasperation all of a sudden.

"What? Why are you giving me that look?" Ember asked defensively as they reached their dorm room door.

Sherry sighed. "Even when you can admit your feelings for him, you have to be difficult about it. You couldn't just accept you're in a relationship and like it, could you?" Sherry shook her head, stepping into the room and flicking on the light switch.

"Hey, it's not that... well, not completely. There's genuinely some things we-" Ember stopped, bile rising in her throat and the air escaping her lungs. Sherry had turned to face her already, before observing the room, in order to give her a judging glower.

"What? What is..." Sherry turned and saw it too.

Ember felt like she was honestly going to throw up, her blood ran cold and her limbs went numb. Tears sprang to her eyes and rolled down her cheeks, and before she could start hyperventilating, she screamed. Sherry - just barely visible in her blurry peripheral vision - just stood still as stone, obviously too shocked and horrified to move or speak. Ember covered her mouth with her hand, her stomach spasming, wracked with waves of nausea and chilling horror.

She barely noticed when Ricky and Reid burst in the door not fifteen seconds later. Ricky went right for Sherry, but when he saw the mess, he stopped and swallowed, disgust clear on his face. He swiftly turned back to Sherry and practically carried her from the room, arms around her protectively, whispering soothing words over and over. Ember's vision was too blurry from tears and the shaking to distinguish anything but a pool of red and black in her line of sight, and she could barely get enough breath. Someone was pulling at her arm, trying to take her away, but she wouldn't - couldn't - move a muscle. Slowly, Reid's voice came blurrily to her ears, and she finally understood what he was saying.

"Ember. Ember, come on, we need to get you out of here. Now, come on. It's OK. It's OK. Everything will be OK." Reid's voice was worried and slightly panicked, filled with the same disgust as Ricky's face had displayed. Even vampires had limits to their gruesomeness, she supposed distantly.

Ember wanted to yell at him that it wasn't OK, how the hell could it be OK! There was a mangled, dead crow on her bedroom floor, wings twisted grotesquely and blood seeping out of it onto the carpet! How could that be OK? But she could only gasp through her tears, feeling cold and numb.

Eventually, Reid gave up on trying to make her cooperate gently, and just lifted her in his arms as she continued sobbing. She didn't fight him as she might've usually at the indignity of being carried like a child. She clutched his t-shirt and curled into his chest, letting him take her wherever it was he was taking her.

All the while, he muttered to himself too low for her to hear properly, and occasionally made a remark to her, meant to be soothing. It didn't help.

Ember was surprised to open her eyes to see clean white floors and pale lavender walls around her. Bright lights lit the sterile, cold room and she realised she was in a harsh, rough hospital bed. She tried to sit up, glancing down the rows of empty beds on one side, and at the drawn moss-coloured curtain on the other side.

She was in the infirmary.

She tried to sit up again and felt vertigo hit her, so she lay back dizzily. Her eyes were sore and her head hurt a little, but other than that she was fine and couldn't understand why she was here. That was, until the images hit her a moment later; the mangled crow, the twisted wings, the blood on the floor, the lifeless empty shine in the crow's black eyes.

Born Dark

Nausea roiled in her stomach but she swallowed it back, determined not to throw up. The helpless tears came once again to pour down her face and she felt something in her heart wrench.

Who would do that? Who would do that to an animal? What kind of sick, evil person would kill a crow that way? And why would they put in her room? Some kind of ghastly, twisted practical joke? An atrocious, disgusting prank?

She realised as she asked herself the questions that there was no possibility other than the theory that someone had done it intentionally. It couldn't have been that the bird flew in the window and hurt itself somehow, or that it was simply a coincidence it had been in her room specifically. It was meant for her. There was no way it was directed at Sherry, because nobody hated her. Some people disliked her just because of her association with Ember, but it was Ember that people hated around here. But who would hate her enough to do something like this? Who would be sick enough to do it?

"Oh, crap! You're awake!" Reid's voice echoed in the near-empty infirmary and she turned to see him rushing over to her from the open doorway in the opposite wall.

"You'd have preferred I stayed unconscious?" Ember choked, a weak attempt at her usual wit.

"No, of course not. But I wanted to be here when you woke up to make sure you were OK. You fainted halfway here and I was worried." Reid's blue eyes bore into hers, conveying all his anxiety and concern. Ember felt her lip tremble and bit down on it, trying to repress more tears. Reid wrapped his arms round her, holding her to his chest and planting tiny, soft kisses in her hair. It was such an unfamiliar thing for him to do, so bizarrely gentle and despite what they'd said to each other yesterday, Ember couldn't help but feel startled by it. This is the kind of thing a boyfriend would do, her mind whispered, and she frowned, unsure exactly how she felt about that. It was so new to her.

"Don't worry. We'll find who did this. I promise, we'll find him." There was grim, furious determination in Reid's voice. And for the first time, the fact that he was a cold-blooded vampire scared her a little. She didn't want to think about what he might to do to whatever sick bastard he found guilty of this horror. But she let him hold her, drawing strength from his care and determination, no matter how unsettlingly foreign it was to her.

A short while later, Reid was sitting in a padded plastic chair, pulled up next to her bed, one hand twined with hers on the sheets. His long fingers tapped a rapid, random beat on the back of her hand.

"So, when do I get out of here?" Ember asked eagerly, looking round at the too-clean infirmary walls and floor. She'd never liked hospital-type settings like this. They were too emotionless, too bleak and sterile. The strong smell of bleach and metal put an uncomfortable tang on her tongue.

"Now, if you want. The nurse wanted to check in on you in a half hour and give you some sort of medication for anxiety, but I can pull some strings." He smiled and Ember knew that he didn't mean pulling strings the way a normal person did, the way a human did. Vampire compulsion was sure to be his charismatic tool, with, perhaps, the aid of his charming smile. Ember smiled back at him and nodded. Reid went off to find the nurse, and Ember sighed.

She was starting to get over the horror of what had happened, and now she was getting angry about it. She wasn't so much angry at the fact the bird had been put in her room, meant for her, but more at the sickness of the way the bird had been killed. How could anyone do that to an animal? She thought once again, fury building up. A knot of flame locked in her chest, and she gritted her teeth. Maybe she'd give Reid some ideas of how to deal with the sick son of a bitch who did this when he found him? Nobody should get to mangle a bird like that and get away with it. Detention wasn't enough. Expulsion wasn't even enough. He should suffer the way the bird did.

"Ember," Reid's concerned voice pulled her from her gruesome train of thought. His wide eyes and pinched mouth let her know he'd been in her head again, and she felt the anger drain away faster than it had come on. Sometimes her temper swung wildly like that, mostly when she was tired or already upset.

"I just can't stand it! How could anyone do that to a bird? It's the most sick, twisted, evil, repulsive, damned awful thing I've ever seen!" she spat, curling her fingers into the blanket on her lap.

"Ember, relax. We'll find out who did it, and why, and then we'll deal with them accordingly," Reid said calmly, shrugging as if it were no big deal. Ember supposed, to a vampire, a dead crow possibly wasn't a big deal. She was overreacting slightly, but she was an animal-lover and tended to be a bit sensitive on the issue of people hurting animals.

"I'm just angry, is all. And…" She paused thoughtfully. She'd never fainted before last night but she was sure she shouldn't still be dizzy, her head shouldn't still hurt and the nausea she felt should've gone away by now. She knew these symptoms well, realised the cause of them also accounted for her sudden temper snap. "And I need caffeine before I bite someone's head off. That's probably why I'm all crazy," she offered as an explanation for her mood swing.

Reid just looked at her for a moment and then said, very soberly. "You know caffeine is a drug, right? Your addiction to it is rather unhealthy."

Ember scoffed, rolled her eyes. "You sound like my mother," she grumbled. Reid just grinned.

"The nurse said you can go but you have to take one of these before you go to bed tonight." He held out a little orange bottle of pills. She eyed the bottle with disdain before snatching it and shoving it in her pocket.

Reid helped her off the bed since she couldn't touch the floor - her feet dangled several inches above the shiny, linoleum floor. This amused Reid a great deal, it was clear on his face, but he refrained from mocking her for once. Ember glared at him anyway, knowing he wanted to laugh, but he didn't seem to care.

It wasn't until they were halfway back to her room that Ember's sluggish mind spat a few real thoughts out, thoughts that didn't pertain to Reid or how unreal he looked walking beside her.

"Wait, where's Sherry?" she asked, suddenly panicked and desperately worried about her friend.

"She's OK. She's with Ricky somewhere, probably the library. She stayed by your bed for a little while, didn't want to leave, but the nurse said she'd let her know when you woke up." Reid frowned for a second at that and then smiled, shrugging it off. "Well, you can tell her yourself I guess. If we can find her," he added.

After a moment of thought, Ember decided Sherry was probably just fine and she could go to find her, and check on her, later. Reid started walking again, not holding her hand but wandering along very close next to her - she had a feeling he wanted to hold her hand but didn't dare in case it stirred up more rumours if they were seen. He stopped at the door to his room and caught her hand – very briefly - to stop her from walking past it.

"Hey. In here, Firefly." He nodded toward his door hand on the door handle. Ember paused and glanced down the hall toward her room.

Then she shook her head. "I need to see my room." She knew the room would've been thoroughly cleaned by now and she wanted to banish the images she had of the crow on the floor. Reid looked at her with a concerned expression.

"I don't think that's a good idea," he said quietly.

"Please. I need to see it all clean again to get rid of the horrible images. Please?" she insisted. Reid looked ready to argue, but then Ember looked up at him pleadingly, and saw his resistance crumble. Slowly, Reid nodded and led her down the hallway toward her own room, though he clearly wasn't happy about it.

Reid opened the door ahead of her and took her hand firmly in his as she stepped in beside him.

The carpet was unmarked, not a single stain or drop of blood, no dark feathers left on the floor. Ember breathed a sigh of relief but, behind her lids when she blinked, she could still see the wrung out bird.

"Better?" Reid asked, glancing around nervously as if someone might've been hiding in the corner, waiting to attack. Fortunately, they were the only two people in the room. Ember nodded and went to sit on her bed, longing for the comfort of her own possessions. Reid closed the door and followed her, eyes searching her expression for any sign she might freak out again. But she stayed calm and, feeling a little childish, reached under her bed for her teddy bear. OK, so even the toughest chicks needed something sentimental. Ember hugged the fuzzy teddy to her chest and saw Reid smile, shaking his head in disbelief.

"I never would've thought it. Ember Jennings has a teddy bear. And I bet you sleep with it too, don't you?" he chuckled, apparently entertained by the notion.

"Shut up," she muttered, the command muffled as she spoke into the teddy's head. She lifted her head to stick her tongue out at him. Reid merely arched a brow. Ember felt very much like a small child right now, but that feeling went away quickly as Reid leaned over to kiss her chastely on the lips. She dropped the teddy and shifted closer to him, snuggling into him instead. He put his arms around her and just held her there, his breath soft on her hair and his solid body comforting next to her. Again, it was such an unknown comfort for her, and it made her heart beat a little faster being held against him like this. But slowly, she began to relax, quite happily breathing in his warm scent until her eyes fluttered closed.

Born Dark

Ember woke up sometime later, wondering how she could've fallen asleep fully dressed and on top of the duvet. Then she remembered the crow and the infirmary, and then sitting with Reid, his arms around her and her fingers curled into the front of his t-shirt. It was going to take her a while to get used to that sort of thing, she realised.

When Ember opened her eyes, gentle green ones met hers, instead of the bright blue she'd been imagining. "Hi, Emz. Feeling better?" Sherry asked, her voice almost a whisper. Ember sat up, rubbing her eyes tiredly. Her eyes stung, and the skin under them was tender from crying earlier.

"Yeah, I'm just fine. How are you?" Ember had been worried about her friend earlier too. Honestly, how had she fallen asleep so easily amidst so much turmoil? Surely Reid had drugged her or something, or maybe he'd compelled her. Somehow, she suspected she'd just been more tired than she'd realised. She didn't often faint, and it had taken a lot out of her.

"I'm OK," Sherry said simply. She didn't need to add more, because Ember could see the lingering sweetness in her eyes that meant she'd been with Ricky recently. Of course.

"Ricky took good care of you, I heard. I'm glad." Ember gave a weak smile and yet again felt that tug of guilt. She was starting to think it might be a permanent thing, the guilt. She wished she could tell Sherry what Ricky really was, she had a right to know.

Sherry just nodded and smiled a little. Ember glanced at the clock; it read 7:43am.

She hadn't thought about the time since she'd awoken in the infirmary earlier, but she realised she must've been out for a while down there. And she must've been out for at least a couple of hours here. Exhaustion and horror were taking their toll lately.

"It seems Reid took care of you, too. He was still here when I got in about an hour ago, and you were completely out, sleeping like the dead. He told me he didn't want to leave until someone else was here to keep an eye on you." Sherry grinned, gave Ember an expectant look. Ember just rolled her eyes. She felt a hint of a smile tug at her own lips, though, before she rummaged under the bed for her coke. She took a swig from the bottle to help wake her up, and then went to the bathroom to freshen up.

She closed the door behind her and examined herself in the mirror. Oh, boy, she thought miserably, seeing her gaunt reflection staring back at her with heavy blue eyes and unusually pale skin - pale even for her. Her hair was a wavy mess and she felt unclean, thick with exhaustion. "Shower time." She muttered to herself, and walked back to the other room to gather up clean clothes. She thanked God it was a long weekend and she didn't have school again until Wednesday. She just couldn't have gone to school today.

She grabbed clean clothes and her hairbrush, and headed for the shower again. Sherry was already absorbed in whatever she'd started watching on her laptop, so Ember figured she could take her time in the shower, hoping the hot water would blast away the tension in her muscles. She closed the bathroom door, and locked it behind her before flipping on the shower and beginning to undress.

Ember emerged from the shower a long time later, feeling refreshed and ready for nearly anything. She dried off and wrapped a towel around herself, brushing her hair into a wet ponytail and securing it with a hair bobble from the collection by the sink. She rifled through the pile of clothes she had on the floor and realised she'd forgotten to take out a clean bra in her hurry to hop in the shower.

Sighing, she opened the bathroom door and walked into the next room, headed for her dresser. She noticed right away that Sherry was gone - probably with Ricky or off to the library to study for her next English essay - but someone else was in the room instead.

Ember immediately felt embarrassed and uncomfortable, standing in just a towel while Reid lounged against the closed door, looking… well, his expression changed quickly when he saw her, turning from a quiet amusement - which probably meant he had something planned, a reason for being here that would surprise her - to something like hunger. Not the bloodlust kind of hunger, though.

"Um, hi. You're back already." Ember was clutching the towel to her with white knuckles, and resisting the urge to simply run back into the bathroom. Reid didn't reply, but his gaze began to wander all over her, raking every inch of exposed skin, and Ember blushed furiously. Her stomach fluttered.

She'd had guys tell her she was pretty, or occasionally that she was hot; she sometimes got admiring glances in the street, but she'd never had a guy so blatantly undress her with his eyes before - not that he really had to use his imagination much, seeing as all she was wearing was a thin, cotton towel which left most of her legs bare for him to see. It was unnerving and flattering at the same time. Then again, that was just Reid for you anyway.

"Uh, Reid? Hello?" She adjusted the towel, tugging it up higher and tighter. Waves of heat were rolling up her face, but there was a different kind of heat sinking into her stomach. She swallowed, watching Reid's eyes stroke lines down her body and back up again. She could practically feel his gaze like a tangible thing, like cats paws brushing her skin. It made her shudder involuntarily, and she knew he noticed. He grinned devilishly at her, his eyes dark.

"Yes?" He raised his brows, finally meeting her eyes again. Ember opened her mouth, but no words came out. She wasn't really sure what to say. His ogling had thrown her mind into a tizzy and she'd forgotten whatever it was she'd been about to say. She closed her eyes briefly, hoping that if she didn't look at him, she might be able to think again. But when she opened her eyes, she gasped, flinching back, her towel slipping a little as her fingers spasmed reflexively. Reid was right in front of her, though she hadn't heard or felt him move; he was close enough to touch, close enough that if she just took a step forward, she'd be able to reach up and slide her fingers into his hair. Oh, for God's sake, control yourself! She determinedly took a step back, despite the urge to move the other way and touch Reid, kiss him and press herself against him. Stop it!

"Why are you here?" she asked, a little more unsteadily than she'd intended. Reid took a small step back and feigned hurt, covering his heart with one hand.

"Don't you want me around anymore? I thought we'd gotten past this?" he teased, grinning. But when Ember only rolled her eyes in response, he sighed dramatically. "I've got a surprise for you. I think you might like it but you should probably get dressed first." He paused then, tilting his head as his eyes drifted over her once more. He added mischievously, "Unless you'd rather stay here and enjoy some other surprises?"

Blushing, Ember pushed away some very inappropriate thoughts and looked away from him. "I'll get dressed," he said bluntly, brushing past him to get to her dresser.

She didn't worry too much about him seeing as she pulled underwear out of the top drawer - after all, he'd actually stolen her underwear not all that long ago. Of course, that didn't stop him trying to snatch it from her, chuckling with delight. Stubbornly, Ember held onto the bra she'd taken out of the drawer, and whirled away from him before he could catch it. She locked the bathroom door once she was in, just in case. She wasn't entirely sure it was completely beyond him to secretly watch her dressing.

"So, where are we going exactly?" Ember asked, peering out the window at the hazy fog rolling over damp, browning fields as they drove by in the Aston Martin. She tapped her fingers nervously on her leg, wondering where he was taking her.

"I told you, it's a surprise." Reid smiled mysteriously, his blue eyes lighting up. He didn't say anything more, and Ember didn't bother asking, knowing he wouldn't tell her. Of course, she could always use a little feminine power and make him tell her, but that would likely lead to other things and Ember wasn't sure she could restrain herself. Plus, tempting Reid like that would be like baiting a shark with chum; he wouldn't be able to resist, and wouldn't be happy unless he got what he wanted.

Ember was puzzled, though, when they pulled up at a rickety wooden fence that surrounded what looked like an old abandoned house. It was big and dark and appeared to be falling apart, but it certainly had that creepy quality that made her fully believe there was something supernatural around it. The mist rolling in across the unkempt garden added to the effect. She half expected a ghost to come howling out the door as they approached it and entered.

NIGHTMARE APPROACHING

H.G. Lynch

Born Dark

Ember

Inside, she found it wasn't nearly as treacherously battered as the outside seemed to be. They stepped through the mouldy entryway into a large, open-plan foyer, with a rotting ceiling that seemed to be shedding plaster and filthy paint in flakes like grimy snow. To their right was a wide archway set into the dusty walls, and beyond it was a huge, empty space. Floorboards crouched unevenly amongst the dust and dirt, litter such as beer cans and smashed bottles were the scattered remains of private parties of daring students. The wooden panelling of the walls was visible through the torn and peeling wallpaper, too faded and murky with age to have a colour or pattern. Cobwebs clung to the corners of the room, drifting from the beams across the ceiling like dripping syrup. Rusted copper pipes showed through a ragged hole in one wall, like the exposed veins of the house.

On their left, there was rickety wooden staircase, leading up to the floor above, the hand railing rotted away until it looked as if it would collapse at the slightest touch.

Ember followed Reid across the foyer, and stopped in front of a heavy, battered-looking metal door, set into the wall under the staircase. The door was large, dented and scorched and oddly out of place in the sagging, ancient building. There was a set of padlocks securing the door shut, though it appeared that somebody had tried to smash the locks, judging by the twisted mess of them. Confused and anxious, Ember looked at Reid. He simply smiled back, and reached under the collar of his shirt for something. When he pulled his hand out, he was holding a set of thin, shiny keys on a chain around his neck. Ember wondered how she hadn't noticed the chain before.

Swiftly, Reid used his collection of keys to unlock the door, and dropped the heavy padlocks to the floor. He yanked on the steel handle, and the door lurched open with a low groan and a squeal of the hinges. Beyond the door, there was a set of stone steps, leading down into darkness. On the cobweb-dusted stonewalls, delicate candelabras were bracketed, empty of candles. Reid moved onto the top step, and began to descend, but Ember hesitated.

Several steps down, Reid realised she wasn't following, and paused, turning to look up at her. He was far enough down into the darkness that his face was covered in shadow, a mask of white turned up to her. His hair gave a dull gold shine, and only his eyes were clearly visible, as glowing blue pools in the gloom. "Are you coming?" Reid asked, his voice echoing faintly up the stone stairway. He stretched out one hand to her, and she saw him smile reassuringly. Slowly, she smiled back, and reached for his hand, stepping down onto the crumbling stone steps. His warm fingers closed around hers, and he led her down the stairs, only Ember's footsteps echoing from the stone around them.

The temperature gradually dropped, and the darkness enveloped them so completely that Ember could hardly see the ground beneath her feet. Eventually, Reid dropped her hand, and looped an arm around her waist, steering her easily down the steps that she could no longer see. Once, she slipped, and felt Reid's arm tighten around her as she clutched at his t-shirt. Her breath puffed out in surprise. As Reid steadied her again, she looked up, and found him smiling down at her, his eyes bright even in the pitch black.

"Are you taking me to a dungeon or something?" Ember whispered as they began moving again, the oppressing creepy feeling forcing her words out quietly. Reid just smirked and shook his head.

When they finally reached the bottom of the endless staircase, Ember paused in both awe and surprise. The room they had descended into was as beautifully eerie as anything she'd seen in movies, with heavy leather-bound books on shelves along the walls and a large stone carving in the middle of the room. The stone was carved with a large dip in the centre, like a scoop had been taken out of the rock. The resulting hollow was blazing with fire, making light and shadows dance and flicker like ghouls around her. It was dim and musty, and felt subterranean, but Ember thought it was wonderful.

However, what surprised her was that there were already three people in the room. Ricky, Brandon and Perry were seated around the room in wooden chairs, various expressions of surprise on their faces as they looked at Ember and Reid. Ricky stared aghast at them, while Brandon and Perry looked shocked and angry.

Ember felt suddenly out of place, like she'd intruded on a secret meeting, and whispered to Reid - despite the fact the rest of the occupants of the room could probably hear her as if she were speaking out loud - "Do they know I know?" She shifted back behind him just a little, uncomfortable as they continued to gaze unhappily at her.

"Well, they do now," Reid replied quietly, his voice holding a tone of amusement. He reached back and wrapped an arm round her shoulders. He led her forward and swung out a little wooden stool for her to sit on, placing it next to one of the empty wooden chairs that he sat on himself. Then there was there racket of several voices shouting at once.

"Reid, What're you doing?"

"Are you nuts? Why is she here?"

"How much does she know?"

The outbursts came from Perry and Brandon, while Ricky just gave her a shy smile and a wave. He didn't seem to have a problem with this, so why should the others?

"Brandon, you know she knows. She was there that night with the witches, remember? What was I supposed to do, compel her?" Reid meant the words mockingly, she could tell, but they came out harsh like a snarl. His face, though, was impassive as marble in the flickering firelight.

"Yes! That's exactly what you were meant to do! Don't you realise how much danger she could put us all in?" Brandon yelled back, exasperated and furious. Ember felt a little hurt by this; she'd thought of Brandon and Perry as at least polite acquaintances, and here they were trying to convince Reid to erase her memory. But under the hurt, she was angry too.

"Danger?" Reid scoffed incredulously, "If anyone's in danger, it's her! Or haven't you heard about the incident with the crow yet?"

Reid's blue eyes held that inhuman glint, like fire reflecting off a sword, and the sliding ribbons of firelight dancing over the sharp angles of his cheekbones only made it scarier. His expression was vicious, making it clear he wanted to fight Brandon over this. Ember got the impression that Reid would fight Brandon over a differing opinion of ice cream flavours, though.

"What crow? What are you talking about? It doesn't matter now. We need to blank her memory or else-" Brandon started, sounding a little tired all of a sudden.

Ember cut him off with her own protests. "Excuse me! Stop talking about me like I'm not right here!" she snapped. "And if you dare try to blank my memory I swear to God I'll stab you with a pencil! Just like a tiny stake, right?" She heard Reid snicker at that, but she continued her rant anyway, ignoring him. "I'm not going to tell anyone what you are, so relax. And just in case you missed it, I'm here with Reid. Doesn't that kind of tell you something? If I really had anything against you guys being vampires, I wouldn't have let Reid drag me here, would I?" Ember came to a stop and breathed out heavily. She stared hard at all of them, and smirked.

She seemed to have stunned them all with her outburst. Ricky had been around her enough to know she had an explosive temper and she wasn't to be messed with, but Brandon and Perry had had very little idea of that until now. Reid was grinning like a maniac, pride and victory and smugness all over his face. Obviously even he hadn't entirely expected her to lash out like that, but he clearly found it amusing to see Brandon stunned that way. He started laughing, a sound that echoed off the walls and made Ember smile. Ricky was first to recover and he grinned at her boldly.

"I think she's right. They both are. I know Ember enough to know that she won't expose our secret and if she's with Reid, she has a right to know." He sounded a little sheepish at the end, despite his strong words. Ember knew what he was thinking of: Sherry. She could see the doubt form in his eyes. And she felt again that twinge of guilt at keeping this from her best friend, but pushed it away. Reid was still chuckling next to her, and Ember gave Ricky a genuinely grateful smile for being on their side. Brandon and Perry slowly stopped being stunned by her outburst but still didn't seem happy about any of this.

"It's not a good idea, but… for now, we'll leave it alone and just see how it goes. Maybe it would help if you explained the thing about the crow?" Brandon said, looking almost resentful at Reid and Ricky - mainly Reid - and sitting back in his chair.

After that everyone sat down and Reid and Ember relayed the crow incident, with Ricky throwing in a few comments. When they were done, Brandon and Perry looked almost as horrified as Ricky had when he'd first seen the mangled bird, but they recovered quickly this time and began plotting out ideas to catch whoever had done it. Ember wasn't sure why they were so eager to catch some sick prankster, especially one that had terrified her, seeing as they appeared to hate her now. But she appreciated the help and figured they were doing it for Reid more than anything. Ember thought it was really too bad Sherry wasn't here. She would've loved it, the creepiness of the stone-bound room. It was a pity she didn't know about any of this. Yet.

"Um, Ember? I know you haven't said anything to Sherry, but I was just wondering… how are you handling that? I mean, considering how close you guys are, I imagine it must be pretty hard?" Ricky approached her just as they were leaving falling into step beside her while Reid was already hopping into the car. A light drizzle had begun falling from the steely clouds, and Ember pulled her hood up to shield her from the rain.

"Hard? No, it's not hard at all, hiding a life-changing secret about my best friend's boyfriend from her when I only see her every day." Ember knew Ricky didn't deserve the heavy sarcastic remark, but she was tired and he'd just asked her about the exact thing that annoyed her most about this situation. Fortunately, Ricky didn't take it too hard. He just gazed at her evenly with blue-green eyes, a crooked, humourless smile touching his mouth.

"OK, I know it sucks. And I want to tell her, I really do but… I just don't think it's the best idea right now. I mean, it was an accident that you found out, and it's not like you and Reid had anything going on then, but it's more complicated with me and Sherry. I really care about her and I know she trusts me. How would she react if I suddenly came and said to her that I was a vampire? Seriously? She'd freak and probably never talk to me again. I don't want to hurt her and I really don't want to scare her off." He truly did make it sound like there was no other option. Ember wanted to growl at him. She sighed, pausing at the door of the Aston Martin and turning to him.

"Ricky, I know. I know you don't want to hurt or scare her, and I know it's safer for her not to know but… this is a huge deal. And I think you're underestimating her ability to cope. I didn't exactly freak when I found out, and I already had every reason to hate Reid. Sherry feels much the same way I do about vampires, and I honestly don't think you'd scare her off. As for the trust thing…well, that might be damaged but if you really do care about her the way she cares about you, I have no doubt you two could fix it. The only two reasons I don't tell her, are because I don't want her in danger and I don't feel it's my place since we'd be talking about you as well. It's your place if you want her to know and, as unhappy as I am about keeping the secret from her, I won't tread on your turf," Ember finished glumly, guilt sweeping through her again. But Ricky just nodded. His expression caught between gratitude and guilt, and walked off to his Audi.

Once in the car with Reid, Ember tried to relax. She'd honestly enjoyed hanging out in the vampires' secret den, despite her newfound dislike for Brandon and Perry. The place was certainly awesome, and Ember wondered if she'd ever be allowed to read some of those big, leather-bound books. Surely they were full of interesting stuff about mythical creatures, which Ember could probably spend hours trawling through gladly.

"What was that about with Ricky?" Reid asked sounding a little piqued. It almost sounded like a hint of jealousy laced his tone, but Reid didn't seem like the jealous type.

"I was telling him where to find me tonight so we could go have sex behind Sherry's back. What do you think it was about?" she snapped sarcastically, making Reid grimace. He didn't look all too convinced she was being sarcastic and she had half a mind to find matches and set the boy on fire. Surely that would kill a vampire? It did in her books. She growled under her breath and Reid sighed, starting the car.

"You always seem to end up in a bad mood around me." It was a simple statement but Reid sounded a little hurt. That just sent another wave of guilt over Ember and she tried not to snap at him again.

"Sorry. I'm just peeved that Brandon and Perry seem to think I'm going to run off and scream 'vampire' to the whole school, or turn around and stake them or something. And the guilt's killing me over not telling Sherry. She's my best friend and we don't keep secrets from each other." She sighed again, and rolled down the window as they started back to the school. "Anyway, I am actually glad you took me here. It's probably the coolest place I've ever seen. Very creepy, very cool," she added, lightening her tone so that the words didn't sink like the titanic. The cool air blowing in through the open window was refreshing and soothed Ember's temper a little, letting the hot anger seep out. Reid didn't reply for a long moment.

"Brandon and Perry are idiots. I didn't think they'd lash out at you like that. Me? Yeah, I expected them to thrash me later but I honestly haven't ever seen Brandon talk to a girl that way before. Asshole." Reid frowned, looking pretty peeved. It made Ember feel a bit better, and she hid a grin.

"Yeah, well… at least I got to give him an earful. Next time it'll be a mouthful of fist," she said with a shrug. Then she broke into a helpless grin. Reid smiled at that and dropped the conversation, but Ember could feel him glancing at her the whole ride back to the school, like she might disappear if he looked away for too long.

Tuesday was miserable. Ember was alone for a good part of the day, since Reid and the guys were out trying to find whoever had put the dead crow in her room - She didn't even ask how they were doing that. She wasn't sure she wanted to know. Plausible deniability was always a good thing - and Sherry was… well, she actually had no idea where Sherry was. She'd been gone by the time Ember had even woken up and she hadn't left a note. Ember wasn't worried though; sure her friend was probably off to the gym or the library for the day. But it left her alone with time on her hands, which led to boredom.

She thought through her options of things to do for the day: Swimming? Skateboarding? Neither of those was fun on your own. Go for a walk? She glanced out the window and grimaced. It was typical autumn weather outside, windy and wet. Normally she wouldn't mind walking in that, but she had nowhere to go on a walk, no destination, and she didn't feel like wandering aimlessly around campus where she might run into people.

Ember sighed, leaning her head in her hand. She wanted to be out with the boys, finding out what sick freak killed the crow, but Reid had ensured her she would be better off here. Of course, she'd argued and the only way he'd gotten her to stay behind was by physically restraining her, tying her feet together so she couldn't run after him. It had taken her too long to get out of the ropes (or rather, the tie he'd used) to even think of going after him.

Damn it, she thought, grabbing her hoodie and pulling on her boots. She'd go to her tree, cold or not, because she just couldn't stand to sit in this stuffy, dull room any longer.

Sitting in the damp, cold tree, twenty feet up from the soggy, pine needle and leaf-riddled ground, Ember groaned with boredom. A sharp blast of wind whipped the loose strands of her hair across her face, and made shivers run through her body almost like spasms. She watched the golden leaves swirl in little twisters on the ground below, and a flock of sparrows danced across the sky in an enrapturing pattern. Ember wished she had a camera with her.

Listening to the rustle of leaves and the whistle of wind around her, she was swept into an old memory.

***

It was the summer holidays back in Scotland, and she was camping with her family in Aviemore. Having escaped the watchful gaze of her parents, she'd gone off to find Owen - her friend since childhood, and son of a family friend. His parents had come along with hers on the camping trip and Owen and Ember had been inseparable the whole week - until they got caught trying to tie a rope ten feet up a tree to make a swing… after dark. They'd gotten in so much trouble for being reckless and stupid: their parents said they could have gotten hurt, or broken a bone if they had fallen. They could have hanged themselves, or gotten lost in the dark. Blah, blah, blah. But Ember was a master at escaping her parents' watchful eyes, even at nine years old.

"Owen! Come on! We're going to the hideout!" Ember had called to him, hiding behind his tent. A small, dark-haired boy crawled out the back of the tent and grinned up at her from the grass.

"Hey, Ember! How'd you get away from your mum and dad?" Owen whispered, scuttling up from the ground and chasing after her as she ran for the nearby cover of trees.

"I'm a ninja!" she whispered back, pausing to pull a karate pose.

The children laughed and continued running until they reached their 'hideout'. It was really a circle in the dirt outlined by rocks and sticks, and filled with fern leaves. But to the nine year olds, it was their ultimate sanctuary. Nobody could find them here.

"What are we going to do now?" Owen asked, respecting Ember as leader as always. Even as a kid, Ember was stubborn and demanding. And Owen… well, he was the sidekick with the big, cute eyes.

"Let's play hide-and-seek! You can be seeker this time!" Ember giggled, before running off into the trees, leaving a grinning Owen to put his palms over his eyes and count to twenty.

"I'll find you Ember! I will!" he called after her, still shielding his eyes. "I'll find you!"

***

A brutal lashing of wind shook Ember's branch, returning her to the present. She grimaced to herself; she hadn't thought about Owen since… when was the last time she'd thought of him? Before he'd gotten in with Scott Halen, surely?

Scott Halen had moved in next door to Owen when he was twelve, and Owen had taken to him like a duck to water. They'd become good friends but Scott was a bad influence. A rough kid with anger issues and no respect for authority. Ember had thought he was cool too, for a while, but when he started getting Owen into trouble - stealing cigarettes, graffiti spraying and vandalising property - Ember had run the other way and tried to take Owen with her. But Owen was in too deep, too sunk into the thrill of danger and recklessness. Ember had lost a friend, but gained a sense of just how dangerous it was to ignore rules and laws. Not that she often kept that in mind. She'd left Owen behind, smoking and cursing at her back as she walked away from him just before she had her parents call the cops on her once-upon-a-time-friend-turned-bad-boy.

"Ugh. Idiot," she hissed to herself, feeling the pinch in her chest as she remembered the way those big, cute eyes had turned cold and narrow. "It was his choice," she muttered to the air, as if she were trying to convince the wind rather than herself, glaring into cloudy sky.

Sighing, Ember climbed down and made her way back to the dorms, feeling nostalgic and irritated. She wondered what Sherry had been doing all day.

"Hey, Emz! I've got surprise for you!" Sherry was immediately on her feet as Ember slunk into the room, kicking off her muddy boots. After the chill of outside, their dorm room was exceptionally warm. Even the bright, yellow glow cast by the ceiling light seemed to give off tangible heat.

"A surprise?" Ember glanced at her friend suspiciously and tossed her boots in the wardrobe, unzipping her jumper with one hand at the same time.

"Well, two actually. One, I know you'll love. And the other I'm not so sure." Sherry's grin faltered for a second but she stuck it back on easily. Ember dropped onto her inviting, cosy-looking bed and faced Sherry uneasily. Ember didn't much like surprises. They often turned out to be bad news.

"Oookay?" She rolled her eyes when Sherry instructed her to close them and hold out her hands.

"Oh, come on! Please?" Sherz pleaded, bouncing in place. Ember sighed and complied, and instantly felt cool metal dripping onto her palm. Opening her eyes, she saw a long black chain curled on her palm, with a set of shiny, silver fangs attached to one end. Ember's eyes went wide - both at the beauty of the necklace, and the irony of Sherry's ignorance - and she grinned at her friend.

"Oh my God, It's lovely! What's this for?" she asked, hugging the green-eyed girl tightly.

Sherry laughed and shrugged. "Just something I thought you'd like. And I thought you deserved it, for all the crap you've been dealing with lately. Plus, I know I haven't been around much." Her easy smile dropped slightly and Ember felt guilt hit her in the gut, wrenching her stomach like nausea.

"Aw, it's OK Sherz. You have every right to spend time with Ricky! And anyway, I've been... handling Reid." Ember made the last two words into an unhappy groan, but Sherry just gave her a knowing look.

"And by 'handling', you mean?" Sherry giggled, arching her brows meaningfully, watching Ember clip her new necklace on with a smile.

"I mean, keeping him in line. And maybe having a little fun at the same time," Ember added shyly. OK, keeping Reid in line was actually part of the fun, but she wasn't sure Sherry would understand that. But Sherry grinned, apparently pleased that the relationship she'd insisted had to happen was working out so far.

"That's what I thought. Now, do you want your other surprise?" Sherry held up a letter in one hand and waved it. Ember took it from her, opened it, and read the first line. And then groaned in horror.

"No! Why now? Why now?" she muttered, her eyes glued to the paper in her hand.

"I'm guessing it's from your mum? But what are you talking about?" Sherry looked puzzled but amused. "She's coming for a visit next week!" Ember hissed throwing the letter down like it had bitten her.

Sherry's eyes went wide but replied calmly, "Well, we do have the whole of next week off school, remember? It's the Autumn Dance, and they need the extra time to set up."

Ember hadn't heard any of this yet, but her mother apparently had. How was that even possible?

"What dance?" She asked blankly.

"We were told about it last week. But of course, you weren't listening to anything last week, were you? You were caught up in bitching to everyone who came near you, and avoiding Reid." Sherry sighed at Ember's bleak expression. "Anyway. Your mum's coming next week. Feel free to squeal or scream." Sherry grinned, distracting Ember successfully, for now.

"She always chooses the worst times! We've got some mad, crow-killing prankster on the loose and Lord only knows what's really going on with me and Reid. We're not in a relationship as such, I don't think, but..." Ember shook her head. It was all so complicated. She didn't feel comfortable pinning a distinguishing label on what she and Reid had going. It was almost a relationship, but conventional rules didn't really apply when your would-be boyfriend was a vampire.

"Seriously? I thought you'd sorted it out? You're just like a couple, but in a really dysfunctional way. Just like your friendship was," Sherry commented wryly and Ember shot her a glare.

"We're... oh, I don't even know. But whatever you'd classify us as, my mum cannot know. She'll either be overly excited and giggly, 'Oh my God, my little girl has a boyfriend!' Followed by a hundred typical questions. Or she'll disapprove, 'Ember, you're far too young to be with a boy like that! He's a bad influence; you should keep away from him!' Yadda, yadda." Ember rolled her eyes with a sigh. Sherry sighed too, though clearly not for the same reason.

"You worry too much. How do you plan on keeping it from your mum? Sure, you can try to avoid Reid all you like while she's here, but she'll probably figure it out anyway. And I'm fairly sure Reid won't like the idea of staying away from you for a whole week," Sherry laughed.

"He'll live. Trust me. But if you say one word about me and Reid to my mother, I'll shoot you," Ember warned and Sherry held up her hands in mock surrender.

"OK. I'll keep my mouth shut. But I'm dragging you to the dance next week," Sherry insisted and Ember started to protest. Ember knew it was futile though. Sherry had that determined look in her green eyes that said she'd physically drag Ember to the dance if she had to, and probably have Ricky help her. Well, there was no way she could fight off Ricky if Sherry brought him in.

"Fine," Ember agreed eventually, very reluctantly. Sherry grinned in victory, and Ember glared. Great. Next week's going to be very busy, she thought bitterly.

The rest of the week passed in more or less the same frustrating, boring fashion. Reid and the guys were out prying answers from every possible being they found, searching unwaveringly for the crow-killing freak; so far no luck. Sherry and Ricky spent a little time together but he was out almost as often as Reid.

Ember vaguely wondered if Reid was avoiding her, but he made it clear whenever he dropped in that he'd rather be with her and he was only taking such a big role in the hunt for her sake. He still wouldn't let her come along and that irritated her, but she had other things to worry about.

She spent more time with Sherz than she had in a while; they watched movies and chatted and even went ice-skating one evening - Sherry fell a few times but got the hang of it quickly, while Ember showed off, using the skills she'd picked up in the few ice-skating lessons she'd had years ago. They were both freezing and damp from falling by the end, but they'd had fun.

Ember simply thought a good deal of the time, wondering about ways to escape going to the upcoming dance, dreading her mother's visit, and sometimes daydreaming. Well, actually, a lot of it was flashbacks to old memories, more than daydreams really. Ever since she'd thought of him on Tuesday, Ember kept having thoughts of Owen. It was strange. It reminded her a little of when she'd been having dreams about Reid, before she found out what he was. Only, with Owen, it was always memories. No dreams, nothing made up, just things that had happened in the past. It frustrated her.

The weekend was a little better. Reid decided to stop the search for the crow-killer just for one day, and spent a few hours with her on Saturday. Ember warned him of her mother's impending visit, explained in no-nonsense terms that he was not to let her mother know that there was anything going on between the two of them. He just gave an easy, devil-may-care smile and agreed… sort of.

Lying on the floor, with her hands folded behind her head, she looked up at where he was relaxing on her bed, and she asked about the impending dance. "So, what's with this Autumn Dance? I've barely heard anything about it. Sherry's making me go." Ember grimaced at that last comment, but Reid simply chuckled. He rolled over to look down at her, placing his chin on the backs of his crossed hands.

"It's just like any other dance really. Music, food and drink, decorations. Everyone dresses up to look good, they get dates and dance and all the other normal stuff." He sighed, a world-weary expression on his lovely face. Ember groaned, leaning her head back on the carpet, crossing her arms defiantly over her chest.

"I can't even remember the last time I went to a dance. I hate them. But Sherry's planning on using brute force, I'm sure. She'll probably get Ricky to drag me there if I fight." She shook her head despairingly, then smiled charmingly up at Reid, "Any chance you could spring me from the hellish prison I'm bound to endure?" She gazed at him hopefully, all but batting her lashes. But Reid shook his head in negation, grinning as if her impending pain amused him. Cruel boy, she thought, though she felt a small smile on her mouth at his sadism. It seemed they had that in common.

Born Dark

"Sorry, nope. Ricky, I'll fight, your best friend, though - not a chance. Would it help if I said I was going too?" he asked, tilting his head as he stared down at her, fine strands of his blonde hair falling carelessly into his eyes. He didn't bother to push them back.

Ember put on a show of thinking about her answer to that, tapping her chin with her finger, and eventually said, "Nope. Doesn't help. It's still going to be a stupid dance. I'm still going to have to wear a goddamned dress," she sneered the word 'dress' like it was some horrible disease. To her, it might as well have been. The day she willingly slid into a girly, lacy dress was the day hell froze over. If she had her own way, she'd wear jeans and band t-shirt to every event she went to. But Sherry would never allow it.

Reid, propping himself on his elbows, looked at her thoughtfully for a moment, letting his eyes run over her. Then he beamed crookedly, showing a bit of fang.

"What?" Ember asked, shifting uncomfortably, puzzled by his obvious delight. The pale afternoon light streaming in through the window lent a shimmer to his fair skin, and lit the powder-blue walls to a shade that almost seemed to move with the restless shadows of the clouds drifting across the face of the sun outside.

"Just imagining what you'd look like in a dress. I'm definitely going to this dance now," Reid laughed and Ember shook her head, sighing. So there was to be no rescue from this dance; she was doomed to attend, and wear a pretty, pretty dress and pretty, pretty make-up and... Ugh. Yuck. The thought alone made her shudder with disgust.

Reid rolled off the bed and came to kiss her, his soft, teasing lips making her head spin. His hands slid down her body and clasped her hips, and her hands found their way into his silky hair. After a long, breathless moment, Ember pushed him away. Instantly, she regretted doing so. She wanted so badly to kiss him again, seeing his hair slight ruffled and his mouth darkened sensually. Somehow, she controlled herself.

"Can't you go one day without feeling the need to tempt me?" she sighed, smiling. It was a stupid question, she knew, because he'd gone two days in a row without doing this to her, but still. It was like he just couldn't get enough of her, and she never let him have much. It was more than self-consciousness, but also a degree of self-respect that stopped her giving in to him. He didn't pressure her, but he made it clear he wanted her. Oh, he made it abundantly clear. He may not be human, but he was still a guy, so she figured she could cut him a little slack on that.

He hovered over her, gazing languorously at her beneath him, and smiled slowly. "I can. I just don't like to. Why is it you so easily resist? Am I losing my effect on you?" he asked tauntingly, but with a seriously curious hint to his tone. She supposed that was to be expected, seeing as he'd likely never had to wait for a girl to give herself to him. They willingly threw themselves into his bed, usually. Lightly, Reid ran a finger down the side of her neck to her collarbone, leaving her skin warm and increasing her heart rate just a little. Nope. He was not losing his effect.

"It's not easy. Trust me. It's… it's a little like having a chocolate cake in front of you that you aren't allowed to eat. You want it because it's yummy, and even more so for it being forbidden, but you resist it because you know you should," she explained, gazing past him at the ceiling, letting her eyes follow the pattern of cracks in the paint. She folded her hands on her stomach in a false show of calmness. Her heart was still fluttering in her chest, and if he didn't move off her soon, she was likely to sneak one more taste of the chocolate cake. Reid laughed, whether at her absurd comparison, or just at her, she wasn't sure. She didn't really mind. It was just good to hear him laugh, warm and sweet and melodious. She still heard a bit of the usual Reid arrogance in it but he wouldn't be himself without his arrogance.

"Good to know." He grinned, leaned down to press a kiss to her forehead, and then got gracefully to his feet. "Now, if you're sure you can live without me for a bit, I've got vampire business to attend to." He reached down his hands and helped her to her feet, then hugged her tightly for a moment. She could feel the hardness of his compact muscles through his t-shirt, and bit her lip so she wouldn't have the urge to kiss him again. Reluctantly, it seemed, he pulled away from her and moved toward the door.

"Oh, no! However will I go on without you?" Ember murmured sarcastically, rolling her eyes again. Reid shot her mock-dark look and then slipped out the door, closing it behind him. Ember sat down on the end of her bed, and sighed, staring at a blank spot on the wall. She was alone again, with nothing to do. Boredom seemed to be her constant companion recently. You'd have thought having a vampire for a boyfriend would've led to a more exciting life - apparently not.

Well, now I have time to worry about my mother's visit in two days' time. Fantastic. She groaned aloud, and flopped back, reaching up and dragging her pillow over her face.

H.G. Lynch

HELL IS A BALLROOM

H.G. Lynch

Ember

Sunday. Who'd have thought there was still shops open at three in the afternoon on a Sunday? Not Ember. But, Sherry had dragged her out of bed two hours ago, tossing clothes and a hairbrush at her and saying they were going shopping. It wasn't a question or a request. It was a demand. So Ember had shrugged on the clothes, tied up her hair, slapped on a little make-up and shoved her purse into her only handbag - a ragged, black shoulder-slung bag with a skull on it.

Now, it was just after three, and Ember's feet ached and her head hurt and she would've done about anything if it meant she could go back to the dorms now. This was the eighth dress store Sherry had dragged her into. Ember was feeling distinctly mutinous as she watched Sherry trawl through dress after dress on the railings bordering the shop walls.

"How about this one?" Sherry held up a long, elegant dress that would've been nice if not for the colour. Pink. Ember shuddered. This was the sixth pink dress Sherz had tried to convince her of so far, and Ember was going to slap her silly if she tried another one.

"No pink! For the last time, it's bad enough you're making me go to this dance, let alone trying to make me wear pink!" Ember growled, glaring at the green-eyed girl, who ignored her obvious bad mood and whirled away to scan enthusiastically through yet more dresses. Sherry, of course, already had her dress picked out; a lovely knee-length, turquoise, strapless dress that made her eyes glow and her skin look radiant. She had matching accessories already, too. This shopping trip was especially for Ember, who couldn't really give a damn what she wore to the stupid dance. She'd insisted that she could simply wear her jeans and a pair of heels, but Sherry wouldn't allow it – and, apparently, neither would Reid.

"This one? Come on, it'd look great on you!" Sherry was now holding up a silver dress, ankle long with sequins.

"Sequins? You're taking the piss now." Ember tended to get short-tempered whenever she had to go shopping. She loathed shopping. Today was no exception, but Sherry brushed it off yet again. Ember inattentively trailed after her friend, to shop after shop, looking at dress after dress.

Eventually, they came to a slightly more promising store and Sherry went right for the brightly-coloured dresses on one rack. Ember, however, hung back and let her fingers run over the racks absently. Until she caught a glimpse of what looked like sapphire-blue material. Sure enough, when she held out the dress, it was the deep, rich colour of sapphire. It had spaghetti-straps and a tight bodice, flaring into an elegant, slanted skirt, sexy but not too revealing. It had a low back with corset-type lacing, and silver, curling lines were embroidered up the side. Ember stared at the dress in amazement; finally, a dress that she actually wanted. The miracles never cease, she thought with a sardonic smile.

"Oh, wow! That would look stunning on you!" Sherry breathed from beside her, making her jump in surprise.

"If I get this one, can we go home?" Ember recovered her composure fast, pretending like she was indifferent to the striking silky dress.

"Yes. Go buy it. Now." Sherry pushed her toward the checkout, keeping an eye on her while she paid to make sure she didn't ditch it and run off home. Which, Ember admitted, was exactly something she was likely to do.

"Try it on!" Sherry insisted as soon as they got into their room, pulling Ember's new dress from its bag and throwing it at her.

Sighing, Ember slipped into the bathroom to put it on. It fit perfectly, hugging her tiny waist and accentuating what little curves she had. Stepping into the other room, she glanced in the full-length mirror inside the open door of the wardrobe, and she had to admit it looked really very good. She could imagine it would look better if her hair was done up nicely and she was wearing heels, but even so it was pretty.

"Oh my God, I bet Reid's going to be drooling over you on Wednesday evening!" Sherry enthused, examining Ember from head to toe.

"Hardly," Ember scoffed, but couldn't help grinning at the idea. She imagined Reid seeing her and suddenly looking star-struck, gazing at her like she was the sexiest girl on the planet. She felt herself flushing, and Sherry gave her a knowing look. Ember just shook her head and muttered, "Can I take this damn thing off now?"

It was half past eleven at night and Ember was staring at the ceiling of her darkened room, listening to Sherry's soft breathing and the wind whistling outside the window. She'd been well on her way to falling asleep when a horrifying thought struck her. Her mother was coming tomorrow! As much as she loved her mother, Ember dreaded the questioning and the cooing she'd endure. Questions about everything: Her friends, her classes, her well-being, whether or not she had a boyfriend…

Ember groaned inwardly as she imagined the kind of grilling she'd get if Mrs Jennings figured out there was something between her and Reid. She imagined her mother's scrutinising gaze and the way she'd nit-pick about anything that was off, in her room or in her stories. Anything that suggested she had a boyfriend. Of course, she'd also have to hope to hell nobody let the rumours leak while her mother was here, and she'd have to find a way to explain why she hadn't made any other friends.

Sighing, Ember rolled over and pulled her duvet over her tightly. Worry about it tomorrow, she thought tiredly, tomorrow is the day the hell starts.

Nine am. Standing in the freezing school parking lot, Ember was huddled into her thickest black jumper and shivering in her ratty Vans. The trees shook their branches, showering down a rain of bronzed leaves like glitter. The leaves scattered across the ground, swirling around Ember's feet.

"Are you shaking because you're cold or because you're nervous?" Sherry put a soothing hand on her arm and grinned. Ember grinned back, trying to stop the chattering of her teeth.

"Both," Ember replied shortly. It was true, she was nervous. She'd spent over half an hour tidying every inch of their room this morning, hiding every Kerrang! magazine and bottle of coke. Folding all her clothes, including her underwear, neatly in the drawers and hanging everything in her wardrobe perfectly on the hangers, and making sure no posters were squint. She knew none of it was necessary, as her mother was never overly worried about the neatness of her room but Ember had felt compelled to do it all anyway. Her mother was sure to throw a fit over the clothes she was wearing, though. All black. Again. Just like she had before she'd left. Ember's indifference to real fashion was a thorn in her mother's side.

Carol Jennings was a deceiving person, light-hearted in company, polite when she had to be, but when it came to her daughter she was protective, if more than a little harsh. Ember had loved the freedom of choice that being away from her mother had given her, since nobody tried to 'girlify' her anymore. Except Sherry, but that was only on rare occasions like for the upcoming dance.

"Hey, Demon. Still standing in the snow, I see?" Reid's voice floated over to her and Ember cursed under her breath. Why did he have to be such a pest? He knew she was waiting for her mother, and he just had to come see for himself what Mrs Jennings would have to say to her daughter. She wasn't sure if he was just too curious for his own good, or if he was deliberately there to annoy her. She guessed it was both.

"Well, it's not actually snowing. It's September, not December." Ember rolled her eyes and shrugged off the arm he slung round her shoulders. Reid pretended to be hurt for a moment, but she ignored him.

"You look cold. Just thought you'd want the body heat." Reid grinned at her in a typically devilish manner, and she sighed. He had such a one-track mind sometimes.

"I thought we agreed you'd keep a lid on it while my mum's here," she mumbled, turning away from the bright spark in his blue eyes.

"Well, your mother isn't here yet and I need to get in as much physical contact as I can until then." He slipped his arm round her waist, pulling her against his chest. Despite herself, Ember giggled quietly, enjoying the feel of his warm body against hers amidst the chilling autumn breeze. Reid put his mouth to hers before she could say anything - or protest - and kissed her hotly. All traces of the cold were wiped from her body and the feeling of his warm, soft mouth on hers eradicated rational thought for a moment. What had she been worrying about before? She was sure it was important but she couldn't…quite…grasp what it was…

"Uh, not to interrupt your exchanging of body heat, or anything, but Ember that looks like your mum's car," Sherry snickered and Ember pulled abruptly away from Reid. She heard a muffled chuckle and then an uneasy cough, an attempt to cover the chuckle. Ember leaned around Reid and looked over to see Ricky standing on Sherry's other side.

"Hey Ricky. Decided to come see what the fuss was about?" Ember gave him a smile and he nodded, smiling back. She turned her attention back to the blue Mazda pulling into the parking lot. Sure enough, it was her mother's car. Ember took a deep breath and braced herself for the start of the show, elbowing Reid in the ribs as he tried to take her hand. He got the message and sniggered.

"I'll get you back for that later, my little Demon," his voice was low and seductive, and it was the first time he'd used her nickname possessively, with the 'my'. She almost gagged but simply rolled her eyes at him. Glancing quickly at

Ricky and Sherry, she realised they weren't holding hands either. But before she could comment, a familiar woman stepped out of the Mazda and started walking toward them all with a bright smile and light in her eyes. Ember swallowed and straightened up. Here we go.

Carol Jennings was almost as short as her daughter, but with dark hair and more curves. She could be friendly and spunky when she felt like it, but Ember had a gut feeling that her mother would be less than friendly if and when she worked out there was a thing going on between Reid and Ember. The woman's green eyes gleamed as she approached the small group. Ember wanted to groan, knowing there would be questions about the boys. She'd so hoped to at least keep Reid away this morning. Even the best laid plans…

"Oh, Honey! It's so good to see you! It's been so quiet at home without you!" her mother chuckled, wrapping her in a tight hug. "And Sherry, good to see you too." She moved to hug Sherry and the other girl stood awkwardly. Ember rolled her eyes. Mrs. Jennings moved on to examining the boys, and Ember's amusement drained away quickly. Oh no. "And I see you girls have made some new friends. I'm so glad." Mrs Jennings sounded extremely enthusiastic about it, introducing herself to the boys simply as 'Carol'. The boys replied politely and Ember almost gaped at Reid, not having known he could show such class as he shook her mother's hand and brought it to his lips like some knight in shining armour. But she caught the mischievous glint in his eyes and the teasing grin tugging at his lips as he shot her a glance. Her mother didn't notice, of course, but she didn't need to apparently.

"Ashton? Ah, yes, I've heard about you," she said to Reid, slight disapproval pinching her mouth. Ember swallowed a groan, wondering how the hell her mother knew about Reid. Probably, she guessed, the same way that she'd known about the autumn dance. However that was.

"My reputation precedes me I suppose. What exactly have you heard?" Reid dropped the false polite smile for a more natural cheeky grin. Ember didn't want to hear this conversation, but she held her tight smile with some effort.

"You're a scoundrel. I hope you haven't been corrupting my daughter," Mrs Jennings sounded light-hearted enough but Ember could see the cautious, dark look in her green eyes. Damn, I'm screwed.

"Mum! Shut up!" Ember hissed, feeling heat flood her face. But she was also trying not to laugh at how her mother had picked the perfect word to describe Reid: Scoundrel.

Reid grinned, amused as ever. "No, Ma'am. Don't think I could if I tried. Ember is extremely stubborn. I'm afraid she'd rip me to pieces before I had the chance," he said boldly, giving Ember a sly glance. She whacked his chest and glared, but his teasing words and her violent reaction seemed to have eased her mother's worry a little.

The woman laughed. "Same Ember as always then. I'm guessing with your attitude versus hers, you're more like a punch bag than a friend," Carol smiled, and Ember sighed, relieved her mother wasn't going to stress about her 'friendship' with a notorious bad boy - for now, at least.

"Can we go now? It's freezing out here." Ember hugged her arms to her chest and shivered dramatically. Mrs Jennings followed her daughter and Sherry, bidding goodbye to the chuckling boys.

"So, anything you want to tell me about those boys?" As soon as they were in Ember's room, her mother began the questioning. The shreds of hope that her mother had believed they were all only friends, the shreds that Ember had been clinging to, vanished.

Sherry looked away shyly but Ember replied calmly. "Nope. Not really. Ricky's nice. Reid's an ass. That's all there is to it." She shrugged and flopped onto her bed. She pulled her bottle of coke from under her bed and took a swig from it, watching her mother grimace. She'd always hated Ember's caffeine addiction, thought it was unhealthy. Ember didn't care.

"Come on, I'm not stupid girls. I was a teenager once. You're old enough to have boyfriends and I'm not going to preach to you about that kind of thing." Carol smiled pleasantly, taking a seat next to the desk in the far corner of the room. It's a trick, Ember's paranoia screamed, she's lying! Admit your relationship with Reid, and she'll eat you alive! Ember knew her mother too well, knew she'd accept Sherry's relationship, but then, Sherry wasn't her daughter. "And anyway, Ricky and Sherry are clearly together. It's obvious as daylight." The woman added, giving a keen glance to the now-blushing Sherry.

"How'd you know?" Sherry asked quietly, twisting her fingers together nervously on her lap.

"The way you looked at each other. Thought I didn't notice, did you? Well, I'm glad you've got yourself a nice boy, Sherry." Mrs Jennings did seem glad for the girl, but a puzzled look came across her face as she turned back to Ember. No!

Don't even start! Ember pleaded silently. "It was easy to tell what kind of relationship Ricky and Sherry have, but as for you and Reid..." she trailed off, green eyes searching Ember's face curiously. Ember scoffed, though her stomach was knotting anxiously as she spoke.

"There's nothing going on between me and Reid. Trust me," she lied, hoping her face wasn't turning pink. Her mother didn't look convinced, so she knew her hopes hadn't been fulfilled.

"Uh-huh? You can't lie to me about this sort of thing Ember, you know that." Carol's voice wasn't scolding or condescending, it was simply a statement: a true one at that. Ember had never been good at lying about guy problems and such to her mother, because those were the things that embarrassed her to talk about. "Ember, are you worried that I'll disapprove? I mean, I'd be happier if you were with someone less wild, but if he makes you happy." Carol smiled weakly and Ember felt herself flushing, with both embarrassment and nausea - why did her mother have to make it sound so... Romantic? Blegh. She's still lying! Ember's mind warned her. She definitely disapproves.

"Mum, there's really nothing-" Ember began to lie again helplessly, not wanting to even think about explaining the unofficial relationship status between her and Reid.

But her mother cut her off, "Are you seeing him, Ember? I mean, physically. Is that why you won't tell me?" Mrs Jennings sounded suspicious and coldly critical all of a sudden. Ember gaped at her mother, eyes and mouth wide in offended shock. Of all people, her mother should know that Ember wasn't like that. But apparently not, though.

"WHAT?" Ember choked. Heat flooded her face, burning in her cheeks. She was sure she was as red as a tomato.

"There was just something in the way he looked at you that made it clear there was a physical attraction between the two of you and if that's all there is to it, it would explain why you're so reluctant to tell me anything."

The woman's voice was hard, her eyes sharp. Behind Carol, Ember could see Sherry's 'I-don't-want-to-be-in-the-middle-of-this' expression.

Ember, almost speechless, burst out with, "Mum!" She didn't know what else to say. She was stunned. Her mother didn't flinch. "Look, Mum, it's not like that! I mean, yes, I think he's... but it's not like that!" Ember spluttered helplessly, her eyes stinging with hurt tears. How could her mother think that!? Memories of Reid's hands on her hips, his mouth on hers, the burning under her skin she felt whenever he touched her, went swiftly through Ember's head, and she shook them away. Those images weren't helping one bit.

"Have you had sex with him?"

It was a direct, demanding question and Ember screeched, "WHAT?" Sherry, on the bed behind her mother, was smothering silent hysterical giggles now, while still looking like she didn't want to be there. Apparently Mrs Jennings was fine with Ember having a boyfriend - as long as she didn't have a sex life. Fun. Ember laughed nervously, incredulous and sure her mother had to be joking. The woman looked deadly serious though.

"You're serious!" Ember gasped, "No! NO! No, no, no! Oh my God, how could you even ask? How could you even think that I'd…" Ember stammered desperately, her face flaming. Oddly, she had this pit-of-her-stomach feeling that the occupants of the room weren't the only ones listening to this conversation. But her mother looked convinced at last. Her eyes had cooled and her mouth was no longer a blade-like, thin line.

"Well then, why are you trying to lie to me? I can tell there's something between you and Reid." Why did her mother have to choose now to be perceptive?

Ember groaned but answered anyway. "It's complicated," she said shortly, hoping her mother would let it go. Her mother looked at her expectantly though, obviously wanting more information. What was she supposed to say? That her and Reid had started out enemies and had played cruel pranks on each other until Ember got fed up and then found out Reid liked her, and she eventually worked out that she liked him too, but they didn't want to become a mushy couple like Ricky and Sherry, so they played about with their usual witty banter and some touchy-feely-ness. Oh, and of course, Reid's a vampire. Yeah. She'd have fun trying to explain all that to her mother. 'Complicated' was an understatement.

"I can't explain. It's too confusing. It gives me a headache just thinking about it," Ember replied eventually, shaking her head like she could shake away the confusion. Her mother gave her a knowing, sympathetic look but let it drop. I'm going to die this week, Ember thought to herself, resisting the urge to smother herself with a pillow to save time and humiliation.

An hour later, they were all caught up on gossip and news, and Mrs Jennings went to unpack her things in the visitors' dorm.

Born Dark

Once she was gone, Ember sighed and was about to complain about how her mother hadn't even noticed how obsessively tidy their room was, when a knock at the door cut her off. Groaning, she went to open the door, knowing what was coming next. "You were listening," she stated unhappily as Reid wandered in, grinning.

"I was curious." He shrugged, closing the door.

"Of course you were." Ember rolled her eyes.

"I'm, uh… going to the… library," Sherry muttered quickly and shot out the door abruptly. Ember gazed after her, confused. She'd bolted like the room was on fire. As Ember turned to give Reid a questioning glance, she realised there was a fire - in Reid's blue eyes. He was looking at her in that burning, hungry way that she'd seen a few times but never got used to. Something occurred to her at that point.

"You weren't listening, you were in my head!" she accused, remembering the few images that had popped up when she'd been trying to explain her attraction to Reid to her mother. Colour filled her face, and she bit her lip.

"I'm surprised you didn't feel it," Reid crooned, running his fingers down her temple, along her now-pink cheekbone.

"I was too-too stressed to…" Her words faded as he brought his mouth to hers. She felt her bones melting as his soft mouth moulded with hers. Reid pulled back to whisper in her ear.

"You know, I was a little surprised your mother picked up on our… attraction, so easily. But then again, I have quite a bit of trouble holding back around you…" Reid murmured against her jaw, making her shudder. "For example, right now, I'd like to hold you tight and kiss you until you're dizzy…" His voice was husky and so sensual that he might as well have been taking her clothes off, because she was about ready to do it herself. Obviously, Reid couldn't even keep up the 'just-friends' charade for a single day. Then again, her mother had already worked out there was something between the two of them so it didn't really matter. But this was unprecedented, this level of intimacy. Ember swallowed nervously, her heart beating an erratic rhythm in her chest.

"But I'm not going to because that would be unfair on you. You have no idea how much of a concession that is on my part," Reid continued, sliding a hand to her butt and squeezing, eliciting an unintentional, soft sigh from her. As devilish as he was, Reid didn't usually say things like what he was saying right now, and it was driving her mad. "It's almost impossible for me to just hold you like this when I know that, really, you want more," he whispered, one hand still on her butt while the other snaked round her shoulder blades. He spoke into her neck and she felt sparks fly over her skin, her heart rate increasing until she was sure her heart would stop at any moment. "Do you have any idea what kind of effect you have on me?" he asked, his cool breath spilling over her neck and making her shiver with pleasure.

"No idea what so ever," Ember replied breathlessly as he kissed her throat, touched his teeth to her skin teasingly. She felt the sharp edges of his fangs. More sparks, more flames and more tingles. Her skin was prickling. Using the hand on her butt, Reid pushed her hips more firmly into his and her eyes widened as she got a very good idea of just what kind of effect she was having on him at the moment. She bit her tongue so hard she tasted blood.

"Now do you realise how much I want you? How much I hate your damned self-control? How much I have to hold back around you?" His voice was a purr in the curve of her neck, his lips brushing her skin as he spoke. Ember was too breathless to reply, and almost too far gone to realise he was desperately trying to seduce her out of her common sense. Almost. She was about to protest but lost the nerve as he gently nipped her flesh in his teeth. She gasped, felt rationality slipping away from her, out of reach. She very nearly dropped her control completely as his hand slid up under her shirt to her bra clasp. His skin was so warm and smooth on hers, felt so good.

"Reid-" she breathed, finding some semblance of self-control and ready to resist. Unfortunately, before she could protest, someone else did for her.

"Ember!" A sharp voice cut across the room, and Ember cringed. Oh, shite! Please, God, no! Ember felt her face burning as she leaped away from Reid and turned to her mother. Mrs Jennings, standing in the doorway, looked furious and shocked, her face red with anger and her eyes glinting. Ember searched desperately for the words to make this torture end. "Mum, look, we weren't- I mean, I wasn't- We weren't going to..." she gasped, trailing off as she saw the darkness in her mother's eyes.

"I'd thought better of you Ember. I believed you earlier when you said you hadn't. But now I'm not so sure." Mrs Jennings shook her head in disappointment at her daughter. The woman had only been here a few hours and she was already making Ember's life hell. This was more or less what Ember had dreaded to start with. Someone just kill me now, she thought wearily.

"Mrs Jennings, it wasn't Ember's fault. She was about to stop me I know she was. We weren't going to do anything more, I swear it. Whatever Ember told you about our... um, relationship, she was telling the truth. Your daughter has outstanding self-respect and I'd never degrade that."

Ember had almost forgotten Reid was still here until he spoke in her defence. She felt a tiny, grateful smile touch her lips. Mrs Jennings, though, still looked unhappy; in fact, even more so as she turned her glare on Reid. "Well, yes, I can believe she would contain herself appropriately. It's you I'm worried about."

Ember wondered achingly what had happened to her mother's earlier playful mood. "Mum! He's not pressuring me or anything!" Ember gasped at what her mother was implying, blushing furiously at the words she forced herself to say. This is ridiculous! Reid looked stony-faced, clearly unhappy and angry at such accusations. But he controlled his temper, presumably for Ember's sake. Seeing his anger reminded Ember of her own explosive temper, and of the fact that this was her mother. The woman she'd fought with countless times since she was able to talk. It didn't make a difference where they were or why she was here, Ember wanted to argue back. It was in her nature. "And anyway, I'm sixteen! I'm legally old enough to have sex if I want to! It's my life and my body to do what I please with!" she practically screamed the words viciously at her mother's astonished, furious face.

"Ember Jennings, you will not talk to me that way! And if I find you've been having sex with this boy, I will-" Hearing her mother speak to her like she was a small child, pissed Ember off beyond description, but she'd gotten good at channelling her anger into snide, smug answers.

"You'll what?" she smirked, deliberately making her tone cold and arrogant. Her mother seemed at a loss for words and, shooting her daughter a murderous glare, turned on her heel and left, slamming the door behind her hard enough to rattle the bookcase against the wall. Ember grinned in triumph but it was forced. She wanted to punch something repeatedly.

"Jesus, I thought you only spoke to me and the school bitches that way." Reid sounded both impressed and a little shaken. He obviously hadn't expected her outburst any more than her mother had. He was right to be shaken. Ember sometimes wondered if she should get some therapy, anger management classes.

"Yeah, well, I had to learn my wit somewhere. And practicing lines in arguments against her was the best way," Ember replied bitterly. She and her mother had always had a strained relationship because she'd always felt neglected next to her younger brother; the ever-perfect, angelic, Josh. Her brother was smart and well mannered and had little trouble keeping his temper in check… when their parents were around. The rest of the time, he was the little brother from hell.

"Look, I'm sorry about this. I really didn't mean us to get caught and I didn't mean to get you in so much trouble." Reid was actually, seriously apologising, and sounding sincere doing it. Ember looked at him and saw that his expression was one of guilt and regret.

Ember took a deep, deep breath and let it out slowly. The burning rage in her chest was starting to cool, but her hands were trembling. She curled them into fists, closing her eyes and counting to twenty. When she opened her eyes again, Reid was watching her cautiously, like she might explode again. She forced a reassuring smile. Though he clearly didn't buy it, Reid smiled back tensely, and told her that he had things to do. She suspected he just didn't want to be around her until she calmed down, likely fearing she'd take out her anger on him. Truth was, she probably would. She let him leave without any protest, and gritted her teeth.

As soon as he was gone, Ember picked up the nearest non-breakable object - which happened to be a hairbrush - and lobbed it at the wall. It hit with a satisfying thud and tumbled to the floor. She felt a little better for that and sank to the floor herself. What was she going to do now? She had to apologise to her mother… eventually. Not right now. They both needed to cool off first.

That was when Ember realised her outburst may have been reinforced by the warm hormones swimming in her system after Reid's attentions. Damn. That would explain the dizziness too. She sighed and apologised pointlessly to the wall where she'd whacked it with the hairbrush, returning the hairbrush to its desk. Why was her life so damned complicated all the time?

Tuesday, 21 September. Ember, reluctantly, apologised to her mother and explained what she'd walked in on.

"Mum, I swear, we were going to stop right there just as you walked in. I let it go a little too far that time, but that's the furthest we've gone at all! I know I'm not ready for that yet and Reid knows it too. He would stop the second I asked him to, no matter how much he…" Ember shut up, realising she was probably not helping by continuing that sentence.

They were in her mother's temporary room in the visitors' dorm, and Ember stood by the door, ready to make a hasty retreat. The rooms in the visitors' dorm were exactly the same as the rooms in the students' dorm, only dustier, since they were rarely used. Mrs Jennings sat on the bed and didn't speak, stared at Ember with narrowed eyes and a cold, shut expression. Ember grew exasperated quickly.

"Oh, come on! You know I hate talking about this stuff! Don't make me explain again! We weren't going to have sex! We have not had sex. We will not have sex!" She didn't mean that last part really, but she was throwing her whole gamble into this one. She needed her mother to believe her. But obviously, eventually, when she was ready, she and Reid would... yeah. She stopped thinking about it before the blood rose to her face.

At last, Carol sighed. "I'll believe you on that, just because I know you Ember. I know how responsible you are about these things. I just worry about you because I've heard a lot of stories about Reid Ashton, from mothers of girls he's been with. And from teachers. I don't want you to be another one of them." Her mother's expression was unreadable. But that did explain the mystery of how she'd known about Reid, and most likely, about the dance too. Ember had forgotten her mother was friends with a friend of one of the teachers here. Great. Fabulous. *She'd going to be keeping track of me, isn't she?* The bitter, paranoid part of Ember's mind muttered to her.

"I won't be. Trust me. I don't think he's ever had to work so hard to get near a girl in all his life," Ember laughed a little, recalling the many pains she'd put Reid through to get up to this point. Carol smiled slightly, but she still looked tense.

"I can imagine," she said simply. "But if catch the two of you again. There will be consequences." Her voice left nothing to argue and Ember nodded solemnly. Her mother dismissed her and Ember practically ran from the room, breathing a sigh of relief once she was out. New day, new worry, she thought, glad the most painful part of the day was over with. Or rather, an older worry.

"Have you got any leads on the crow-killer yet?" Ember asked impatiently. Somehow, in the midst of her worries about her mother, she'd overlooked the whole dead-bird-in-her-room thing for a couple of days. Reid looked discouraged, his blue eyes showing his disappointment.

"No. We've chased down every lead we had, and all we got were dead ends. It's just that, as much as a lot of people hate you now - thanks to your snarky, witty remarks - they're all too shallow to have the guts or brains to pull a prank like that." He grimaced and Ember thought it looked strange on him; He looked so much better when he smiled. She sighed and folded her arms, thinking seriously.

"Well it hasn't happened again, and I'm pretty much over it anyway. I still want to kill whoever did it, more for the sake of the bird than myself. I guess we could let it go." It hurt her to say that, the fury for the suffering and pain the crow must've endured by the hand of the sick freak who had killed it welled up inside her. But she had other things to focus on and she couldn't hang on to anymore stresses. Reid was looking at her like she was crazy. Maybe she was.

"Don't look at me like that. I'm just not going to waste any more time on this. I'm not giving the twisted bastard the satisfaction of having me constantly on edge. Either it'll happen again or it won't. And until it does, I've got bigger issues." Ember knew she sounded perfectly calm and rational, but inside she was fuming. Reid seemed to sense that.

"Very... sensible. Pity you don't mean a word of it." Reid rolled his eyes, obviously having picked up on her hidden anger.

"I do mean it!" she insisted, then frowned. "Well, sort of. I just don't think it's right to waste energy worrying about one more thing. I've already got my mum and this dance to worry about, plus there's still the matter of reality not being what it should be and the whole thing bet-" Ember shut herself up, realising her next words could be taken the wrong way. Reid just stared at her with narrowed eyes.

"Yes? 'The whole thing bet-'... between, maybe? As in, between you and me?" He arched a brow at her and she turned away, biting her lip. "Uh-huh. That's what I thought." Ember couldn't tell what he felt about that because his voice was deceptively calm.

"Look, I didn't mean-" she started, turning back to look up at him with big blue eyes.

"Yeah, I know. It's complicated. Normally I enjoy making other people's lives more difficult but with you I actually feel bad," he sighed shaking his head in what Ember was sure was mock-despair.

"You know I'd rather have a more complicated life than one without a sexy vampire boyfriend, right?" She grinned, trying to cheer him up. He raised his brows at her, his face showing mild surprise. Then Ember realised what she'd said, and covered her mouth with her hand. Honestly, she hadn't meant to call him that, not out-loud. In her head, she usually referred to him as her boyfriend, but the reality was a little more complex, and she'd never actually called him that to his face before.

But all Reid said in response was, "Yeah, I know. And I'm sure I wouldn't be anywhere near as happy if you decided to uncomplicate your life." He smiled almost sweetly, and his words were just a little sappy.

Ember rolled her eyes. "You need to stop reading girls' magazines. I don't," she smirked and he chuckled. Ember felt better seeing him smile again, and reached up on her toes to kiss him chastely. Of course, being who he was, he grabbed her around the waist and turned her chaste kiss into a more heated kiss. Ember pulled away regretfully, and placed a restraining hand on his chest.

"Last time, we got caught remember? It was yesterday so don't you dare say 'No, I don't remember'. Control yourself just for this week and next week you can do just about anything you like to me. Just about!" she added, holding up a finger warningly as he opened his mouth to make a typically Reid-like remark, his eyes brightening mischievously. He slumped back and groaned in disappointment.

"You're mean," he muttered, pouting. Ember bit her lip, noticing how lovely he looked when he pouted like that. She was starting to doubt her own ability to control herself for a whole week.

"I'm sensible. Now, shoo! I've got things to do and if you get caught in here, my mum will rip my head off, and yours too." She shoved against his chest, trying to push him from her room.

"Does she hate me that much already? Normally it takes more than one day for someone to want to kill me." He shrugged but moved toward the door.

"Yeah, well, she's heard plenty about you, and if I didn't like you so much, I'd still hate you too." Ember smirked and waved to him as he wandered off down the hall.

Sighing she sat back on her bed and wondered how the hell she would deal with her mother's seemingly instant hatred of her b-... of Reid. Even if only for a week. And she still figured there was a way out of tomorrow's dance. She just hadn't thought of it yet. Lying on her bed, waiting for Sherry to return from her rendezvous with Ricky, Ember pulled out her MP3 player and plugged the headphones into her ears, hoping to drown out her thoughts and worries with loud rock music.

Sherry

In an empty visitor's room, Ricky and Sherry were a little busy. Clothes were scattered on the floor and both teens were breathing raggedly, kissing and whispering to each other. The room was dim, because Ricky had closed the curtains. The door was locked, just in case Reid decided to show up.

"Sherry..." Ricky's voice was deep and husky as he murmured into the skin of her shoulder. He'd de-robed her of all clothes but her underwear, and he himself was stripped to his thin, sky-blue boxers.

"Mh?" Sherry breathed, feeling his lips on her skin and the hot waves rolling through her.

"Sherry, I... there's something I need to tell you," Ricky said hesitantly and Sherry was instantly worried. Those words coming from a boy's mouth were never a good sign. She froze as he pulled away from her, and helped her into a sitting position. Whatever he had to say must've been important, because it was very clear he would've rather continued down the path they'd been on.

"Ricky, I swear if you tell me you're married, I'll get Ember to bitch-slap you into the next country," Sherry warned, only half-joking.

"No, no, nothing like that. But it is something about me, something you really should know before we... get any more serious." Ricky looked uncertain and uncomfortable - and utterly gorgeous, with his brown hair rumpled and his muscled chest on show. Sherry waited patiently, her heart thudding in her chest from anxiety now, no longer lust. Ricky sighed.

Ricky

How was he supposed to tell her this? He'd been wanting to for some time now; ever since he'd had that chat with Ember and she'd said it was his choice, his responsibility to tell Sherry. He knew he needed to. He couldn't keep lying to Sherry about what he was, he cared about her too much for that, but if she was to turn away from him in disgust... well, he wasn't sure what he'd do.

Finally, Ricky got up the guts to tell her, letting the words come awkwardly to his lips. He couldn't look at her while he said them, not wanting to see whatever emotion would show in her lovely green eyes - he only knew it wouldn't be happiness.

"Sherry, I'm... I'm not human. I know how it sounds, but I... I'm a vampire. I know you probably don't believe me but I can show you. I don't want to scare you and I didn't tell you before because I don't want to put you in danger. There are rules and reasons for not telling you, and I was worried about how you'd react and Reid made Ember promise not to tell you. She said it was my place and nobody else's to let you in on the secret. And I decided I care about you far too much to keep lying to you, no matter what the consequences might be later." Ricky let out an anxious sigh but didn't look at his girlfriend yet. He realised he'd rambled hopelessly after getting the crucial word out.

When Sherry didn't answer for a while, he turned to look at her and saw the disbelief in her pretty green eyes. Cautiously, Ricky pulled back his lips to expose his fangs to her. He heard her gasp, and was about to try to explain it all to her, but he didn't get the chance. Sherry flew off the bed, dressed faster than even he could track, and was out the door in a flash. His only thought after that was, CRAP!

Sherry

Sherry was furious and upset as she ran, tears on her cheeks and not caring where she was going. She had to find Ember, but she knew she wouldn't be in their room. She headed outside, anger and hurt and sadness pulsing in her. How could Ember have kept this from her? It was the biggest secret there could be, and Ember had hidden it from her for the sake of her own boyfriend! She might forgive Ricky, understanding why he hadn't told her, believing he'd lied to keep her safe. But Ember? There was no reason Ember should've lied to her. No good reason. Sherry felt like her world had been tipped upside down, and she needed to scream at someone, needed someone to explain it all. But first she needed to find Ember.

Ember

Ember was on her way back from her tree, having been sitting in it for almost an hour now. She was avoiding her mother, and killing her boredom at the same time. She almost wished this Tuesday would end quickly, but she knew tomorrow would be worse. She still hadn't thought of an escape plan for the dance.

She'd only been walking for a few minutes when a familiar voice called to her, stopping her in her tracks,

"Ember! Hey, wait up!" It was Sherry's voice but she'd never heard that accusing, cold tone in her voice before. Not directed at her. Turning, Ember saw Sherry, her expression furious and tears drying on her cheeks, stalking toward her in angry strides.

"Sherry, I thought you were out with Ricky? What are doing here?" Ember asked, trying to sound calm, despite her shock at her friend's biting tone.

"I was with Ricky! He told me about the little secret! How could you keep this from me? I thought we were best friends!" Sherry's green eyes were vicious and sharp, just like her words. Ember gaped for a moment, hurt and horrified - had Ricky really told her?

"What are you talking about?" She felt the need to deny it until she was sure. She wouldn't stick her foot in her mouth and spill this secret without knowing for sure that Ricky had told already.

"Don't act like you don't know! Ricky told me everything! I can't believe you chose your boyfriend over me! You kept this secret - for him! I thought we wouldn't let guys come between us? Ever! I guess I was wrong!" Sherry practically screamed the words in her face, a verbal knife stabbing her heart. Ember felt her eyes fill and her lip trembled. How could Sherry react like this? She should've been able to understand. Ember hadn't wanted to keep the secret, she really hadn't.

"Sherry, I-" she started to explain but Sherry held up a hand to cut her off.

"I don't want to hear it! Why don't you go screw your precious boyfriend, like the two-faced slut you are?" And with that, Sherry turned on her heel and stormed off, leaving Ember in shock with tears running down her face. She felt like someone had punctured her heart, letting a rush of misery fill her and choke her lungs. Sherry had never spoken to her like that before, never insulted her like that, not even when they had big arguments - which wasn't often. What was she supposed to do without her best friend? It would be like walking with a broken leg. Painful.

Ember retreated slowly and carefully crawled back up her tree. Only once she was safely perched thirty feet up, could she let herself cry over what had just happened. She couldn't believe it. Ricky had told Sherry, and Sherry had turned on her. It seemed they were both thinking the same thing though: How could she?

Reid

"Ember?" Reid called out, knowing full well she was here somewhere. He couldn't remember exactly which tree she normally sat in, so he was opting for the call-until-she-answers method of searching. Unfortunately, she wasn't answering. He could smell her scent so he knew she was nearby, but the rustling of the leaves and the whistling of the wind prevented him from hearing any sign of her. He couldn't pinpoint her location in the dense mass of trees and bushes.

"Ember! Come on, I know you're here!" He was a little worried. Why wasn't she answering him? Did he do something wrong? That was usually why people stopped talking to him, but he was sure he hadn't done anything to upset her. She'd been fine when he left her earlier. What if she was hurt? After all, there were big animals in this forest, or she could've fallen out of her tree. Reid didn't want to think about that, it was a chilling idea that made his heart ache. He was about to try to do a mind-sweep to find her brainwaves when the wind died off for a moment, long enough for him to hear what he'd been searching for.

Ten feet left and thirty feet up, Ember sat in her tree, and she was crying. Frowning, Reid made the jump straight up to the branch next to hers easily. She didn't even notice until he spoke. "Ember?" Reid tentatively put a hand on her shoulder, perching on the branch next to her. She flinched and turned away, rubbing at her face furiously.

"What're you doing here?" she asked in a thick, hoarse voice. It was clear she'd been crying for a while then. Reid felt fury flare up inside him, along with the sensation of tightness in his chest at seeing his girlfr-... at seeing Ember this way. It wasn't often this girl really cried - unless she discovered a mangled crow on her bedroom floor - and right now she looked devastated.

"Ember, what is it? Did someone hurt you? I swear I'll rip them to bits if they did!" He growled fiercely, clasping her wrist in his hand. He expected her to turn shimmering, wet blue eyes on him, but she kept her head turned away as she spoke.

"No. It's OK. Just forget it." Her voice shook and it was clear she was repressing another round of sobs. He desperately wanted to make her happy again, unable to stand the way her tears made his heart ache. "Ember. Is it something I did?" He didn't think it was, but he had to be sure. Ember shook her head violently in negation.

"No. Of course not."

With an internal sigh of relief, Reid continued. "Then who hurt you? Please, talk to me," he murmured, reaching out a hand to her face. She jerked away slightly and sighed as he made a soft, hurt noise - unintentionally. She let him put his fingertips delicately to her face and turn it toward him, and bit her lip without meeting his gaze. Reid almost snapped, ready to go and maim whoever had made his Ember this upset. He'd never seen her so broken. Her cheeks were tear-stained and her eyes were red-rimmed, beads of tears clung to her dark lashes and her mouth quivered before she bit down harder on her bottom lip. Reid, unable to help himself, put his fingers to her mouth softly and smoothed out her lower lip before she could bite it so hard it bled.

"Ember, please, tell me what happened?" he almost begged the words in a tender whisper, feeling the pained expression on his own face. She shook her head, and folded her hands in her lap limply. She bit her lip again, and Reid grimaced. It'd be such a pity if she gnawed that lip too much. He'd never get a chance to kiss it again at this rate.

Eventually, he sighed, giving up for the moment. "Come on. Let's get you back to the dorms. It'll be getting dark soon and it's freezing up here." Before she could protest, he gathered her up in his arms and leapt into the air, soaring downward. He landed with a muffled thud, taking the force easily and without dropping the girl in his arms. She looked up at him with a mildly stunned expression and he smiled lightly. "Faster than making you climb." He shrugged and began to put her down, but she clung to his shirt. She pouted slightly and snuggled into his chest, making his heart jump and ache at once. He felt an adoring smile touch his lips and kissed her forehead lightly, carrying her back to the dorms like she weighed no more than a rag doll. To him, she didn't. She was a slight, feminine bundle in his arms, a delicate girl he felt he needed to protect, as he'd never wanted to protect anyone else in his life.

Somehow, Ember fell asleep in his arms before they got back to the dorms, but he didn't mind. All that crying must've tired her out, He thought. He didn't want to wake her so he carried her up to her room and tapped on the door softly with his foot. He waited for Sherry to open the door, and let himself feel the warmth of the beautiful girl curled against his chest. She was so amazing it made his heart throb sometimes.

"Reid, what the- Oh my God! What happened? Is she OK?" Sherry's angry expression melted into concern and fear for her friend.

"She was really upset about something before I found her. She fell asleep before I could get her back here. I didn't want to wake her," he explained shortly, as Sherry moved back to let him in. He placed Ember on her bed and folded the duvet over her carefully. She was breathing softly and evenly, but every so often her expression would crumple like she was having a nightmare. He hated to see that, but he was sure she'd be alright with Sherry now. He turned to bid Sherry goodnight but her face showed guilt and still fear and it bothered him for some reason.

"What's up?" he asked almost casually, but his brow was furrowed.

"I, um… it's just… I was so angry at her earlier. I felt like she betrayed me for you. But now I feel really bad for that." The green-eyed girl frowned and took a deep breath. Slowly, he realised she hadn't taken her eyes off Ember as she spoke; she was avoiding looking at him.

"Why were you-" he started to ask why she'd been angry at Ember, but as Sherry's eyes flickered to him, he understood. Click. "Ricky told you." He wasn't sure how he felt about that. His eyes returned to the sleeping girl on the bed, suddenly feeling awkward.

"Yeah. He told me. You're one too, right? That's why Ember started getting that strange look in her eye whenever she saw you. Like you were some sort of amazing creature she couldn't comprehend. I get it now. And I understand why she didn't tell me. She didn't want to put me in danger." Sherry looked at Ember, too, warmth and gratitude and friendship in her eyes.

Reid was starting to feel a connection to Sherry; they both cared for Ember a lot, in different ways. But he was stuck on what Sherry had said about the way Ember looked at him, like he was amazing. He had noticed it but he hadn't really believed it, mainly because that was the sort of thing he didn't believe he really saw until someone confirmed it to him. He always thought he was imagining it, mistaking lust for deeper emotions. Not that he'd ever felt like this about anyone before - but for his Ember to look at him that way… He smiled and had the overwhelming urge to wrap his arms around the sleeping girl.

Sherry was looking at him as if she knew what he was thinking, and she smiled gently. "She really does care about you, you know. I don't think I've ever seen her so…" Sherry trailed off, shaking her head lightly. Reid just nodded, but he was still smiling to himself. He dropped a kiss on Ember's head and left, nodding goodnight to Sherry as he went. He'd find out tomorrow what had upset his little demon so much.

Ember

Ember woke up the next morning with a headache and sore eyes. Her pillow was damp and her hair was a mess. Sighing, Ember hauled herself out of bed, not even glancing at the empty bed on the other side of the room. She swept up some clean clothes and headed straight for the shower, hoping the warm water and steam would relax her, and help her think.

Once she'd washed her hair and scrubbed her skin raw with her favourite shower gel, she folded herself on the shower floor and let a few more tears escape. They were invisible in the spray of scalding water pulsing from the showerhead, but she felt them run on her cheeks. Slowly, she realised she needed to think; she couldn't just sit here and cry all day.

What was her biggest worry? She'd figure that out first. Well, her mother was an issue, but not hugely important, just annoying. She'd be gone in a week, and how much damage could she really do in that amount of time? Not much surely. The crow-killer was also an issue but she'd promised to give up that fight, no matter how much it still pissed her off. Vampirism and vampires being real? Well, huge deal, yes, but a problem… nah. She'd been dealing with it so far, and it wasn't like she hadn't suspected vampires and witches existed before anyway. She kind of liked that they were real. Although she wasn't sure how Sherry would see it once she calmed down.

Ember sighed as she thought of her best friend. She was sure what Sherry had said yesterday had simply been heat-of-the-moment insults. She hadn't meant them… had she? It still hurt. But it wasn't the insults that really hurt Ember; it had been the cold, hateful look in Sherry's eyes. Could she really have meant what she'd said? Ember had never seen Sherry so vicious, so dark, so angry - at least not with her. That was definitely her biggest problem right now. She could handle her mother, she could handle Reid and his vampirism, she could even handle the crow thing - with some effort - but she couldn't handle not having her best friend. The only person in the world Ember really trusted with all her heart. But she didn't know how to fix it. And at the same time as being hurt, she was really, really angry. She wanted to lash out at Sherry, explain it all to her with expletives thrown in, wanted to hurt her back. But she wouldn't do that. Even if Sherry hated her now, Ember wouldn't hate Sherry. She'd ignore her until she calmed down, but she was going to hang on to her pride. She wouldn't talk to Sherry until she apologised. No matter what the situation, or who the person she was dealing with was, Ember wouldn't be doormat.

Feeling a little strength come to her with her decision, Ember stepped out of the shower and got ready to face what was sure to be a long, painful day.

It was evening, and Ember felt awful. She didn't want to be here. Girls in pretty dresses and guys in suits and smart shirts wandered around, some dancing to the slow music playing from the massive speakers at one end of the hall. The ceiling was strung with orange and gold streamers, and posters of autumnal scenes, such as a bronzing forest and a bright pumpkin patch, adorned the walls. Ember groaned internally.

The excitement over how nice she looked in her pretty new dress had worn off quickly after only a few minutes at the dance. Now, she was sitting alone at a table in the corner of the room, feeling lonely but trying not to attract attention. She wanted to be alone and mope. She didn't even know why she'd come to the stupid dance anyway. It had seemed like a good idea in the fleeting moment she'd stuck her pride before her feelings.

It didn't take long before Ember spotted her mother, mingling with a few other parents who'd come to visit this week. The woman wore a classy, knee-length black dress that looked good on her. Always fashionable, her mother. Ember ducked lower in her seat, not wanting to endure the awing and cooing she'd no doubt receive if her mother saw her here, and wearing a pretty dress no less. It would be humiliation city, and Ember wasn't sure she could muster a smile at all right now.

Luckily, her mother didn't seem to be looking for her, obviously not suspecting her daughter would come to the dance. Not so luckily, Ember noticed who Mrs Jennings was now talking to; Sherry and Ricky. Something in Ember stung at seeing her best friend, so beautiful and happy in a gorgeous dress with her gorgeous boyfriend. Ember suddenly desperately wanted to run away. Run anywhere, away from the dance, away from her now-broken friendship. But as she turned to do just that, Ember caught a glimpse of a more than welcome sight.

Lurking in the shadows against the far wall, looking every bit the dangerous, gorgeous bad boy he was, Reid was lounging casually. A thankful smile spread delicately across her lips as he met her gaze with glowing blue eyes and made a discreet beckoning gesture. She obeyed gladly, something in her chest fluttering at the way he acted so mysterious, and scuttled swiftly past scantily clad girls strung onto tipsy guys, to the other side of the room.

As soon as she reached him, Ember threw her arms around Reid, surprising him and herself. Normally, he was the one eager to show affection. But Ember needed him right now, and welcomed his warm arms wrapping around her tentatively.

He murmured into her hair. "You look stunning." Ember sighed a breath of relief. Reid pushed her back so he could look at her properly and she could see the thoughts forming behind his eyes. "If I didn't know you any better, I'd think you were an angel." He smiled sweetly at her and pulled her back against his chest. She stood in his arms contently, not caring about the whispers and giggles or any of her other problems, just for a little while.

Reid

She really did look like an angel, dressed in sapphire silk, her skin creamy and radiant against the deep colour. Her hair flowed in soft, caramel waves around her face and shoulders, and her eyes were wide and entrancing. The dress hugged her petite figure perfectly, and showed off her sexy legs. But she was still upset about something.

Reid didn't ask what it was that had upset her last night, because, as curious as he was, he didn't want to upset her more. He couldn't stand to see her cry again, especially not when she looked so lovely tonight. So he just held her, protecting her from everything else by simply wrapping his arms round her and letting her forget the world. And he knew that was what she was doing, forgetting everything else; He could tell by the way her breathing softened and she relaxed against him. He'd deal with punishing whoever had hurt her at a later date. For now, he was happy just to have her in his arms.

Born Dark

Carol

Carol was surprised to hear that Ember had come to the dance. She hadn't seen her daughter here yet and it was very unlike Ember, but Sherry had said she'd seen her come in. Carol turned her attention to searching for her daughter. And soon spotted her, feeling both anger and awe flare up inside her.

Her daughter looked gorgeous tonight, in a stunning blue dress, and she looked perfectly content in the arms of Reid Ashton. Carol still didn't like that boy, but he seemed to really make Ember happy. She just hoped he cared about her as much as she did for him. Mrs Jennings watched her daughter for a moment and saw Reid whisper something in her ear, making her blush and giggle. Carol grimaced, only imagining what kind of dirty comment he would have made to make Ember blush that way. She was going to let it drop - for now - though, until she caught the tail end of whispers behind her.

It was a group of girls, dressed in skimpy pink and black dresses, and plastered in make-up, but upon hearing her daughter's name, Carol tuned into their conversation,

"…heard she gave him a blow job in the Boys' Locker Room the other night. I can't believe her nerve. And she called Kara a slut!" The girls burst into whispered giggles, and Carol felt rage seize her. Not only were these girls talking trash about her sweet, smart, innocent daughter, Carol wasn't entirely convinced that what they said was a lie. It was that boy's fault. He was corrupting Ember, ruining her innocence and destroying the clean reputation her daughter once held.

Furiously, Carol headed toward her daughter across the hall.

Ember

"Uh-oh. This can't be good." Ember caught sight of her mother steaming toward them, fury written across her face. "Uh, hi mum. You look nice," Ember said pathetically, smiling weakly as the angry woman stalked up to them.

"Ember, you're coming with me. I don't want you around this boy anymore," her mother snapped, grabbing her arm. Ember yanked it away and pressed herself closer to Reid. Not tonight, she begged silently, Please not tonight mum. "Ember! He's a bad influence. I can see it already. He's corrupting you, just using you like he has every other girl." Her mother was livid, but Ember wasn't going anywhere, even if the tears building in her eyes spilled over.

"Too late for that. He's already screwed her in just about every place in the building." A harsh whisper and laugh came from a passing girl. Kara. Fury welled up in Ember and she glared at the ugly, red-headed troll with unconcealed contempt.

"Shut the hell up Kara. I'm not the one who gave Randy Olsen a blow job behind the dumpster at TipTap two nights ago," Ember spat, not caring that her mother was right next to her, already fuming. Kara gave her a sneering look and walked away, her heels clapping against the polished floor.

"Ember! What do you think you're doing? You can't talk to people that way!" Mrs Jennings' mouth was wide in shock at her daughter's unruly outburst.

"I'm freaking surviving, is what I'm doing!" Ember hissed, turning cold, fiery eyes on her mother, "I've been putting up with so much crap lately. Stuff like that, the rumours, and a hell of a lot of other crap, and the last thing I need is you trying to take away the only person I have left!" Ember gripped Reid's arm hard, vaguely wondered if she was hurting him. She dismissed the thought; he was a vampire. He could stand a few claw marks.

"You have Sherry! Your best friend! She's-" her mother started to argue but Ember felt tears spill down her cheeks and lashed out viciously.

"No, I don't have Sherry! You should've heard what she said to me yesterday! It was almost worse than what some of the bitches around here have been saying! She hates me, and don't ask me why because I'm not telling you. I don't want to talk about it. But Reid is the only person I have right now, and whether or not you think he's corrupting me, I don't give a damn! I'll do what I want, and what I want to do right now is get the hell out of here." And with that, Ember whirled and stormed out, dragging Reid with her. Thankfully, he didn't resist. She was pretty sure she couldn't have budged him if he had, and her exit would've been much less dramatic that way.

Absently, Ember was aware she was crying, but at the same time she was too enraged to control it. She wanted to punch and kick at something, and scream and shout. Her mother was such a cow sometimes! Did she really have to try to control everything Ember did? You'd have thought she'd learned a long time ago that the more she pushed Ember to do something, the more Ember would push back and do the opposite. It was just how Ember operated, and always had.

"Ember." Reid's voice made her slow but she didn't stop walking, despite the fact she wasn't sure where she was going. But when Reid halted, she did too. He stopped dead in the hallway and twisted his arm so that he was the one gripping her instead. He looked down at her, and she glared up at him. "Ember." Reid didn't seem to know what to say, but his blue eyes held every unspoken word. It made her cry more, seeing the love and worry and sympathy for her in his glittering eyes.

Reid stood for a moment and then swept her up into his arms, carrying her while she sobbed silently into his chest. She knew she never should've gone to the dance.

Reid

Eventually, they reached her room, and Reid laid Ember out on her bed, settling beside her and stroking her hair tenderly. He'd wanted to know what had upset her so much, and now he knew, and he had no idea how to deal with it. He'd promised to hurt the person who'd done this to her, but she wouldn't want him to hurt Sherry, he knew. And Ricky would kill him if he tried. Plus, he didn't usually hurt girls - unless they were witches trying to kill him and his friends.

Of course, he knew why Sherry would've yelled at Ember: Ricky had opened his damned mouth, and Sherry had ended up feeling betrayed by Ember. He just knew that that was why it had happened, even if he wasn't sure of specific details. Like what exactly Sherry had said to Ember. It didn't matter really. All he could do was comfort Ember and help her get through this until Sherry realised she'd made a mistake. And as for Mrs. Jennings... well, what he would do about her was unclear, but he had some unpleasant ideas that he was sure Ember wouldn't agree to, no matter how mad she was at her mother.

Reid knew there would be another vamp meeting either tonight or tomorrow, depending on how long it took Ricky to get up the guts to tell Brandon he'd let Sherry in on the secret.

Sure enough, three hours later, Reid was sitting on Ember's bedroom floor, watching her sleep, when Ricky poked his head in the door. He looked sheepish, as if he was sorry for intruding. Reid thought he had a lot more to be sorry for than that.

"Hey, Reid. There's going to be a meeting in a half hour," Ricky was whispering, having spotted the sleeping girl on the bed. He paused, chewing his lip, and then added, "I told Sherry-"

"Yeah. I know," Reid's tone was dark and clipped, and Ricky looked taken aback for a moment. He was dressed in a tux, his top button undone and his tie loose. He must've just gone right to Brandon after the dance - otherwise Brandon and Perry had been at the dance too and Reid just hadn't seen them. Probable.

"What are you doing here anyway? Ember's sleeping." Ricky needlessly pointed out like Reid was so stupid he couldn't work that out for himself.

"I'm making sure she's OK after what happened tonight. And after what happened between her and Sherry, I guess, too. You should've told Brandon right after you let Sherry know. And you shouldn't have let the girl go running off either!" Reid was still whispering but it was more like a hiss, his eyes cold as ice as he glared at the youngest of the vampire boys.

"Reid, what're you on about?" Ricky tried to glare back but just looked upset. Reid didn't often get really mad at Kee, but the brunette boy's idiocy and gentle nature had ended up getting Ember hurt.

"Apparently, yesterday after you told Sherry, your girlfriend ran off to scream at Ember. I don't know what exactly she said, but Ember was in tears, thirty feet up a tree when I found her. She was crying again tonight because her mother yelled at her for being with me, and because she saw Sherry. She was ready to run out of there after seeing you two, until she saw me. Then her mother screwed that up!" Reid had risen and was advancing on his friend, ready to push him out the door and continue the argument outside where he wouldn't wake Ember.

Ricky looked hurt - and surprised. Reid knew why he was surprised: Reid was seriously defending an upset girl against his own best friend. It had never happened before, but that was because he hadn't known Ember before. He'd never cared about a girl this way before. When she cried, it hurt him too, somehow. But he hadn't lost his bad boy edge, or his reputation, and he knew it. Ricky knew it too, knew Reid could kick his butt halfway to China. Ricky backed out the door as Reid advanced, the younger boy holding up his hands as if in surrender - or protection. He'd need it if Sherry and Ember couldn't reconcile soon.

"Reid, come on, man. It's not my fault! I needed to tell her and I wasn't going to stop her running from me if she wanted to! That would've only scared her more! I'm sorry Ember got upset, but what did you expect me to do? Hold Sherry hostage till she calmed down? It took her four hours before she came back to talk to me again after I told her!" Ricky was still whispering, not wanting their private argument to be overheard by students now returning from the dance. His aqua eyes were bright with defensive anger. Unfortunately for him, Reid was far angrier, and Ricky wouldn't stand up to him in a real fight.

"Ricky, I think you should leave right now. Before I really hurt you. You know I can, and I will. I'll see you at the meeting," Reid growled. Ricky, with his jaw set but his eyes calm, just nodded sharply and walked away. He knew when an argument against Reid was pointless; he'd learned when not to push the older boy. Smart kid.

Reid watched Ricky stalk off down the hall and turn the corner, probably headed to wherever he'd stashed Sherry for the time being. Who'd known how much strain a relationship could put on a friendship?

H.G. Lynch

There Are More Things In Heaven And Hell...

H.G. Lynch

Born Dark

Reid

Once again, the basement of the old, abandoned farmhouse was alight with candles and flames and full of swirling dust motes… and raised voices. Brandon had been lecturing both Reid and Ricky for nearly an hour, despite already having lectured Reid before. Apparently, he felt the need to reiterate himself seeing as Ricky had re-opened the issue and now Ember wasn't here to defend herself. Fortunately, Brandon didn't aim any hits specifically at Ember - Reid would've ripped his head off for it if he had. All the blame was pointed at the blond boy himself and Kee, but Reid had long since learned to tune out Brandon's raving. Ricky on the other hand, looked angry and upset at the same time. He didn't get yelled at a lot, and it hurt him when he did. And, by God, this was some verbal thrashing Brandon was giving tonight.

Watching the flickering orange flames and the dancing black shadows on the floor, Reid let Brandon's voice fade to a buzzing in the background, instead hearing the crackle of the fire and the hum of his own thoughts. His own thoughts, though, soon dissolved to just a stream of empty consciousness. He was just staring blankly at the floor when Brandon threw the book at him. Literally.

"OW! Hey, what was that for?" Reid yelled, rubbing his arm and glaring from the offending leather-bound book to the Golden Boy who'd thrown it.

"For falling asleep while I'm trying to explain to you why what you did was stupid!" Brandon almost yelled but he seemed to be yelled-out.

"You already gave me that lecture and Ember handed your ass to you in that argument! Ricky's the one who needed the lashing. Especially after how his little girlfriend reacted to the news!" Reid sent Kee a glare, and Ricky flinched at the hostility in Reid's voice. Brandon looked taken off-guard, his expression becoming wary and puzzled.

"What happened?" he asked, anxious curiosity in his voice. Reid kept his glare on Ricky,

"Oh, so you haven't told him yet? Well, after he let Sherry in on the secret, she went straight to Ember to bitch her out because Kee here let it slip that Ember already knew." Reid smirked darkly, feeling a vindictive satisfaction at the guilt in Ricky's eyes, adding a feral curl to his lip like a tiger baring its teeth.

"So? What's the big deal? So Sherry got pissed at Ember for not telling her. You were the one who convinced her not to tell and I wasn't going keep lying to my girlfriend!" Ricky shot back, flinging his arms out in an exasperated, defensive gesture. Reid snarled, and Brandon came and put a hand on his chest warningly. It was so, so hard not to break Brandon's hand.

"Reid, just chill out. I understand you're upset that Ember's hurt but it isn't Ricky's fault. And this is girl business; they'll figure it out on their own soon enough. All we can- all you can do, is comfort Ember. And all Ricky can do is let Sherry ease into the whole new perspective. Fighting isn't going to help anything," Brandon spoke calmly, in that logical tone that irritated Reid because when Brandon spoke like that, he was usually right. Slowly, Reid backed out of his attack stance and Ricky lowered his hands, both of them retracting their fangs.

"Fine. Is this meeting over? I need to feed." Reid didn't wait for an answer. He stalked up the dusty, echoing stairs and out into the chilly autumn night.

"Reid! Wait up!" Ricky called after him as he stormed toward the darkened trees. Reid didn't stop walking, swiftly weaving between the trees and bushes. He really didn't want to talk to Ricky right now, not when he was so pissed off. He needed to blow off some steam first, before he snapped Kee's neck. "Reid! Come on, Man! Stop!" Ricky grabbed his arm, trying to pull him to a stop.

"Ricky, let the hell go before I break your hand." Reid snarled, glaring pointedly at the hand gripping his arm. Ricky slowly uncurled his fingers and pulled his hand back while Reid made to start walking again.

"Reid, look, I know you're ticked, but it's not my fault what happened with Sherry and Ember! They'll work it out on their own, and you can't blame me for what Sherry said. Her mouth, her words, her choice. All I did was tell her I'm a vampire. I didn't control how she reacted!" Ricky stumbled backwards, walking in front of Reid, holding up his hands defensively while Reid kept walking.

"Yeah, all you did was tell her you're a vampire... and let it slip that Ember already knew! You could've kept that to yourself! We could've played it so that it looked like Ember found out the same time Sherry did. Ember could've acted it out and the whole thing would've been a giggly, girly, explore-the-world type thing for them! And Ember wouldn't have gotten hurt." Reid glared at the dark-haired boy. Ricky groaned in frustration.

"Reid! I know you lo- you care about the girl, but come on! You know this isn't my fault but you're-" Ricky started rambling again but Reid's sensitive ears picked up something beyond Ricky's voice. He halted, tilting his head to listen better.

"Shh. Shut up a minute Kee." Reid held up a hand to silence his friend, listening to the faint grunting and lapping noises beyond the trees.

"Reid, what're you-" Ricky started again but Reid put a hand over his mouth roughly.

"Kee, shut the hell up. Listen to that..." Reid jerked his head in the general direction of the noises. It certainly didn't sound like normal animal noises; it sounded more like... a wolf, or some large predator having a snack. Nothing around here was that big. Reid glanced back to Ricky, who met his gaze with even, confused eyes.

Reid jerked his head sharply and took his hand from Ricky's mouth, making hand motions to direct their plan of attack silently. Ricky nodded and started creeping round one way while Reid crept round the other. They circled the source of the noises and, using the perfect synchronised moves they'd developed years ago, pounced in on the most unexpected scene.

Before the creature could react, Reid had it pinned to the ground, knee on its lower back and holding its forepaws in the dirt, while Ricky pinned the back paws. And really, it wasn't an animal. Being half-human and half-wolf, a werewolf was just a creature. And one of which that was fairly easily recognisable at the minute.

"Get the hell off me!" the werewolf snarled in a thick, distorted voice through long, sharp teeth.

"Well, well. Joseph Rian. What d'ya know? The rapist is also a werewolf." Reid jerked the boy's head back by the coarse brown fur on the back of his neck. It wasn't hair anymore really, and it grew down his back, covering his lower spine and melting into the supple limbs of a wolf. Joseph snarled incomprehensibly and Reid twisted the boy's head to the side at a painful angle, making the creature whine in agony.

"The bitches said you'd never find out! How the hell did you figure it out?" the half-human, half-wolf creature growled. Reid was taken off-guard, unsure what the werewolf was talking about. Joseph seemed to notice Reid's lapse in focus and took the chance to kick out, knocking Ricky off and trying to throw off Reid, too. Unfortunately for the wolf, Reid was faster and stronger than he was, and simply pulled back against the boy's wrists, twisting his arms back and pushing against his spine with his knee until it cracked loudly. Joseph let out another whine and snarled.

"What are you talking about, Rian?" Reid snapped, pushing the boy into the dirt on his stomach again and twisting his arms up, holding him down by pressing his foot into the boy's spine. Standing over Joseph, Reid glanced back at Ricky, who was brushing himself off and glaring at the writhing, snarling bastard Reid was pinning. "You OK?" Reid asked, and Ricky nodded, coming to stand in front of the helpless wolf-boy.

"Good. Now answer the question mutt!" Reid jerked on Joseph's arms, making him howl in pain.

"Not a chance! They'll kill me!" he whined.

"If you don't start talking, telling us what and who the hell you're on about, I'll kill you!" Reid hissed. "Have you ever had your blood drained against your will? It hurts like a bitch. Or so I've heard. Maybe we should test that right now?" Reid and Ricky both flashed their fangs, Reid flipping the wolf-boy so he could see the cold glint in his vampire eyes. He pressed his foot down on the wolf's chest, crushing the sternum while Ricky grabbed and bound his furry wrists above his head, rendering him almost immobile. "Where'd you get rope?" Reid asked Ricky, baffled, and Ricky grinned in response.

"Jacket pocket. Been carrying it for a while. Don't ask." Ricky shrugged. Reid shook his head, faintly amused. It made him wonder what else Ricky carried around randomly.

"Whatever. Now talk wolf, or I break your ribs one by one until you spill the info." Joseph growled but it ended in a whine as Reid stomped on his chest and Ricky stood on his bound paws in the dirt. They felt no guilt in hurting a supernatural rapist. How the hell he wasn't in jail already was beyond them, but the ability of wolves to scare their way out of crap like that could be incredible.

"The witches! They hired me to plant the dead bird in the girls' room! They want revenge on you bloodsuckers, and they said…" Joseph trailed off, shutting up. Reid felt fury boil up inside him, and heard a sharp, meaty crack as he stomped down hard on Joseph's shoulder.

"Keep talking!" he snarled as the wolf let out an agonised howl.

"They said I'd get the girl, Ember, if I helped them! They wanted to lure you two out but they hadn't finished the plan yet!" Joseph whined, his green eyes fearful and pained under the dark, thick brows.

"What was the rest of the plan?" Reid growled through his teeth, getting more infuriated by the second. He unnecessarily dug his heel into the wolf-boy's third rib on the right, threatening to snap it and send it plunging into his lung.

"I don't know! They never told me! I sweeeear!" the boy wailed, ending it in a choked howl as Reid thumped him in the side of the face.

"Don't give me that bullshit! What was the plan?" Reid was seeing red and the bloodlust was welling up in him uncontrollably. He could smell Joseph's blood, warmer and thicker and muskier than human blood. He was sure it would taste disgusting, but any blood would do.

"Reid, calm down! We can't get information from him if he's dead!" Ricky warned. But Reid knew Ricky, at least partly, just didn't want to kill the boy. His guilt reflex was too easily sprung. Reid, though, had no such compunctions. It wasn't Ricky's girlfriend that was going to get attacked if this monster got loose.

"I don't know what the rest of the plan is! I DON'T KNOOOOOOOOW!!!" Joseph shrieked, writhing in terror as Reid flashed his fangs, longer and sharper than usual in his fury-fuelled bloodlust. Reid considered for a moment and decided, through his red haze, that the wolf was telling the truth.

"Fine. But if you ever go near Ember again, I will not only drain you of every drop of blood, I will break every bone in your body first. That's two hundred and six bones, snapping one by one. Got it?" Reid kicked the boy across the face, and slammed his foot into the wolf's ribs. He heard a few sickly cracks and smirked, before darting down and gripping the boy's thick hair. Reid savagely yanked Joseph's head back so that his throat was exposed. Viciously, he sunk his throbbing fangs into the boy's neck, hearing Joseph's agonised howls and screams as he thrashed. Reid held him down easily, drinking the thick, tangy red liquid that poured out of the puncture marks. He'd been right in his earlier assumption; the werewolf's blood tasted awful, too salty and bitter.

Eventually, Ricky pulled him off and held him steady. "Reid, that's enough! That's enough! Let's go!" Ricky yelled, dragging the blonde boy away with great difficulty. They left the broken, beaten werewolf to lie in the dirt and recover, and Reid wiped the blood off his chin and mouth, retracting his fangs. He felt calmer since releasing his anger and the bloodlust was satisfied. Now it was time to relay what they'd discovered to the girls. Hopefully they'd stop fighting if he explained his newly formed theory.

Images had come to him through memories in Joseph's mind while he'd been drinking - it was easy to pry into a mind while you drank from the person. Most of the time, they sent images and messages unintentionally and you didn't even have to dig into their head. The werewolf boy had seen the witches morph like freaky alien chicks, right in from of him. The witches were capable of shape-shifting spells… They could take on the form of anyone, given the right ingredients. And Reid suspected that was exactly what they'd done.

Ember

"Ember? Ember are you OK?" A whisper came to Ember's ears and she felt a hand touch her arm lightly. She pulled her eyes open, longing to see the blue gaze and sensual mouth of the boy she'd come to trust and adore. It was hard to believe she had once hated Reid so much, and seven weeks later, she loved spending time with him, missing him when he was gone.

But it wasn't glittering blue eyes that met hers as she blinked in surprise. Ember scowled at the green-eyed girl in front of her, and flinched away from the hand on her arm. Sherry looked genuinely worried and upset, and a little hurt at Ember's reaction. "I saw you and Reid leave the party. You looked upset, and I wanted to come see you but Ricky said I should wait until Reid left." Sherry frowned and pulled her hand back slowly. Ember very nearly broke down at the utter concern and sympathy emanating from her friend. But she quickly remembered what Sherry had said to her two days ago, and clenched her teeth to keep back the tears.

"What happened? I mean, I saw your mum… you had an argument?" Sherry sat back and looked at Ember from the floor, while Ember pulled herself into a sitting position. Why was Sherry acting like nothing had happened? She was trying to comfort her as if she hadn't called Ember a two-faced slut forty-eight hours ago. Ember didn't say anything, but she could feel the puzzled, angry expression on her own face.

"Come on Ember, talk to me. You're obviously upset with your mum. It was about Reid, wasn't it? And I know that the thing with the crow's still bugging you." Sherry's green eyes suddenly turned from deeply sympathetic, to excited. OK? Ember was officially confused. Sherry took a deep breath, and then said, "And Ricky told me. I know you know, too. About… them being vampires. I found out on Tuesday, and I wanted to talk to you about it but you were sleeping when I got in and Reid said you'd been upset, and today I was so busy with Ricky and getting ready for the dance, and you left before I could talk to you there…" The green-eyed girl stopped rambling, sighed, and stared expectantly at Ember. Ember just gaped for a moment, baffled. Had the argument on Tuesday been a dream? Had she imagined it? Because Sherry seemed to honestly mean every word of what she was saying.

"Uh, what do you mean?" Ember eventually choked out unable to think of a witty remark or biting comment. Sherry looked at her with confusion now, a crease forming between her brows.

"I mean, I know you know Reid and Ricky are vampires. We so need to talk about that. But if you'd rather talk about your mum or-"

Ember cut her off. "Wait… I already know you know. Did you hit your head or something? Do you not remember what you said- no, wait, screamed at me on Tuesday after you found out? You called me a two-faced little slut and then walked away! And now you're acting like that never happened." Ember wanted to throw something at her friend, but she used all her self-control to keep her hands balled in fists in her lap. Sherry looked at her with blank shock.

"Ember, what are you talking about? I did come looking for you, I did want to yell at you, but I never found you on Tuesday! And you can't honestly think I'd ever say something like that to you?" Sherry gasped, looked hurt by the mere suggestion. Something in the back of Ember's mind was rattling, trying to tell her something important, but she ignored it. She was too confused, too angry to listen to it.

"Well, unless you happen to have an exact doppelganger who knew precisely when you found out about the vampires, and knew you'd first come to me because I already knew about it…Uh, yeah. That's honestly what I think!" Ember was slowly regaining her sarcasm but it hurt to try to use it against her best friend. She had enough to deal with without fighting with Sherry.

"Ember, I swear to you, I did not see you after I found out on Tuesday! Not until I'd talked to Ricky again, and then you were sleeping when Reid brought you back. Ask him, I was seriously worried about you! I felt bad for wanting to yell at you, but I never actually did yell at you! Not until now!" Sherry was yelling now and Ember flinched. Her voice wasn't hostile, just pleading and frustrated. Ember took a deep breath, making a great effort to calm down. Sherry obviously didn't want to fight like this, but Ember always had a short temper. She would control it for the sake of her friend, no matter what they were arguing about.

"OK. Let's just think about this rationally. I am positive it was you - or someone who looked exactly like you - that came and yelled at me. She knew you'd found out, she knew I was in on the secret, and she knew we're best friends. If you're saying that you honestly never found me on Tuesday… Then we have a serious problem." Ember frowned. Two weeks ago, this argument would've continued in the same infuriating pattern - Sherry denying the encounter and Ember insisting it happened - but after having discovered the existence of vampires… well, doppelganger conspiracies didn't seem so insane. "I think we need to-" Ember started and was abruptly cut off by a familiar smooth voice.

"Talk to the vampires?" Reid grinned, strolling into the room, closely followed by a grimacing Ricky.

"Were you at the door or in my head this time?" Ember mock-scowled. Reid just laughed and Ricky waved weakly at the girls.

"You took my advice. Well done Kee," Ember grinned at Ricky, who chuckled.

"Oh no! Don't you start calling me that, too!" he replied despairingly, folding himself on the floor next to Sherry.

Ember grinned. "Well, Kee's no worse than Demon. And I know you call me that too, behind my back, so don't pretend like you don't." She held up a hand to stop his undoubted denial and he shrugged sheepishly.

"I see you two have made up? Good. Ricky and I have discovered something interesting," Reid smirked, sprawling on his stomach on her bed next to Ember. He ran his fingertips up her arm and she slapped his hand away. He feigned pain, clutching his hand to his chest. She rolled her eyes at him and sighed.

"What did you discover that was so important you felt the need to interrupt our reconciliation?" Ember asked, shooting a wry look at Sherry, who smiled back. Ricky was currently clasping one of Sherry's hands in his, gazing at her with clear love in his bright eyes. It was sickly sweet and made Ember want to gag.

"Well, it appears that those witches we caught decided to get revenge on us by messing with you two." Reid wasn't grinning anymore, so much as just baring his teeth.

"And you know this how?" Ember enquired, surprised.

"You remember Joseph Rian?" Ricky asked solemnly, and Ember nodded, gritting her teeth. "We interrogated him after we found him chewing on a rabbit out in the forest earlier. Turns out, he was working for the witches, and he just so happens to be the one who put the dead crow in your room." Reid grinned, but it

Born Dark

was a malicious, dangerous grin, and his eyes glinted in that inhuman, scary way they sometimes did.

"Reid, what did you do to Joseph?" Ember asked warily. Reid just looked at her, suddenly pulling an angel-innocent expression, with a sweet smile and clear blue eyes.

"Nothing he can't recover from. Eventually," he replied smoothly. Ember shuddered a little but also sighed in exasperation. He was a vampire after all, and at least he didn't kill Joseph, but it was still a little scary imagining Reid violently ripping at the helpless boy. Her temples itched. "He wasn't helpless! He's a damned werewolf!" Reid suddenly burst out looking at her like she'd just said a lion was no more dangerous than a kitten. Clearly, he'd been prying in her head again.

Ember scowled at him, and muttered, "Stay out of my head."

"What? Werewolves, witches! Oh, come on!" Sherry was staring at all three other occupants of the room with horror written on her face.

"You didn't tell her about the witches?" Ember clucked her tongue at Ricky, who shrugged. "That was how I found out," she said to Sherry. "I was watching a group of girls, who turned out to be witches, when these two, plus Brandon and Perry, came onto the scene flashing fangs and flaunting superhuman speed," Ember explained, shoving Reid's arm playfully. He grinned, flashing his fangs at her as if to make a point. Two points actually. Ember looked away quickly. "Of course, they didn't know I was there until they'd secured the witches - who happened to be trying to hurt the vampires. And then someone decided to try to talk to me, twenty feet up a tree, by magically appearing right behind me. Silently. Lucky I didn't freak out and fall off my damned branch," Ember continued, arching a brow at said 'someone'. Reid shrugged nonchalantly.

"Hey, I thought you might jump and run if I didn't try to explain it. And climbing just took too much time," he said.

Ember sighed, but Sherry still looked in shock. "So, yes, witches exist too. And apparently so do werewolves. Great." Ember glanced at the boys serious again. "I'm surprised you guys didn't notice this before. It can't be easy to hide 'lycanthropy' from a group of vampires?" she commented dryly.

"Yeah, well, he was good at hiding it and we don't investigate animal scent trails in the forest." Reid rolled his eyes, but he was clearly unhappy with his own ignorance. Sherry was slowly absorbing all the new information, her eyes narrowing thoughtfully.

"OK. Can we press pause for a moment? So vampires exist. My boyfriend and my best friend's boy-" Ember glared sharply at the green-eyed girl talking. Sherry made an exasperated noise, "-OK, my boyfriend and Reid are both vampires. Witches exist and they, what? Are using Ember and I as a means of getting revenge for the vamps beating them up? Great. And of course Joseph Rian the Werewolf is working for them. Did I get everything?" Sherry's eyes were bright with intense light, expectant and a little incredulous.

"Everything but why Joey decided to work for the witches." Ember nodded, and turned to the boys for an answer to that final question. Reid, for once, seemed to be reluctant to speak. Ricky was the one who answered her.

"He wanted to get back at you for... well, for what happened that night at TipTap and he wanted to get back at Reid for beating him up that night," Ricky said quietly, his expression sympathetic. Ember felt sick, remembering that night. Joseph had attacked her and Reid had come to the rescue at the last moment. Recalling how, for just a moment, Reid had been her hero, Ember smiled at the blond next to her. Reid was too busy brooding to notice.

"So, what do we do now?" Ember asked, unsure what their next move would be.

"Well, we took care of Joseph. I'm fairly sure he won't be a problem anymore. But as for the witches, we don't know what they'll try next. They might opt for more lotions and potions, more illusions and trickery. Or they might just decide to grab knives and stakes." Reid shrugged, and his blond hair fell into his eyes.

"Fantastic. We have vindictive, vengeful witches after all of us, who may or may not want to kill us," Ember said, heavy on the sarcasm.

"Actually, they definitely want to kill me and Ricky. It's whether or not they'll kill you two as well that we're not sure of. They might just use you two to get to us. Draw us out." Reid's eyes were cold but his tone was light. Sherry gazed at him with wide green eyes, like he was insane. He was, of course, but that was beside the point.

"Hmm. What you're saying basically is that we have no plan of attack, no plan for defence and no information to make those plans. Fun. Does that mean for the next couple of hours we can actually relax a little then?" Ember was tired, and she knew Sherry was dying to talk to her in private about the whole situation.

After a moment, Reid nodded. "Fine. But don't leave the room and don't split up. We've got to go talk with Brandon and Perry anyway." Ember nodded in agreement and Sherry did too. Then Reid sat up and leaned over, putting his mouth to hers and kissing her with a little more intensity than was polite in company. But when he pulled away, it was clear Ricky and Sherry didn't mind because they were also engaging in some serious lip-locking. Ember giggled under her breath and watched the boys leave, sending Reid a sweet smile as he winked at her.

Thursday morning was… well, almost relaxing. Ember woke up early to find Sherry poring over her notepad. "What'cha drawing?" Ember yawned, brushing her hair off her face.
"Nothing really. I'm actually just doodling." Sherry shrugged lightly, never taking her green eyes from her notepad.
"Well, must be some serious doodles if you're concentrating so hard on them," Ember joked and pulled herself from her bed to stretch. Sherry just smiled, but continued scribbling. A quick peek over Sherry's shoulder as she made her way to the bathroom let Ember see that Sherry was indeed doodling, but the page was covered in fierce eyes and bloody fangs and the word 'vampire' in various different texts.
Ember grinned, amused. She had to admit, she'd been doing some gory drawings herself since she found out what Reid was. Having a vampire boyfriend was good for inspiration sometimes.

When Ember emerged from the bathroom, clean and fresh and fully dressed, Sherry was frowning. She was twirling her pen absently in her fingers, and the page in front of her was covered with black lines.
"You know, you never did tell me what you were arguing with your mum about?" The green-eyed girl looked up at Ember speculatively. Ember shrugged and tossed her pyjamas in a heap on her pillow before collapsing onto her bed and sighing.
"My mother seems to be under the impression that Reid Ashton is a bad influence, and is not only corrupting my reputation but also unbalancing my sense of self-respect and… well, she thinks I'm having sex with him," Ember summed up in less complex terms.

Sherry blinked, but without missing a beat, asked, "Are you?"
Ember flinched, surprised at the burning curiosity in her friend's voice. She wasn't offended as she might have been had anyone else asked, because she knew

her relationship with Reid had pretty much been a mystery to Sherry up until now. Sherry wasn't asking to be nosey, or for gossip, or so she could judge. She just wanted to know what was happening in her best friend's relationship. So Ember threw her a casual smile. "Nope. I don't think we're quite at that stage. Everything's still pretty complicated, and... I know Reid wants it - he's Reid after all. Infamous man-whore. Bad boy. Male." Ember rolled her eyes. "But I don't think I'm ready for that. How about you and Ricky? You must be getting pretty hot and heavy by now?" Ember, too, was only interested in her friend's life, not looking for gossip. Curiosity was her ever-present weakness.

Sherry blushed but smiled. "We haven't gotten to that yet, but yeah, we're getting pretty... close." The green-eyed girl giggled and Ember laughed with her.

"Well, well. Go Sherz." Ember grinned, and then added in a serious tone. "And how are you handling everything? You know, with the whole reality-being-thrown-out-the-window thing?"

Sherry sobered up and just nodded. "I'm doing OK. It was a shock at first but I'm getting over it. Sort of. Hearing you guys talk about it so casually yesterday made me feel like I'd been dropped into some private club by accident. I think it'll take a while before I get so comfortable with it. How long did it take you to get over it?" Sherry asked eagerly, her eyes alight as she beamed. Ember brushed hair off her face in a nonchalant movement and bit her lip for a second.

"Well, I'm totally insane you realise, and you know I've always kind of believed vampires and things existed so I mean you can hardly compare," Ember rattled, avoiding answering directly, but Sherry gave her a knowing look that shut her up. Ember sighed. "I got over it in about a day really. Pretty much anyway. Little things like the fact that werewolves exist still get me, and sometimes I wonder if I've completely lost my nut, but mainly the thing that gets me is just Reid. Whenever he shows his fangs, it hits me like lightning and I think, 'Wow. He really is a vampire. They really do exist and my sort-of-boyfriend is one of them!'" She paused, rolled her eyes, "And then he kisses me and I forget what I was thinking about for a while," Ember tacked on the end, grinning.

"The fangs don't scare you at all? Even a little?" Sherry enquired. Ember shook her head.

"They did to start with but, you know me, I like fangs. They're sexy, not scary," she laughed.

Born Dark

"I've only seen Ricky's a couple of times, and they freaked me out a bit. But I'll probably like them too once I'm used to them," Sherry confessed, looking a little sheepish.

They sat in silence for a while after that, Sherry returned to her doodling and Ember sank into her own thoughts, wondering what to do about her mother. Ignoring her was always an option, but she knew she'd feel bad afterwards since her mother wouldn't be back until the October holidays. Albeit they were only a couple of weeks away, but still. Two weeks was a long time to be hurting, especially when it was your own daughter that did the damage.

"What do you want to do with the rest of the week off?" Sherry piped up, breaking Ember's train of thought. Ember was kind of glad, though, for the distraction.

"I don't know. We still have the issue of the witches trying to possibly kill us to deal with. But aside from that, I've got no plans." Ember thought of a few things they could do but her mind still lingered on her mother. Surely she should do something fun with her before she left?

"Ice-skating? Shopping? Cinema? Um, picnic? We never got round to considering that double date thing properly." Sherry suddenly seemed cheered by that idea and Ember groaned. She'd been pitching her protests about the idea for a double date when they'd found that damned dead crow in their room. She'd totally forgotten about Sherry's sickly sweet romance plans. "Oh, come on, It doesn't have to be like a normal double date, with candle lit dinners or anything. I mean, our guys are vampires after all! Nothing normal about that. You don't even have to think of it as a double date, just think of it as us all hanging out together." It was clear Sherz was going to keep pressing this; the excitement was glowing in her emerald eyes. Reluctantly, Ember agreed, nodding slowly.

"Fine. But I swear, the minute it gets all lovey-dovey orientated, I'm leaving," Ember warned with a sigh. But Sherry squealed in delight.

"Yay! We'll make it Friday and we can go.... um..." Ah ha! Something to slow down her plans. No destination, no activity plan. But, of course, Reid had been listening again, whether at the door or in her head, Ember wasn't sure.

He simply strolled into the room casually and flashed a devilish smile. "Swimming?" He pitched the idea so smoothly that it almost sounded reasonable.

Sherry liked it. "Yeah, swimming! We haven't been swimming in ages and the leisure centre is only a half hour's drive away." Ember hated to burst the girl's bubble but there was no way she was going to parole around in a wet bikini with

Reid anywhere nearby. He may have been her sort-of-boyfriend, and they may have engaged in a little bit of physical teasing, but she was not going to tempt him further and she was sure seeing him in wet swim shorts would do nothing for her own self-control. She could still vaguely remember seeing him swimming that day she'd stolen his clothes from the Boys' Locker Rooms. It was certainly a distracting sight.

"Couldn't we do something, I don't know, that wouldn't involve getting half naked and soaking wet?" Ember rolled her eyes and pushed Reid away as he slung an arm around her. He pretended to be hurt for a second but then chuckled, a warm gleam coming to his blue eyes.

"What, worried you won't be able to control yourself around me like that?" he teased. Yes.

"No, I'm worried you won't be able to - or won't want to - control yourself. Last I checked, you were still the ever-touchy-feely Reid Ashton. And a public pool is not the place for your antics," Ember smirked and propped her feet up on his lap as he folded himself on the end of her bed.

"Do you understand the word 'privacy'? You seem to always be listening to our conversations," Sherry mused, light-heartedly.

"You always seem to be talking about me in some way or another," Reid shot back with a grin.

Ember rolled her eyes. "Back to the matter at hand please?"

Sherry sighed at her this time. "I want to go swimming. I'm sure Reid will behave himself for the sake of everyone else." Sherry gave him a cold, sharp glance and her tone insinuated it wasn't an assumption as much as an order.

"I guess I'll have to. I'm just not sure Ember will behave." Reid smirked at her.

"I'm sure I'll manage somehow," she muttered sarcastically, and was abruptly pulled against his hard, warm chest for a smouldering kiss. Her lips parted instinctively under his, bubbly things stirring inside her.

A few seconds later she was released and managed to gasp, "What the hell was that about?"

Reid grinned, gracefully rolling off the bed. "Mother alert. She'll be here in… eighteen seconds. I've got to go." And with that he flitted to the window, threw it open and flung himself out it. Sherry gasped, gaping at the window with wide eyes and Ember just called "Show-off." down to him from her bed. *I heard that!* Reid's voice answered in her head and she laughed. She'd said the same thing to

Born Dark

him the night she found out his secret. It was becoming a private joke. Sherry stared at her for a moment until she explained.

"He replied, in my head. Telepathy is handy on occasion." Ember shrugged but Sherry still looked dumbstruck. "Didn't Ricky expl-" Ember was cut off as her mother entered the room.

"Ember, can I talk to you?" Mrs Jennings asked gently, but her face was stern. Fabulous. Sherry excused herself and left the room. Ember was half tempted to call her back to rescue her, and mention that this was her room too and she shouldn't have to leave just because Ember's mother wanted to lecture some more.

"What do you want?" Ember snapped harshly, glaring coldly at her mother.

"Ember, I know you're upset about last night. But I truly believe there are better guys out there for you. Ones who will look after you and not put you in the middle of awful rumours." Mrs Jennings said calmly, sitting delicately on the end of Ember's bed. Ember got off the bed.

"Those rumours started way before me and Reid were together. They were going around practically since day one and they just got kicked up a notch is all. I defend myself perfectly fine and I don't care what those bitches say about me anyway. I don't need protection and I hate being looked after, you know that! It makes me feel like a little kid. And you don't know anything about Reid anyway, aside from the rumours. But, as has been proven in my case, rumours aren't always true! He's a lot smarter and sweeter than anyone gives him credit for. And you know what? He did take care of me, last night after you bitched at me at the dance!" Ember was getting angry again and she didn't care about her language in front of her mother anymore.

"Ember, language!" Carol chastised. "And you know I'm only looking out for what's best for you." Carol was taking a less vicious approach now, obviously realising that yelling wasn't going to get anything done. Ember snorted.

"Yeah. Whatever. You don't know what's best for me at this school. I know how things work around here and I'm handling it. What's best for me is having Sherry and Reid by my side. If you want me to be happy here, you need to let me handle my own life. There's nothing you can do or say to make me send Reid away. He means a lot to me." Ember raised her chin, facing her mother squarely and showing that she meant every word. Her mother looked surprised, and disappointed. She sighed, frowning at her daughter.

"Fine." The way that she said it told Ember that she was most definitely not fine with it, and she wasn't going to give up. Not yet, anyway. The woman was impossible.

After a few moments of silent glaring - a battle which Ember won thanks to her startling ability to appear threatening even to her mother – Mrs Jennings left, slamming the door behind her. Once she was gone, Ember groaned, bit her pillow to keep from screaming. Then she plugged in her MP3 player, hoping to distract herself and calm herself before she smashed something.

Sherry

"Ember was trying to explain something to me before her mum came in. She said something about Reid replying to what she said but in her head. What did she mean?" Sherry was sitting, cross-legged on a table in the library. Lately this was where she'd been hanging out with Ricky, just since she found out he was a blood-sucking mythical creature. It wasn't that she was scared of him - she still adored him, still wanted to be with him - but she just wanted to be safe. And the library, though quiet, usually held several people doing homework, making it the best place to discuss secrets and still be safe.

"Oh, well… strong vampires, especially born vampires, we can communicate telepathically. We can read minds and sometimes pinpoint peoples' brainwaves. We don't do that stuff usually, though. It's dangerous, we could get caught and Brandon doesn't like us using our vamp-magic. But Reid… well, he's Reid. He ignores the rules." Ricky shrugged, stretched out on the floor, with his back against a shelf of books about the History of the Steam Engine. This was a fairly deserted area of the library, with only a few people studying at a nearby table, too far away to hear their whispered conversation.

Sherry considered this new information for a moment, trying to absorb it calmly the way Ember did. OK, so what if Kee could read her mind and talk to her in her head? Hadn't she always wondered what it would be like to have a vampire as a boyfriend? Yes. So why should it be such a big deal in reality? It shouldn't. The internal argument seemed logical, but then again, logic was hardly suitably applied to this situation. Her boyfriend was a real-life vampire for Christ's sake!

Sherry looked down at said vampire and examined him. He was still the same Ricky she saw before: same soft brown hair the colour of chocolate, same lightly tanned skin, same sweetly boyish smile and the same deep, gem-like aqua eyes. "Hmm," was her simple, thoughtful reply. She was a little curious to know if he'd ever read her mind, but she didn't think it mattered. He already knew how she felt about him, vampire or not. There wasn't anything in her head he couldn't know.

"You're not, like, freaked out or anything, are you?" Ricky asked his gentle mouth pinched nervously.

Sherry shook her head. "Not really. Ember said she freaked out when Reid tried to read her mind. Not because she found it freaky, but just 'cause she gets all defensive over privacy and stuff. She's handling all this like it's practically nothing. It's insane. But then again, she's always been a little crazy." Sherry smiled fondly at memories of her friend's nuttiness. Like the time, when they'd both been seven, and Ember had insisted they sneak into the nursery garden at their primary school. She'd scrambled over the high wall that separated the play park from the neighbouring apartments' land, slunk across the far edges of the private garden, climbed the gnarled tree at the far wall, and then hopped the metal fence into the nursery garden. Sherry hadn't been sure whether her friend was incredibly brave for trespassing like that, or just insane.

Presently, Ricky chuckled. "So I'd noticed. She'd have to be crazy to have fallen for Reid," he murmured.

"Well... how do I put this nicely? Reid's a stubborn asshole." Sherry grinned and Ricky laughed, blue-green eyes twinkling. Sherry continued, "But Ember's the same way. They suit each other. She really does care about him. And as far I can tell, he cares about her. It's nice to see Ember getting involved in romance without gagging at it," she added, shaking her head hopelessly. Ricky grinned, looking as radiant and sweet as ever. Sherry felt her heart do a little flip.

"So that explains the face she makes whenever I'm around you. She doesn't like the romance. That's a shame. I rather enjoy it." Kee beamed and Sherry caught a glimpse of his fangs. He abruptly turned away, retracting them and then looking back at her sheepishly. "Sorry," he mumbled.

Sherry frowned. "You don't need to apologise. I need to get used to it," she said calmly.

Kee just nodded. "So, I know we've discussed a lot so far - the powers, the blood drinking, and the superhuman abilities - but is there anything else you want to know?" he asked seriously, but gently. Just then, something popped to her mind and Sherry blushed helplessly. She remembered the conversation she and Ember had had this morning, after Ember had explained what her argument with her mother had been about. She hadn't thought about it at the time, but maybe vampirism had an effect on the mechanics?

"Sherry? What's up? You look like a beetroot all of a sudden," Ricky chuckled, distracting her. She realised there was heat in her cheeks and she was biting her lip nervously. Ricky was looking at her curiously, a smile playing about his mouth.

"Nothing. It's nothing," she said dismissively, cringing at the high, breathless note to her voice.

"You're lying. You've got a question. What is it?"

For a moment, Sherry wondered if he was reading her mind but then realised he wouldn't need to ask what her question was that way. He could just read her expression. Sherry shook her head, refusing to speak, and Ricky got off the floor. He came and stood in front of her, gazing at her with a suspicious, quizzical expression. He carefully took her hands in his, and let his aqua eyes bore into hers, and Sherry felt her heart skip a beat.

"Please tell me?" he murmured, pouting. He looked so gorgeous and adorable, and the shimmering of his lovely eyes was making her stomach melt. She couldn't say no to him, not when he did that her.

"I was just wondering if there was… if vampires can-" she stuttered in a whisper, feeling her face burn, and dropping her gaze to their entwined hands.

"What?" Kee prompted when he realised she wasn't going to finish her sentence. Sherry shook her head, biting her lip again. Ricky released one of her hands and brought his fingers to her face, brushing a lock of hair behind her ear. Something in her chest fluttered and her eyes flicked to his reflexively. "Please tell me. Please?" His glittering eyes were so warm and deep and trusting.

"I was just wondering if… if vampires could… you know, with humans… if it was possible to…" Sherry looked away embarrassedly. But Ricky caught what she was trying to ask and chuckled under his breath.

"Oh, that. Yeah, it's possible. Reid isn't known as a man-whore just for his crude comments and charm." Sherry suddenly felt like an idiot for not having realised that, but she could never think clearly around Ricky. He was always too much for her, too overwhelming, too amazing for her mind - and body - to handle. "And I may be nicknamed 'Kee' but I'm not as innocently babyish as that name suggests. For example, I have no qualms over inappropriate behaviour in a library," Ricky added, wrapping his arms round her and kissing her sweetly. Sherry broke away regretfully, giggling.

"Kee, we'll get caught," she breathed, but he just kept kissing down her jaw, his fingers finding the bottom edge of her shirt and sliding up under it. A shiver went through her at the feel of his fingertips on her bare skin, just above the waistband of her jeans.

"So? You were the one who wanted to make sure there were other people around, just in case. Your choice of venue, not mine," he murmured into her skin, making warm shivers running down her spine.

"Ricky," she gasped in shock and delight as his hand moved up her back, his fingers played with straps of her bra and his mouth was softly teasing against her neck. His lips on her neck made her nervous, but it was the same nervousness she'd experienced before she'd discovered he was a vampire. Whether or not he occasionally drank blood - apparently, unlike Reid, Ricky chose to drink from blood-bags from the local blood bank - he was still her Ricky. "Okay then, can we please go somewhere less... public?" She tried to pry him off but he refused to let go of her. She sighed in exasperation, despite the insane hammering of her heart and the rushing of adrenaline in her blood. Really, she was anxious that they might get caught, but the idea gave her kind of a thrill somehow.

"Actually I've got to be somewhere in the next sixty-four seconds. I'd better run. I'll see you later." Ricky pulled away glancing at his watch and grinning at her.

"What? You kiss me and get me all bothered and then you just leave me here?" Sherry held out her hands, palms up, in a helpless gesture.

Ricky laughed. "Yup. That's pretty much it."

Sherry muttered, "Jerk," as she watched his retreating back. He glided to the library doors and pushed them open, letting in a faint breeze of cooler air.

I am not! Ricky called back, only the voice sounded in her mind, bypassing her ears. Ricky wasn't even in the room anymore. The doors had swung shut behind him. Sherry wasn't sure whether to smile or shudder. Now she understood what Ember had meant when she said Reid had answered in her head. Telepathy. She was going to have get used to that, too.

Ember

That night, Ember fell asleep quickly, and just as quickly tumbled into a bizarre dream. It had been days since she'd thought of Owen, having been distracted with problems like her mother and the argument with Sherry that didn't really happen. She'd given up on the idea of convincing her mother that Reid wasn't a bad influence. Reluctantly, she'd gotten over the crow-killer thing, knowing that Reid punished him appropriately. The shape-shifting, vengeance-seeking witches were still an issue but until they tried another attack, of sorts, that worry could be put on hold.

Her biggest worry at the moment was a typically human, every-day issue - well, if you could call a double date at a swimming pool with two vampires, one of whom was the school's most infamous man-whore, typical and every-day. And now, that worry was being transferred into her dream.

***

She was standing, waist-deep in pool water, dressed only in her best blue bikini. That wasn't the strange part. She wasn't alone in the pool. That wasn't the strange part either. The strange part was the other person in the pool, gazing at her with familiar eyes.

"Owen?" She couldn't believe it. Owen was standing in front of her, looking as coldly dangerous as he had the day she walked away from him four years ago, only in the dream he looked how he might now, at sixteen. And she couldn't deny he was, well, attractive. With silky black hair sticking up in disarray, and a smooth, muscled chest on full display. Not as nice a physique as Reid's of course, but still, not bad.

"Hello Ember. Nice to see you again." The words came from the boy in front of her, but she barely recognised the voice. If not for the incredible eyes, she might not have believed it was Owen, even in a dream. This was a first though; Owen had starred in memories dredged up in her thoughtful moments recently, but not in any of her dreams. And seeing him as he might be in reality these days was a little scary. She wasn't sure what to say to this dream-Owen - after all, last time she'd seen him in the real world, he'd been spitting expletives and slurs at her back, while smoking on a cigarette. But he didn't seem to have changed much since then, judging by the coldness in his eyes and the hostility in his voice.

"What, don't you want to see me? I thought we were friends once upon a time." There was an edge to his voice aside from the hostility, an edge she recognised easily by now. Arrogance.

"We were until you became a delinquent thief. Did you get into drugs after I left you, or did you just start nicking cars?" Ember bit her words off sharply, glaring at Owen. Despite their odd setting, and state of undress, she wasn't going to take any crap from an old-friend-turned-criminal.

"Hmm, I see you haven't lost any of your spark. I'd begun to think you'd gone soft after you walked away from me. You know, I never stopped thinking about you. You were always there in the back of my mind whenever I stole something, whenever I spray painted a wall, whenever I smoked a cigarette. You would pop into my head, yelling at me that I was being an idiot." Owen sounded totally calm - and totally insane.

"Right. Glad to know I didn't slip your mind. Why are you here?" Ember took a step back, feeling the smooth water on her stomach as she moved. Vampires in reality didn't bug her, but an old friend in a dream... that was freaking her out. Maybe she was the insane one?

"I wanted to see you again. I've missed you, you know. We were such good friends, could've been more if you hadn't turned your back on me. And right now we could've been together, still in Scotland, watching seagulls fly over the North Sea, seeing the moonlight shining on the water." Owen stepped toward her quickly and put his arms around her. She struggled but she couldn't break his hold.

"Owen, get the hell off me. I walked away from you for a reason. And right now you sound completely insane. I haven't seen you in four years and I wouldn't want to be with you. I never would've wanted to be with you. You're a lying, cigarette-smoking, thieving punk!" Ember kicked out at him and he finally let go - sort of. He pulled back but gripped her shoulder with one hand while his other hand traced her bare side. She growled and snatched out of his grip, giving him a backhanded slap across the face. The force of it snapped his head to the side. "Do not touch me," she warned in a low snarl.

Unperturbed, even with blood rising to the handprint on his cheek, Owen simply smiled. It wasn't a pleasant smile, so much as a leer. "Oh, come on. You know you can't resist. You love the bad boys. You always did." Owen gazed at her with smouldering eyes. Ember had a good reply to that one.

"Yeah. You're right. I do love bad boys. I guess that explains why I like my boyfriend so much," she smirked. Owen looked mildly irritated for a moment, but recovered fast.

"Yes, well. If you like him so much, why do you still refuse to really accept him as your boyfriend, except inside your own head? You make up reasons, excuses for not using the word openly, as you should. You tell yourself it's complicated, when there's nothing complicated about it." Owen shook his head, his black hair scattering ink drops that melted into the water around him. "Are you ashamed of him? Is that it?"

Shocked, Ember spluttered, "No! Jesus. Where do you get off, saying-"

"If you like him so much, why haven't you had sex with him?" Owen's appallingly personal question, and his certainty of it, took her off-guard. It took her a moment to regain balance but that was all it took for Owen to apparently confirm his theory to himself. He pressed her, eyes intense. "Come on, answer me. Why haven't you?" He was grinning like a lunatic and it was a little worrisome. Ember recoiled, taking another step away from him. He followed her. She gulped nervously, trying to remind herself that this was just a dream. But it just felt so real.

"How do you know I haven't? Reid is... well, he's not shy of physical intimacy, and he is the hottest guy I've ever laid eyes on. Why wouldn't I?" she retorted with a bravado she didn't feel, putting her hands on her hips. She was starting to feel uncomfortable in her lack of clothing and it seemed she was discussing her non-existent sex life with too many people these days.

"I know because I know you. And because you managed to argue against me without actually using the word 'sex'. It's almost like you're shy of saying it." The spark in Owen's expression was really pissing her off now.

"How would you like me to prove it then? Describe where, when and how we did it? Would that make you happy?" She was bluffing of course, but he didn't know that. And there was no way she'd ever tell him those kinds of details anyway - dream or not - and he didn't know that either.

"Actually I was thinking you could just prove you have no issues with physical intimacy. I'm sure your boyfriend really has no compunctions about it, but you do. You always have, ever since we were kids. You never liked letting people hug you, or hold your hand. But, if you really aren't so shy of physical contact anymore, maybe you could just let me near to you." Owen had his hands on her again before she could move. One hand on her hip, the other on her shoulder blades. She squealed in protest, disgusted, and pushed him away. He stumbled, splashing up water that rained around him, soaking his hair so that black ink dribbled down his cheeks like dark tears.

"What part of 'I have a boyfriend' don't you get? Wait, this is my damn dream! You're not here, and you have no business being in my dream. Especially like this! Get your hands the hell off me and go away!" she shrieked, slapping at the darkly grinning boy as he tried to step toward her again. He paused, tilted his head, and winked at her.

"I'll see you soon," he murmured. She wasn't sure if it was threat or a promise, but it freaked her out anyway. And then he was gone, leaving her confused and angry. The dream dissolved around her and she faded into the normal blackness of sleep.

H.G. Lynch

Chlorine Dreams

H.G. Lynch

Ember

"No, I'm not coming out!" Ember was curled on the bench in her changing room, knees tucked up to her chin.

"Ember, come on. You agreed we could go swimming! And you didn't have a problem with being seen in a bikini before! Why now?" Sherry called to her, rattling on the door. No doubt she was trying to unlock it with a coin. Ember shivered in the cool air blowing down from the air-conditioner, and curled her toes against the smooth wood she sat on. Why now? She thought bitterly, because now I have a boyfriend, and he might not like what he sees.

"Because!" Ember replied shortly. She was feeling queasy, nervous that… well, that Reid wouldn't be so impressed when he saw her in a bikini. She wasn't as full-figured as normal teenage girls, and next to Sherry's curves, she'd look like a stick. It normally didn't bother her, but she had someone to impress now and being stuck in the middle of two gorgeous guys and one beautiful girl, she was bound to look like a scrawny twelve-year-old.

"That's not an answer. Come on, nobody's going to say anything. I wish I was as skinny as you, you know that!" The door rattled again and then a clinking, like a coin being dropped on the slippery tile floor.

She heard Sherry whisper, "Damn it." And saw a hand reach down to pick up the coin from the small gap under the door. One of the boys murmured something too low for Ember to hear, but it suddenly flew open and she flinched. Sherry grinned at her and Reid arched a brow at her, smirking. Damn it!

"Are you going to come out on your own now, or will I have to carry you and toss you in the pool myself?" Reid asked, crouching slightly as if ready to pounce at her. He looked stunning, in simple black swim shorts, with his smooth chest bare and his blond hair tousled. His hipbones curved teasingly into the waistband of the shorts, and Ember averted her eyes, feeling warmth rise to her cheeks. Reid's eyes, though, seemed to hold a spark of mischief as he grinned at her and she half expected him to flash his fangs.

When she didn't answer him, he sighed and took a step toward her. She stuck out a foot to hold him back, uncurling and pressing herself into the corner. Her foot pressed into his stomach and he just glanced down at it, then back at her with an, 'are-you-serious?' expression.

"Don't. No, don't. Don't!" she warned him as he grabbed her ankle and pushed her leg to the side, reaching for her with his other hand. But her pleas went unacknowledged. He grasped her arm and, with a deftness and quickness that startled her, flung her a foot off the bench and caught her in his arms. She let out a yelp of surprise and then hissed at him, struggling against him pointlessly. "No, put me down! Put me down! I'll walk!" I'll run. Away from here, she thought as she tried to prise his hand off her knee. She felt a prickling at her temples and cursed the vampire holding her.

"You're not running anywhere my little demon. You are going in the pool whether you want to or not," Reid murmured in her ear, his breath touching her hair, making her heart flutter for a second.

"Stop riffling in my head!" she snarled as they approached the edge of the pool, slamming up her mental walls to block him out. They were at the deep end of course. Fabulous.

"I wouldn't have to if you were more cooperative. I had to know if you would really walk to the pool or if you were lying again," he muttered, his mouth still close to her ear. It was very distracting, made it hard to stay indignant.

"Well, I have no choice now do I. So you can put me down now." She looked up at him with fierce blue eyes, trying to look innocent but failing. Her lip curled angrily, despite her efforts.

Reid smirked at her and pressed a kiss onto her lips before whispering. "Put you down? I don't think so."

Ember scowled. "Put me down right now or I'll screeeeeeeeeeeeee-" She broke off with the promised scream, but not because he didn't put her down. He did. In a way. He threw her into the pool.

She plunged into warm, chlorine-bleached water and swirled about helplessly. Her hair swam around her face, feeling like silk on her shoulders and neck. It took her a second to reach the bottom of the pool and she instantly whirled upright, pushing off with her toes and bursting to the surface. She gasped and choked, flinging her hair off her face and rubbing water from her eyes. *I'm going to kill him for that.*

"Reid!" she shrieked up at the laughing blond, still watching from where he'd thrown her from. Sherry and Ricky were laughing too, and if she'd had something to throw at them, she would've done so.

"How's the water Emz?" Sherry called down, grinning. Ember flipped her off and proceeded to turn and swim away from the giggling group, heading for the shallow end. She heard a splash and a yelp behind her as she swam, meaning that Sherry had been pushed in, too. Another splash a moment later, followed by a chuckle and Sherry's scandalous giggles. Ricky had jumped then.

Ember reached the shallower water and turned, sitting on the tiled pool floor to watch her friends. She noticed there weren't many other people here, surprisingly. A few elderly people, a handful of young couples with infants and a couple of kids their ages, but that was all. And of course Ricky and Sherry, splashing each other in a sickly sweet show of love. Ember rolled her eyes, and then focused on the gorgeous blond boy still standing on the poolside.

Just as she flicked her attention to him, Reid met her gaze, grinned and lifted his arms over his head. She got a great view of his chest that way and she bit her lip, wondering if he could hear her heart skip from here. Then he dove from a standing position into the warm, rippling water. He looked wonderfully graceful as he did it, landing with only a minor splash and popping to the surface a moment later. He flipped his wet blond hair out of his eyes and ran a hand over it. God, he could pose for a 'Beach Babes' calendar, she thought, tilting her head back to look at the ceiling. It was arched and mirrored, reflecting her own pale form back to her. Just for a moment, she thought she really didn't look all that bad.

"Something fascinating up there, or just trying to avoid looking at me?" Reid asked, playfully dripping water over her shoulder. She hadn't noticed him coming up next to her, too fixed on her own reflection to detect his right beside her, and she jumped a little, sending ripples of water flowing. Unhappily, she turned to him and glared. He was grinning at her.

"Jerk," she accused and glanced away.

"I'll take that as the latter," he said nonchalantly. Ember frowned.

She watched her own fingers swirling in the water as she replied. "You're mean for throwing me in. I would've rather jumped myself or stayed in the changing room," she pouted, hoping for some apology. For a while, Reid didn't reply, and she assumed he was thinking of something witty to say.

Instead what he said eventually was, "Why?"

She looked at him, confused, "Why would I rather have jumped myself? So that I didn't choke and nearly drown. And because I hate-" She started, arching a brow at him, but he cut her off.

"No. Why would you rather have stayed in the changing room? You agreed to come swimming, albeit reluctantly, and from what Sherry was saying up there, it sounds like you enjoy swimming. I mean, you wouldn't have done five years of lessons if you hated it, right?" He sounded confused now. His eyes were probing her face, looking for answers she doubted he'd find.

"I do like swimming. Usually. But this is meant to be a double date. Not one of the many things that was on my bucket list." Ember rolled her eyes, but he frowned at her, his blue eyes intense. She tried to ignore the way he looked so cute with his wet hair ruffled and sticking to his forehead.

"Again, you agreed to it. Why the last minute change of heart?" he insisted. Growing more embarrassed by the reason for her reluctance, Ember wished he'd just drop it. The way he was looking at her was starting to make her think she'd been stupid to imagine that he wouldn't like her body; there was plain desire on his face as he lazily looked her over, as if he hadn't really noticed her lack of clothing until now.

"Why all the questions? I'm here and I'm in the pool now," Ember shrugged, watching Sherry and Ricky banter on the metal ladder bolted to the wall at the other end of the pool. Feeling uncomfortable and unconfident, seeing Sherry's lovely figure and the way Ricky clung to her, Ember chewed her lip and resisted the urge to curl into a ball to hide herself. She wasn't resentful of her friend for looking that way, but she was a little jealous. She wished she could have a real, girly figure. It wasn't something she often thought about, because she usually liked the way she looked, and she didn't care that guys didn't undress her with their eyes like they did the other girls. But just sometimes, like now, it got to her.

"But you're not happy. What's wrong?" Reid persisted with his questions and she almost wanted to hit him, but she had a feeling the lifeguards wouldn't like that much. She just shrugged, hoping he'd let it drop now. But when she felt her temples prickle, she slammed up her mental walls and glared at him. He wasn't going to drop it then. Damn him and his insistent curiosity. "If you'd talk to me, I wouldn't have to try and pick answers out of your head," he smirked, but it looked forced. That was when Ember realised that he wasn't asking out of curiosity, he was asking because he cared. He truly wanted to know why she was unhappy, perhaps so he could fix it. She could see it all in his eyes, a lovelier, bluer blue than the pool water. She sighed, half-realising that he knew she'd give in all along - him and his damned good looks were irresistible. Maybe eventually she'd stop cracking whenever he gave her that deep, intense stare that made her feel like her soul was melting inside her.

"If I tell you, you'll laugh at me," she muttered, feeling his fingertips running over her arm lightly. He was watching his own hand, which made it easier to speak. He shook his head, a silent promise not to laugh. "Fine. I just... I-I'm not..." She couldn't work out how to word her explanation without sounding like a total loser, so she scowled at the water for a moment and then held out her arms, "Well, look at me," she said simply, frowning. Reid's eyes flickered to hers for a moment through his dripping blond hair.

"I already have. And if I do it again I'm afraid we might get kicked out for what I'm likely to do to you," he said quietly, a smile playing about his mouth as he returned his eyes to his hand, tracing her arm again. It took her a second to understand what he meant, her mind working slowly as it sometimes did in uncomfortable situations.

"What... What are you likely to do?" she asked in a shy whisper, glancing between him and her toes stretched out in front of her. Now Reid really grinned, a bright mischievous grin, and his eyes glowed as they met hers again.

"Trust me, I shouldn't say those things in a public place. You might get embarrassed and blush. And then I'd really have a problem containing myself." Ember bit her lip and felt the heat colour her face as she imagined the kinds of things he might say. Her skin felt suddenly acutely warm all over. "Mh-hm. Just like that," Reid murmured, brushing his fingertips up the side of her neck to her cheekbone. "You're so goddamned sexy, you make me feel like-" She shut him up by putting a hand over his mouth.

"Shut up. I get it," she mumbled, giggling. She was pretty sure she didn't need to hear the rest of what he was going to say; It would only make her feel more bubbly and squirmy inside. And they were in a public place. His eyes bright, Reid licked her hand childishly and she yipped. "Ew, Reid!" She wiped her hand on his shoulder and he laughed. "Childish much?" she added, splashing water over him.

"Well, you don't want it be a double date so let's make it a play-date." He grinned at her and splashed her back. She hesitated, trying not to laugh but he'd successfully cheered her up and gotten her over her bout of self-deprecation, and he'd done it without being condescending or rattling off mushy compliments. Eventually she gave in, giggled and leaned in to kiss him. Once her mouth was just few centimetres from his lips, she pulled back abruptly and sent a huge wave of water spraying over his face, and tried to crawl away quickly. Reid made a disgruntled, surprised noise and growled.

"Hey! That was just plain mean!" He caught her ankle as she made her getaway and dragged her back through the water to land across his lap. "I think you should apologise for that," he whispered, his mouth right at her ear, his arms wrapped round her, warm and solid compared to the swishing water.

The sharp blast of a whistle pierced the air, but Reid didn't even look around as he released her and held up his hands as if in surrender, so the lifeguard could see clearly he'd let go of her. The lifeguard did not look like a happy woman. Ember bit back laughter and scrambled off his lap, standing and splashing her way to deeper water. She had no idea where Ricky and Sherry had gone, probably around the back of the little diving platform at the far end. It was private behind there, and out of the view of the lifeguards.

Ember waded into waist-deep water and took a deep breath, holding and ducking under the water. She blew out the breath and sat on the bottom of the pool for seventeen seconds - she was counting - and then rose up again. She swept her wet hair off her face and turned to look for Reid. He'd disappeared too. Hmm. Ember was about to go in search of him when a hand caught hers, dragging her off toward the jacuzzi.

"Sherry and Kee are at the jacuzzi. They want us to come over before we cause trouble." Reid grinned, clearly not adverse to the idea of making trouble.

"How do you know that? Telepathic link to Ricky?" Ember trailed after the blond boy, slyly eyeing his back; the way the muscles moved smoothly and the water ran in rivulets down from his shoulders. She let her eyes follow a drop all the way from the nape of his neck to the rim of his shorts, following the supple curve of his spine, and took the chance to look a little lower. She bit her lip, admiring. *Nice butt, huh?* Reid's smug comment sounded in her head and she flinched in surprise, feeling a fresh blush rise to her face.

"I thought I told you to stay out of my head," she hissed, embarrassed at being caught ogling.

"I wasn't in your head. I just know you, and I know you like what you see." He smiled brazenly back at her as they reached the edge of the jacuzzi. Ember stuck her tongue out at him. He was right, of course, but he didn't need to know that.

"What're you two talking about?" Sherry was snuggled against Ricky's chest on one side of the jacuzzi. It was a big jacuzzi, round and large enough for ten people. And they had it all to themselves. Nice.

"Nothing. Reid was just being an pest," Ember chirped, sliding into the bubbling water and settling across from Ricky and Sherry. The water, she was pleased to note, was very warm, almost hot, and the bubbles sprayed against her spine from one of the jets.

"Liar. Ember was checking out my butt," Reid laughed, ignoring Ember's glower.

Ricky chuckled, shaking his head. "You shouldn't encourage him, Ember," he said lightly.

"Why do you always choose the worst times to be truthful?" Ember glared at Reid, who rolled his eyes and slipped in beside her, slinging an arm over the edge of the jacuzzi, behind her shoulders.

"So, Sherry, how you handling the whole vampires-werewolves-witches thing?" Reid asked, curious but casual. It was obvious he wasn't fully paying attention to her answer; he was stroking lines over Ember's shoulder, playing teasingly with the strap of her bikini top.

"Um, OK. I think. I haven't run screaming or lost my mind yet so I think I'll be fine." Sherz smiled, her gaze flicking to the brunette boy beside her. *Something tells me she wouldn't cope so well if not for Ricky*, Ember thought fondly. Despite Ricky being one of the unnatural, he still had a calming effect on her friend. Ricky, she supposed, was just one of those innately soothing people.

"Oh, and Ricky filled me in on the telepathy thing." Sherry was talking to Ember now, and Ember remembered they had been about to discuss that yesterday before her mother barged in. "I just wish I knew when he was reading my mind. I have to be careful with what I think now." The green-eyed girl glanced at Kee, who only smiled innocently. Ember frowned. Sherry couldn't feel it when Ricky was reading her mind, but Ember could always tell when Reid tried to read hers: that prickling sensation. Reid had said, when she'd first discovered her ability to feel telepathic intrusions, that it wasn't normal for a human to feel it, but having that confirmed made Ember feel a little freakish.

"Ricky, could you just try something for me please?" Ember asked politely, sure that this was going to sound very strange to him. Ricky looked confused, but happy to help as he nodded.

"Sure," he agreed amiably. Ember hesitated, thinking of tricky but innocent things like maths calculations.

"Could you try to read my mind? I just want to test something." Ember smiled lightly, and Ricky gave her bewildered look. But he obliged. Ember felt a prickling at her temples and put up her mental blocks; *Might as well test two things at once*, she thought. Ricky looked taken aback, more bewildered than before, and Sherry looked almost as puzzled. But Reid was looking at her questioningly, though he knew exactly what she was doing now.

"How did you do that?" Ricky asked quietly. He stared at her intently, searching for an explanation on her face, like it might be written on her forehead in red ink.

"You mean I blocked you, too?" Ember asked, knowing the answer, but needing confirmation.

Ricky nodded, pursing his lips thoughtfully, and then blinked. "Wait, 'too'? What do you mean 'too'?"

Reid chuckled next to her and patted her on the head, which Ember responded to with a slap to his chest. "Well, Ricky boy, it seems Ember here has the ability to block us out of her head. And she can feel it when we try to pry. It's a pain in the butt for me but…" Reid shrugged. Ricky looked amazed.

"You can feel it? How? I mean, what's it feel like?" he enquired, curiosity and wonder alight in his eyes. He ran a hand through his hair, itching his head.

"Just like a prickling at my temples. But I can block out the intrusion by just well, imagining a stone wall around my mind basically. It's weird but it works." Ember grinned, thrilled at having stumped yet another vampire. She wondered what Brandon and Perry would think of this. Meanwhile, Sherz was looking lost.

"Wait, why can you feel it and I can't? Is there something wrong with me or something?" Sherry pitched her brows up in a worried expression.

Ember shook her head quickly. "No, no. I'm the freak. We aren't meant to be able to feel it. Right, Reid?" She turned to him for confirmation and he nodded, but his eyes were glued to her and a thoughtful expression was plastered to his face.

"This is… well, weird. I've never heard of a human being able to feel telepathic things like that, let alone block them." Kee was examining her now, like a scientist with an experiment. Great. *I'm the vampire version of a scientific oddity,* she thought grudgingly.

"Maybe I'm not human," Ember joked. "Now, can we stop fussing about my messed up mind and talk about something… oh, I don't know, normal perhaps?" She rolled her eyes, and Ricky laughed, but Reid was still watching her thoughtfully. She wanted to ask him why he was staring at her like that but his gaze changed when he realised she knew he was still gazing at her. His eyes darkened and became just a little hazy. She opened her mouth to ask what he was thinking but when she felt his hand on her leg, she got an idea. His fingertips trailed up from her knee slowly, and a shiver of heat travelled down her spine. His blue eyes were fixed on hers and a sensual smile curved his soft mouth. His hand crept up further but when his fingers reached halfway up her thigh, she caught his wrist. Butterflies battered her stomach, and she had to take a deep breath to cool her trembling nerves. She chanced a glance at Ricky and Sherry, hoping they weren't looking. Luckily they were absorbed in an enthralling conversation of their own.

Ember leaned close to Reid and whispered, "If you can't keep your hands in decent places, keep them to yourself." She let him feel her lips on his cheek before she placed his hand back on his own leg. He gave her a devilish look, flames dancing in his eyes.

"Would it make a difference if there weren't other people here?" he murmured, a mischievous gleam coming to his blue eyes along with the flames. Ember stroked her fingers down his side and across his abs teasingly, and sweetly seductive smile on her lips.

"Not a bit," she answered silkily. And before she could react, his mouth was on hers, kissing her in a way that was warm and sweet, but with a wild edge that made Ember's head spin. A deep cough from the other side of the jacuzzi, along with a giggle, brought Ember back to her senses and she pushed Reid away. She blushed and let her hair fall around her face like a dripping screen, trying to calm her heart rate. Ricky was looking uncomfortable but amused, while Sherry was giggling under her breath.

"I do not want to know what you two get up to on your own, if that's how you act in public." Sherz laughed and Ember blushed deeper, feeling heat in her face.

"Hmm, don't I wish," Reid said dryly with a sad sigh. Ricky arched a brow inquisitively and Reid opened his mouth to say something, but Ember elbowed him in the ribs - guys and their need to chat about their sex lives. It was so stupid.

"Say one more word and I'll..." Ember cut off mid-threat and switched to telepathically threatening him, *I'll make sure you never get close to what you'd like to do to me. Got it?* Reid glared for a moment but Ember just raised her brows expectantly, twisting her legs away from him so they no longer touched.

"Fine," Reid pouted, but it was clear he was conjuring plans for later. Probably trying to find a loophole in her threat. It wouldn't do him any good, because he could find a way of talking to Ricky about their escapades - or lack of - in any loophole, but she could still keep her body away from him no matter what. He couldn't win.

"OK. If you two are done with telepathic threats, maybe we could go check out the flumes?" Ricky grinned, and Ember wasn't sure if he'd heard her mental warning or if he could just guess. She hoped it was the latter, though that still left her feeling a little uncomfortable.

"Flumes it is," she piped up, excited by the idea of trying out the water flumes in a new pool. She wondered if they'd be as good as the ones back home. Maybe they'd be faster!

Reid

Reid bit his lip as he watched Ember climbing the stairs to the top of the flumes. He was lagging behind with Ricky, who was rattling on about something, but Reid really wasn't listening. He was busy watching the way Ember's hips swayed as she walked up each step. So she wasn't as curvy or busty as the usual sixteen-year-old girls, but he'd had enough of those girls anyway. She was sexy in a more delicate way, and the way she denied his touch just added to the wanting. He'd love to trace the curve of her hips, the dip of her tiny waist, her long legs, with his fingertips, but she wouldn't let him. He was the vampire, but she had control over him. It was sweet torture.

"Hello? Reid? You're not listening are you?" Ricky shoved his arm, bringing him out of his entranced ogling for the time being. Blue-green eyes fixed on him with exasperation, and Ricky sighed.

"What? No. I've got better things on my mind." Reid grinned his usual devil-may-care smirk. The brunette boy just rolled his eyes.

They reached the top of the stairs and found there was no queue. He, of course, knew these flumes well, having been swimming at this pool since he was four. 'The Caterpillar' was the bumpy one, 'The Snake' was the winding one with lots of loops and 'The Shark' was the super-fast, 60 degree angle one. And the look on Ember's face said she couldn't wait to try them all. Her eyes were glued to 'The Snake', but Sherry dragged her toward 'The Caterpillar'.

Reid hung back, leaning against the cool tiles of the wall to watch them. The tiles under his feet were slick and the air was chilly, but it didn't bother him in the least. Gooseflesh was rising on Ember's arms, though, and he smiled a little. *She's so fragile*, He thought with a pang. It made him want to look after her, take care of her, but despite her human fragility, she was too fiery to let him. She'd

Born Dark

take of herself, he knew. And she'd eat you alive if you ever hurt her, a little voice whispered in his head. It didn't amuse him. He frowned briefly. Then I'll make sure I never hurt her, he vowed silently.

"You go first." Sherry insisted, pushing Ember to the mouth of the flume excitedly. Ember laughed and sat down at the flume entrance, water flowing over her pale skin in clear ribbons.

"You sure? It looks awful scary," Ember teased Sherry, who ducked and pushed the girl fiercely. Ember shrieked but then laughed as she flew down the tunnel and disappeared. The remaining three of them all turned their attention to the TV screen on the wall near the stairs, where it showed the exits of all the flumes; live feeds wired from cameras at the bottom.

After nearly a minute of watching, a girl flew out the end of one flume in to the deep pool at the bottom. She plunged under the water and came up a moment later, grinning and wiping water out of her eyes. She looked to be laughing and glanced at the camera, giving a thumbs-up and wading out of the pool. Sherry laughed and shot down the flume herself. Reid expected Ember to come rushing back up the steps to try the next flume, but she waited at the bottom for Sherry.

"Why do they do that? They always wait for each other." Reid was puzzled. He'd seen groups of girls occasionally wait for each other if they had things to discuss or somewhere to be, but he'd never seen two girls constantly stick by each other like that.

"They're best friends. Probably closer than we are to Brandon and Perry most of the time. Friendship links them that way." Ricky shrugged. "Plus, they're girls. Who knows why they do anything?" Kee laughed, his eyes still on the TV screen. Sherry slid out the end of the flume and splashed into the water, coming up to the surface quickly and laughing as Ember ran in to throw water over her playfully. It was cute and a little childish the way they acted together, so natural like they were sisters, not friends. Both girls on the screen turned to the camera and made beckoning gestures. Reid and Ricky looked at each other and grinned. Ricky wandered to the mouth of 'The Caterpillar' and Reid went to 'The Snake'. They'd go down different slides at the same time so they'd come out the bottom at the same time, surprising the girls. Once they were sitting at the mouths of the flumes, they nodded to each other and pushed off, flying into the flumes simultaneously.

The warm water sloshed over Reid as he slipped around the familiar curves and twists of the flume, the tunnel being pitch black in some parts and shimmering with light in others. Until he flew out the end and was swallowed by the deep, warm waters of the pool. He pushed to the surface and slung his hair off his face, turning to Ricky, who was laughing next to him. The girls were giggling on the edge of the pool and Ember took a running jump into the water, sending a spray of it over him and Ricky. Reid felt a tug on his ankle and toppled over backwards, losing his footing on the slippery tiles underfoot. He felt hands on him again, pushing against his chest to keep him under the water's surface. He grabbed the wrists and yanked Ember to him, wrapping his arms around her and bringing her back to the surface with him.

"Trying to drown me? Or did you just want an excuse to put your hands on me?" he chuckled into her ear, brushing her wet hair off her face. To his surprise, she wrapped her arms around him in return and hugged him tightly. Then she tilted her head back and kissed his jaw, his neck, the hollow at the base of his throat. Sparks flew down his nerves, making him feel jittery inside. God, how did she do that to him?

"Maybe both," she whispered against his chest, her lips soft and warm on his skin. He tried to think of a witty comeback but his mind kept flicking to other lines of thought. He trailed one hand lightly, teasingly down her spine, and expected her to pull away or mutter a warning for him to 'move his hand before he lost it', but he felt her lips curl in a smile against his neck.

"Did you hit your head on your way down the flume?" he murmured into her hair, trying to think of a reason not to pull her flush against him and kiss her again. It was so tempting, his every primal instinct snarling for him to do just that. Somehow, he restrained the urge.

"Nope…" She lifted her head and her lips brushed his as she spoke. "I'm winning a bet." She whispered against his mouth, her fingers running across the nape of his neck, sending delicious shivers down his back. When she leaned back, he tried to catch her lips with his, but she chuckled and slid her other hand down his spine, way down, making him pause. Heat spilled through his body, and he wondered, just for an instant, if she would really dare.

Then her words registered in his head, just as she pushed him, hard. He stumbled and fell under the water again, too stunned to right himself for several seconds. While under the water, he could see Ember's long, slender legs and dainty feet. Curious to see if she was ticklish, he began to reach for her, but pulled back. She'd likely kick him if he tried to tickle her.

When he re-surfaced at last, Ember and Sherry were laughing, eyes on the big clock on the wall above them. "Ten…Eleven…" Ember was muttering. Shaking water out of his ears, he caught the end of them counting, and glanced at Ricky for some explanation. He just grinned and shrugged. Helpful, Reid thought sarcastically.

"Well, ten seconds. OK, you win," Sherry announced to Ember, who beamed at her friend. The green-eyed girl pulled a sulky expression, and then broke into a grin as well.

"What the hell are you two talking about?" he asked, finally bringing himself out of the pool. Ember smirked at him, though he saw her gaze briefly follow the lines of his body, before returning to his face. It made him want to smile, knowing she was as attracted to him as he was to her.

"We made a bet that I could keep you under water for ten seconds, without using physical force to hold you there. If she won, I had to agree to another double date, a proper one. If I won, which I did, she had to cut down on the mushy lovey-dovey-ness when I'm around. So, no more gag-worthy sop-fests while I'm in earshot!" Ember laughed and Sherry mock pouted.

"Damn it. I was going to arrange for a candle-lit dinner or something." The green-eyed girl looked honestly disappointed for a moment, and then giggled as Ember made a gagging noise.

"Yeah, well. Just as well I won. You know I'd actually rather stab myself with a fork than do a candle-lit dinner," Ember muttered, folding her arms over her chest. But Reid wondered just how much of Ember's act had been for the bet, and how much had been just for her.

Ember

It was nice to be dry and clothed again as they all headed home. Ember was a little tired after the day's events, and she knew it would take an extra shower when she got home to wash the chlorine smell from her hair. But it had been fun and seeing Reid in swim shorts was enjoyable to say the least. She ran her tongue over the roof of her mouth at the remembered sight.

Right now, curled in the backseat of Ricky's BMW, Ember relaxed. She could almost pretend like her life was normal. She could practically forget that her boyfriend was a vampire and her best friend's boyfriend was also a vampire, and that there were shape-shifting witches after them all. Lazily, Ember gazed out the window to the velvet dark sky and glittering stars, observing the pale glowing orb that hung over the tops of the pine trees. Night-time was so beautiful. So peaceful. She wished she could stay awake long enough to watch the stars all night long.

***

"Oh, great. You again," Ember muttered, instantly irritated by Owen's entrance into her sleep. But at least this time she was fully clothed. They were standing in the forest, and Owen looked the same as before: cold, menacing, dark.

"I'm here to warn you. You shouldn't go into the forest at night. You'll regret it," Owen said in a low voice. A warning? Sounded more like a threat. From a dream-person. Right.

"Mh-hm. And I'm going to take your advice why?" Ember rolled her eyes. Owen sneered.

"Because the witches will get you if you don't," he said it dramatically, like someone in a horror movie. Too bad her life was already a horror movie, so it didn't scare her. Plus, this was a dream… or maybe a nightmare, but either way it didn't make a difference to her what the hell this guy said. "I'm serious Ember. I don't want you getting involved with those witches. They'll get you into trouble… because of who you could be!" Owen looked perfectly serious, and almost concerned. And again, he sounded as insane as last time. Nutter, Ember thought in exasperation.

"Fabulous. I'm grateful for your concern and all, but I'm not going to take advice from a crazy person. Can you go away now?" Ember smirked, making a sharp shooing motion with one hand. She expected him to scowl and walk away and the dream to end. That's not what happened. Instead, he strode over and kissed her roughly, hugging her tightly to his chest. Ember felt fury fill her chest and she pushed against him, yanking his head back by the hair - or attempting to. No matter how hard she shoved or tugged, he didn't budge. Stupid dream-person!

He moved his mouth to her ear at last and whispered, "I really have missed you." The words were surprisingly gentle, honest-sounding, but Ember didn't care. She threw out her fist to collide with his face, but her hand went through him, like a bullet through smoke. And he dissolved into mist before floating away. That's when the dream ended.

***

Born Dark

Back in reality, Ember sat up in her bed. She assumed Reid must've carried her in and put her in her bed to avoid waking her; the sweetie that he could be sometimes. Frustrated with her dreams, Ember growled at the ceiling and threw back her covers. If these dreams kept up, she'd never get a good night's sleep again. She might even be afraid to go to sleep.

Irritated, she got out of bed and wandered to the window, opening it silently and peering out. The fresh smell of the cool night air helped calm her down, and the sweeping darkness was soothing. Ember propped herself on the windowsill and leaned her head back against the frame, eyes closed. Why Owen had started appearing in her dreams, she had no idea, but it certainly was annoying, if harmless - damage to her sleep patterns aside. At least the scented night air will chase off the nightmare, she thought tiredly. She let her mind drift.

"Oh, sweetie. I wish I didn't have to go yet. I never got the chance to take you shopping!" Mrs Jennings was pouting in disappointment but it was clear in her green eyes that she was glad to be going home, even if it meant leaving her daughter here. It would only be two weeks before she was back, and Ember was planning on enjoying those two weeks of freedom, before two more weeks of hell came back to her - the October Holidays.

"Yeah, How awful," Ember muttered sarcastically as her mother squeezed the air out of her lungs with another bone-crushing hug. The woman smiled and pecked her on the head before turning and giving Sherry's arm a squeeze.

"I hope you can keep her out of trouble. And take care of yourself."

Sherry nodded with a polite smile. Ember saw her mother glance around behind them slyly, and knew what she was looking for or rather who. But the boys were still in bed at ten on a Sunday morning. Thank God.

"Well, tell the boys I said it was nice meeting them. And I'll be back in two weeks, remember." Mrs Jennings glanced sharply at Ember as she said it, making it clear it was a warning. Ember tried not to scowl,

"I know, I know. Tell Dad and Munch Monster I said 'Hi'," Ember smiled at using the nickname she'd given her younger brother. Carol smiled and nodded, before turning and getting in her car. Ember watched her drive off and once she was safely out of sight... "YES! Finally!" Ember punched the air and almost fell to her knees in the parking lot, despite the wet ground. Sherry laughed and shook her head disapprovingly.

"You should miss her, you know?" she muttered.

Ember grinned helplessly, "Yeah? Well, I can't miss her when she's here, can I?" she quipped. Sherry just rolled her eyes and they made their way back to the dorms.

The rest of Sunday was uneventful. Ember had thought Reid would be dying to get back to her side, seeing as they had no reason to fear getting caught, but he apparently had other things to attend to.

Monday and Tuesday were painfully slow and boring, being back at school. When it came to the middle of the week, Ember was almost relieved. Just two more days until the weekend! She thought longingly. Two more days and she could sleep past 7am. If only she had something to do this weekend. She sighed, unhappily. She had the feeling Reid might be avoiding her; three days and hardly anything more than a few five-minute drop-bys. It was strange, considering usually he couldn't stay away from her. Maybe she was getting clingy? Oh Dear God, no! She grimaced and Sherry nudged her.

"What's up? You look horrified," she giggled. Ember just shook her head mutely, glaring down at her scribble-filled English jotter. Sherry shrugged. "Well, it looks like you're being signalled," she murmured, jerking her head toward the left and a few rows down. Ember followed her glance and saw Reid grinning up at her. She tried to force a smile in return but it must not have been convincing because Reid's smile fell and he looked a little hurt. Aw. How cute.

What's wrong? Reid's voice came to her mind and she bristled at having him in her head again. She threw up her mental blocks and glared at him for a moment, before scribbling a note. It was more dangerous than telepathic notes but at least she could lie on paper.

Nothing's wrong. I'm just bored to death here.

She folded the paper and tossed it to Reid. He caught it nimbly in his long fingers and gave her a look before turning to read the note.

A minute later, the note landed back on her desk.

OK, if that's all it is.

Ember scowled at the note. The words seemed, somehow, almost sharp, uncaring. She could imagine the way he might say them, with a shrug and a cold smirk. She'd expected a joke or witty comment or something, but no. Damn it. I'm over-analysing again, she thought, frustrated. The bell rang, effectively ending her worrying for the moment. She had Biology next. Great.

Reid

Damn it. He couldn't stand this. Three days and it was already killing him; four days technically. He'd been busy on Saturday and he'd gotten into a little trouble, and since then, he'd been trying to stay away from Ember. For her own good.

***

He'd been out in the woods, feeding on a blood bag - he preferred fresh blood from the source but he couldn't bring himself to feed on any girl but Ember. Though he wasn't feeding on her either. What was a guy to do? When he'd been interrupted by a cold female voice.
"You're awfully brave to be out here alone, vampire," the woman speaking looked vaguely familiar, with cropped hair and sharp, grey eyes.
"Oh, of course. Because I'm terribly afraid of the random women running around," he sneered, tossing the blood bag to the ground carelessly and scuffing pine needles over it. The woman's face glowed with hatred.
"You don't even know who I am, do you?" she spat. Reid shrugged,
"I'm guessing I screwed you and never called afterwards?" He shrugged nonchalantly. The woman's face twisted in disgust and horror - and more rage.
"NO! I'd never sleep with a blood-sucking monster! I'm one of those witches you attacked, you disgusting freak! And I swear you're going to regret that!" Oh. Now he remembered her. He hadn't really been paying attention to her that night. He'd sensed Ember up in the tree and he'd been more focused on finding a way to get her out safely.
"Right… wait, how do you even remember that night? We blanked your memories!" Reid hadn't considered that before. Even when he'd heard from Joseph that he'd been working for the witches. Nobody had wondered about how the witches had remembered anything. Smart Reid, He thought, real smart.

"Trade secret. We have ways to prevent compulsion. Too bad for you and your friends. You'll regret messing with us!" the witch hissed and Reid set his jaw in annoyance.

"Say it again, I think I missed it the first time," he muttered, rolling his eyes. Witches with a way to protect against compulsion could be a real problem, but he wouldn't let her see it worried him.

"I'm serious, vampire! We're going to strip you of everyone you care about, starting with your little girlfriend. How do you think she'd enjoy being a mouse? I think it would suit her." The witch smiled a nasty smirk and Reid felt fury flare up in his chest. The bitch was threatening his Ember.

"You won't touch her or I swear to God, I'll rip you all apart limb by limb and burn your mangled corpses," his voice was deadly quiet as he spoke, and he could feel the dark glint in his eyes, the lengthening of his canines. The witch backed off a little as he slipped into an attack stance, but she snarled one more thing before she fled.

"You know she doesn't love you, right? You're a monster! What girl could love a monster? None! She's acting because she's terrified of you! She's going to turn on you! And if she doesn't… she's only in danger because of you! Soon, you'll realise you're going to get her killed!"

And then the witch was gone. But her words seemed to echo in his head. 'You're going to get her killed'. It struck him with startling clarity, and painfully so. The damned witch was right. It was his fault Ember was in this mess! His fault Joseph had put the dead crow in her room, his fault she was being hunted by vengeful witches, his fault she was in trouble with her mother - that last one was hardly important in light of the other issues, but still it was a problem he'd caused. Maybe her mother was right? He was a bad influence. He brought danger to Ember, and soon enough she'd start to consider things… like mortality. What if she asked him to turn her? He couldn't do that to her. He couldn't make her what he was. Could he?

That's when he'd decided to stay away from her for a while. For her own good. If he wasn't around her, the witches might leave her alone. Maybe she'd realise she didn't want him anymore, and she'd get herself out of this mess. He could handle that - maybe - but he hoped it wouldn't come to that.

**

And that was why he'd forced himself away from her since Saturday because some stupid witch had hit a nerve. But there was no way in hell he was risking getting Ember turned into a mouse or worse, even if it was killing him to stay away from her. He knew she'd been upset about something in English and his curt reply to her note hadn't helped, but maybe she'd avoid him for a week or so. Just until he could track down the witches and rip them to shreds.

Unfortunately, his body ached for her, and so did his heart. She was so exciting and fiery; when she wasn't around everything was cold and dim. There was something in her that was magnetic to him, something fierce and bright and beautiful. And Dear God, if he had another dream about her in that damned bikini, he was going to lose his mind. His attraction to her wasn't purely emotional after all. If they hadn't been in a public place on Friday… As it was he'd barely controlled himself. He'd so desperately wanted to stroke every inch of her body, feel the heat of her soft skin on his, hear her whisper his name… Stop it! He jerked himself out of it. He wanted to storm down to her room and wrap her up in kisses and touches to make her dizzy. But that would ruin his plan to keep her safe. So he lay on his bed, trying to block the impure images that rushed to his head, and hoped he could sleep for the next few days. Dreamlessly.

Ember

Thursday. Four o'clock. The forest. Ember was sitting in her tree, thoughtfully watching the clouds flow across the grey-blue sky. Her dorm room had seemed oppressing, so she'd come out here to think. She was wondering about her dreams of Owen, about what he'd said and why he kept showing up. The last time she'd had strange dreams like that, they'd been about Reid, telling her what he was. Perhaps these dreams were trying to tell her something too? But she hadn't seen Owen in four years; he was a stranger to her now. Why would he be the one trying to tell her things? Things that, in reality, he had no idea about. Analysing dreams was never comforting in Ember's mind. They always seemed to tell her dangerous or scary things.

"So why do I bother?" she sighed aloud, resting her chin on her knees, her gloved hands wrapped round her shins. The caw of a crow nearby sent shivers through her, and she had to shake off the images the sound brought to mind; blood and feathers on her bedroom floor. Eventually that image would stop filling her with anger and sorrow. Or at least that's what she hoped. For now, her Owen encounters in her sleep were more distracting. They confused her to no end, and worried her just a little. They were only dreams but, as she'd learned, dreams could be prophetic. What if Owen's warning was true? Maybe she really shouldn't be here on her own?

With that thought, she glanced around her. At the creaking pine trees and swaying oak trees, the misty sky and sodden ground. She listened to the chirp of birds and the rustle of leaves, the whisper of the wind and the whipping of branches. She felt the sharp, cold air on her face, blowing loose strands of hair across her cheeks and forehead, felt the rough bark at her back and the warmth of her thick jumper. No. Nobody could hurt her here surely? Even witches couldn't get her in this peaceful place. Not when she was twenty feet off the ground in a tree. Twenty feet up felt like a whole other world to her today. Like she was free in her own reality, where there was nothing but the surrounding nature. That's why she'd chosen here to think about the things that worried her. They couldn't hurt her if she was here, but she could think about them safely. The only person who could get to her here was Reid.

Ember bit her lip, suddenly feeling a little upset atop her confusion over her disturbing nightmares. She was starting to think Reid really was avoiding her. She'd tried to catch him after English class today, but he'd taken off so fast she'd only glimpsed him rounding the corner to the Art department. He'd been so lively and flirty on Friday and then snap, he'd started this. Had she done something? Surely she hadn't been clingy recently? She knew how that could drive him away - hell, it'd drive her nuts if anyone even suggested she was clingy. She didn't stick to any guy like glue, no matter how much she cared for them. But then, why was Reid avoiding her? She wouldn't track him down and ask. That would be stupid if she really was being clingy. Instead she'd give him some space and hopefully he'd come back to her when he wanted to. It'd give her a chance to redeem herself in the eyes of her oft-neglected friend. She knew she'd been quite unsocial to Sherry the past few days, and Sherry had tried to make time for them to hang out all weekend. Even when Ricky had shown up to take her out on Saturday morning, she'd declined in the hopes that Ember would watch movies with her. Ember had felt bad about being anti-social to her friend, but those pesky dreams were irritating her.

"OK," she muttered out-loud, straightening up. "Give Reid some space, hang out with Sherz and forget the dreams." She decided firmly, stretching out her cramped arms and legs. Carefully she clambered down the tree, wondering if Sherry would be up for a horror movie night tonight.

"Ouch!" she cursed as she jumped from a few branches up and hit the ground awkwardly, stumbling against the tree trunk. She scowled and brushed off the leaves and bark from her jumper before turning to walk back to the dorms. But apparently fate had decided to intervene in her newly-made decisions, because Reid was suddenly standing in front of her now, looking solemn. "Oh, hey. What's up?" Ember smiled weakly, unsure whether or not to hug him.

"Ember, we need to talk." His voice was dull, and his blue eyes were unusually dark. His devil-may-care smile was missing, replaced by a tight frown. Ember was immediately suspicious.

"OK. What about?" She dropped her smile and narrowed her eyes, feeling a chill blossom in her chest. He hesitated, looking away from her.

"I... I've realised something..." he began slowly, his voice emotionless as he started to walk around her - at a distance. She waited patiently, watching his feet as he stepped gradually round to her right. "I know this might come as a shock, babe, but I... I don't..." He paused, and Ember had to push away from the tree and turn to see him now. He was standing a few feet back behind the tree, facing her with sympathy on his face. He looked rueful as he said. "I don't want you anymore. It won't work with us. I'm a vampire and you're not. We're so different and ...you just aren't what I want." His words were almost cold, sharp but blunted by his gentle tone. Ember felt a stinging heat in her eyes and they filled with tears that she tried to blink back.

"Are... are you breaking up with me?" she asked in a whisper, the chill in her chest froze round her heart. This was shocking to say the least. She knew he was being distant but she never expected this. How could he have changed his mind since Friday? She hadn't done anything wrong; she hadn't changed.

"Yes. I'm breaking up with you. I'd say 'let's be friends', but I don't think that's a good idea. You should just... try to stay away from me. It's better for us both." Reid brushed blond hair off his face, tugging down his black beanie and adjusting his fingerless gloves casually. Tears ran down Ember's cheeks and she hastily wiped them away.

"Reid, where did this come from?" she almost wailed but her voice cracked.

"I met one of the witches on Saturday and she said some things. And I realised she was right. We're just not right for each other. I can't look after some little human, and you can't survive in my world. You might act like you're fine with it but I know deep inside you fear me. It's why you've stuck with me, despite not caring that much about me. But I'm making it easy for you now. I'll leave you alone, and you can be safe without me." Reid didn't look at her, just gazed off into the trees. She had a sinking in her stomach, and an ache in her chest. Her head hurt all of a sudden.

"What about Ricky and Sherry, huh? They've made it work! Why are you listening to some stupid bloody witch?" Ember shrieked, more tears escaping. Reid shrugged.

"It's different," he said shortly, as if it was an answer. Ember opened her mouth to argue, but something in the cold set of Reid's jaw, and the way he wouldn't look at her, shut her up. She shut her mouth and stalked up to him slowly. She ignored the tears running down her face, and stood just a foot from him until he turned to meet her gaze. She threw out one hand with all the force she could muster and slapped him across the cheek, hard. It made a sharp cracking noise and his head snapped to the side.

"I hate you," she hissed through gritted teeth. Then she turned away and sobbed softly, letting the tears run freely as she ran back to the dorms.

Once she was close to the edge of the trees, Ember allowed herself a sneering smirk and wiped away the fake tears drying on her face.

Ember thumped on the dorm room door and waited impatiently for it to open. The second it opened and she confirmed who it was behind it, she threw out her hand to slap the boy. But he was far quicker than her, even when caught by surprise, and he caught her wrist inches from his face.

"Whoa! What was that for?" Reid exclaimed, blue eyes wide in surprise.

"Why the hell didn't you tell me you had a run in with a witch on Saturday?" She snatched her hand back and shoved him back inside the room, following him in and shutting the door. He looked at her in shock and opened his mouth but no words came out. "Well? That's why you've been avoiding me, isn't it?! For God's sake, I thought you were smart!" Ember sighed exasperatedly, longing to punch him.

"Wait, how did you find out?" He blinked and grimaced in confusion, running one hand through his hair. Before she could answer, he was suddenly holding her arms and peering into her face intently. "Have you been crying? Oh my God, that's not because of me, is it? I didn't mean to-" he started, guilt swelling in his lovely blue eyes. Ember waved him away.

"Shut up a minute. Yeah, I was crying, but I was acting. I'm good at that remember? I had a run in with a witch myself, only she was pretending to be you." Ember rolled her eyes and he let her go, abruptly angry. Sometimes, his mood swings were worse than a girl's.

"What happened?" he growled.

"You broke up with me! How could you?" Ember whined, pretending to cry again. And then she removed her hands from her face and smirked up at him dangerously, amused by the startled expression on his face. She arched a brow and saw the corners of his mouth twitch.

"And you knew it wasn't me?" he asked boldly, sitting back on his bed.

"Yep. To start with I thought it was you. For like, five seconds. But then the not-you person, called me 'Babe' and I realised you'd never be stupid enough to call me that. Especially if you were breaking up with me." Ember smiled innocently as Reid chuckled.

"And how do you know I won't break up with you? How do you know I didn't send the witch to do it for me?" he teased, trying to look serious but failing miserably. Ember grinned and walked over to him. She pushed his shoulders back so he lay flat on the bed and sat astride his lap, leaning over him. She bent close to him and breathed against his lips.

"Because you haven't had me yet," she whispered seductively, running her hands over his chest. It was fun to watch his pupils dilate and see his lips part as his breath quickened. She smirked and planted a tiny, teasing kiss on his mouth before moving off him. He groaned and closed his eyes briefly, not moving from his sprawled out position.

"You're cruel, you know that? I've barely seen you in four days and the last time I saw you, you were in that goddamned bikini, and now you tease me like this? Demon!" He sighed and pushed himself into a sitting position again.

She shrugged. "Your own fault. You were stupid enough to listen to a witch and stay away from me. You had me a little worried so this is your punishment." Ember grinned and sat down on Ricky's bed casually.

"C'est la Vie," Reid muttered and then focused again. "So, how did you figure I'd seen the witch on Saturday?" he asked seriously.

"Oh, she said you had. Well what she really said was, 'I met one of the witches on Saturday and she said some things. And I realised she was right. We're just not right for each other'," Ember quoted dramatically. She snorted. "Whatever she said to you on Saturday, she was not right. I don't care if she rattled off a hundred reasons for us to not be together. I have one reason for us to stay together, and it should beat them all," Ember said smartly, meeting his curious gaze evenly.

"And what might that be?" He asked his eyes alight. Ember smiled genuinely and leaned over to stroke his face gently.

"I care about you. And I know you care about me, too. Even if our relationship is complicated, that much is true and simple." She saw his blue eyes glow and a sweet smile spread across his mouth before he kissed her. It was a different kind of kiss to usual; it was slow and sweet and gentle. And it made her heart ache - in a good way. He pulled away and looked at her, brows pitched up worriedly.

"You know I was only avoiding you for your own good, right? The witch threatened to hurt you, said I would only put you in danger. I guess I forgot that you can fight for yourself." He smiled a little but his eyes were full of remorse. "And it was nearly impossible to stay away from you that long. I kept getting images of you in the bikini. My dreams have been pretty lurid since Friday." And he was back to being same old Reid. Ember laughed and he flashed a dazzling grin before pulling her over to him and sitting her down on his lap sideways. She leaned her head on his chest as he held her, and she could feel the warmth of his skin through his shirt, and hear the beating of his undead heart. That witch was wrong. Vampires and humans weren't all that different. They both bled, and killed and loved. It didn't matter that one was prey and the other the predator. All that mattered were the emotions. And of course, the fangs were important. Just because they were so damn hot.

After an hour or so, Ember left Reid with the excuse that she had homework to do. It was a lie – well, she did have homework to do, but that wasn't why she was leaving their cuddling session. She was leaving because she kept thinking about that damned witch and the way she'd been trying to play her and Reid apart. It made her furious. So furious, in fact, that she returned to the forest in search of a confrontation. If nothing else, she wanted to slap the witch stupid or, at the very least, give her a good earful of insults. Not that it would do any of them any good, but it might make her feel a little better, and it would show the witches she wasn't fooled by their plot, their games. She wasn't giving Reid up without a fight. She'd spent too much time figuring out she cared about him to let anyone mess it up now.

Born Dark

So she ducked out of the dorm building, careful not to slam the door, and stormed across the parking lot and into the trees. Her feet flawlessly remembered the path to her tree, dead brown leaves crunching under her boots. She felt certain that the witches would show up if she just hung around for long enough, but she didn't feel like waiting, so as soon as she got to her tree, she snapped off a branch nearly as thick as her wrist and started to shout.

"Hey, witchy! I know you're out here! Why don't you show yourself, you pathetic coward! And no disguises this time! Yeah, that's right, I knew it wasn't Reid! You're not as smart as you think, you magical freak!" she yelled, knowing that witch was still hanging around. She could feel it, sense someone else nearby.

And then she heard the snap of a twig behind her and she spun, pointing her branch like a sword out in front of her. The tip hovered at a girl's throat, just above the collar of her green shirt. The girl had wavy brown hair and doe-like brown eyes. Ember recognised her as one of the witches immediately and narrowed her eyes to a glare. The girl just stared back with an annoying kind of innocence, her hands staying by her sides. Ember didn't lower her branch as she spoke, though she wasn't sure how much damage she could do with it if the witch decided to attack her. Reid would kill her if he knew she was out here, picking a fight with a witch, but it needed to be done; Ember wanted to make it clear to these witches that just because she was small and human, that didn't mean she wasn't a threat. It didn't mean she wouldn't fight them every way she could. They were threatening her and her friends, and she wasn't going to stand for it. Ember had never taken threats very well – about as well as she took commands, which wasn't well at all. She dealt with them even less well when they were aimed at those she cared about.

Ember smirked thinly at the witch, lifting her chin and jabbing the end of her branch into the girl's throat just enough to make a point. "Hello there, witch," she spat the word like it was an insult. It might as well have been. Ember was currently ranking the witches somewhere below Kara, and just slightly above Joseph the Werewolf. She took a close look at the brown-haired girl. She looked completely normally, pretty enough, even a little plain. She looked harmless. But Ember knew she wasn't. "I take it you're the one who thought you could fool me with your little disguise. It was a neat trick, but there's something you should know if you want to pretend to be my boyfriend: He wouldn't dare call me babe." Ember stepped a little closer, invading the witch's personal space. The girl's eyes narrowed at last but she didn't so much as twitch. That was a smart move, because

Ember was very tempted to do something nasty with this branch the second the witch showed the slightest sign of attacking.

"You want to know why he'd never call me babe?" Ember continued, ignoring the dark look the witch was giving her. She'd had scarier glares from her mother. She went on without waiting for the witch to answer. "He wouldn't dare because he knows it would piss me off. He really doesn't want to piss me off. Not just because I'm his girlfriend and he cares about me, blah, blah. No, he doesn't want to piss me off because bad things happen to those who annoy me." She wasn't thinking of Kara or even Reid himself, but of a girl who'd bullied her at her last school. One day, Ember had gotten so fed up of the bullying that she'd collected some spiders from her garden and carried them to school in a plastic container. Then, when the girl had left her bag unattended for a moment, Ember had loosed the spiders into her schoolbag. When the girl picked up her schoolbag, the spiders crawled onto her hand and up her arm. The screaming had been heard all the way across school. And, of course, nobody had seen Ember do it, so she got away with it, but she made sure the girl knew the spiders were from her. That girl never bullied her again.

Ember smiled viciously at the memory. People so often underestimated her. This witch had done the same, and now look where she was – on the end of a very pointy stick aimed at her jugular. And she did not look happy about it. "Guess what witchy?" Ember crooned in a sugar sweet voice, the one she used when she was really, really angry. She'd worked out that it disturbed people when she used the voice while smirking at them. Usually, they shied away or stared at her like she was crazy. The witch's expression didn't change, but it didn't dissuade Ember from lifting her branch to tap it against the girl's jaw, like a Victorian teacher might have done to chastise a student not sitting properly in class. "You pissed me off. So now bad things are going to happen to you. Do you understand?" Ember tipped her head down to glower sinisterly at the witch through her lashes. The witch looked murderous. It only made Ember smile more. Until she heard the crunching of leaves under feet behind her.

Keeping her branch steady at the brown-haired witch's throat, Ember whirled, wishing she had another weapon as the three other witches slunk out of the trees around her, stalking her like a pack of wolves. She recognised the crop-haired one as the leader and met her glare with even fierceness. The ginger girl, with her wild mane of orange hair, had a lethal look about her, so Ember kept track of her in her peripheral vision, but she didn't take her gaze off Croppy, because she knew the others would not attack without some signal from their leader. Both Ginger and Rainbow stopped when Croppy held up a hand, confirming what Ember had thought.

Ember gritted her teeth, determined not to show fear. She was outnumbered now, surrounded, and nobody else knew where she was right now. If something happened to her, if these witches attacked her or kidnapped her, how long would it be before somebody started to worry? An hour, two, more? She pushed away the thoughts, focussing on the witches instead. Panicking wouldn't do her any good. But maybe she could find a way out of here, make a break for it. If she could just get close enough to the dorms, she'd be safe. Surely the witches wouldn't follow her across the parking lot in broad daylight, not with other students milling about. Of course, if worse came to worst, she could send Reid a telepathic yell for help. She wasn't sure he'd hear it from this distance, but it was worth a shot if she got desperate.

"Well now," Croppy said, smiling a condescending little smile that made Ember want to rip her face off, "I guess our little plan didn't quite work, did it? But you know what, Ember? It doesn't matter because here you are, all alone, and here we are. And you've rather annoyed us as well, siding with the vampires." Croppy frowned, shaking her head as if in disappointment. Ember continued to glower at her, uncomfortable because she couldn't see the brown-haired witch or the one with the rainbow streaks in her hair properly. Either one could lunge at her and she probably wouldn't have time to react.

But Croppy continued to talking in a sincere sort of voice that made Ember bristle. "But, Ember, this doesn't have to end badly for you. If you walk away right now, leave the vampires to us and don't interfere, we can overlook your…indiscretions. We'll leave you and your friend alone."

Ember made a disgusted sound. "And what will you do to the vampires?" she asked, although she already knew the answer.

Croppy didn't even hesitate before answering in a flat tone. "We'll kill them. But that shouldn't matter to you. They are predators, killers even, who feed on innocent humans. They manipulate them with their mind powers and then they suck their blood. Vampires are evil creatures who must be gotten rid of. Help us, help us destroy them, and we'll give you whatever you want. We can teach you spells that work for humans, we have money, we have power."

For a moment, Ember made a show of considered her offer, and then smiled sweetly. "Thanks but no thanks, witchy. I think I'll stick with my blood-sucking boyfriend. However, I will give you a piece of advice in return for your kind offer: Back the hell off, because vampire or not, I bite too." And with that warning, Ember threw down her branch and began to leave. She made it four steps toward Ginger, who was baring her teeth angrily, and just for a second she thought they might actually let her leave.

And then Ginger leapt at her and she knew Croppy had given the order to attack. Ember barely dodged the red-haired girl's fervent attack, spinning out of the way at the last second. But Rainbow came at her from the other side and knocked her flat to the ground. The air burst form Ember's chest in a rush and she struggled to gasp for air. Rainbow had her wrists pinned to the dirt, holding her down, but Ember pulled up a knee and slammed it into the witch's stomach. With a yelp of pain, Rainbow rolled off her, clutching her stomach. Ember scrambled to her feet and tried to run. She heard someone breathing right behind her and threw herself aside just as the brown-haired witch tried to snatch her. She kept running, weaving agilely between the trees. She knew this route well by now, and the witches didn't; it made it easy to outrun them, skipping over slippery patches of mud hidden under fallen leaves, avoiding rocks buried in the undergrowth, hopping on raised roots instead of tripping over them.

Through the trees ahead, she could see the grey of the school building. She willed herself to make it that far. Her lungs were bursting, her legs burning, and she didn't dare look over her should to see how far behind the witches were. She still hear them behind her, several pairs of feet kicking up rustling dead leaves and snapping branches. One of them yelped and Ember guessed she'd tripped over one of the tree roots.

She was almost safe now, the edge of the trees just metres ahead, but then something strange happened. One moment she was just running, hearing her own ragged breathing and feeling the wind rushing past her as she ducked branches, and the next she staggered to a halt as prickle of warning shot up her spine. Instinctively, she spun, must in time to see a bizarre orb of blue light flying toward her. She threw up her hands, not having time to move out of the way. The orb smashed into her hands, and she expected a jolt of electricity, maybe her skin burning off, but all she felt was a tickle and some warmth against her palms.

Blinking in surprise and confusion, Ember lowered her arms and stared at her hands. They were a little red, but otherwise fine. No scorch marks or welts or anything. She glanced up and saw the witches standing some distance away, staring at her, incredulous. Apparently they'd expected more to happen, too. But nobody had time to ask any questions like, "Why aren't you singed to a crisp?" or "Did you just try to kill me?" because, at that moment, the vampires showed up. Out of nowhere, they were suddenly at her sides, flanking her protectively, Reid and Ricky. She wasn't sure how they'd known where she was, or that she'd been in danger, but that didn't matter. They were here.

Now facing two angry vampires, and with their magic clearly malfunctioning, the witches didn't seem so keen to tussle. They turned to flee, and Ember thought Reid would go after the, but as he took a step forward, the witches suddenly vanished. Poof. Just like that, gone into thin air. Ember was sure it was an illusion, they were just using some sort of invisibility spell or something, but it surprised Reid enough that he turned back to Ember instead.

He stared at her with narrowed blue eyes and she thought for certain he was about to lay into her for recklessly endangering herself by coming out to the forest, but all he said was, "Are you okay?" She nodded, mute. He sighed and looked to Ricky. "Do you suppose we scared them off for good this time?" he asked, without much hope in his voice. Ricky just frowned and Reid shook his head. "I thought not. But at least they'll think twice about coming after Ember again." He grinned abruptly and gave her a look that made her suspect he'd known she would come out here to confront the witches.

She smiled back at him hesitantly. "I warned them it was a bad idea to piss me off. I think they may have gotten the message," she said. Reid laughed, slipping his hand into hers. Even Ricky chuckled.

They turned to head back to the dorms, Ember feeling just a little proud of herself for standing up to the witches and more than a little glad she didn't get killed. They were almost at the entrance to the dorm building when Reid turned to her and said, "You know, you'd make a great vampire."

Ember split into a grin. "Damn straight I would."

Reid laughed again as he pulled open the door to the dorms and Ember couldn't help but wonder if he really meant it, that she'd make a great vampire. She hoped so, because she fully intended to become one.

H.G. Lynch